INTO THE CITADEL

INTO THE CITADEL

BOOK I OF THE DYSTOPIAN TRILOGY

JAMES HARRISON
CAMPBELL

Into the Citadel: Book I of the dystopian trilogy

This is a work of fiction. Names, characters, places, and incidents are either the product of the author's imagination or are used fictitiously. Any resemblance to actual persons, living or dead, or to events or locales, is entirely coincidental.

For more information, contact the author at jamesharrisoncampbell@gmail.com.

First paperback edition: December 2023

Book Design by Maryam Sadiqa and the Author

ISBN: 9798850786960

www.intothecitadel.com
(site design by Michael@avs.business)

Also by James Harrison Campbell

RED MASK

Book II of Into the Citadel

MOUNT OF POWER

Book III of Into the Citadel

INTO THE CITADEL

PROLOGUE

The end of civilization began randomly enough, with an innocent muezzin's cry broadcast from a minaret towering over the Pakistani city of Islamabad. A timer was started, fifteen minutes were allowed for crucial military command and control personnel working across town to leave their desks and consoles for sunset prayer, then a fiery chasm opened and consumed the world.

The year was 2034, by the old Christian calendar, and a raging storm of hatred and destruction was upon the earth. The shadowy organization believed to be called by its members simply *Qadar*–Divine Destiny–and thought mortally wounded by the assassination of its latest front man, had lashed out with an orgy of murder and mayhem that took the Pakistani, American, and French presidents, the Swedish prime minister, the Saudi king, and hundreds of others. In retaliation, neo-Nazi-fired mobs killed tens of thousands of Muslims in Paris, London, New York, Stockholm and elsewhere, unknowingly playing out the second act in a masterpiece written by the apocalypse-seeking cult and its wealthy benefactors. The third act, years in preparation, came in Pakistan as the world's eyes were upon Europe and America. First the traumatized Pakistani government, uncertain of its own ability to keep its nuclear arsenal secure, yielded to international pressure to temporarily move most of it into special terrorist-proof depots–the very facilities long-since infiltrated by secret Destiny supporters within the military–then scores of bombs and warheads already made transportable and concealable for the sequestration were–within minutes of the muezzin's call in the capital—bloodily stolen.

As darkness fell across Pakistan, the militaries and intelligence services of the world shifted into controlled-panic mode, but too late. The weapons were gone. Three months later, in the final act, warheads smuggled into Israel and to high points in one-hundred-twenty-three of the world's infidel cities were simultaneously detonated, punishing centuries of accumulated blasphemy and setting the stage for the worldwide caliphate.

Things didn't go according to script, however. Recalcitrant nonbelievers—down to individual submarine commanders, missile crews, and bomber pilots—arrogantly fought back, destroying holy places and population centers in the Muslim world. Then beggar-thy-neighbor set in. Commanders still receiving satellite imagery and comparing the level of destruction, one country to another, independently concluded the world was in ruins, but not uniformly. Those with remaining nukes silently looked to their compatriots and agreed: it must be *our kind* who survive the holocaust. And so the genocidal leveling began and reigned until all the bombs were gone.

That took a week, then things got worse.

Even as radiation poisoning and starvation began to kill billions of country people and those who'd fled smaller cities in time, billions more were assailed by wave upon wave of infectious disease. Many such—influenza, polio, smallpox, anthrax, shudders, Ebola, Marburg, SARS—were well known and not usually dangerous to advanced societies, but almost no one was immune now, and in the chaos new variants spread rapidly. Others were new, perhaps escaped or released from military bioweapons labs or even from private ones attempting to engineer genocides of their own. Refugees trying to flee outbreaks inadvertently spread them, until the whole world was infected and dying.

The remedy occurred to everyone eventually: withdraw into smaller and smaller communities and kill trespassers and all who become ill. Within a few years the plagues dwindled and the earth's population stabilized at the edge of extinction, survivors and their children living mostly in isolated villages and developing their own ways and dialects and beliefs.

As generations came and went, technology and history and learning died away—difficult to maintain in the circumstances but also hated and feared as the very things that had brought the holocaust. Religion fractured into thousands of sects and cults, often at war with each other. Some people clung to their best understanding of the old ways, but most rejected them and gave their allegiance to new explanations, new systems of social organization, and new intermediaries who promised to intercede for them with the divine.

In a village on a river called Husson, the priesthood of the god ZAH ruled. In earlier times it had been as chaotic as the rest, then one day a frustrated old man, known thereafter merely as The Chaplin, donned an immaculate white suit that no one had seen before and stood all day at the edge of the village, staring at a grove of trees at the top of a hill that all shunned because it was where the sick had once been taken to be quarantined or killed. Villagers tried to speak with him and when he wouldn't reply they murmured among themselves and marveled at the suit's shiny gold buttons and colored ribbons over the heart and the embroidering on the shoulder-boards matching the decoration on the white hat and at the impossibly white shoes. At twilight he had started forward only to be held back by his wife, who asked where he was going. I am summoned, he'd said, and she'd released him. That night fire had engulfed the summit and all had thought the Chaplin killed, but in the morning he'd descended through the smoke and embers just as he'd ascended, except for the jagged Z-symbol burned into his forehead and the sheathed sword at his side.

The god ZAH had given him the sword, he proclaimed, to force obedience to his will. ZAH had revealed that he'd punished and cleansed the world because, in the instant of infinite time that was human history, his creations had impudently sought not just to *praise* and *obey* him, as was his will, but to *understand* him. They'd arrogantly created truth-seeking religions and philosophies and technologies as if they were gods themselves. Now they were reduced to their proper station and would be suffered to live only if they stayed there, respectfully shunning esoteric knowledge and following the guidance of his representatives.

ZAH had made the Chaplin and his wife and their descendants his priests and priestesses, to be styled Lords and Ladies, the villagers were told, and he'd left a protocol for living that was at first resented but later avidly accepted when its benefits became apparent. By ZAH's order, the priests said, village girls were not allowed to marry and bear children until they'd first borne a priest's child, who could in turn be elected to the priesthood or attain other favored position. Priestesses could likewise couple with unmarried commoners and bear priestblood children, with similar benefit to the children, even when they were unwanted and given up to be raised by, and in the service of, the state. Many sought the security and comfort this elevated social status brought and readily offered their frequently unhappy sixteen-year-olds. Over time the practice created an ever-larger and more powerful elite as all tried to elevate their progeny and therefore themselves—many adopting elements of fashion and behavior from eras only they were permitted to learn about—and the stage was set for expansion and for domination over less-effective systems of social organization.

Today, as in the Chaplin's time, ZAHism's greatest obstacle and enemy is *knowledge*—of the world before the Cleansing and of all that ZAH found intolerable in his ungrateful creations—so the priesthood ruthlessly suppresses it for all but its own elite. As it grows and eventually makes its home in the abandoned but partly intact city a few hours' float down the Husson, it establishes a Ministry for the Suppression of Error to find and consign to the ovens not only secret hoards of books and other prohibited materials, but also those unbelievers who have collected and studied them. Peaceful ignorance prevails.

Still, for some, curiosity lingers and love overcomes fear.

1 - Ronnie and Jenna

Firstportage Village - year 106 of the Age of Obedience

Twenty-Six days," Ronnie said flatly, breaking the silence as he and Jenna walked in the evening on the wildflower-strewn village common near their families' homes. Jenna entwined her fingers in his.

"Yes," she said, glancing away at the scattered cows and horses and goats in the field with them.

Before the somber mood had descended, they'd been bantering playfully in French, as they'd done in secret since childhood. Then a teasing and inadvertently suggestive remark had fallen from Jenna's lips before she could stop it and they were back to the subject they'd been trying to avoid.

"It's just *sex*, Ronnie—it doesn't *mean* anything. Every girl has to go through it.... Besides, you'll be chosen soon, too. Then we can be together."

"Yeah, but you're going so far away. Maybe you'll fall in love with some handsome priest—never come back." He self-consciously touched his still-sparse beard, aware that the clergy were mostly clean-shaven.

That made her stop and look up at him. "If they're handsome," she said, "then you don't have to worry, do you? —you know I only like the ugly ones." He put his hands to her waist and drew her closer.

It was an old joke, but it still pleased him. Family lore had it that the

Citadel priestess who'd once coupled with Ronnie's father had been dissatisfied with the result and left her baby to be raised by the father and his new wife, a woman whose own priestchild had died and who was happy to be a mother again. It was said the fashion of the moment was for babies who could be expected to grow up pale and slim and elegant, and Ronnie, named Rondak for the mountains to the north where his ancestors had sheltered during the Cleansing, was unacceptably broad boned and strong featured and dark haired, even if he did have the favored blue eyes. Inevitably he became known as "Big Ugly," affectionately, or simply "Ug."

"And I like the skinny ones," he said, looking down at the swell of breasts squashed against his chest, belying *her* childhood nickname of "Bean," or more formally, "Stringbean." She took pleasure in his gaze and the feel of him against her until she started to blush, then pulled away and tugged him into an amble toward the woods. Glancing over his shoulder toward the small house some hundred paces away, he saw his mother sit back from her gardening to study them.

She needn't worry, he thought; they wouldn't go into the woods today; the risk–and their desire for each other–was too great, for both knew enough to know what they desperately wanted–with every fiber of their nearly sixteen-year-old beings.

As the law required, Ronnie and Jenna were innocent in the most important sense, but they knew about sex, having watched every manner of creature engaged in it and having secretly and repeatedly met in the past year to practice it. The self-control that kept them from going further was born of fearand responsibility–for a momentary lapse could mean death for themselves and their families. As all knew–as the Protocols dictated by ZAH to the Chaplain more than a century before stated–16-year-old virgins were for the priests. Girls could neither marry nor bear other children until they'd first been "blessed" with a priest's child, and unmarried boys were obliged to service any childless priestess who desired them. Once a boy and a girl who'd already birthed a priestchild married, the obligation supposedly ended, but the priesthood was all-powerful, and the people couldn't read the Protocols for themselves anyway.

Most people, anyway.

Like their parents and siblings and about thirty others in the village of hundreds, Ronnie and Jenna were book-reading Freethinkers, cursed of ZAH and his priesthood along with practitioners of banned religions old and new and subject to losing their heads in the market square should their education be discovered. For unauthorized and undisciplined learning had the potential to whet the appetite for esoteric knowledge—to encourage doubt of received wisdom and to nourish the desire to understand the true nature of things, even the nature of ZAH himself—the very effrontery that had brought the Cleansing, according to the Teachings.

Ironically, the Teachings were even better known to the Freethinkers than to most, for one of the many ways they covered their secret lessons and discussions was to camouflage them—whenever witnesses were about—as a sort of lay catechism wherein the instructions of the clergy were parroted, which flattered even as it mystified the none-too-smart local priest. There was always something about these polite, reserved children that he couldn't quite put his finger on—something in the eyes ...

If he'd known that Ronnie and Jenna spoke strange languages together to preserve a sense of the breadth and variety of the world, known that they knew and shared with others its history before the Cleansing, discovered the secret library that Ronnie's parents kept spread out in the attic and the chicken coop and in the carpentry shop, he would in apoplectic outrage have consigned the whole family to the inquisitors, who would over a few days of screaming and begging have identified the other heretics. Which was why the young lovers would not go into the woods today, nor do anything to attract attention to themselves or their families, before Jenna's scheduled departure for the Citadel, where reports of her auburn-haired and hazel-eyed beauty had caused her to be summoned.

As the couple walked, Jenna took her hand away to clasp it with the other one in a pose familiar to the younger Freethinker children and spoke in her schoolteacher voice: "Let's be *practical,* Ronnie. This will be *good* for us, *and* our families, *and* the others. You and your birth parents might be priestblood, but my parents are not. They've always been suspected and looked down on for being refugees from the last pogrom in the mountains, their obedience questioned, and that affects *me.* But now you and I will have a child to raise who's connected by blood directly to the *Citadel,* just as you are; even if *you* don't know your birth mother, you can be sure the Citadel knows of *you;* the elders say they keep track of such things. My priestchild will make us *safer*–give our family more *opportunity* in life. Don't you see?"

"I *know* all that, Jen; I listen to the elders too–*and* the priests. Priestblood binds us into one people–binds us to ZAH through his elected, and blah, blah, blah. I don't *care* about any of that right now. I just don't want to *lose* you!"

They had come to the far side of the common meadow and stopped to gaze ahead in unseeing thought. Before them the woods began and soon rose abruptly up and over the remains of an embankment that once extended to left and right all the way around the village to the river. It had been hastily built during the Cleansing, when diseased and desperate and dying multitudes shuffled across the land. Over the decades much of its structure–comprised mostly of steel-bodied vehicles and large chunks of outlying buildings that had been destroyed to deny shelter to the strangers–had rusted and rotted and collapsed upon itself, becoming home to many small creatures. In truth it had never been a defensible barrier, merely a border between village and not-village, between neighbors and strangers. Sick and starving refugees had called over it or stood atop it to plead for help, only to be driven away or to be killed with makeshift weapons if they attempted to descend. Men and women of the village had cursed God and wept as they slew whole families to save their own. When the strangers had stopped coming and the world had grown so quiet that the river's wreckage-made first cataract could be heard from a mile away, the villagers had gone into the woods to collect the disintegrating corpses and burn them on great pyres. Now the barrier marked the beginning of a sylvan wilderness extending west mostly unbroken for a thousand miles—a wilderness in which two young lovers could certainly lose themselves.

Suddenly the birds in the trees were stilled and the couple's dangerous thoughts were interrupted by a deep, penetrating vibration in the air. Turning, they saw the distant figure of Ronnie's father Bern standing at the edge of the meadow in the light of the lowering sun and swinging a flashing axe about his head on a swivel-jointed wrist strap. It was a slender bush axe, its blade long and hooked at the end and sharpened on both sides, and it sang. Bern the woodworker and village engineer had discovered how to give it voice by cutting tuned air channels into the hickory handle where it met the blade, and the result was a thrumming sound so deep it was more felt than heard, a sound that set distant dogs to barking and caused livestock to raise their heads from grazing. Father and son had used two of them to communicate their positions when separated in the woods, and now father was using his to fetch his son back from the edge of the abyss. Adding to the sense of urgency were the figures of Ronnie's mother Marta and his little brother Bo staggered beyond his father, and of Jenna's mother Hermione standing in her kitchen doorway not far away.

Ronnie raised a hand in acknowledgement and the sound stopped as Bern caught the axe handle in his left hand but remained watching. After a moment the others went about their business and neighbors' curtains fell back into place. Now Ronnie faced Jenna and took both her hands.

"I just don't want to lose you," he repeated, calmly this time.

Jenna fixed her mesmerizing eyes on his. "You're not gonna lose me, Ronnie, and I'm not gonna lose you. The Citadel is only two days float from here—it's not in *China*, for ZAH's sake! I could be back in a few months, if you'll take me with a big belly."

"I'll take you any way I can get you."

"So it's settled, then?"

Now Ronnie caught behind the question a hint of the sadness and tension she must be feeling and realized how selfish he'd been. Though Jenna was only two months older than he, she'd always been the mature and sensible one. Spreading his arms, he tried to rise to the occasion.

"I'll be waiting for you and your big belly with open arms."

She went into his embrace and they stood gently rocking, back and forth. After a time she looked up at him.

"We didn't finish our lesson. Say the words to me– the ones I like."

"You mean, *"Te quiro?"* he teased.

She shook her head, her eyes come alive.

"Ich liebe dich?"

Another slow head shake.

"What about ... *Je t'aime?"*

"Those're the ones. Say them again."

She'd often chided him for not using an amazing memory for more than parlor tricks, so now, wanting to show he'd been paying attention after all–that he remembered their every moment together–he let the playfulness pass from his face and said, *"Je t'aime, et je t'aimerai, de tout mon cœur, pour tous les jours, jusqu'à la fin des temps,"* promising love, with all heart, for all days, till the end of time.

"*Moi aussi,*" said Jenna, offering her lips.

2 – Villain's Houseguest

In the market square it took only the rhythmic tramp of a dozen soldiers, marching purposely, to still the two or three hundred morning shoppers and vendors, now standing frozen with goods and parcels and baskets in hand. When it became apparent that their destination was Jenna, Ronnie stepped in front of her.

"Whaddaya want?" he demanded of their officer, who'd raised his fist to his men in a "hold" gesture.

"None of your concern, boy. Stand aside!"

"I asked what you wanted."

The officer was momentarily taken aback by the youth's apparent fearlessness. Then he remembered himself and raised his chin.

"In the name of ZAH," he cried for all to hear, "I require the virgin Jenna. Now, stand aside!"

"No. It's not time."

Sputtering in disbelief, the man hesitated, then, seizing his sword scabbard with his left hand and splaying the fingers of his right in signal, yelled, "Ready arms!"

Hands went to short swords and broke them free from scabbards but did not fully draw them. Marketgoers moved back in alarm, all knowing there was no middle ground between drawn sword and slaughter. If the officer now called Fight!, Ronnie would be dead and maybe Jenna too.

Seeing Ronnie's hand move to his back where he wore a knife sheathed crosswise, Jenna surged forward to grab his wrist and move in front to put her other hand in his chest.

"No, Ronnie! Don't fight!"

She pushed and struggled and said his name several times before he met her eyes. They silently pleaded with him—for their own lives and futures and for their families. When she saw the madness dissipate and felt him relax, she patted and fussed over his disarranged shirtfront to keep his attention on her, then turned to the officer with dignity.

"Shall we go?"

The man glared over her shoulder at Ronnie long enough to let him know how lucky he was, not to be arrested or chopped to pieces. When he took his hand from his weapon and called "Reverse order!" his men snicked their swords home and parted into facing columns. As he escorted Jenna through the aisle thus created, the others fell in behind by twos and tramped back out of the square. Jenna never looked back.

When the murmuring began, Ronnie looked around and saw mostly fear and shame. Many of these people had known Jenna all her life, but they hadn't stood up for her, and now they couldn't meet his eyes. Of the ones that did, some communicated exasperation, as if to say, What did you expect? –it's the law! while others, particularly women who'd had the misfortune of having to couple with the odious village priest, smirked. But here and there, as he kept scanning the crowd, he met the sympathetic and comforting eyes of brother and sister and elder Freethinkers.

There were at least a dozen in the square. Here was Master Lamar the one-armed lamplighter—who had been sharing his passion for military history with Ronnie since he could first hold a wooden sword—today carrying his wife's basket as that kind lady also glanced his way. There was Mistress Rostova the language tyrant, the oldest person in the village at fifty-six, staring at him as expectantly as if she'd just commanded him to conjugate an obscure German verb, whose importance lay not in its present usefulness but in its world-expanding effect on the minds of her special students. And watching with outright hero-worship from a nearby porch were the twelve-year-old twins Colin and Carin, who helped in their father's business of portaging boats past the nearby first cataract of the Husson and who were scheduled to receive a math lesson from Ronnie that very afternoon, under cover of cleaning the chicken coop. Seeing how scared they were by what they'd just witnessed, he winked before turning away, eliciting uncertain smiles.

Hurrying home, Ronnie thought about the soldiers. As usual they were men not originally from Firstportage, but they *were* part of the local garrison–about half of it, in fact. At least they weren't likely to be the ones who would transport Jenna to the Citadel. But why take her today? nearly a month early? and so unceremoniously?

He went straight into the carpentry shop next to the house and found his father noisily sawing a piece for a loom he was making for one of the neighbors.

"Dad! They've taken Jenna!"

Bern stopped sawing and turned from his work. He was still taller than his ever-growing son and robust instead of lanky, but with the same eyes.

"What's that?" he asked.

"They *took* her, Dad! Soldiers! In the market! We have to get 'er back!"

Bern put down the saw and took his son by the upper arms. "Calm down. Take a breath.... Now be precise and quick like I taught you. Tell me."

"In the market. About twelve soldiers–garrison soldiers. Came right for Jenna–no explanation–ready to fight."

"Did it seem to be about the Circle?"

"Don't think so–they demanded the *virgin* Jenna–and there were other Circle members in the square, not bothered."

His father briefly looked away in thought.

"All right," he said. "Go tell your mother to make herself

presentable and gather my meeting clothes and come to Jenna's house. I'll go there now. Go!"

"Should I change too?"

"You're not going. If I know you, you were none to accommodating to the soldiers. Best you stay out of sight and out of mind for a little while. Your job right now is to make sure the library is buttoned up, then come to look after Juli."

"But–"

"No 'buts'–this is a moment for subservience and diplomacy, not confrontation. Now go!"

Ronnie stamped out angrily, but Bern's mind had already moved on. Working the pump handle to fill the reservoir and wash his rough hands and stubbled face, he glanced around his shop. On his worktable was a scrap of bark with calculations scratched on it. He broke it apart and tossed it out the window into the garden and started for the door, only to stop and backtrack to lift a tray from his toolbox and retrieve a piece of ancient paper carefully hidden within.

He stared intently for a few seconds at the picture cut from an old magazine, committing the design of the dining table depicted to memory, then he ate it, looked around once more, and left.

When Ronnie arrived at Jenna's house after making sure the library was secure, he found a tear-streaked Hermione helping her elderly husband Clarence with his coat and a confused seven-year-old Juli crying in his own mother's arms. He immediately stooped to tie the old man's boots, knowing how severely arthritic he was.

As Clarence steadied himself with a hand on his shoulder, Ronnie remembered that he wasn't arthritic in the way of some people, but from being beaten nearly to death during the last pogrom, when troops accompanying evangelizing priests had poured out of the Citadel and garrison towns to find and destroy heresy, especially in the mountains to the north. As Jenna had revealed to him, her mother had been just fourteen at the time, best friend to Clarence's daughter and aspiring wife of his eldest son. When an advance party surprised their mountain hamlet and found books and schoolwork in all the six homes there–a girl's poetry, beautifully penned and signed with a flourish, a boy's annotated copy of Tremblay's history of America in the twenty-first century–the males were killed outright and the females violated. Saved by her precocious beauty, Hermione had been taken to the priests with other girls as spoils of war. She was arbitrarily determined to be sixteen and thus rightfully theirs, but she'd cut the throat of her fifth rapist and fled back to her hamlet, by then reeking of death. Among the bodies of his wife and all his children, she'd found Clarence bludgeoned and broken, but alive. Tearlessly, unable even to pause and accord respect to their loved ones, she'd gathered food and weapons, made a litter out of branches and old coats, set fire to all the houses to consume the remains of the dead, and drug Clarence a half mile to a tributary of the Husson, where she wrestled him into a tiny boat that was kept overturned in the nearby brush. Two days later, when a tattered houseboat had approached, she'd strung her bow and nocked an arrow she'd made herself, but it was only a family of river-borne tinkers, who fed them hot food and accepted their small boat in exchange for a few coins and an introduction to the family of portagers who worked the first cataract of the Husson. The young couple who would become parents to Colin and Carin admired Hermione's finely crafted arrows and in turn introduced her at Firstportage Village to a fletcher who was struggling to keep up with a growing population of hunters, and they had paid work.

At least Hermione did. Clarence, once a stonemason, never fully recovered, but he did what he could, and the first thing he could do for Hermione was to marry her, and quickly. Already pregnant from rape but unable to explain this and the circumstances of her arrival, she'd first presented herself as an orphaned but ZAH-loving sixteen-year-old virgin to the lustful local priest, and then married Clarence as soon as Jenna was born. By then they'd been recognized as educated and invited into the Freethinker Circle and were relatively safe. Clarence gathered material for arrow shafts in woods and on riverbank and

Hermione prepared and fletched them and affixed points fashioned from metal scrap by Little Smithy—still called that even though Big Smithy had been dead for years. Jenna helped from the time she was five, first gathering feathers and later learning to shoot to test the final product.

Little Juli, whom Ronnie now took on his back from his own mother's arms—she didn't like to be carried "like a baby" by him—had been a surprise to everyone, except, presumably, Clarence and Hermione. Those who knew their history had assumed their marriage was one of two people who cared very much for each other but probably didn't have relations. So when Hermione happily got a big belly and Clarence developed an uncharacteristic spring in his step, friends were delighted; it seemed to mark the last stage in their resurrection as human beings, symbolized by the wedding bands Clarence made for them both out of a length of gold chain they'd been paid for some work.

Now what they had made was endangered because Brother Bal, ZAH's current chief representative in the village, had drawn attention by reporting Jenna's quality to his superiors in the Citadel, knowing that he'd be in trouble if he tried to keep one such as she for himself. Any problem with the process of getting her down the river and into the hands of the Matron of Virgins at this point could cause an investigation into all concerned, which in the case of the two Freethinker families could be their end.

Bern wondered out loud what could have caused this move by Brother Bal.

"The kiss," said Hermione, sitting in her best clothes with her face in her hands. Marta, her hand on Hermione's shoulder, nodded.

"What, dear?" said Clarence.

"In the meadow—they kissed.

"So? Lots of teenagers kiss."

"Not like that," she replied. "It was a lovers' kiss, and they were so close to the woods, and it was near dark. Maybe one of the neighbors suggested something to Bal. We all know how he feels about Jenna."

They contemplated that for a moment, then Bern stood with purpose. "Let's go."

Clarence and Hermione were fugitives who had settled far from the river and village center to reduce the chance of being recognized, so it was normal for them to be treated with a little distance as they walked toward the temple, but for Bern and Marta it was a different story, or should have been. Marta was village-born and had been popular all her life, and Bern had come from the mountains with his widowed mother as a boy and helped in her custom-weaving shop until she could get him apprenticed to Mortise the Carpenter. Both were priestblood and therefore respectable, but today even their neighbors would do no more than briefly meet eyes and nod sympathetically before ushering their children inside and going about their business. Only the widow Syl the butter-maker came out on the road to walk a distance with them while railing against the old lech Bal, which she could get away with only because her product was in demand and because she was thought to be crazy. "I'm not, you know," she'd once confided to Bern with a conspiratorial wink, which he returned.

In ten minutes they were at the temple, a column-fronted wooden building set on an artificial hillock in emulation of the Mount of ZAH downriver, where the god had first revealed himself to the Chaplin; the convent, where unmarried priestesses resided, and the priesthouse, for single priests, were to left and right. Walking across the audience court where the priests interpreted ZAH's will to the people as they saw fit, rain or shine, the others nervously urged Bern to take the lead. He stepped to a bell mounted on a post near a flight of stairs and lightly rang it with a small hammer suspended on a chain. Presently a pinch-faced young woman came out onto the porch, raising her hood over her hair. She wore the grey, ankle-length robe of a sub-priestess, or "sister," and Bern, being quite tall, could look over the edge of the porch to see that her shoes were scuffed and down-at-heel.

"Yes?" she said irritably.

"Sister, can we see Brother Bal?"

"What about?"

"The virgin Jenna, daughter of Clarence and Hermione." He gestured toward the silent parents.

"Can't they speak?"

"My wife 'n me're neighbors—priestblood. They ask us ta talk fer 'em."

The sister made a put-upon noise, paused a moment to demonstrate her gate-keeping power, and disappeared inside.

Bern knew Bal wouldn't come out right away even if he wasn't busy, but that they had to maintain themselves in respectful and expectant pose for the eventual emergence of the great man. It was believed among the Freethinkers that Bal couldn't even read or write, but he had wielded the sword of ZAH over Firstportage Village for fourteen years. As time had gone by and he'd continued to be denied the black robe of priesthood—which he wore anyway when superiors weren't around—he'd become more capricious and dangerous, but the merchants and tradesmen, especially the Freethinkers among them, had learned to work with him, and now they did their best to keep him on station: better a corrupt and incompetent priest they knew than a competent and interfering one they did not.

Bern doubted that the name he'd been given was reference to an old god whose worship was heresy, but it wasn't so unusual. During the depopulation and displacement of the Cleansing, family names had become superfluous and given names problematic. Old-fashioned ones like "Clarence" and "Hermione" suggested an acquaintance with books or an affinity for the old ways and brought suspicion when they were borne by strangers. New ones were thought up to replace them, often based on familiar objects or places or trades or creatures and sometimes comprised simply of evocative sounds. Thus the son of upwardly mobile one-time illegal forbidden-zone scavengers had become Bal, and the daughter of rapist priests, whose mother wanted to name her Elizabeth after her own murdered mother—until new friend Marta convinced her otherwise—had become Jenna.

Finally the man stepped onto the porch, wiping his mouth with a cloth napkin and tossing it aside; he wasn't supposed to reside or dine in the temple itself but ostentatiously did both. He was tall and thin and clean-shaven, with his greying hair dyed black, and had an olive complexion that could be observed in numerous of the village's firstborn children, though he might never have noticed; he only became interested in the young when they began to mature.

Now his contemptuous eyes scanned the spectators who'd begun curiously to collect at the back of the audience court before coming to rest on the unwelcome visitors.

"Well?" he intoned.

"Lord Bal," said Bern, going along with today's black-robed masquerade as a full priest, "thank you fer seein' us."

"Yes? What is it?"

"The virgin Jenna, lord ... she was s'possed ta go to the Citadel at full moon—on 'er birthday—but this mornin' she was ... took away.... Her parents ..."

Bal looked over their heads in a bored fashion. "She will be with the sisters until her departure."

"But lord," said Bern, "she do sumpin wrong? Do she need ta be punished?"

"Not your concern," said Bal, beginning to turn away. "She's with us now."

"With respect, lord—"

Bal slowly turned back with such a baleful glare that Bern changed what he was about to say.

"It's jes thet, she was gonna help me with sumpin I was makin' fer the temple, lord."

"For the temple?"

"Yes, lord ... a fine dinin' table, wit carved legs."

"And chairs?"

"Course, lord—four chairs."

The greedy man considered. "She will stay with the sisters ... but her mother may visit after breakfast—tomorrow." Again he started to turn away.

"Ever day, lord? 'til she leave?"

"A long table, and eight chairs."

"Don't have that much matched wood, lord. Six chairs?"

Bal hesitated for effect, nodded, and went back into the temple.

Bern breathed a sigh of relief. So Jenna's sequestration was only about jealousy or a desire to keep her from running away, nothing more serious. She would go to the Citadel for a few months as scheduled, come back and marry Ronnie, and life would go on as all expected. The four turned for home with resignation.

As Bern and Ronnie labored over Bal's new table, Hermione made her morning visits to Jenna, delivering her favorite clothes and pastry treats and the greetings of loved ones and taking away stories of convent life. The convent was where much of the priesthood's and village's business was conducted by the dozen or so sub-priestesses, or "sisters," who possessed literacy and numeracy in varying degrees. In such a small village as Firstportage it was also where childless sisters and visiting priestesses could entertain unmarried young men, if they desired, and where priests and sub-priests bestowed their blessing upon virgins, all in the cause of binding together the community of ZAH and incidentally providing servants and soldiers for his service. To Jenna's surprise and the surprise of Hermione's post-visit audience—consisting of Bern, Marta, Clarence, and Ronnie—there was also all manner of cross-coupling not mentioned in the Protocols and Teachings, including between brothers and sisters, sisters and sisters, and even between one of the village's five brothers and various young men of the village. It was remarkable that any of the priesthood's work got done,

Jenna had laughed to her mother, but at least she was only expected to help with the housework and gardening.

Then one morning Jenna's laughter rang false and her smile was strained as she sat with her mother on a bench by the garden wall.

"What is it, daughter?"

"The priest that came with yesterday's caravan–Lord Nils–I heard him talking to a sister, trying to impress her, I guess. I think he was talking about a new pogrom– Keep smiling, Mom!"

Hermione tried to stifle the fear provoked by that word. "Tell me," she said tightly.

"He told her he was a very important person, responsible for making preparations for 'a holy mission,' he said, 'ordered by ZAH himself.' He said it would involve thousands moving on the roads, and the garrisons and clergy had to be prepared."

"What else?"

Jenna casually looked about before replying. "For each town, there would be a list of suspected heretics. When they were confirmed–he said 'when,' not 'if'–their properties would be divided among the priesthood. He said he would be rich."

"And the heretics? Did he say–" she smoothly dropped into the middle of a description of little Juli's latest antics as a grey-robbed sister came around a corner, walked past, and went through a gate.

"No names," said Jenna. "He mentioned money-lenders and jewelry-makers and rich landowners.... Said they were all cursed of ZAH–Freethinkers."

"He said *Freethinkers?"*

"Yes. What should we do, Mom? I'm scared."

Hermione was silent a moment, then, "Did he say when?"

"No."

"We have to find out. Maybe one of the Circle can talk to the traders...." She turned on the bench to look at her daughter appraisingly.

"What?" said Jenna, discomfited.

"Does this priest talk to you?"

"No.... Well, he *looks* at me sometimes. I'm a nobody. Why?"

"You're a woman. A beautiful woman."

"What?... *Oh* ..."

"Can you do it, baby?"

"I don't know *how*, Mom."

"Again, you're a woman—you'll figure it out." When her daughter continued to stare at her uncertainly, she took her hand and went on. "Sometimes, when our lives are in danger, and our families are in danger, this is the only way we can survive, or fight. And maybe you won't have to give yourself. You're smarter than any stupid priest. Figure out what *he* wants ... and use that to get what *you* want.... Understand?"

Jenna's eyes teared up. "Mom, *I can't.* I'm only *fifteen!"*

"Sixteen," said her mother, looking stern, then softening.

"Look at me, daughter, and listen.... Sixteen years and nine months ago I used a piece of broken glass to cut the throat of one of the murdering priests who may have been your father, felt his blood pour over me, pushed his body off in order to escape, to make a life ... to make *you* ... and to raise you with a love that would make the circumstances of your birth irrelevant. I had just turned fourteen.... Believe me, you can find the strength, if you have courage."

Jenna knew the story, but before now it had seemed to be about some Freethinker heroine from history, not her own mother. This time, listening intently, she had stopped breathing. Finally she gasped a ragged breath, blinked a few times, and suddenly her eyes were clear. Looking into them, Hermione saw a sight so moving that her own eyes teared. In the time it took to take seven slow, centering breaths, Jenna, by an act of will, transformed herself from a mere precocious child into a grown woman.

"Don't cry, Mom," she said calmly, "it's going to be all right."

Putting her hand to her daughter's cheek, Hermione said, "Welcome to the rest of your life, my love. May it be a happy one."

3 - Flee or Die

There was no fighting a pogrom. One could only flee—or die. But flee where? and when? and with whom? Jenna's initial intelligence had enabled the Freethinkers to make preparations—to cache food, clothing, weapons, and coin at three locations in the forest, to consolidate and conceal in a shallow cave much of the Circle's precious library of forbidden books in the hope it could be recovered one day, and to make a plan of escape from the village—but the secret had to be closely held. Even though Freethinkers were trained from childhood to keep secrets without seeming to, no one wanted to run the risk of a Circle child, distraught at the prospect of losing a non-Circle playmate or first love, compromising everyone.

Nor could others in danger be warned directly. There was not really much overlap between the Freethinker Circle—comprised mostly of craftspeople and modest merchants—with the "money-lenders, jewelry-makers, and rich landowners" of Jenna's intelligence, but some such were friends and neighbors. In secret conference, the de facto leaders of the Circle concluded that the labels "freethinker" and "heretic" would simply be applied to anyone the priests and the village mayor wanted to rob, to make the targets legally defenseless before the representatives of ZAH. As Bern pointed out to the others collected around the lantern in his home—with windows covered and Ronnie listening from the attic stairs—only two Circle members really fit the description: Nan the vintner, whose winery had become the biggest for many miles, and Gowda the merchant, who supplied goods and financing to the traders who plied the roads. After weighing the safety of the Circle against that of friends in the targeted groups, it was agreed that each Circle member should decide whether to give warning, knowing that, if they misjudged, they risked torture and death not just for themselves but for everyone.

"Now," said red-headed Rooster, "we just need to know when." And with that all eyes went to Bern, who gazed into the lantern's steady flame.

"We're working on that."

Jenna raised her eyes, met those of the black-robed figure coming toward her, and shyly looked down again. Soon she was looking at a pair of fine leather boots. She rose gracefully from the garden bench to the level of the faux-jeweled Z-symbol suspended from a chain around the man's neck and stood with hands clasped in front.

"What are you doing out here, child?" asked the priest.

"Nothing, lord," she answered guiltily. "Just thinking.... Am I needed inside?" She glanced at the passage into the scriptorium and anxiously back to meet his eyes, then down again.

"No," he said, pleased by her deference.

The seconds went by as she felt him study her. Soon her cheeks and throat and the exposed swell of her breasts were crimson with embarrassment. Finally she gathered her courage and looked up, seeing malicious amusement in a clean-shaven and handsome face.

"May I be of service, lord?"

He continued openly to appraise her.

"You have very nice manners for a country girl," he observed.

"My mother would be pleased to hear you say so," she replied bravely, now smiling slightly. "She says I'll need them."

"Why is that?"

She looked confused. "I thought you knew, lord. I thought that was why you look at me sometimes."

"Knew what?"

"That, on my birthday, I am for the Citadel–for the high priests."

His slight smirk faded into an "Oh," and he involuntarily took half a step back. She seemed to misunderstand the reaction, plopping down on the bench dejectedly.

"That's what I was afraid of," she said miserably.

"What?" he said, sitting beside her.

"That I wasn't pleasing enough.... You're the first high priest I've ever met, and I hoped I was making a good impression."

"High ...? Actually, child, I'm not–"

"That's what I was thinking about. *You.* People say that high priests are old and ugly, but *you*'re not. I was thinking it would be nice to receive a blessing from someone like you. Hoping ..."

He was open mouthed at the plainspokenness of this girl. "You're not afraid?"

"I *was* ... then I saw you and Sister May."

"Saw what?"

"When you gave her your blessing in the laundry room ... and did the other things. She's only two years older than me, but I could tell she liked it."

"You were spying?"

"I was ... *trapped* ... in the back ... but I did peek a little bit." She lowered her eyes. "I'm sorry, I just wanted to see what a high priest liked. Are you angry?"

There it was again: 'high priest.' Lust struggled with self-preservation, but he couldn't help asking one more question.

"How did watching us make you feel?"

She appeared to consider, shifting on the bench, then looked up at him, lips slightly parted.

"I wanted to be Sister May."

ZAH! Save me from this girl! he silently cried. Adjusting the folds of the robe in his lap and looking away, he desperately tried to focus his mind on the penalty for doing what he wanted. To get control of his reckless appendage he imagined it being cut off with exquisite slowness and ceremony, along with its accessories, and stuffed in his mouth; then, with his nose clamped shut and just about to suffocate, to have his head sawn off with a dull saw, all in front of an assembly of fellow clergy.

Regaining his composure, he looked at her ruefully and announced, "That would be lovely, my dear, but I'm not a high priest—not for a few months yet. See?" He momentarily moved the dark blond hair from his left ear to show that the lobe was unmarked. Then he raised his hand to push the voluminous hair over her right ear and she turned it to him, exposing a neck perfect for kissing. When he took her earlobe between his thumb and forefinger her eyes fluttered and her lips parted again. He smiled.

"Your single stroke of ZAH's symbol means you have one priestblood parent. Two strokes for two parents, and three for elevation to the priesthood. High priests have the bottom stroke on the left ear, the Messengers have the middle one, and only the Sword of ZAH has the top one. See? No high-priest stroke."

Unexpectedly, as he displayed his unmarked right earlobe, she reached and gently took hold of it and lightly kneaded as he had done. No mere girl had ever been so forward with him, and he was momentarily transfixed by her closeness and her touch. Then the spell was broken by the passage arm-in-arm through the garden of the impressionable Sister May, now looking heartbroken, and the unimpressed and unbedded older sister, Olive, looking disapproving.

He took Jenna's hand from his ear but held on to it. "You're going to get me in trouble," he said.

"I'd *like* to get you in trouble."

He laughed at boldness, but then grew serious. "I'm responsible for making arrangements for a very important event—here in Firstportage and to the north. After that I'll be elevated to the high priesthood, I'm sure. Then I won't be so easy to get in trouble."

She squeezed his hand. "Can you do this event before I leave at full moon? Then maybe I could stay with you."

Looking into her eyes, he momentarily forgot himself. "No ... it's scheduled for three days *after* full moon. You'll already be gone."

She looked down sadly, then up again. "Well, I still have ten days. Can I do anything to help you?"

He was surprised at the offer. "I don't know.... Can you read and write?"

"No, of course not," she said, taking her hand away, insulted that he would think such a thing. "But I know numbers–all the way to one hundred–that's the number of arrows my family sells in a bundle."

He took her hand back. "I didn't mean to offend. It's just that I see you in the scriptorium."

"I just bring clean paper and ink and clean up."

"I see," he said, then, "If the documents the sisters create were numbered on the corner, would you be able to put them in order?"

"Documents? What do you mean?"

"I mean, if you had a stack of papers and each one had a different number, could you switch them around so that the little numbers were on top and the big ones on the bottom and you could count right through them?"

She frowned in concentration, trying to visualize such an operation, then brightened and squeezed his hand.

"Yes! I could do that!"

Jenna's intelligence was horrifying to the Freethinkers. Three days after she'd given the crucial date to her mother, she'd told her of the documents she'd been able to scan while collating, pretending repeatedly to lose her place and restarting until the senior sister began to look at her curiously. Three pieces of information were particularly disturbing. First, on the day, advance units of the Citadel main force would sweep past Firstportage, up the river roads, on the pretext of chasing bandits, in order to establish roadblocks to hamper escape to the mountains. Second, they would pre-secure and man containment areas, such as animal pens and village squares, where suspected heretics could be concentrated. And third, they would systematically exterminate Freethinkers and other undesirables, interrogating those first-seized for the identities and locations of those still at large. Worst of all, the documents seemed to have a generic quality to them, as if they were meant to be used with minor variation all over the realm of ZAH, all at the same time.

The realization that this could be the worst calamity since the Cleansing concentrated minds and hardened hearts, and sympathy for others in the path of destruction had to be discarded. The thirty-something Circle members and a handful of friends would be unlikely even to save themselves, much less others. Their best hope was to congregate at the two meadow-side houses between dark and moonrise on the night before, move together into the woods, and hope that the next days' chaos would temporarily cover their absence and their escape. All had agreed not to speak of a route or destination until everyone was well away, knowing that one caught-and-tortured member could compromise even the most carefully thought-out plan. The only consensus was to strike deep into the western woods to avoid searchers coming from the river road and settlements, and eventually to turn north, crossing or following tributaries of the Husson into the mountains.

Once this general plan was agreed, there was little left to discuss, save the one subject all were avoiding: Jenna.

Three nights before full moon, Ronnie could stand it no longer. He rose from his listening perch on the attic stairs and marched into a meeting that was breaking up without having discussed her—again.

"So," he said, as three or four Circle members were preparing to take their leave, "what's been decided about Jenna?"

The adults exchanged looks that discomfited Ronnie and the visitors continued to make their exit, except for Clarence and

Hermione. When the door was shut, Bern motioned his son and the others to chairs around the table where the group had been talking. Ronnie took his seat with a certain foreboding.

"Son," began Bern, "everybody is thinking about her, worrying about her. She's risking her life every day to help us all. Now, her mother has discussed various escape options with her, but there's a problem.... She's afraid to leave the convent before her transport to the Citadel."

"What?" said Ronnie, his voice rising. "Afraid?... Jenna?... I don't understand. Hermione says the back gate where the trash barrels 're kept has an inside latch. She can get out no problem! Tomorrow night! I can be waiting for her and take 'er to the woods to wait for the rest of you. What's she afraid of?"

"She's not afraid for *herself,"* his father continued patiently, "she's afraid for *us* ... that if she runs away, it'll draw attention to the Circle—maybe cause the kind of dedicated pursuit they wouldn't be able to mount once the main operation starts. And she's right: not having enough readers in the officer corps means communication breaks down when things get chaotic. But if Jenna and her family and our family are the only targets, they could catch us. That would be the end for all the Freethinkers of Firstportage."

"But—" said Ronnie, distraught.

"It's *true*, Ronnie," Hermione joined in, "I saw it when I was a girl, when the main target was the mountain settlements. When forces were concentrated and the objective was well understood, they were efficient, but once units started to lose touch, they lost focus and started to do their own thing. Then it was just anarchy, and that made it possible for some people to get away." Her hand sought Clarence's as she spoke; he looked pale and frail. "That's why there are still Freethinker settlements in the mountains, because Citadel forces become disorganized before they finish their task, *if* they have many tasks."

"I can't *believe* this!" Ronnie almost shouted. "You're talking about military history, I'm talking about *Jenna—our* Jenna." He started to get up. "I'm not going to—"

His mother grabbed his forearm. "Honey, listen to Hermione. I'm sure she's not finished." He glared at her for a moment and sat back down.

"So she refuses to do anything that would bring attention to us before the operation," said Hermione, "but that's not the end of it. She asked me to obtain a special potion for her, and I did. I'll give it to her in the morn—"

"Potion?" gasped Ronnie, incredulous. "You mean *poison?"*

"That's—"

"*Listen,* Ronnie! —just *listen,*" urged Hermione. "The potion is what some girls use to end illegal pregnancy—yes, it's poison, but in small doses it only makes you sick, very sick, which is what she would have to be to delay her departure. If she takes it, she'll be sick by nightfall, and they'll quarantine her. Even if she recovers in a day, she can pretend to be delirious until the operation begins, then escape in the confusion."

Seeing hope warring with doubt and fear in Ronnie's face, she added, "You can be there to guide her out, if your parents permit."

Ronnie turned to them with a plea in his eyes, and they both nodded.

"You'd have to move very quickly to find us in the woods, son," said Bern, "or we could be separated—forever. Understand?"

"Yes, Father. Yes, Mother. Thank you."

As she listened to the sound of horse hooves and carriage wheels in the forecourt of the Temple of ZAH next door, Jenna fingered the small porcelain vial in the pocket of her skirt. Glancing around the garden first, she took it out and shook it at her ear. Much more than four drops, which was all she'd been told to put on her muffin when she was ready. She pulled the cork to smell it and found it odorless. Nils appeared at the passageway to the scriptorium with a sheaf of papers in hand, but he was only flirting. She slipped the vial back into her pocket as he retreated inside.

She'd allowed herself to be discretely and not so discretely kissed and rubbed against a few times in the last two days. Her first kisses had been amateurish, but thanks to his tutoring–or so he thought–she'd improved. Now he couldn't get enough of her, to the consternation of the older sisters and the jealousy of the younger ones. He was so infatuated that he had countermanded Brother Bal's order to terminate her mother's visits.

When he came out of the passageway again, she moved the parcel her mother had brought to make room and he sat down. She could see he was excited about something.

"What is it?" she asked. "Am I needed?"

"In the worst way, but later," he teased. "I've just received the Citadel dispatches, and there's a note from a colleague. He says the Council of Messengers has approved elevation to the high priesthood for all priests in the field who perform well in the present mission. That means we don't have to wait to be together! I might even be able to take you as my wife right away, since you're priestblood. What do you think?"

Jenna was speechless, but not at the young priest's surprise marriage proposal. For the briefest instant she'd let her eyes drop to the papers which he held in his lap, and gone cold.

"I ... I don't know what to say, Nils." She fell against him and he put his arm around her. "It's like a dream," she murmured, reading the document.

Suddenly, the usual soundscape of the convent was disturbed by authoritative voices answered by deferential ones, by hurrying feet, and by the unmistakable clatter and clomp of armed men. As Nils withdrew his arm and Jenna straightened up, a grey-robed Brother Bal strode into the garden, followed by Olive, the senior sub-priestess. Then an enormously fat figure in black and two flanking aides emerged from the passage and Nils bolted to his feet, almost spilling the papers. Six black-helmeted and black-armored guards took positions just within the garden as whispering sisters and servants filled the passage beyond.

The fat man stood glaring for several seconds at the face and straight-ahead eyes of the mortified priest, who'd instantaneously come to his senses upon seeing him.

"This the girl?" demanded the fat man, not looking at her.

"Yes, Excellency," confirmed Bal.

"And she's been working in the scriptorium?"

"By Lord Nils's order, Excellency," said Sister Olive.

Now he turned his malevolent gaze on Jenna, and she stood up.

"Can you read, girl?"

"No, sir– I mean Excellency," she said, copying the others, "but I'm learning to make pages."

"Pages?"

"She can count, Excellency," explained Olive, "to a hundred, she says."

"I put the little numbers on top and the big ones on the bottom, and ..."

The fat man took the sheaf out of Nils's hand, glanced at the top document, and blanched. Nevertheless, after flipping through the pages he handed them to Jenna.

"Show me."

Jenna took the pages, sat down on the bench and started to look through them as the fat man closely observed. Her finger repeatedly fell on numbers in the text and she tried to make sense of them and to put the pages in the proper order, but soon she was sniffling and her hands were shaking.

The fat man turned to look at Bal, who, covering for his past incompetence, confidently said, "I've known her most of her life, Excellency; she's a good girl," by which he meant she couldn't read or write, and that he'd been successful in preserving her for her virgin's duty.

The fat man looked down at her shrunken and embarrassed figure, took back the papers and handed them to an aide, and turned to the senior sister. "Keep her out of the scriptorium, and no visitors until she leaves." Then to Jenna, "Go to your quarters, girl," and finally to the young priest, who'd become glazed-eyed with impending doom, "*You*, come with me."

At the end of the garden and about to turn a corner, Jenna looked back to see the guards fall in behind her slump-shouldered would-be husband as he passed out of sight.

"I'm sorry," she whispered.

Long after the sounds of iron-wheeled carriage and horses on courtyard stone had receded, Jenna sat in her tiny room with the porcelain vial in her hand. Death was in the air and unavoidable, but she was loth to make herself the first subject of others' pain. News of her own death might indeed serve to expedite the flight of the Freethinkers, but how could she be sure? It might only give pain without purpose.

Was there another way?

Ronnie and Bern emerged from the woods under gathering clouds to be met at the edge of the common meadow by T-Rex, the part-wolf, part-wolfhound guardian of the home when the men were away. The scene was quotidian: the two with bush axes in hand, returning from a day of clearing new growth from around numerous trees in the forest—trees that had been husbanded for eventual harvest by the childless Mortise the Carpenter and that, by tradition, had passed to Bern and remained his property as long as he demonstrated dominion by keeping their root fields clear to the dripline. Under cover of this habitual activity they'd been able to check on and supplement the three escape caches and to make a stretcher for Jenna in case it was needed; now there was nothing to do but wait for the third day hence, when Hell-on-Earth was scheduled.

The men had worked without speaking, both aware of how much Jenna must be suffering at each moment: aching, vomiting, shitting herself and her bedding, being cruelly confined to her room to live or die as she would—a misery that none of those who loved her could help her through.

By the time they'd crossed the meadow, blood-orange sun had blinked out west and veiled moon had risen east. Hermione showed herself at her kitchen door, ready to join them for a nightly consultation while T-Rex guarded the younger children from the back porch of her house. By the time the men had shed their packs and dirty boots and washed their hands and faces, five steaming mugs of tea were on the table and Clarence and Hermione were coming through the door.

Ronnie looked from his mother to the new arrivals and asked, "Any news?" by which all knew he meant news of Jenna.

"No, Ronnie," said Hermione. "Not since morning. She has the potion; if she took the drops with food at midday, she'll just be getting really sick now. Maybe they'll come for us during the night, or maybe they'll tell me in the morning when I visit. We just have to be ready to act our parts."

The worry in Ronnie's eyes was painful for all to see. "Was she scared?" he asked.

"Not at all," Hermione lied. "Told me to tell you not to worry—and she gave me something for you," she lied again.

"What?"

"You have to stand up to get it. Come here."

Mystified, Ronnie rose and went around the table, where Hermione unexpectedly wrapped her arms around him and squeezed with all her strength then kissed him on both cheeks. She hadn't kissed him since he was about twelve and he was embarrassed, until Clarence and the others chuckled in good humor.

To cover as he extricated himself, he talked about the comfortable stretcher he and his father had made so Jenna could be carried until she regained her strength, and about his reconnoitering of the warren of alleys behind the convent, through which he was prepared to bring her on his back once she came out the back gate.

In mid-word he stopped to cock an ear, as did the others.

There it was again! T-Rex's unmistakable hybrid bark, this time closer; he'd come off the porch toward them. One more confused bark, and then a chorus of yelps and whines and other excited utterances.

Ronnie marched to the door and threw it open. Seeing by the cloud-filtered moonlight a grey-shrouded figure with a tail-wagging T-Rex insanely dancing about, he grabbed the axe propped on its hooked blade-end beside the door and stepped onto to the porch.

"Who goes?" he demanded in a grown man's voice, prepared to chop down any attacker even as his father came through the door behind him with a lantern in one hand and his own axe in the other.

The figure stepped forward into the lamplight, lowering the hood of a stolen robe of a sub-priestess of ZAH.

"C'est moi, cher prince–ne me tue pas!" Don't kill me!

"Jenna!" said Ronnie hoarsely as he threw the axe to the ground and moved to enfold her in his arms. In a moment she was being hugged from all sides with a mixture of affection and consternation. What was she doing there?

"Let's go inside," she said. "C'mon, Rex."

Ronnie bent to retrieve the axe. "He has to go back to work, Jen. The kids are at your house."

"Oh, right," she said, then bent to rub T-Rex's face and speak affectionately to him before pointing him back to his post, whereupon he trotted dutifully into the dark.

Once the door closed behind them, Jenna became serious. "I only have a few minutes. I–"

"What?" cried Ronnie. "No!"

"*Listen*, son," commanded his father.

She started again, quickly recounting all that had transpired after her mother left that morning, leaving out her playacting with Nils for Ronnie's sake. When she described the fat man, she saw Bern nod.

"You know him?" she asked.

"Sounds like one the traders describe. Grotius, head of the Ministry for the Suppression of Error."

"The *Error Minister?"* said Marta in disbelief, "in our little village?"

"Not a good sign, I'd say," mused Bern. "Go on, Jenna, about the documents."

"I was able to absorb only one order. It seemed like something to be passed around and signed by different people—maybe to show they'd read it. Already nearly full—about twenty signatures."

"You said 'order,'" noted Bern. "What was the order?"

"Just one thing: to advance all operations by one day, to daybreak on the second day after full moon."

They stared at her a moment, then met each other's eyes in understanding of the emergency adjustments that had to be made. Her lifesaving mission accomplished, Jenna started to back toward the door.

"Now—"

Ronnie grabbed her hand and tried to control his desperation. "Jenna, Jenna ...,' he began in a reasonable tone. "Please ..."

"No, Ronnie. Don't make this harder. I can't stand it." Her self-control faltered and her voice and eyes betrayed her anguish at parting.

"Just come over here a second," he urged, leading her across the room beside the low fire where the teakettle still warmed.

As the young lovers held hands and spoke urgently, the adults, to give them privacy, began discussing how best to spread the new intelligence Jenna had brought. Soon, though, something passed unspoken between the two women, who took their men by the arms and murmured quietly. Finally, Hermione took the lead.

"Jenna, honey."

"Yes, Mom?"

"It's early, and still pretty light out; you could attract attention. You should stay here—with Ronnie—till it clouds up more. We're all going over to be with the children."

The two looked to the others in turn, then silently to each other.

Hermione stepped closer with her arms open and Jenna went into them. Then it was her father's turn. The dignified but now-frail man held her with a tenderness he seldom displayed, brushing a stray hair over her ear and kissing her forehead. Looking into his eyes, she knew she'd never see him again.

Bern and Marta embraced her together. "Thank you, brave girl," said Bern. Marta added, "If we miss you in the forest, find the mountain people's message stone, like your mother told you, and look for the smoke of cooking fires in the forest. We'll be waiting there for you."

As they turned to speak to their son, Jenna surreptitiously extracted the little vial from her pocket.

"Here, Mom," she whispered, "I won't be needing this."

Alone, and with all the time in the world, the lovers simply held hands and looked at each other, lost in the moment. Finally, without letting go, they went about the house extinguishing candles and lowering the lantern, and thence into Bern and Marta's bedroom.

The sisters who resided at the convent were surprised not to be joined for breakfast by their guest, who was normally an early riser. Eventually Sister May—her jealousy abated by the fall of Nils—was sent and found her sound asleep. Soon a drowsy Jenna learned that Nils had been jailed, that Bal seemed to be wearing Nils's black robes in Minister Grotius's presence, and that all of them but Bal would caravan that night to the Citadel in the forecast moonlight, Jenna riding with Sister Olive as chaperone. Today was her sixteenth birthday and she was officially virtual chattel of the Priesthood of ZAH until she bore a child, and she fervently hoped Grotius would not exercise his high priest's prerogative in a moving carriage before they even reached the city. She didn't know if another man would be able to discern her changed status.

She spent the day in anguish over what she was putting Ronnie through, imagining him pacing nervously as all but her mother awaited news of the illness that had suddenly stricken her—news they would not receive, for there would be no illness. Would he ever come to understand her decision? —the decision to hold the Circle's safety and that of her own unborn children above passion? She ached for a sign of forgiveness she knew might never come.

At nightfall Jenna was relieved to find herself still unmolested. At moonrise under a clearing sky, the newly elevated Lord Bal saw the caravan off—wearing Nils's faux-jeweled pendant, she noted—and they were away on a trip of about fifty miles, planning to rest at Westmount Hamlet opposite Mount of ZAH Village until late morning and to arrive at the Citadel by end of day.

Jenna gazed out the open window at the dim, blue-grey countryside, thinking about her night with Ronnie and about what might become of him now. Hard times were upon them, and only the meek or the very brave might survive. Ronnie was already tall and strong and she had seen him fight, but only in defense of her or others, and always stopping himself before anyone was seriously hurt. Could he fight men like those in this column? —black-armored paramilitary troops of the Error Police? Like her, he'd barely been out of Firstportage in his life, and he'd certainly never been in armed combat.

As the moon mounted higher, the caravan forded a shallow creek on its way to the Husson a few hundred paces to the east and started moving along an escarpment on their right. Suddenly the night creatures went silent and the horses grew skittish. Troops and passengers looked around nervously while Jenna struggled to maintain her composure. Soon a deep bass thrumming began to suffuse the night and she looked out the window to see, on an outcrop back from the road, a solitary figure, shirtless and swinging an object about his head, writhing his lithe torso and arms to get maximum effect from his instrument. Sister Olive leaned across to see. "Who's that?" she said peevishly. "What's he doing?"

"Probably just a crazy shepherd boy," said Jenna.

Most of the column was already past, but the guards behind were affronted by the display and took up its challenge, launching a few arrows at the impudent youth. Even at the distance, some came within inches of their target, but still the boy played on, until the soldiers laughingly berated each other's bowmanship and stopped wasting arrows.

Sister Olive, still craning across, said, "That's one strange boy."

Jenna smiled to herself. "Yes ... unique in all the world, I'd say."

Finally realizing that the boy was looking directly at *them*, Olive reached across and dropped the leather curtain over the opening.

Jenna's little smile faded as she leaned back in the seat, still able to hear the strange music of Ronnie's magical bush axe. In a moment, after Olive had resumed her seat and her interest in the river side of the road, she slipped her forearm past the curtain and held her hand up in farewell. Instantly the sound stopped.

On the escarpment, a panting and weeping Ronnie held the suddenly stilled axe across his body, watching the silver-moonlight-bathed hand until he could see it no more

4 - Fateful Turning

By the time Ronnie reached his home and his bed the moon had almost set again. He'd seen a faint light in his parents' bedroom window as he approached and under their door as he entered, but it had gone out within minutes.

He tried to rest for the long day and night ahead but couldn't fall asleep. In his troubled state it seemed that darkness had no more descended than it lifted again as the sky outside began to lighten. Soon he heard his parents moving about in the common room, his father probably lighting the fire in the iron stove as Ronnie himself should have been doing and his mother beginning to prepare breakfast. He gave up trying to sleep when he heard his sleepy-voiced little brother ask from his loft where Ronnie was and be hushed by their mother. Soon he heard Bo climb down his ladder, spend a few minutes in the lavatory, and then head for the henhouse to gather eggs.

He lingered in a hopeful half-dream of Jenna on her traveler's cot at the inn across the river from Mount of ZAH village, still sleeping peacefully, now safe from the army attack. When he let the dream go and sat up, he found himself still in the clothes he'd put back on after bathing in a moonlit stream on the way home. He pulled his boots on, combed his hair with his fingers, ruffled his little beard, and made his appearance–but he was too ashamed to take his place at table.

He'd never disobeyed his parents about a serious matter, but the evening before, with the caravan still unformed and long after Jenna's illness should have been reported, he'd grown so frantic for news that

Hermione had told him about the return of the poison and what she thought it meant, trying to persuade him to honor her daughter's wishes. Instead, he'd impulsively defied all to snatch up his axe and head for the convent, leaving them to prepare for the consequences of his likely arrest. It was the kind of irrational act that all Circle members were raised to disdain, and he couldn't believe he'd been the one to commit it.

"I'm sorry," he said now. "Mother, Father ... I'm sorry."

Bern studied him a moment, then nodded his acceptance. "It's all right, son," he said. "Let's put it behind us and move on, as we must."

"I guess I just went a little crazy," he explained. Bo looked back and forth, already chewing.

"Love will do that to you sometimes," said his mother, skillet in hand. "Dangerous stuff–best avoided, for the most part." She slid the huge omelet onto his plate. "Now sit down and eat; we've a long day ahead."

Ronnie told of seeing Jenna in her carriage from a vantage point near the south river road, and of her farewell, stripping away the drama. When he got up to take the dishes out to T-Rex for a good licking and a wash at the pump, he encountered Hermione and told her too, her eyes intent on his, mining them for the truth.

"She did it for all of us, you know," she said hoarsely, and now he became aware of her appearance–the yellow-tinged and greasy face, the stained teeth, the unkempt hair, the dirty gardening clothes.

"I know–I can honor that now.... Are you okay, Auntie? You don't look well."

"That's the idea."

"What?"

"Ready, Herm?" said his mother, coming out of the house with Bo trailing behind. She was transformed. Now, instead of the fresh face she'd worn at breakfast, she looked like someone who risen from her deathbed for some last-minute shopping: skin grey, eyes blackened, wearing clothing that smelled and looked to have been left in the pigpen for a few days.

"Ready as I'm gonna be, I guess."

"You *sound* sick," said Marta, gathering her things. "Perfect."

"You don't look any too healthy yourself, girl. Here—let me fix that hair."

She raised her fingertips to Marta's head, but instead of smoothing her hair in place she contrived to artfully disarrange it.

"There. Now you look like a real plague carrier."

Looking between the two women, Bo grew alarmed. "Are you sick, Mama?"

"No, honey," she assured, "we're just playing. I'm fine."

Ronnie smiled weakly at the scene, which might have been comical if it weren't so deadly serious. When he'd gone to recover the frying pan from T-Rex and stood washing it at the pump, the two women went by arm-in-arm with their market baskets. As they passed between their houses and approached the path, their progress became less sure-footed. Soon, he knew, after a few sniffles or discrete coughs into raised kerchiefs, word would fly around the marketplace that their two families were diseased, possibly dying, and must be avoided until whatever afflicted them had done its work, or not. That would guarantee they'd have no uninvited visitors for a while, even if, after a couple of days, friends and neighbors might start leaving life-sustaining parcels by the path.

As the morning wore on, Clarence reinforced the impression of illness with his stiff movements about their two houses. Only he wasn't faking. Ronnie knew him to be no more than fifty-five years, but he looked and moved like a man of seventy or more, thanks to the near fatal beating he'd once taken from the priests' goons. As Ronnie chopped wood and took care of other outdoor chores so he could raise an alarm if necessary, his father and Clarence labored to hide their part of the precious library, in the determinedly optimistic hope that it could one day be recovered.

Seeing Clarence falter with a fat parcel, Ronnie parked his maul in the tree-stump chopping-block and started toward him, but then waited for him to get up the two steps and through the door of Bern's workshop. Ronnie half turned to give T-Rex a signal and followed.

"How's it goin', Dad?"

His father raised his head from below floor level. "You post Rex?" he asked.

"Yeah. He knows something's up. He's on the job."

"Come see, then."

Ronnie went to where the tongue-and-groove floorboards had been taken up to expose an area the size of the bed he slept in at night. "Looks dry," he remarked, looking into the stout, yard-deep box he'd helped his father build and bury a couple of years before. Constructed of oak planks and cross-planked inside with cedar, it was more than adequate for the books piled about, especially since the schoolbooks would be buried in a hole already dug in the chicken coop.

"Shall we?" said Bern, gesturing at the stacks. As Clarence struggled to rise from a chair, Ronnie grabbed up a stack and handed them to his father. "Can I do this part, Uncle C? I need the exercise." The already tired man started to protest, then settled back.

"Remember these, Dad?" said Ronnie as he touched volumes in the next stack. "Lamar gave 'em to us after his son died.... Sun Tzu, Machiavelli , Clausewitz ... biography of Alexander of Macedon ..."

"He gave them to *you*–hoping you'd learn what he was trying to teach his boy–but don't get sidetracked, son. We've got a lot to do before nightfall.

Ronnie handed over the stacks one by one, trying to ignore the heavy, five-color world atlas, Audubon's bird book, Graves's *I, Claudius*, books by Chaucer, Angelou, Stephen King, Shakespeare, James Patterson, Dibenadetti, Rowling, Koshiba and more, finally the even more dangerous books of history and religion and philosophy and–with greatest difficulty–three small wooden boxes made especially to protect the fragile treasures within: nearly two hundred comic books from the century before the Cleansing, donated by a family run out of new young people to enjoy them or scholars to study them,

By the time all the stacks were put away, Marta and Hermione could be heard greeting T-Rex and then the door opened.

"How's it going?" asked Marta.

"Good," said Bern. "There's a little extra room–for keepsakes and such. Ronnie's chess pieces ... your mother's quilt."

"We got some fresh tea before they ran us off. Wanna cup?"

Behind her, Hermione was looking at her husband, who hadn't risen from his chair. "Not for us, thanks," she said. We've got a lot to do."

At this, Clarence rose as gracefully as he could and took his wife's meagre market purchases. As the mismatched couple left the workshop and headed to their house, the others glanced at each other but did not speak the obvious.

At the fletcher's house, as it was known, little Juli stood in the doorway looking as discomfited by the break in routine and her parents' appearance as Bo had earlier, even if she couldn't have expressed why.

Once inside, Hermione said, "Why don't you rest awhile, dear. I'm going to mend your winter coat."

"I'm fine. Just wanna check the cabinets–see what we still need to pack."

Juli fetched the sewing basket and sat at her mother's feet as she took the heavy coat onto her lap and set to her task. Clarence moved about, opening and closing doors, rummaging around. With his back to the others he worked at something for a moment, then resumed his rummaging.

Finally he stepped to the door.

"Be right back," he said over his shoulder.

"Can I help with something?" said Hermione, her eyes on her work.

"Not this time," said Clarence at length, then he turned to regard his wife and daughter until Hermione raised her head.

"What?" she said with a quizzical smile.

"Nothing ...... I was just admiring you both."

Hermione's mouth opened slightly in surprise. She blushed and looked back to her work, smiling. "Thank you," she said, then low to her daughter, "Daddy's admiring us. Say 'Thank you.'"

Pleased if slightly mystified, Juli turned her head and said, "Thank you, Daddy."

"You're welcome." Then he went out and closed the door.

Hermione concentrated on her task, turning the coat inside and out to check her progress on a loose shoulder seam, following one stitch with another until she had finally tied off. Putting the coat aside, she rose and went to the window, but saw only T-Rex near the chicken coop. She turned back to ponder what errand had been suggested by what Clarence had found or not found in the cabinets. Her eyes were drawn to one high cabinet and, unbidden, her feet took her toward it. She opened the door and studied the disarranged small bottles and pots, the mortar and pestle. Then she saw it–a short length of gold chain with bits of broken silk thread at one end. She knew instantly what it was, what it had replaced in the cabinet, what it meant.

At that moment, in the chicken coop, beside a pile of dirt and a hole dug to bury more books, Ronnie wrestled as quietly as he could with a violently dying Clarence. Minutes earlier he'd seen the old man cross from his house to the coop on some mission. When a banging had erupted from within and startled chickens hurried out noisily, he'd laid down his maul to investigate and found Clarence writhing on the ground against the wall, the small vial in the dirt beside him. Ronnie had rushed to him, then started to go for help, only to feel Clarence's steel grip on his arm.

"No, Ronnie! Don't leave!"

"But ..."

A full-body spasm and a shudder and a stifled groan went through the contorted man, then, "Help me finish it, Ronnie! Don't let Hermione– Oh, oh ... *Zaaahh!*" he moaned, convulsing in agony.

Compelled by the beloved man's last wish and great need, Ronnie clapped his hand over Clarence's mouth as he yelled and stared with wide-open, desperate eyes. When the spasm subsided, Ronnie grabbed a rag off a hook and lay down behind him, putting an arm under his head and wrapping his legs around to keep him from kicking the wall. When the next wave came he put the rag to Clarence's mouth and felt him bite on it as he wailed.

When the shuddering started finally to diminish, Clarence said with perfect clarity, "Make me presentable, Ronnie, and ... ah ... ah ... aahhg ... no-no-no-no–" and he was babbling and vomiting and yelling into the cloth again. This time the trembling didn't stop and breaths came shallow and labored. As Ronnie felt the life wrung out of Clarence's frail body, he began softly to cry.

"Don't cry, Ronnie," rasped the old man. "Don't cry."

When he didn't say more and didn't spasm again Ronnie thought his ordeal was over, but then Clarence turned his head slightly and whispered, "Jenna ..."

"What, Uncle?"

"Protect ... Jenna ..."

He's fading, thought Ronnie, forgetting that Jenna was already gone.

"Promise!"

"I promise."

The last forceful utterance seemed to bring on a final convulsion as Clarence's spine arched and his hands turned into claws. Then suddenly he stopped moving, frozen in agonizing death. Against his bony back, Ronnie wept.

In the house, Bern wondered why the sound of his son's woodchopping hadn't resumed and went to the door. Seeing no Ronnie but only T-Rex looking agitatedly into the coop, he went to investigate and came upon a scene momentarily beyond understanding.

"Ronnie! What happened? Are you hurt?"

"He's dead, Dad," blubbered Ronnie. "He took Jenna's poison. When I found him, he asked me to help him be quiet, so Hermione ..." He yielded to fresh tears.

Bern, on his knees behind Ronnie, reached over and felt for a pulse at Clarence's throat, then, finding none, pulled his son into a seated position and embraced him.

"There, son. Don't cry any more. You did a brave thing and I'm proud of you."

"But–"

"Hush, now. What's done is done. Time now to–"

"CLARENCE?" shouted Hermione from her porch, the gold chain clutched in a fist at her chest.

In the coop, Bern stood up quick and pulled Ronnie up with him. "Listen," he said urgently. "I've got to get her in the house and tell her before she sees him like this. What you need to do is to massage the signs of pain away and wipe him clean before I bring her out. Can you do that, son?"

"Yes, Dad."

"Good boy. Get to it."

"Don't scream," said Bern quietly, once he'd stepped from the coop to redirect Hermione's determined march toward the house and–once inside–gotten between her and the door. Instead of screaming, she tried to get around him, but when he blocked her and held her at arm's length to let his eyes communicate the hopeless truth, her face contorted and she fell against him. Marta, watching the scene and understanding intuitively, came to embrace them both. Young Bo, even though he wasn't sure what the crying was about, joined in.

By the time Marta and Bern had walked Hermione between them into the coop and Ronnie removed the blanket he'd draped, Clarence had been made to look like a man peacefully sleeping. Hermione knelt and put her hand on top of her husband's, crossed on his chest. She no longer cried, but simply looked. Finally, she raised one lifeless hand and placed under it the piece of gold chain that had been his wedding band, though, ever considerate, he'd surely meant for her to have it to spend during the flight to safety.

It was clear to all that Clarence had meant to be buried where a hole was already dug, and so it was done. Then, there being no time or choice, preparations resumed. The books from the coop were packed away with the others, the tight-fitting lid hammered back in place, tarred, and covered with enough depth of earth that it would never be accidentally disturbed by a plow. Laundry was hung out to dry, long-burning fires prepared, fruits and vegetables gathered as well as could be expected of two sick families. Young Bo and Juli were kept occupied or napping all day so that once they and other children were surprised with the information that they were about to go on a nighttime walk in the woods, and that Uncle Clarence would meet them later, it would be too late for word to slip out to non-Circle friends. Bo may have understood the truth, about Clarence, but at least he pretended to believe.

By late afternoon a few of the seventeen Freethinkers who would depart from the location had started to arrive, all relieved by the increasingly cloudy sky, which would make pursuit by the police less likely, if any informer summoned them. By sunset all had collected in the common room of the Woodmaker house and were being tied together, family members lightly to each other and parents taking their places holding onto a common knotted rope, with the subdued Hermione and confused Juli placed in the middle by unspoken consensus. Most were lightly dressed and unburdened, their equipment and provisions already cached in the woods, and, despite the loss of Clarence and the deadly seriousness of the occasion, a certain picnic-going levity was being maintained, whether for the children or themselves. Finally all was in readiness. The long-burning fire was started in the fireplace and lanterns were extinguished. As firelight flickered across the faces of adults and children who had known and supported each other all their lives—all of whose lives would be forfeit if they failed—the house fell silent.

Ronnie, with his young eyes and ears and his intimate knowledge of the forest trails, would lead, with his mother and brother behind and his father at the end of the rope to look after anyone who might stumble or panic and let go of it. As the last of the sun's light faded, Ronnie opened the door, took up the bush axe leaning against the wall beside it, and led the way out; his father closed the door behind himself and murmured for T-Rex to follow.

The seventeen, plus one outlandish-looking wolfdog, walked single file across the common meadow, hands on those before them in the partly obscured moonlight, taking small steps and frequently bumping into each other until a rhythm and a pace began to develop. At the rampart Ronnie chose an easy path over the collapsed and overgrown vehicles and rubble, one that had been trod by generations of hunters and woodspeople. For a few minutes he stayed to such well-known forest thoroughfares, but then veered onto mere deer-paths, and then through heavy brush into close passages that he had established in recent days or that only he knew. Then, as the backlit clouds spread out above them, he stopped and turned back.

"We're here, Dad," he said quietly.

"Everybody okay?" asked Bern just as quietly and received reassuring murmurs from the adults.

"We're in a glade," he told them, "about the size of the temple forecourt. We're going to stretch out till the rope is taut and sit down or lie down until we have light to move faster. When you're settled, you can let go of the rope. Go ahead, Ronnie."

Soon all were in the grass and making themselves comfortable. Now low conversation began among family members and between neighbors. For the first time young children were able to ask parents what was going on, but these were children who from early ages had been taught that the world was a dangerous place in which safety could be found only with others of their kind; reassured that they were with the people that loved them and that all would be explained later, many cozied up to their parents and fell asleep.

Ronnie, mentally and emotionally exhausted, thought he would never sleep soundly again, but as soon as he put his head on his backpack and started thinking about Jenna and the promise he'd made to her father, he was out like a snuffed candle. He didn't even feel T-Rex settle against his leg.

Moonlight woke him some time later and he sat up to see others already moving about. By the time it began to yield to daylight, the now mostly untethered fugitives had retrieved the supplies cached by his father and him over the past week and reached the high ground to the northwest, where two smaller groups were to meet them. From a rocky outcrop they would be able to see parts of the village and river road, and perhaps make sure there was actually an attack before committing themselves to the wilderness. Many of the group, unable to go back to sleep in this moment of decision, found niches from which to await the morning sun and see what it would reveal. Bern and Ronnie shared one such niche.

As the eastern sky began to lighten, Ronnie spoke.

"Dad?"

"Yeah?" said Bern, his eyes scanning downriver. When nothing more came, he looked back. "What is it?"

"Have I been a good son?" Said Ronnie. "Have I done my duty?"

He'd never in his life uttered such questions. His father turned to give him full attention.

"Yes ... and yes," he said. "What's on your mind?"

Ronnie took a ragged breath, let it out. "I can't go with you," he rasped.

Bern didn't speak for a long time, but only looked. Finally, clearing his throat, "You may never find her, you know. Never even get into the Citadel."

"I know, but I have to try. If *we* can't return home, then neither can *she*, and she may not find us in the mountains."

They fell silent again, as first one bird in the trees below sang out tentatively and was joined one by one by others with more confidence. As the disk of the sun broke the horizon and lit their place in the rocks, Bern withdrew a leather pouch from his shirt and took from it a short tube closed at one end and with a cap at the other. Unscrewing the cap, he shook out a rolled sheet of the Temple of ZAH's finest stolen white bond. He smoothed it out and looked at it for a moment, then handed it over. As Ronnie perused it, he broke into an incredulous grin. It was a travel pass—forged, of course—for one Rondak of Firstportage, apprentice woodworker, in route to Citadel City to take up employment with one Oswald Woodmaker. It had an elaborate "Z" symbol at the top and was signed by Nils, Priest of ZAH. Beside that presumably dead man's signature was a round stamp with the image of what looked like a masked bear—incongruous, to be sure, but quite impressive.

"Hermione's idea," said Bern, "from Jenna's description of official documents."

"Where'd you get the stamp?"

His father, already rummaging in the pouch again, extracted a smaller pouch made from an animal's bladder and spilled from it several coins, three of which were gold, one of which depicted the masked bear.

"This is half the family's fortune," he said. "What's left of it, anyway." He picked one gold coin with a man's head and the word "Kruger" on it and held it up. "Give any one of these three to Owlly—that's what he's called, by the way—so you won't be a burden on his family. Cut pieces off the others if you need to. Don't let anyone know you have them." He poured them back into the pouch and handed it over. "If you suspend this above your privates by the cord it'll be less likely to be discovered. Do it now."

"Thanks, Dad," said Ronnie, lifting his shirt to tie the cord around his waist and putting the tube in a leather pouch slung over one shoulder.

"You're welcome.... Now, I'd best go and break the news to your mother. You watch for– What?! ... What is it?!"

Ronnie was suddenly alert and pointing to the southeast.

Darkness lingering in the river valley had obscured the dust clouds on the road, but it could not obscure fire. In the distance, where lay the hamlet in which Jenna's party would have rested the night before, two and then three tiny points of light could be seen. As they watched, a merged column of smoke rose into the sunlight.

Rising higher, the sun began to reveal the dust clouds of cavalry and wheeled vehicles and marching men. Now Ronnie's sharp eyes discerned the formations moving on the road.

"Look, Dad! They're already north of Firstportage! and ... look there!"

More fires breaking out–right in their own village!

Without getting up and exposing himself more than necessary, Bern craned around until he spotted a stout, short-limbed and necked boy nearby.

"Turtle! Do you see?" The boy nodded, wide-eyed.

"Stay low and don't run. Find Lamar and tell him, and tell him to get everyone ready to leave as soon as the others arrive. Understand?"

"Yes, Uncle Bern."

"Go!" he commanded, and the boy turned his broad back and moved off purposefully.

Bern had hoped the other two groups would make it to the outcrop before moonset but had known they might have to stop short in the woods. Still, they couldn't be far away. Now he scanned the trees and willed them to hurry.

"Your mother knows, Ronnie," he said as he watched. "She was just hoping things would work out differently."

"What'll you do now?"

"Make up a plan as we go along, so no individual can compromise us if they're captured." Captured and tortured to death, he meant.

Bern scooted shoulder to shoulder to his son. "Listen to me now, and don't forget.... You've studied military history, and you're a brave boy, but now you must be *smart* and *resourceful*–without letting anyone know how smart and resourceful you are. The Circle must flee *before* the priesthood, because we're too many to hide, but *you* must flee *into its domain*, and *ever closer to power*. The priests look to the horizon for threats, and they can overlook those under their noses, especially if those threats reside among people they need, like bureaucrats and soldiers and craftsmen. So let this attack wash over you, then get as far behind the front as quick as you can. Those in the rear will assume you belong, especially if you act like you do. Got it?"

"Do you think I'll be safe to walk the road?"

"My biggest worry is that you'll be conscripted for the army if you're so exposed, so try to find some kind of camouflage–I can't say what that might be, but–"

Ronnie had gone on point again, and Bern's attention swiveled to the wood's edge some fifty paces away where Ronnie was looking and intently listening. Soon, Bundy the portager emerged cautiously and then extended his arms and broke into a grin when he was greeted by others who stepped from hiding to usher him and his party out of sight.

"That's a relief," said Bern, leaning back against the rock. "Just six more now."

As the two resumed watching the attack unfold, it became apparent that troops were being moved in wagons on both sides of the river–fast.

"There's a lot of 'em, Dad. You think they're in the woods yet?"

"It's a lot of territory ... maybe just the main trails at first."

Seconds later a cry came from the trees just in front of their position. Bare feet ran, branches snapped, and suddenly a dark, wild-haired teenage girl crashed from the brush and fell hard, nearly losing the dagger she had in her hand. Instantly, a muscular, thick-headed dog charged out of the trees and was upon her, biting her about the back of the neck and shoulders as she screamed and fought. Ronnie grabbed the axe lying next to him and broke cover, as did others.

The half-minute it took him to reach the girl was an eternity in which the vicious beast bit and shook her even as she stabbed at it with the dagger. By the time Ronnie was in striking distance, the dog had bitten her in the face and throat and blood poured from her.

Fearful of hurting the girl, he violently slammed the butt of the axe handle into the dog's side. The animal broke its grip to confront him and immediately yelped as an arrow struck and protruded out of the opposite side of its neck. As it writhed and pawed in helpless pain and fury and the bowman above nocked another arrow, Ronnie kneeled to the girl.

It was Betta, Jenna's best friend, and she was beyond saving. As he helplessly tried to staunch the bleeding, she looked up at him.

"Ronnie ..."

"Hush now, Bet," he said, easing the dagger from her hand. "We've got you."

"Ronnie ... they ..."

Bern was at Ronnie's shoulder. "Betta, honey," he said gently, "where are the others?"

"Dead," she said, her eyes tearing. "All dead.... My mother ... they ..."

Bern nodded in understanding. "Do the soldiers know we're here, Bet?"

She moved her head side to side, fading.

Bern looked around at the scene, into the woods, at the others arrayed upslope. He went to the now-dead dog and broke the arrow's protruding head off to pull the shaft out and hide it in the brush. By the time he looked at Betta again, Ronnie was gently closing her eyes.

"Come here, son," he said, drawing Ronnie away to stand close, face to face. "We have to leave her here to be found, or they'll think the dog is still tracking. As it is, they–" He stopped, mouth open.

"What is it, Dad?"

"Don't move, son.... Let me look past you ... yes ... in the trees ... about thirty paces ... a man in camouflage ... a scout, probably.

Ronnie stiffened. "If he's a scout, then–"

The man sensed he was compromised and bolted. Hearing his sudden flight, Ronnie spun and gave chase.

"*Go*, Dad! I'll get 'im!" he yelled on the run, his axe counterbalanced in his right hand or held crossways to breach thick brush with the handle.

The man was impossibly fast through the trees, darting this way and that like a startled deer. He seemed to have no weapon–at least none that showed against his forest-hued garment or made noise as he ran.

Incredibly, after a half-mile of charging up brush-covered slopes and careening down them, the man began to increase his distance. Ronnie, used to outrunning nearly everyone, grew desperate. If he didn't stop the scout before he reached his unit and reported, the fugitives would be found and slaughtered. He would have to discard the ever-heavier axe.

Cresting a ridge and barreling clumsily down the other side, Ronnie saw his chance, for before him lay a yard-deep and fifty-foot-wide stretch of a stream that his group had crossed just 1ast night. As the scout tore through the dense brush at the stream's near edge and waded in, Ronnie changed his grip on the axe. By the time he reached the gap in the foliage, the scout was clawing up the opposite bank. In a moment he would be gone for good. Heedless of the drop-off into the water, Ronnie launched his weapon with everything he had left. It tumbled in a shallow arc across the water and with a sickening thud buried its hooked point at the base of the scout's neck. Regaining his feet and splashing across, he found the man sprawled on the mudflat with his limbs all aquiver. His camouflage head covering had come off and he lay facing away, long blond hair matted with sweat. Ronnie, still trying to catch his breath, stepped to the man's other side and bent down.

It was a mere boy, maybe younger than himself, narrow and hawkish of face, his eyes blinking and his mouth working wordlessly. When Ronnie put his foot on his back to wrench out the blade, he gave a great jerk and lay still. He watched the boy's face a moment longer to make sure he would never speak to anyone again, drug his limp body into the creekside foliage, and turned for the fast walk back to let the others know they were safe for the moment, if they hadn't gone too far.

When he reached Betta's resting place, he saw that the dagger had been put back in her hand and all signs of the others had been erased from the scene. No one stood from among the rocks to call or wave to him. He remained listening for a while, then headed for the less-challenging west shoulder of the hill. The rocky ground beyond fell away to where thick woods resumed and then rose gently to the foothills beyond. He couldn't yell, lest his river-spanning voice be heard by pursuers, so, making sure he was well below the ridgeline, he slipped the swivel-mounted leather strap over his hand, took a strong stance, and began to swing the bush axe about his head. Almost as soon as he'd raised the characteristic low hum, he stopped the axe with his left hand and waited.

Seconds later, in the distance, his father emerged into the open and raised a hand. He'd been waiting. Ronnie raised the bloody axe to show the deed had been done.

As father and son stood regarding each other, Marta stepped to her husband's side and others appeared from the trees. She held a welcoming hand out toward him, but when he didn't respond to it, she extended both arms wide and slowly closed them across herself in a gesture of embrace. Hermione and several others did the same and showed the children how to hug Ronnie over the distance. He returned their embrace, then turned south toward the Citadel and was gone.

5 – Traders' Wisdom

Crouching just within the woods in the midmorning rain, Ronnie shivered. He drew his coat closer and his hood down to his brow.

After four days of crawling through brush and hiding in pools of water and in blinds constructed in tall trees and in others thrown together so close beside busy footpaths that dogs took no more interest in him than in the smelly troops they accompanied, he'd come back to the river road. Dead reckoning and a woodsman's skill had brought him to a point a few miles north of Westmount hamlet, just twenty miles or so north of Citadel City.

As he watched the muddy traffic of people and animals and wagons on the road, churning up the packed earthen surface laid atop an ancient highway as they moved in both directions, he shivered again. He'd stopped a mile back to wash himself and his clothes in a creek and was still soaked to the bone, but that wasn't why he trembled.

He couldn't get the images out of his mind–of doomed men and women and children, some holding hands and others long-separated from friends and family, fleeing before the trained-to-be-vicious troops now sweeping through the woods; of adults gleefully swarmed and cut to pieces and the young violated or taken away in chains; of futile attempts to fight back. Below his tree-blind, a bloody-footed woman in tattered pajamas and clutching a silent baby in her arms had fallen with an arrow in her thigh and then struggled to her feet to fight off the two men who'd descended upon her. As one soldier held her, the other broke the arrowhead off in her leg and then began to unfasten his trousers as she screamed for her child. Ronnie had touched the axe secured on his back under his pack and started to climb down but froze when several more men arrived. Retreating to his blind, he'd watched helplessly, shaking in fear and shame and rage, and now he couldn't forget. When several of the soldiers had taken her—even as others suffered violence and ridicule for trying to stop them—she'd died from a spear-thrust to the heart, seemingly staring at Ronnie in the tree above, as if beseeching him to help her already dead baby.

Worst of all, he knew her, as the soft-spoken woman who'd sold her handmade dolls in the Firstportage market, her table always surrounded by happy children.

Shaking the memory away as the rain dwindled and stopped, Ronnie tried to concentrate on the oncoming southbound traffic, remembering his father's admonition to find a way to blend in. After an hour of watching mostly supply wagons and prisoner transports and men on horseback and a couple of trader's vans, he spied a vehicle he recognized. It was a large, enclosed van pulled by four mules, home and place of business to a family of traders with whom his father was at least acquainted. He wasn't sure if that was good or bad, but as it neared, Ronnie moved parallel to the road to a place where it curved, so that he might approach the van mostly unseen by other traffic. As it came into view again, he studied the older couple on the seat, recognizing by his broad-brimmed hat the man who held the reins, from a visit he and his father had made two springs ago to the field where road traffic overnighted and traders conducted business. Then, with a glance in the opposite direction to see no northbound traffic for the moment, he stepped from the trees and raised his hand in a courteous gesture belied by the hooked axe-blade extending above his right shoulder. With a nudge and a word from her husband, the woman on the seat quickly spun and went into the van. The mules walked on unperturbed.

"Master Trader!" called Ronnie from the verge, but the man was more intent on scanning the trees for some additional threat than in talking to the man who might have been set as a mere distraction from it. Ronnie swept the hood from his head and stepped closer.

"Master Trader ... A word, please!"

With a final glance into the trees on both sides of the road, the man spoke to his animals and reined them to a halt. As he did so, a trapdoor opened on the van's roof and a younger man stood through it with bow in hand, an arrow already nocked but not drawn. Then another trap opened and a woman who might have been the man's wife appeared, a loaded crossbow cradled in her arms.

"Whaddaya want, boy?" demanded the driver.

"A ride to Citadel City, sir."

The man snorted derisively, "This ain't no fuckin' taxi service, boy.... Besides, you don't look right. Whaddaya doin' 'long here afoot?"

"I had a ride with a carter, but his vehicle was taken by the army, so I continued on foot."

The trader regarded him skeptically.

"I had a travel pass," Ronnie added, "*have* a travel pass."

The man glanced into the trees again, then back to the boy, deciding. Feeling a refusal coming, Ronnie put his left hand behind his hip to push the butt of the axe handle so he could reach over his right shoulder and sweep the deadly instrument out in a practiced movement. Instantly both bows were sighted on him, ready to let fly, but he only extended the axe, handle-first.

"I offer my axe, sir," he said calmly. "It's a good one. I made the handle from hickory, and the blade is from good antique steel." He hesitated, then, "You sold a piece to my father last year."

The trader stared for a long moment, until he'd placed the then-fourteen-year-old boy who'd accompanied the woodmaker on a spring day and been loaded down with an assortment of old-world-salvage—glass, wood screws, tools, and more.

"The cabinetmaker," he said, remembering the tall, courteous man and also the woman who'd come with him another time,

Ronnie gave no response, but only continued to hold out the axe.

"Let me see the travel pass," said the trader, motioning the others to be at ease. The older woman peeked from the van as Ronnie laid the axe on the ground and fished out the tube. As he stepped forward and handed it up, he started to explain how to unscrew it, but stopped as the trader began doing so.

The man set his still-dripping hat on the seat beside him, revealing a bald head, and spilled the rolled paper into his hand. When he'd gotten it unwound, he looked at it upside down for a moment before righting it and contriving to look perplexed, but Ronnie wasn't fooled. This man could read.

After studying the masked-bear stamp with subtle amusement, he rolled and reinserted the paper in the tube and handed it back. Then he craned to look around the body of the van to see a supply wagon entering the long curve and turned back to where the woman watched and listened.

"Mother?" he said to the door-crack, which opened wider. "This boy needs a ride. What say you?"

She stuck her head out and regarded Ronnie with apparent scorn. "Looks like a pervert 'n a homicidal maniac, ta me."

"So that's a *yes*, then?"

"*Sure*, why *not?* Let's live even *more* dangerously."

The trader put his hat back on and patted the seat where it had lain. "Come aboard."

Ronnie retrieved the axe and offered it as he'd done before. This time it was accepted, inspected without comment, and handed back to the woman. "Maybe Chatter could oil this blade a bit, Mother. Looks like it's been wet for a while."

"Why bother? it's all rusted up," she said, taking it. "Besides, we'll probably all be murdered before we get a chance to sell it!"

The man was Baladur, his wife Hemma, and to Ronnie's immense relief, they had no further questions for him. The mules plodded ahead rhythmically and the entire rig creaked and swayed as the man and boy made small talk about the weather and road conditions, the woman sitting crossways in the low space between the seat and the open door of the van. Soon, Ronnie's head dropped to his chest and he might have fallen off into the road if Baladur hadn't grabbed him by his backpack. He was made to exchange positions with Hemma and fell sound asleep wedged in the small space, but when he awoke he was inside the van, his pack and boots beside him and a blanket draped over him on the narrow straw mattress.

It took a moment to get his bearings. The sound and movement of the rig, the mixed smells of feed and axel grease and of cooking and of all the diverse wares a trader's van must carry. The interior was lighted by the two trapdoors open to the now-clearing sky, their ladders folded out of the way. Willing away the fog in his mind, Ronnie turned his head to look around and met the unblinking gaze of a large man just an arm's-length away, leaning against a pile of sacks. Startled, he struggled to rise.

"I'm sorry," he blurted, "I–"

"That's Chatter," said a voice, and Ronnie turned again to see a young woman sitting in a small upholstered chair, sewing on a piece of leather in her lap. "For Chatterbox, 'cause we can't get 'im to shut up.... I'm Rae."

Ronnie gathered himself to his knees and extended his fist, first to the still-unblinking man, then to the woman. "I'm Rondak," he said, "or just Ronnie.... Thank you for the bed. I didn't realize ..."

"These are exhausting times," observed Rae.

"Yes."

"You hungry?"

"Well," said Ronnie, reaching for his pack, "I have some jerky."

Rae stretched for a plastic box on a shelf and pulled off a tight-fitting lid the like of which Ronnie had never seen before. "Try these," she said. "They're not fresh, but they should be all right. Seems the bakers have stopped baking for the moment."

Ronnie reached in and took one–then a second one after Rae insisted–of the most delicious fruit-filled cupcakes he'd ever tasted.

While he was eating them as slowly as intense hunger would permit, Chatter rose and fetched him a cup of water in a heavy-bottomed vessel and returned to lean against his sacks.

Between mouthfuls, Ronnie looked at the dirty white canvas bags nearly filling the van and asked, "Are those your wares?"

"Official mail," said Rae. "We've been drafted to transport it, like others on the road, since– "

"Booty bags," Chatterbox offered.

"Body bags?" said Ronnie in alarm.

"No," said Rae," *booty* bags. Know what that is?"

Ronnie shook his head.

"Well, better if you ask my dad."

Ronnie accepted the rebuff and went back to breaking off bits of cupcake to see what they contained and then savoring each bite. Chatter continued to gaze and Rae to sew.

After a while, on some unseen signal from Rae, Chatter got up and stepped through the doorway to kneel behind Baladur and Hemma. Soon Baladur entered the van and sat atop the pile of sacks while Hemma followed and lowered herself to the bare floor to lean against them. Ronnie made to vacate the mattress with a "Mistress?" but she waved him back down. He crossed his legs and waited.

"Feel better?" inquired Baladur.

"Yes, sir. Thank you for your hospitality."

The other nodded and considered a moment longer, then, "How old are you, Ronnie?"

"Almost sixteen, sir."

"So you've never seen a big military operation like this before?"

"No, sir."

"Do you understand what it's about?"

"About finding Zah's enemies, I think. Heretics."

"And do you think that's it? –the whole explanation for all this turmoil?"

Ronnie looked carefully into the eyes of the two women and back to Baladur before answering, "Probably not."

"Good answer. Some would say it's about wealth and power, beyond what's necessary to protect Zah's interests."

"What do you mean?"

"I'm a businessman, Ronnie, and businessmen know that war is an opportunity for profit. For soldiers it's also an opportunity for plunder." He waved to the "booty bags."

"You mean ..."

"Yes, these bags are full of soldiers' and priests' plunder—property taken from the people, heretics or not— one regulation-size bag for the lowest rank, up to ten for officers, all numbered and efficiently delivered to the Citadel for safekeeping."

"But ... that's not ... that's not ..."

"Not *right,* you're thinkin'? Of course not, but it's the way of the world—the reason a lot a men go to war." "He hunched over to get closer to Ronnie. "Here's how it works: powerful people start feeling insecure or insufficiently rich and think a war. They need an enemy, real or imagined, so they invent one or they elevate a minor one. Then they get the soldiers riled up with promises and visions of glory and money and power and sex and—"

Hemma made a derisive noise and her husband rephrased. "Theft and murder and rape, in other words. These are mostly ignorant boys who never had anything—never had a girlfriend or wife of their own. Sometimes they're orphans or taken as children and raised by the state. They're not all bad, but they're easily manipulated, and when they're directed in force against an enemy, they can be wild beasts, which serves the purpose of frightening people into submission."

"People like heretics, you mean," said Ronnie, growing hoarse and unsteady as an image of the woman with the dead baby swam before him.

"That's the thing, Ronnie. Freethinkers and others can be labeled as the enemy but then that label can be put on anyone that resists or flees or has property or position coveted by the state. Right now the woods 're full of the bodies of heretics who never had a rebellious thought but just panicked. It takes a lot a nerve to stand at your front door and ..."

Baladur stopped as Ronnie leaned forward to support himself with a hand as his body convulsed. Hemma understood and grabbed the container of cupcakes. "Here, Ronnie," she urged, jerking off the lid just as he let go of the cakes he'd already eaten and kept retching as gentle hands touched his back and shoulders. Then, head down, he cried.

"It's *my* fault," he said miserably at last.

Hemma touched his chin arid raised his tear-streaked face to look into his eyes. "No, Ronnie. Whatever has happened, it's not *your* fault," she gestured toward the Citadel with her head, "it's *theirs.*" She took a cloth offered by her daughter and wiped his face and then set the cloth and the container outside the door as Chatter looked back and again to the road. "Now," she said," sit up and pull yourself together."

Ronnie did as instructed. Soon he gave his attention to Baladur again, but the trader was finished with his political tutorial, so he asked a question. "Why do you *tell* me these things? Why do you even *speak* to me like this? You just *met* me."

"Snap judgement, it's called, and it's something you need to cultivate to survive in that cesspool you're going to. Fleeting contact with thousands of people, and you have to start forming a judgement at your first meeting, instead of over years like you've probably done unconsciously in the village. For instance, it only took Hemma and me one conversation with your mom and a couple with your dad to conclude they were like us, and probably faced the same danger."

"You mean ..."

"It's not necessary to name the enemy, and we'd best not, but I'll give you one more piece of advice: there's no predicting under what circumstances you'll encounter potential friends and allies, so be receptive to everyone, until you've found reason not to be, then disengage without seeming to—offended people can be resentful and therefore dangerous. Understand?"

"Yes, Master Baladur."

"Good boy," said the trader, checking forward out the door, where the mules seemed to be working up a slight incline. "Now, I have a question for *you.*" Ronnie looked up. "How many southbound vehicles went by before you approached us?"

"About a hundred, I guess. I recognized your rig."

"See? That was an instinct based on some judgement you made more than a year ago, from a brief encounter, and it was right. So have confidence in your instincts, and you'll be fine." Baladur looked forward again, then back to Ronnie with some excitement. "Ready?"

"For ...?" began Ronnie as he heard Chatter call to the mules and reign them to a halt, then engage the parking brake.

"Come see!"

"This is called 'All-Boney Overlook,' said Baladur as he led Ronnie toward the crest of a hill, where other travelers variously gawked or picnicked or ran about in play. Then Citadel City came into view, and he was transfixed. Even though he knew there had once been cities a hundred times as big and more, he was still thrilled to contemplate the physical proof of what humanity had once been capable of building. For before him, a few miles distant, across a shallow valley and a glistening, ferry-crossed tributary joining the Husson from the west, stood a hundred structures taller than anything he'd ever seen, in a city containing a hundred times as many people as Firstportage and Mount of ZAH and the other upper-Husson communities put together. Around the core of it was a great wall, and within the wall were the tallest buildings, many of them "taller than an arrow-shot," as people said. Outside the wall on the near side and seeming to bend around the entire city was a jumble of lesser structures, haphazardly arranged, thickest near the main roads leading to portals in the wall. Beyond this jumble was a jagged spiderweb leading to farmland and, at the far side of the city, a larger road going east and west upon which traffic could just be discerned in the afternoon sun.

Then there was the bridge—a gargantuan structure spanning the Husson at the south side of the city, its dramatic effect unmarred by its slight tilt. Ronnie had heard of it, of course, heard the competing narratives of how it came to be the only bridge left standing on the upper Husson, and how it came to be tilted, but he hadn't anticipated its power to symbolize and explain the Citadel's strategic advantage: in a world destroyed, here was a largely intact city at the crossways of a great waterway and a great land road, situated just downriver from the sacred place of Zah's revealing and upriver from the abandoned Great Ruin, the richest treasure-trove of pre-Cleansing salvage on Earth.

"I'm sure you know the official legend," Baladur was saying at his shoulder. "Zah sent a great fireball to consume the flesh of the city but not its bones. Some who'd survived the original holocaust started to build a wall with the materials of outlying structures, but they refused to acknowledge and obey Zah after his revealing and weren't worthy of what they had, so he exterminated them and gave the empty city to the righteous, who moved here from Mount of ZAH. Thus, "All-Boney" became "the Citadel"—behind a completed 40-foot wall—and then "Citadel City," when others came to live in its shadow, providing its food and labor and manufacturers—and its soldiers. Now they say it commands an empire stretching for thousands of miles and across the sea, and that its work will never to done until it controls the whole world, according to Zah's commandment." Baladur looked around before adding," "That's the official version, anyway. The empire's probably got a few holes it, if you ask me."

"Is that the Egg," asked Ronnie, pointing at a distant, lopsided object.

"That's it," said Baladur. "What do you know about it?"

"Just what the priests taught us"

"Which was what, in your village?"

"You know ... that a rival god was incubating its young there. Zah smote it, cracking it open and toppling it from its pedestal, killing the evil within and making the abandoned city safe for his own people."

Baladur snorted, while Hemma glanced about in concern.

"What?" asked Ronnie.

"Sorry, Ronnie," said Baladur. "It's just that, those of us who grow up on the road hear so many different versions of history, we're constantly having to piece it together in ways that are, at least ... *plausible.*"

"What picture did you come up with?"

"Some say," the old trader began cautiously, "that it was Zahist agents who kept factions incited to fight each other in the city, supplying guns and bullets to first one, then another, until they were diminished in number and sick of killing. When the factions decided to meet to make peace, the agents mined the meeting place and killed them all—wrecking the building."

"The Egg," said Ronnie.

"Right" said Baladur, gazing. "Most of the agents got their just rewards, though."

"How?"

Baladur made sure his wife was keeping watch—so *he* didn't have to—and went on: "It's said that a large kill-crew arrived to clear the city of survivors, and then killed the agents too—all but one called 'the Engineer,' who'd mined the Egg. When the kill-crew itself got ambitious and started making demands in advance of the Chaplin's arrival, the Engineer mined the bridge upon which they would await the Chaplin's ceremonial barge, and blew *it* up, *in his sight.*"

"Leaving this 'Engineer' the only one to tell the tale? Then how—"

Ronnie had turned his head toward Baladur and been startled to find himself in eye-contact with one of a trio of soldiers moving among the sightseers. His impulse was to turn away, but before he could act on it, he felt feminine hands slide under his elbows as Hemma and Rae joined him on either side.

"Ain't it, though?" exclaimed Hemma in broad dialect, apparently referring to what had become a beautiful day, freezing him in place between herself and her daughter.

"Uh huh," muttered Ronnie after a moment.

Using Ronnie's head to shield her mouth from the soldiers, she said low, "If you notice them, they'll notice you, dummy, so don't. Look at the other people–at the girls.... And as for you, Master oh-so-careful Baladur, you're making this boy look like a never-been-to-town tourist. This your first time harboring a dangerous criminal?"

"You're right, Mother," said Baladur in mock-contrition, "I'm no good at this. You should probably get a better husband."

"Believe me, I been lookin', fer thirty years!"

Ronnie smiled, the momentary tension fled, and the soldiers passed on.

"Well," said Hemma gaily, tugging at Ronnie's elbow before he could learn more, "shall we take a ferry ride?"

6 - Citadel City

Clean your rig, Master Trader?" shouted yet another boy trotting alongside the van. "Special discount for traders at Oddo's rigwash, just ahead on your left." Baladur waved a dismissive hand. Sitting beside him, Ronnie looked ahead in wonder.

He'd never seen so much human activity or heard such a cacophony of human voices. At Firstportage market, vendors raised their voices only to shoppers passing near their wagons or tables, and hawkers on the road were few and polite. Here, once the road became stone-paved beyond the ferry landing, they ran alongside or even mounted the vehicles unbidden to tout their goods or services, including rig cleaning, animal stabling and grooming, campground rental, coal and firewood, food, mind-altering herbs and drink, games of chance, T-shirts, souvenirs, actual and purported stolen goods, legal advice, money lending, tool sharpening and repair, and, inevitably, themselves: demure or provocatively painted and attired creatures of often indeterminate age and sex, offering services some of which Ronnie had never even heard before. And common to all these entrepreneurs and their minions was a lanyard around the neck or waist from which dangled a small copper medallion with Zah's symbol and other letters and numbers on it, signifying that the bearer was authorized to conduct business and had paid the fee appropriate to the enterprise. Market vendors and craftspeople at home had possessed such devices, but here it seemed that no one at all could earn a living without the priesthood's leave. The symbol adorned even the commercial vehicles and the roadside structures that housed inns and brothels and stables and other such businesses, assuring travelers that they were licensed to receive their patronage.

Stables and rigwashing operations were located on the river side of the road, with pasturage for hobbled horses and mules and donkeys down to the water, and here many vehicles were pulled off to the side, for those planning to enter the Citadel itself were required not only to have Zah's symbol displayed, but to be clean and presentable, and on a muddy day business was booming. Nevertheless, Bil the rigwasher welcomed a valued customer in Baladur and took his vehicle right in. Soon it was aswarm with the proprietor's entire family, who commenced to bathe the van and wheels and the mules themselves and then to water and feed the animals in harness so that they might be refreshed to make their destination before dark. One youngster even set about polishing the brass bell used to announce the van's arrival in each village and hamlet. Ronnie started to help, but when Baladur shooed him away with an embarrassing remark about getting to know some of the painted women eying him, he hoisted his pack to one shoulder and headed toward the river.

Thinking to relieve himself in a clump of bushes beside a huge pipe from which water spilled, he instead found himself accidentally trespassing in what amounted to the front yard of someone's home, for a family was sheltering there. A frail-looking man stepped out defensively and Ronnie halted in surprise. He took in the man's unkempt and desperate look, his worn clothes, the stick in his hand, and took half a step back.

"Excuse me, sir." he said calmly. "I didn't mean to disturb."

The man glanced around for witnesses and moved forward with the stick half raised, perhaps thinking this boy would drop his fat pack and run, but instead Ronnie lifted one hand to stay him while moving the other toward the knife sheathed sideways at his back. The man stared at him for a moment, motionless, then wearily let his stick touch the ground and turned back to call a name. The bushes moved and a very skinny girl of about thirteen emerged—barefoot, wearing a T-shirt and too-big shorts, her dark hair spilling lank over her bony shoulders, her eyes wary.

"This what you come fer?" asked her father.

"What? ... No!... I mean ... no, thank you. I was just ..."

Ronnie was dumbfounded. He'd never imagined such a young girl selling herself, or being sold by her own family, since it was a death sentence for all concerned, according to the Protocols. But he wasn't in Firstportage anymore, and this was a half-starved family living under a bush, all without the medallion that would allow them to be paid for legitimate work or even to fish in the river. Anyway, he was only a passer-by, and this wasn't his business. What could he do about it?

"Excuse me," was all he could get out as he started to turn away. The man dropped the stick and took a step toward him.

"Have you–," he began apologetically, "Have you a coin or two? ... fer the children?"

Ronnie considered. There was no way he could safely retrieve and open the bladder-purse holding the gold and silver coins, which was secured at his groin.

"No coins," he said, now glimpsing expectant eyes through the foliage, "but do you think they might like to share some jerky with me?"

Not waiting for their father's reply, three more children filed out to stand behind him, followed by a haggard young woman in what might once have been a pretty yellow farmwife's dress.

"Can I sit over here?" Ronnie asked, moving toward a jumble of concrete chunks that had apparently calved off the end of the ancient pipe and at some point been purposely arranged. He sat down with his pack between his feet, rummaged in it for a moment, and came out with a bundle the size of a small bread loaf, tied in burlap. When he unwrapped it and held it out, the children surged forward, but their mother let them take only one strip each of the smoked beef, which immediately went to mouth. Then mother and father each took a piece and with obvious difficulty waited for Ronnie to take one for himself, put the bundle aside, and tear off a bite with his front teeth, before they sat down and began eating their own.

As the lip-smacking and then the giggling and childish banter rose over the sound of flowing water, Ronnie looked around at his surroundings. “Never saw a drain you could stand up in before,” he remarked conversationally, taking another bite.

“It’s a’right,” said the father, perhaps mistaking Ronnie’s interest in this “room” of his home, “cep when dere’s rain.”

“So this is just runoff? Where does it come from?”

“Dunno.... Nobody know.” He pointed toward higher ground, where part of the city must once have stood. “Up dere, reckon.”

“You never tried to find out?”

“Find out?”

“Where it leads ... how far it goes.”

The man and woman looked one to the other as if seeking help to understand this strange notion, with its hint of recklessness and perhaps irreverence. Not knowing what to say, they concentrated on their meal.

Ronnie changed the subject. “How’d you come to be here?” The couple exchanged another look before the man spoke.

“Dem books, reckon.”

“Books?”

“Plow up a ol’ bathtub–upside down, tell ya. Toppa sacka tings–books, dey call ’em. Use ’em fer firestarter, give some ta neighbers. Police come–all black-like–call us ’emy a Zah.’ Take our badges ’n say get off.” He touched his chest where his medallion might once have hung or been pinned. “Never mean no harm,” he muttered, looking at the ground and taking another bite of jerky.

Ronnie’s heart ached for these innocent people, who had suffered for the resistance to the priesthood of someone like himself, and he silently vowed to come back and help them if he could. Up at the rigwash, the newly polished brass bell rang, and Ronnie knew it was for him. He left the bundle of jerky with the explanation that he was already at his destination and didn’t need it anymore and made his way back.

Δ Δ Δ

Baladur's business was within the Citadel itself, and he could have entered through one of the lesser north gates, but instead he stayed on the river road to take the long way around to the main south gate. The main structure of the gargantuan, debris-made wall did not extend to the river but instead ran parallel to it well out of flood danger, with the road passing between wall and river. At either end of the main wall were subsidiary walls and gates which allowed the road to be blocked north and south, but today they were open as usual.

Again sitting beside Baladur, Ronnie tried not to gawk as a guard tower rose above the gateway through which they passed and the main wall ran ahead on the right, punctuated at long intervals by more towers and pierced by a couple of openings through which traffic moved. On the other side of the road and lower stood a line of trees and a procession of long, narrow buildings; beyond these could be glimpsed docks built atop ancient sunken barges, some with cranes to serve cargo vessels and others rigged to accommodate passengers. Ronnie now realized that if the two roadway gates were closed, this riverside space could be invested and secured and the Citadel supplied by water.

He couldn't decide what to look at: the vehicles and people on the road, the sail- and oar-powered boats on the water—plus one with a smokestack the like of which he'd never seen—or the wall itself.

The priesthood supposedly restricted knowledge of the past to its own higher members, but this slowly crumbling barrier was a public testament to it, for partly revealed beneath its veil of weeds, shrubs, earth, rust, and animal droppings were such constituents as whole buildings collapsed in place and supplemented by pieces of many others, cars and trucks and busses, tangles of telephone and lamp poles and wiring, piles of mailboxes and traffic lights and furniture and machinery and all the other detritus of the previous age. In places, it had apparently suffered small avalanches of material as its component parts of wood and steel rotted and shifted, the dislodged material merely carted away to leave gouges here and there. At the base of the wall the ground was stained reddish brown from decades of rust seepage and when Ronnie thought about this he realized that whichever ancient storm drains carried rainwater away from the Citadel would surely be red-stained as well. The one drain he'd already see ran clear.

"Don't do it," said Baladur beside him when Ronnie's head began to lift in awe at a particularly tall building looming ahead beyond the wall.

"What?"

"Don't gawk at the tall buildings like you've never seen them. Be cool."

"Oh, right ..." He turned to see Hemma grinning at him and back to the road ahead to put on a seen-it-all expression.

"How many floors is that one?" he wanted to know. It was black, glass and all, though it looked as if Zah's fireball had blown away some of its cladding to reveal white underneath, and some of its missing windows had been replaced with exterior walls in which smaller windows were set. An apparent smokestack had been tacked onto the side, running the building's entire height.

"Forty-four levels. Headquarters of the Ministry for the Suppression of Error–by its official name–controls the Error Police and the army, only one with elevators. Know what that is?"

"Not sure," Ronnie lied.

"Takes people up and down inside. Powered by steam.

"Don't they get burned?"

"Not like that. It turns some gears–that's all I know."

Ronnie's heart sped up and his throat constricted as he formulated his next, most crucial question. He wanted to sound nonchalant, but as he spoke his voice failed and he had to clear his throat and start again.

"Where– Where do they keep girls who come for blessing?" Baladur looked across to study him–see if he was joking. Behind them Hemma's face had turned serious.

So that was it, thought Baladur. A girl. And not just any girl from back home, but one coveted by the high priests of Zah. Dangerous stuff.

He should really claim ignorance.

"There's more tall buildings up the hill, blocked by the wall right now," he said instead. "Some are barracks–for the army and the Citadel Guard. Some are for government workers and such. But at the top is a big old building with spires and such." He gestured with his hands. "The Palace of ZAH. That's where the messengers live and commune with the god and give audience. The building to the northwest of it, with the columns, is where the virgins stay. They're not allowed visitors, and going there uninvited is suicide. In fact, any kind of interference with the high priests' business is suicide. Understand?"

"Sounds like a place to avoid."

"If you want to keep your head, yeah."

As the van came up on the first opening, traffic slowed to permit northbound and southbound vehicles to be alternately directed toward the guard station by a woman in uniform standing on a small round platform in the middle of the road. Baladur bade Ronnie look inside as they passed, but casually.

"This part of the city is ancient," he said, "but you still need a permit and friends to live inside the wall. My business is through the last riverside gate, past the Water Gate where tankers cross to take water from the river, but since you can't go in, we're going around to the main one on Citadel Square. It's closer to Owlly's."

Ronnie had been absorbing all he could of what he could see through the gateway as they moved around a line of mostly commercial vehicles waiting to turn, but now his head snapped back.

"You know him?" he asked, aware that he'd never mentioned the name on the fake travel pass that Baladur had pretended not to be able to read, *or* Oswald's nickname.

"Heard of 'im. Pretty sure his place is in Woodmaker Street, against the wall west of the square. If not, just ask around that area for 'im.... And one more thing: these city police are suspicious, and smarter than the country variety; they may not like the look of your pass. So I suggest you lose it, or say soldiers took it from you at the overlook. There's a lot of confusion right now so they won't be surprised, but the good thing is that the city needs craftspeople. They're not going to arrest you or drive you off if you've got work."

"I understand.... How about now?"

"Good a time as any."

Ronnie rotated the pouch under his shirt around to the front to extract the tube and the pass and began casually to tear pieces and eat them. He kept the tube as evidence that he'd once had something official.

After passing the Water Gate and the final gate through which could be seen the lower floors of the Black Tower and the tall buildings beyond it, Ronnie turned his attention toward the river, where, as the line of roadside foliage broke for a space, he had to consciously resist pointing.

"What ... is ... *that?"*

Baladur followed his stare and answered with a tone almost prideful: "That, my boy, is the *Wind of ZAH,* largest vessel afloat. They say Zah blew it here from one of the estates downriver, so his priesthood could use it to spread his teachings across the waters. The topmasts retract to clear bridges and get more places. I didn't know it was here."

Numerous vehicles were pulled off the road ahead and people stood in their wagons or atop their van and carriage roofs to get a look at the magnificent vessel, which might have been called a four-masted schooner were it not conspicuously missing its third mast. Under the circumstances, Ronnie felt no hesitation to gawk and stood on the seat as Hemma joined him and Chatter and Rae emerged through the trapdoors. All marveled at the former private yacht's beautiful lines and fittings and at the uniformed crew moving about, oblivious to the sightseers.

Looking beyond to the bridge, which became more worn-looking as distance diminished, Ronnie saw the missing third mast, for it had apparently been hoisted out of its place by a crane reaching over the bridge's side and was being maneuvered to lie lengthwise in a cradle on a barge positioned below, as people crowded at the rail observed. The scale of the whole scene–the ship and mast, the crane and barge, the bridge, the heavy traffic on the road, the wall and buildings impossibly tall, the noise and smell of tens of thousands of people and animals–all conspired to make him dizzy, and he sat down heavily.

"You all right, Ronnie?" asked Hemma, stepping down from the seat to put a hand on his shoulder.

"Yeah.... It's just a lot to take in.... I feel small."

She smiled mischievously. "Wait'll we get 'round the corner!"

The mules walked on unimpressed, even as the disused, looping roadways-to-nowhere of the Tangle loomed overhead.

Eventually the wall ended at another guard tower and gate, and the businesses and houses resumed, looking more substantial and prosperous than those on the city's north and with people to match passing in and out of them.

Some traffic turned at the first street, but Baladur continued past several more until he'd passed under the first span of the bridge next to an abutment and then turned right, through a jumble of repair shops, smithies, and provisioners.

"I want you to get the full effect," he said mysteriously.

Behind them the others had emerged again to watch.

A few hundred yards further on he turned north again into light traffic on the widest, best-kept road Ronnie had ever seen, even now being filled and swept and otherwise tended after the rain. Ahead, beyond two stone columns flanked by imposing government buildings, other traffic moved, and beyond that the road simply disappeared into open space. "Might as well take advantage, eh?" said Baladur.

"Whaddaya mean?"

"The pennant," he said, gesturing with his head at the small triangular flag that fluttered in its holder at the corner of the van's roof behind Ronnie. "It says I'm carrying official cargo and may use restricted roads and such. They take it back when I deliver.... Watch this!"

Indeed, as they approached the intersection, the young woman on her platform spied the device and stopped cross-traffic to let the well-worn, mule-drawn trader's van beneath it pass between the columns and into the square.

"Ain't that great?" laughed Baladur. "I should make one of those to keep for whenever I'm in a traffic jam!"

Ronnie wasn't listening. Instead, he was gripping the edge of the seat as if he might be sucked into the huge open sky above. Hemma, standing behind him, put her hand back on his shoulder.

"It's called Citadel Square, or just 'the Square,' or sometimes 'the porch,' as in 'Zah's front porch.' They say it's three shots long and wide—there's market on the fifth day that fills it up. The lane up the middle is just for official traffic .... What do you think?"

"It's ... *big*," said Ronnie in understatement, looking around. Pedestrians crossed the vast space in all directions and vehicles moved about its perimeter, turning into and out of side streets. Directly ahead lay the main gate—not utilitarian like the others but built to impress, with a stout tower encircled by two levels of battlements from which silver-clad guards watched. Even the adjoining wall was different: well-tended and almost smooth, all its gaps filled and its overgrowth trimmed. Pedestrian passages lay to left and right of the main opening.

"All this was under construction when I was a boy," said Baladur. "The plaza, the surrounding buildings, the gatehouse."

"Where'd they get all the stone?"

"Locally, and from the Great Ruin, collected by the miners, barged upriver by steamboat."

"That's the one with the smokestack?"

"Yeah. Built in the Chaplin's time, when some people still knew how to make such things. I Don't think it works anymore. Nothing like that does."

They fell silent. As the rig trundled forward toward a line of vehicles waiting at the gate, Ronnie became uneasy again. What was he doing here? How could he hope to challenge ... *all this?* ... or even know what to do? Unconsciously, he started bouncing his knee.

Halfway across the square, Baladur pointed off to the left. "See that first street away from the wall? That's Woodmaker Street. I'm pretty sure your Owlly's place is down there, with the other furniture and cabinet makers. This rig can't go down that street and you can't enter the Citadel, so you should get down when we stop and just walk over like you know where you're going.... Is he expecting you?"

"Not exactly."

"Listen, then ... we're going to rest and reload and depart north again day-after-tomorrow, through the South River Gate. If you were to be waiting on the river side of the road at midmorning, you could ride back with us—that is, if ..."

"I'm sure I'll be fine. Thank you, Baladur."

"Well ..."

"Ronnie," said Hemma behind him. "Come inside for a minute." She stepped into the van and Ronnie swung his legs around and followed. Chatter and Rae came down from their perches and the four variously sat and knelt. Hemma reached behind a sack and brought out an object rapped in cloth.

"You obviously put a lot of work into this," she said, revealing Ronnie's axe. "We wanted you to have it back. To remember ..."

Ronnie marveled. It hadn't looked so good since it was made. "My dad and I made it together. It's just like his."

Hemma nodded and tilted it up. "Chatter put a nice edge on it, and Rae made you a cover."

Chatter looked away awkwardly, but Rae enthusiastically showed off her handiwork. "See, Ronnie, this inside layer is oily and keeps rust away, but the outside is dry. Just close it like this." She slipped it over the blade and hooked it closed.

"It's never had a coat before."

"'Bout time," said Hemma. "Now, let's get your pack on."

Baladur asked Ronnie to lead the mules across the last intersection to wait behind another large vehicle blocking the gateway. He made his farewells, watched by the guards at the battlements above, and dismounted with his pack and now-covered axe in place. When the traffic warden gave her signal, he tugged the lead mule into motion and edged the team across and right up behind the other vehicle, just within the tunnel that led under the battlements and through the thick wall.

Here, silver-clad Citadel Guardsmen walked about looking for anything amiss, glancing at and dismissing him as he held the mule's harness. Suddenly he realized that he should be scared: a strange boy in country clothes carrying an axe and standing nonchalantly in the portal of the tyrant's fortress, practically being stumbled over by the tyrant's guards.

The crafty old trader had done it on purpose, Ronnie realized, to inoculate him from fear of this gaping maw and what lay beyond, and of the minions that attended it. He practically laughed out loud as he glanced back at Baladur and Hemma sitting side by side, straight-faced but with amusement in their eyes.

The driver ahead shouted to his animals and his vehicle pulled away. Ronnie walked Baladur's mules forward as if he'd done it a thousand times, but when he reached the far end of the tunnel and halted, he momentarily lost his composure, for there–right there, at the top of the long hill–was the Palace of ZAH, and just beyond it, the Blessing House. He was transfixed.

'Hey! ... Boy!" yelled the guard before him, and Ronnie realized he'd been speaking to him for some time.

'What?" he muttered.

"Your badge! Your Citadel badge! –for the third time!"

"Oh! ... No, I'm not going in."

"Well, get off, then! We got work ta do!"

"Yes, sir. Sorry, sir."

He turned to walk back out of the tunnel with a gruff complaint of "Fucking tourists!" trailing him. As he passed Baladur and Hemma he met their eyes and struck his own heart with his fist.

7 – Sign of the Owl

The outer precincts of the former city had mostly been gathered into the wall, but much of the grid of streets and alleys remained, as Ronnie could see when he came out of the tunnel and turned west to enter Woodmaker Street, where the much-repaired street surface was still bounded by what must have been the original concrete curbs and sidewalks. Beyond these were decidedly non-original-looking one- and two-story structures which often combined utilitarian design with the kind of decorative flourishes harvested by licensed miners from the forbidden zones: spires, arches, elaborate windows and doors and more. Above many such doors were hanging signs depicting house specialties: here a simple wooden chair or an upholstered one, there a bureau or crib or table. Others relied upon evocative symbols or images: a crossed hammer and saw, a beaver, a woodchuck, a woodpecker, and, beyond an intersecting street, an owl.

The street was thronged with vehicles and people and Ronnie had to step behind a wagon parked in a side yard to extract one of the gold coins from his hidden pouch. When he'd put it in his pocket and resumed the sidewalk, he advanced with purpose, but as he approached the intersection, he faltered.

What, again, was he doing here? Who was this Owlly and what should he even say to him? Did Owlly know he was coming? That he existed? His father had surely meant to tell him more, sitting side by side on the lookout in the forest, but Betta's panicked arrival and bloody demise had driven all thought of Owlly out of mind and they'd had no further opportunity to discuss him. What did Owlly know or not know? What was he to his father? Could he even be trusted?

For a moment Ronnie stood at the curb and watched traffic moving in and out of a small passage through the wall to his right, all by foot or sedan-chair, some black-clad and important-looking, others merely prosperous, still others with the dress and demeanor of servants, and he wondered what was so important that all were in such a hurry to get to it.

Standing there in his baggy clothes, a pack and a bush axe on his back, his hair unkempt and his thin beard still a stranger to scissors or razor, he suddenly felt conspicuous and moved on across the traffic to stop at the sign of the owl. As he considered his next move, the noise of the street faded and the familiar sound of sawing came to him from deep within the handsome two-story structure, accompanied by the smell of glue being heated over a fire, which made him homesick, and, perversely, hungry. Still, his feet wouldn't take him the final distance to the door to ask to be taken in.

He looked up at the painted owl as if it could give him advice. He was pondering the enormous eyes when—

"Well?" said a deep, pleasant voice, and he looked down from one set of owl eyes to another, or at least the human equivalent, set in the placid face of a big-headed small man standing before him on the sidewalk with a stack of lumber balanced on his shoulder.

"Beg pardon, sir?"

"You've come a long way, son. No sense turning away now."

"Master Owlly?"

The man gave him a small nod and a smaller smile. "Let's go around back, so I can put this down."

Ronnie, having carried lots of lumber on his own shoulder before, didn't offer to help a man already in control of his burden but merely followed until they'd passed an empty cart and come to a gate that Owlly had Ronnie swing open to a small, wag-tailed, reddish-brown dog and a couple of plump chickens. Once through, he gestured to a stack of sawhorses against the wall of the house.

"Let's have a couple of those over here," he said, and Ronnie lifted them off the stack and placed them the right distance apart for Owlly to stoop between and offload his cargo.

"Now," he said, brushing a hand across his shirt and offering it in an old-fashioned grip, "Welcome, Ronnie, son of Bern and Marta. Let's go inside and meet the family–get you settled in. Get some food in you." He let go Ronnie's hand and started to turn toward a short flight of stairs into the house.

"Master Owlly," said Ronnie, forestalling him, his fingers feeling the gold coin through the rough fabric of his pants, "I just wanted to say ... my father told me to come to you, but it wasn't clear that you would have work for me, so I wanted to say ... if you don't need me, I could ..."

"Don't need you? Wasn't clear? Ronnie, didn't your parents tell you about me? Don't you know what we are to each other?"

"No, sir. My dad started to tell me, but ... we got separated."

"Separated?"

"Yes ... in the forest ... we ..."

"Are they alive?" Owlly asked, suddenly hoarse.

"I think so," said Ronnie, frowning and looking at the ground.

Owlly thought for a moment, then put a hand on Ronnie's shoulder. "Son," he said, "I can see we have a lot to talk about. But there's plenty of time. For now, just know this: You have a home with us for as long as you want or need it, and I'm grateful to be able to give back what was once given to me. So welcome home."

"Thank you, sir," said Ronnie, the tension of the last few days beginning to drain away.

"Now," said Owlly, glancing up to see his wife observing them through the window, "let's go meet the boss."

In the Freethinker world, it was a disservice to share dangerous information thoughtlessly, because to do so unnecessarily burdened the recipient with yet more secrets to keep and increased the chance they might slip out or be tortured out. So it wasn't surprising to Owlly that Ronnie's parents hadn't mentioned him before; Ronnie hadn't *needed to know* the story. But now he did, and so did his own family. He knew Bern wouldn't have sent his son to him if the son couldn't be trusted with the knowledge, so once introductions had been made and a meal consumed and the sun set, the story was told—a story even his own two sons hadn't heard.

"I was five when the priests' soldiers came to my village," said Owlly quietly, rotating his lantern-lit face to his four listeners in his peculiar way. "They gathered everybody and shouted about books they said had been found, but I understood later that it was a lie, because nobody could read. Then they just started killing everybody. Didn't seem to care if people ran—maybe they wanted the fear to be spread. My sister was holding my hand and dragged me away. Couple days later we snuck back, but couldn't find our village. It was gone. Men with mules were clearing an area, almost as big as the square, where there was coal right near the surface—that's what they were after." Owlly looked around to see understanding in his listeners before going on. "So we walked for a couple more days, then my sister carried me. We fell down a ravine and she hit a rock. When she woke up, we kept going. Came to some houses." He looked to Ronnie. "Your grandmother was hanging the wash and saw us—took us in. That's how I came to be a part of your family, raised with your father, who was just a toddler then. He's the one gave me my name, when he first started to talk."

He paused in thought.

"Where's your sister now, Dad?" asked 18-year-old Brod, a robust priestchild of calm demeanor.

"Dead," said Owlly. "Later the same day. She lay down for a rest and just never woke up. The knock on the head, I guess."

"What was her name?"

Owlly looked at his older boy, his 14-year-old son Jak, his wife Nel, and Ronnie, and extended his hands to either side. The others understood and joined hands around the table.

"Angela. Her name was Angela. She was ten."

"Angela," they all said, and were quiet.

When they broke, young Jak spoke up, delighted to be able to ask about things not normally discussed. "How did you and Mom meet?"

Owlly looked to Ronnie, then to his son, smiling. "When Ronnie's grandfather died, his grandmother decided our futures were downriver. We could do anything with wood by then, and a trader friend made an introduction that got us work at Firstportage. So I was in the market one day and this very tall, very pregnant beauty spoke to me, a nobody, and that was that. We married as soon as your brother was born.

"I thought you were cute," said decidedly un-beautiful Nel, who was as sturdy-looking as her priestblood firstborn.

Owlly met his wife's eyes with undiminished affection, then rotated to Ronnie. "And you, Ronnie ... is there anything you can tell us about your family? Do you have brothers and sisters? a girlfriend?"

Ronnie thought about what to say for so long that Owlly misunderstood. "It's all right, son; you don't–"

"Five days ago," Ronnie began, "we were in the forest–my mom and dad and my little brother Bo and our friends. I was telling Dad that I had to come here, and he was starting to tell me about you, but something happened–a scout with a dog. The dog killed a girl–I chased the scout. I got so far away from the group that Dad and I couldn't talk again, but we saw each other at a distance. They were all right."

"And the scout?" asked Owlly, unblinking.

"Dead."

Owlly nodded his relief. "You passed through the lines?"

"I let the *lines* pass over *me*–that's what Dad said to do."

"Good job.... So, why did you say you 'had to' come here?"

"Well ..." He looked down at his hands.

"What's her name," asked Nel at length.

"Jenna ... daughter of Hermione and Clarence."

"*We* know Hermione and Clarence!" Nel said happily, glancing at her husband. "It was Hermione that told me to talk to Owlly that day, pregnant with your Jenna, I guess. Are they here? In the city?"

"Clarence is dead. Hermione is with my parents."

"Oh ... then ..."

"Jenna was brought here alone–on her sixteenth birthday–six days ago."

"You don't mean ..."

"Where is she exactly, Ronnie," demanded Owlly.

Ronnie was a woodsman, always aware of his orientation in relation to landmarks, like the great wall that towered in the darkness over the back yard of the house in which he sat, and which he now sat facing. He met Owlly's suddenly concerned eyes across the table and simply raised his chin, toward the Blessing House.

8 - Redline Alley

Baladur and Hemma had already acquainted Ronnie with the great danger of interfering in the priesthood's affairs, so he'd been quick to assure Owlly and Nel that he wasn't going to do anything to draw attention, like rescue Jenna and bring her to his basement lair on Woodmaker Street. He *did* need her to know where he was—so they wouldn't be lost to each other forever—but he also knew he had as much as a year to make contact, because Jenna, having no home in Firstportage to go to now, would not embark on a possibly fruitless search while pregnant or with a new baby. So he deferred to his new guardians, who insisted he leave to them the subtle and discreet inquiries that might be made of Citadel customers and others, regarding the virgin Jenna, who was "visiting" from their home village.

In the meantime he dedicated himself to learning his masters' business and the peculiarities of their goods and their clientele. In no time he'd satisfied everyone of his craftsmanship and even gained a Citadel work-badge as Owlly's new apprentice. This enabled him to go with the master and his sons on deliveries and installations and even on design consultations where Nel's expertise was especially valued.

The Citadel had overwhelmed, at first, with its scale and its opulence and sometimes its weirdness—such as manifested by The Egg, an unfortunately shaped building that had long ago been toppled and smashed open to expose to ZAH's light whatever evil power it incubated—but Ronnie adjusted—in fact he grew quite comfortable and confident, which created a new problem: it made him more interesting than he wanted to be, especially to the priestesses. And they were everywhere—in the fifth-day market, in shopping streets within and without the Citadel, riding past in carriages or sedan chairs, even coming with increasing frequency into the shop. Having passed his sixteenth birthday but still determined to preserve his affections for Jenna, he sought the counsel of his elder brother-in-bond.

"Walk like this," said Brod, hunching his shoulders, lowering his head, and lurching stiff-legged about the basement where Ronnie slept. Ronnie looked on skeptically.

"That—looks—*ridiculous,*" he said. "You look like an imbecile."

"That's the point, dummy. Priestesses don't want imbecile children, so they'll avoid you—unless they just want to play—then you're in trouble anyway. Stupidity is a turn-on for some of them, especially the older, married ones who think you don't know they have no rights to you."

"You speak from experience," said Ronnie. It wasn't a question, or a joke.

"Well ..."

Ronnie knew that Brod was still single because he was waiting for his 15-year-old girlfriend to be sixteen and priest-blessed and legally marriageable, but he'd seen more than a few priestesses look him over.

"Does Suki know?" he asked.

"Maybe. We don't talk about it. Only about our own future."

"And ... the children you make in the meantime? What of them?"

"You have to put them out of mind, for your own peace," said Brod. "Men of our class are not invited to be in their lives and you'll make yourself crazy worrying about them if you don't accept the fact that you're just seed for these women's wombs—or sport, for that sisterhood of libertines who teach each other how not to get pregnant in the first place, before they ever leave the convent.

Sisterhood of libertines? Despite his commitment to Jenna, Ronnie was curious. "What are they like?" he asked.

Brod considered. "Very clean," he observed. "Beyond that, as different as night and day. Some want a big, stupid bruiser who's rough with them and makes them come, some are actually shy and just want kindness and affection. Those ones tend to fall in love, if you make them *too* happy. That's trouble. Best to stumble around like an imbecile and attract the other kind. Can you do that, my son?"

"I'll work on it," said Ronnie, pantomiming his imbecile walk.

By the time Ronnie had been in the city for three months he'd learned its geography well. Armed with his work medallion and Citadel badge and tool vest, and occasional down-time, he'd trekked all over, always remembering not to stroll but to give the impression of being on his way to the next job, pausing only occasionally to enjoy the view of the countryside from the hill on which the original city had been built. His first lengthy excursion had been across the Citadel and out the north river gate to take a parcel to the family on the riverbank, but they weren't there. The only sign that they ever had been was a farmwife's muddy yellow dress, wadded up and discarded under the bush that was their shelter when the storm drain ran. He'd sat down and started to nibble one of the pastries he'd brought, willing himself to imagine them somehow restored to their former life, but lost his appetite and left the basket on the concrete stool. He'd gone a few times to the depots where traders conducted business with the Citadel, hoping to encounter Baladur, but he was never there either, and other traders became nervous when he got on the subject of conditions in the north, and of the prisoner transports that passed on their way to the Black Tower.

Some days he walked out on the bridge to watch sailors and workers moving about on the deck of the once-again-four-masted *Wind of ZAH,* thinking about all the wondrous sites it was capable of visiting, some perhaps not much different than they'd been before the Cleansing, others as they hadn't been in 100,000 years.

His exploration had also delineated "enemy territory," which started just past Patty's Pub, where Woodmaker Street became Stonecutter Street, in which the specialty was decorative carved stone, practiced in sheds hard against the wall and in surrounding streets. Even though the trades were complementary, and shared much the same clientele, their practitioners did not mix, except at Patty's, where the tables were informally divided among these two groups and their allies. The bar was neutral territory and mature family men and women often consorted there, but when a youth of one group went onto the other's turf, even for a harmless word to a work-colleague, the whole place went quiet until the separation was reestablished.

Ronnie had learned the rules the hard way, not at Patty's but in "Redline Alley," a passage running directly away in front of the pub and dividing the two neighborhoods. One day, eight months after his arrival, dismissed by Owlly for an afternoon, he'd started down the snow-covered alley on a new exploration, only to be accosted by an older stonecutter he'd seen at Patty's.

"What's up, woody?" said the thirtyish man in a none-too-friendly tone as he pulled a trash barrel through a doorway and turned to confront him. "You lost?"

'Jus' passin'," replied Ronnie neutrally, making to move around him.

"Don't think so," said the man, stepping into his path. "You don't belong here." Further down the alley, others stopped what they were doing to observe.

Ronnie stopped too. "Whatchu mean?"

"Redline is stonecutter–you know that. You need to stay on the shop-side streets."

"Never heard it–plus, it don't make sense. This is the shortest way from Patty's to Toolmaker Square–for both of us. 'Scuse me."

He brushed past the man, who now put fingers to mouth and gave three sharp whistle bursts. Soon faces began to appear at doorways and windows, especially on the stonecutter side of the alley. A couple of teenage boys stepped out ahead, then more. Ronnie's hand started automatically to move to his back, but he remembered he no longer wore a knife there, in compliance with city regulations. He hunched his shoulders and plodded on.

His fate was determined when the boys ahead did not confront him but instead let him pass and closed behind. The alley remained clear to the end of the block, but he knew he'd never get there unless he ran, and that wasn't going to happen.

From a building ahead on the right, a string of kids began to emerge one at a time—boys and girls old enough to be expected to fight, if not yet fully grown. Then, as if making way for a dignitary, they drew away from the doorway.

Ronnie knew who would emerge before he did, because only one kid commanded that kind of deference: *Scarface.*

If ever a 17-year-old boy was intimidating-looking, it was Scarface—with a visage once cleaved nearly in two by a machete, leaving a deep cleft that ran from his forehead down the left side of his nose all the way to his jaw, distorting his left eye-socket shape and breaking out some left-side teeth in the process. And it wasn't just the disfigurement but the hawk-like glare that went with it, challenging anyone who would think of making a joke or looking away in disgust or embarrassment.

Ronnie didn't stop to make a joke or look away but instead, as Scarface took a stance to confront him, used the momentum of his fast walk to smash the older boy in his lopsided nose with all his torso-twisting strength.

Nothing could have surprised Scarface more than for the first time in his life to find himself on his back in the middle of Redline Alley. Nor were his crew prepared for the trespasser to smash on through two or three more of them. But then their bloody-faced leader roared them out of their stupor and they swarmed, grappling and punching and kicking until Ronnie was on the ground, then kicking and stomping every part of his body.

As blood splattered repeatedly across the snow and he began to lose consciousness, he made a resolution. Next time, he would make it to the end of the alley.

9 - Blessing House Tales

The long winter of 106-107

Convalescing with nothing to read was boring. Interminable hours of lying on his bunk in the basement, listening to the sounds of the home and workshop above and of the street through the narrow windows set just above ground level– hours of thinking about Jenna.

Visitors helped some. There were the family friends and the adults from the woodmaker side of Redline Alley who'd observed the fight and eventually dragged him through a door to safety. There were Brod and Jak and other teenagers–boys and girls who encouraged him to weave a tale of dragon-slaying and did it for him when he demurred. There were even a couple of priestesses: shop customers who's spoken to him despite his efforts to seem unappealing and who commiserated over his various wounded parts, their interest becoming more than clinical as he recovered.

In the early spring of 107, once he could climb the steps from the basement to the back yard, he resumed light work, sanding and staining finished pieces at the foot of the great wall, which, at this spot, a few feet off the ground, incorporated an entire debris-filled school bus. He knew it was a school bus because the lettering on its side was still readable through the rust and overgrowth: Morningside Middle School.

It killed him not to be able to resume his studies–that the only reading he'd been able to do in the past nine months was three barely legible words on the side of an ancient bus. Worst of all, he couldn't understand why, as the son of Bern and Marta, he wasn't being trusted with the knowledge that Owlly and his family, and numerous of their friends and shop visitors, were almost certainly Freethinkers.

It was in their speech and behavior in private, in their opinions and how they expressed them, even in Owlly and Nel's lack of concern for the wrath of ZAH when he told them where they could find the gold coin they'd earlier refused, if he failed to recover. He'd buried it along with the others, in the dark of night, against the cut-stone wall of the crematorium, the forbidding edifice past Stonecutter Street that was surrounded by a sea of serried berms, beneath which were deposited the bones and ashes of more than two million so-called heretics and millions of the books that had been evidence of their crimes. Since early days it had been the site of quarantine and extermination of Zah's accursed and was therefore feared and avoided by all except high priests and their minions engaged in dark rituals, and, some said, the dead themselves; climbing the perimeter wall and going on the grounds at night took a lunatic, a suicide, or a Freethinker.

He was trying to be patient–to give everyone time to know him as well as they needed, to send him on useless errands and give him time off to wander while they conducted their clandestine affairs–but offended pride was becoming an issue, and something had to give. After all, he hadn't bothered them about Jenna in months, and they had no reason to think he would bring suspicion upon them, as soon as he got well, by charging up the hill with his axe.

"Jenna? From Firstportage?" said the pan-faced young sub-priestess, glancing away from Nel to meet and misunderstand Ronnie's suddenly staring interest from across the room. She smiled, pleased that he was finally noticing her, knowing that she could have him whenever she wanted but that Citadel decorum dictated that she *invite* rather than *force* him, lest she be labeled unattractive and desperate.

"Yes, I met her," she muttered, distracted. "Arrogant little bitch."

"Really?" said Nel, changing her position slightly to draw the priestess's eyes away from Ronnie. "I don't know her, but I understood she was nice."

"Nice? That little whore?... Listen, I've worked at the Blessing House for two years, and I've never seen a virgin take to her duties with such enthusiasm—or get so many priests after her at once. No modesty at all. The other girls thought it was disgusting."

Across the room Ronnie leaned on a heavy table on his fists, his back to the two women. Crashing waves of nausea and jealous rage assailed him, and it was indeed all he could do not to grab his axe and charge through the Citadel gate to cut down every satin-trimmed priest he could find.

"Maybe they don't like her because she's popular," said Nel, massaging the conversation for Ronnie's sake.

"*I'll* say, said the priestess with a sneer. "Snooty, too—putting on airs, like she was ordained herself.... We were glad she left early."

"You mean ..."

"Just a few weeks after she arrived. The matron came to the lounge and told her to gather her things, and she was gone. Looked scared to me—not so uppity."

"Was she with child?"

'All that fucking? How could she *not* be? Missed her second period."

Nel glanced at Ronnie to see he had resumed his waxing, wondering if he knew the girls had to go through a "proof of virginity" cycle before being presented. "So she must have gone home," she said.

"Got married or set up by some rich man, more likely," said the unattractive young woman, a hint of bitter envy in her voice. "She looks the part."

"What?"

"Saw her coming out of a place on Shopping Street—no belly, fancy clothes, fancy carriage, bodyguards—a whole wardrobe's worth of parcels."

"When was this?"

"Yesterday.

10 – Shopping Street

STOP RIGHT THERE!" yelled Owlly to Ronnie's back at the front door, no longer beneficent uncle or father-figure but military commander. "Downstairs! Right now!"

Nel had hurriedly summoned him from the workshop while Ronnie was in the basement retrieving his Citadel badge. It had taken only a few words: Jenna seen yesterday, shopping like some rich man's mistress. Once the gossipy priestess had gone, Ronnie had surged into action, ignoring her pleas.

"Brod, you too!" he shouted over his shoulder, herding Ronnie toward the stairs at the side of the showroom. Once they'd all reached the basement, Ronnie started defiantly to state his case.

"Shut up!" Owlly yelled again, to the amazement of both boys. "Just *shut your mouth* and *listen* to me! You are not going *anywhere*–without my *permission.* You are not going to endanger *yourself,* our *family,* all our *friends,* over a *girl–any* girl. Is that *clear?"*

"But–"

"Shut up! You have already drawn attention to yourself and us through your stunt in Redline, and now you want to charge up the hill to Shopping Street, in your work clothes, wearing *my shop's medallion*–to do *what?* Accost a Citadel girl with a fancy carriage and bodyguards?

"I just want–"

"Shut up! Maybe you'll go door to door, telling everyone how you and your childhood sweetheart–from a village now under martial law as a hotbed of heresy–are meant for each other, searching for each other, even if she's apparently *not* searching!

"I just want–"

"Shut up!... No, go ahead. You want *what?"*

"I just want her to see my *face*–to know I'm *alive*–and *here–waiting* for her."

Owlly thought about that, calming a little. "What if she doesn't care," he asked reasonably, "or tells you she's no longer interested in you. Then what? Are you going to throw a tantrum in the middle of Shopping Street? Get arrested? Get us all arrested?"

Ronnie looked miserable at the thought of losing Jenna, at his general predicament, but he was past crying.

"No," he answered softly. "I'll go to find my parents."

"Your parents ..." Owlly muttered, then turned away to walk aimlessly about the basement for a moment, while the two boys stared at him. Ronnie grew uneasy.

"What ...?"

Owlly raised a hand, but gently.

"There are rumors–reports–that the army established a cordon–a line of ambushes–across all the routes to the mountains, before the main attack. These reports– These reports say that *no one* got past.... That all were killed or captured."

Ronnie stared, his disbelieving mind seeking a thread of hope in what he'd just heard, seizing one.

"Captured?" he croaked.

"All those were taken to local garrisons, or to the Tower. None survived, they say."

Ronnie felt his life unravel, all that he was and most cared for lose shape and substance. He stood immobile, unable to move or cry out. Brod moved as if to put a hand on his shoulder, but did not.

Finally, after the awful news had had time to sink in, Owlly threw a lifeline.

"Our hope must be, Ronnie, that the reports are wrong. Frontline officers and administrators frequently lie to make themselves look good. Your parents are not just any fugitives, they're resourceful: if anyone could make it through, it's them. But even if they did, it's not likely you could find them. Not in the present climate.

Ronnie stirred himself from his paralysis. "They could have left a message."

"You mean on the message stone? It's been scrubbed and chiseled clean, and soldiers are stationed at it, so unless you're talking about something else, that's out."

Ronnie stared in dismay, then moved to sit on a stack of lumber. After a moment, Owlly and Brod sat on either side of him.

"Let's look at the hopeful side for a moment," said Owlly. "*You* may not be able to find *them*, but *they* can find *you*. So you *must* protect your position here. Yes?"

"Yes."

"The other thing is your Jenna. She could be in position to have heard the same reports we have. She may believe you're dead. Which means ... "He paused to let Ronnie work it out for himself.

"Which means," said Ronnie with rising excitement, "none of what the priestess said matters! Jenna's only behaving as if she thinks we're all lost to her!" He started to rise. "If that's true, then–"

"Sit still," said Owlly, clamping a strong hand on his forearm.

"But–"

"Don't make me yell at you again. Just listen." Ronnie sat back.

"Yes, she needs to see your face–and your *toolbox*. If she still wants to be with you, then that should be enough for her to find you. So I'm going to give you a chance to encounter her– Sit down!... I'm going to give you a chance to encounter her–tomorrow–if you will conduct yourself as I say, and as Brod says. He's going to supervise you and you're going to follow his orders. Agreed?"

"Yes, Uncle. Thank you. What do we do?"

Owlly sighed and slapped his knees in resolution. "Have you ever been in Shopping Street," he asked.

"No."

"Well, Brod has—to do cabinet work in some of the shops. So, here's what you're gonna do ..."

"Good morning, mistress," Ronnie said for the third time since separating from Brod, who was now working the other side of the street. "Do you require any cabinet work today? any repairs?"

The elegantly dressed, shod, and coiffed woman glanced his way from her task of arranging garments on a table and saw not Ronnie but a slumping youth in workman's clothes and scuffed boots, with a small Citadel work-badge on his collar and the toolbox at his side suspended by a strap across his chest, hot-branded on its wooden side with the figure of an owl. She opened her mouth to shoo him back out the front door.

"Shelves?" said Ronnie, forestalling her. "Display cabinets? Storage? Sticking doors?"

"Sticking doors?" she echoed. "Yes, as a matter of fact. Over here." She led him to the rear of the shop and showed him the problem. He could immediately see that the guide strip of the dressing room's sliding door was loose and misaligned. He quoted her a price and went to work.

Soon he was finished and out on the street again. He loitered with apparent purpose, as if he were waiting for a late delivery or something. It was the hour when delivery vans and unsightly workers started to dwindle and shoppers to arrive. He faced one direction awhile, then the other, taking in all that was to be seen: two-, three-, and four-story brick and stone buildings—glass fronted at street level—horse- or donkey-drawn carts, mule-drawn omnibuses, hurrying pedestrians, umbrellas blossoming at rooftop restaurants, last-minute streetsweepers, and now a few carriages. Across the street, Brod came out of a shop, gave him a "keep going" gesture with his head, and went into the next establishment.

The pan-faced priestess had said “fancy carriage,” and “bodyguards.” She hadn’t said whether the guards were horse-mounted or in the carriage or on it, but anyway the description didn’t fit anything he could yet see. Sidewalk and street traffic did seem to be building rapidly, however, and as he moved down the street he wondered if it was normal.

Two shops later he was ejected after a well-dressed couple entered and glanced disapprovingly at him as he spoke to the proprietor. On the street he scanned the traffic and was about to move on to the next business when he noticed a city policeman strolling his way, tapping his leg with his truncheon. Ronnie resisted the urge to evade him and looked for an alternative. Nearby was a curbside parking attendant waiting to mount the next carriage to direct its driver to some off-street location—a boy Ronnie’s age, with an entrepreneurial gleam in his eye. He walked over.

“Hey, brother,” he said.

“Yeah?” the boy said warily.

“Been workin’ here long?”

“Little while. What’s up?”

“Nah, jus’ wonderin’. My boss told me go get some cabinet business, but these people ...,” he shook his head. The cop glanced at the two and moved past.

“You’re too late—in the day, I mean. Here, they don’t want workin’ people ‘round after mid-mornin’—specially this week.”

“What’s so special?”

“The *Wind a ZAH?* The ship on the river? They say it’s leavin’ in a few days. All the fancy folk ’re havin’ parties and—” A large carriage pulled up in front of the shop and stopped. The boy, saying “Gotta go!” over his shoulder, rushed to open the door for the two women passengers, to give them a numbered disk, and to climb up beside the driver with a numbered paddle. A similarly dressed girl replaced him at the curb as the carriage pulled away and Ronnie turned to the next shop.

He spent the next two hours alternating between soliciting work from mostly unreceptive and often hostile shop people and making conversation with the parking attendants and the footmen and porters and other loitering servants of the Citadel elite. The conversation kept him on the street, where he could better observe the comings and goings, and he got better at it as he went. By the time he'd traversed the three blocks that constituted the high-end women's shopping district—among whose patrons were many priestesses who contrived as they moved to allow glimpses of rich clothing beneath black robes—he'd become positively engaging. Further down the street lay mostly men's shops and, cops or no cops, he sat down on the curb to wait for Brod to come out of the last place he'd seen him enter.

He was exhausted, he realized. This was the most walking, standing, and talking he'd done since Patty's Pub, the night before Redline Alley. His ribs and guts ached, and when he laughed to himself at his condition, the pain was so sharp that for a moment he couldn't breathe.

But he felt good, like he'd made a good start at finding her. By Owlly's ground rules he had to stop for the day, but tomorrow he could come again at a different time. And then there was the bridge, five days hence.

He'd learned that, besides the private parties, Citadelians were also shopping for just the right clothes and accessories in which to be seen by their peers at the sailing of the *Wind of ZAH*—or just "the *Wind*," as he'd learned to call it—on what was described as a mission to spread the god's truth to the heathen world. While ordinary townsfolk and even most Citadel-dwellers would be barred from the bridge, those of obvious wealth or position or connection would populate it and have the best views—of the ship and each other. If Jenna had somehow become attached to a household with fancy carriages and bodyguards—especially if she herself was guarded—then she might attend, either on foot out the main gate or dismounting from a carriage at the bridgehead with others. That's where he would be.

As he saw Brod come out of a shop and gesture to him, Ronnie looked the other way down the street at the well-dressed men moving on the sidewalk and passing between carriages and shops and remembered what his father had told him about camouflage.

It was Nel the practical romantic who came to his aid. She approved the plan in the face of Owlly's skepticism, she loaned the silver, she even told him where to go and who to talk to and what to say. Thus on the second afternoon, after another fruitless visit to the women's shops and as traffic eased at teatime, Ronnie handed his toolbox off to Brod and entered an intimidatingly refined men's shop, whose layout Nel had designed and whose cabinetry Owlly and his sons had built.

"Yes?" said a prim, middle-aged man without turning from his folding and stacking.

"Are you Master Willum, the tailor?"

"I am," said the man. "Do you have a delivery?"

"No, sir ... I ... I need some clothes," said Ronnie.

"You need some clothes," echoed the man, not unkindly but with a small ironic smile as he turned from his work to look Ronnie up and down. "Are you sure you're in the right sort of shop?"

"Yes, sir. A lady sent me. Said you would know what I need."

"A lady?"

"Yes, sir."

"And does this lady have a name?"

"No, sir. But she gave me this–said I should get a haircut, too." He opened the leather pouch he held in his hand to show a jumble of silver coins. "Is it enough?"

"Oh, I see," said Willum Tailor, visually assessing the amount and understanding. A married woman, a young lover, an anonymous payment–now it was all clear. "Well," he said, taking Ronnie by the elbow and drawing him deeper into the shop, "it depends on what you need. What are you going to be doing?"

"Going to the celebration on the bridge."

"You mean for the *Wind?* In four days?"

"Yes, sir."

Willum nodded. "So you just need one suit of clothes, appropriate for that?"

"And boots."

"And boots."

"And a haircut."

"And a haircut.... Anything else?"

"No, sir."

"Well, yes, then. I think we can accommodate you ... and the lady."

Walking Ronnie into a cutting room where others variously worked at tables or sipped tea, the tailor stepped up uncomfortably close, said "Excuse me" as Ronnie stiffened slightly, and felt his shoulders and arms and torso and looked at his hands and feet and teeth. Then he raised his inspection to Ronnie's face and asked, "Are you still growing? Getting taller?"

"I guess so."

"Well, we'll allow for that. You don't want to grow out of things too quickly. I have a feeling this won't be your last fancy-dress occasion." Then, bidding Ronnie to take off his boots and stand on a raised platform, he turned to the others and said, "Gentlemen, let's create a masterpiece of this young man! We have three days!"

Ronnie was surprised, and a little irritated, to learn what a difference fine clothes, a shave, and a professional haircut made in the way a person was perceived and treated. Whereas before, he could walk down Shopping Street virtually invisible—especially if he was *trying* to be invisible—now, in the long wrap-jacket of "taupe" and sash of "burgundy" (according to Willum Tailor), and his glistening new boots, he was a magnet for other's eyes. At first it made him uncomfortable, and, despite Willum's admonition to "stand straight!" he continued the slumping, stomping walk he'd learned from Brod, a shopping bag containing his work clothes and an extra shirt in one hand and his new overrobe draped over the other arm—but by the time he got to the end of the block he had loosened up. Standing at the crosswalk, feeling the eyes of passengers in passing carriages, he took a deep breath, straightened up, threw the robe over his shoulder, and walked on with the natural ease that was his birthright, past parking attendants who didn't recognize him, women who now openly admired him, police who avoided him, and finally Citadel gate guards who stepped away rather than into his path. When he entered Owlly's shop and got an appraising look and finally a collective nod from his adoptive family, he was ready—ready to confront and win—or win back— the one whose opinion mattered most.

11 - The Bridge and the *Wind of ZAH*

Passing out of the Citadel without a badge on display was one thing—going in, another. But the day-watch guards at the pedestrian gate were no less deferential to the tailored suit and the rich overrobe and the air of entitlement than the previous evening's watch had been. Nor was it difficult for Ronnie to stroll dismissively past the guards forming up in Chaplin Square, before the closed main gate, to join what was already several hundred Citadelians waiting to walk out together on a fine early spring day.

As the crowd of clergy, merchants, bankers, artists, professionals, army and Error Ministry officers, bureaucrats., spouses, lovers, and all their attendants grew, Ronnie kept casually on the move, looking for the one face in the crowd and showing his own, ready at every moment to see the startled eyes or hear the gasp or exclamation or feel the urgent hand on his arm that would signal the beginning of a new life—the life not just of the man he'd now become but of the husband and father he dreamed of being. Yes, he could already see it in his mind's eye: Jenna, the girl he'd been playing and climbing trees and learning and *being* with his entire life, coming to him with joyful tears, the memory of all misunderstandings and misgivings and doubt and promiscuity and betrayal instantly erased, life beginning anew.

So intent was he on seeing her and realizing his vision, that he couldn't see others, but they saw him. He was a new young face suddenly appearing among them—a curiosity to some and a provocation or threat to others. Was he someone's home-bound offspring, normally sequestered but out today for the celebration? Was he a traveler? a lover? a policeman? a spy? Who were his parents? his friends? his connections? Was he useful? Was he dangerous? Was he married?

"Hello," said a voice, and he turned so abruptly that the grey-robed sub priestess who'd addressed him stepped back in surprise.

"Oh, excuse me," he stammered. "I ..."

The attractive, red-headed young woman's contrastingly dark companion nudged her and she went on, "I'm Cinya, and this is Sister Iris."

"Ronnie," he said, helplessly. Then, not knowing how to act with a priestess whose social equal he was pretending to be, he went mute. A slight movement of Cinya's right hand reminded him what he'd seen in the Firstportage market, at the priests' assemblies, and played at with Jenna, and he extended his own hand to bow and raise Cinya's to his forehead, his thick dark hair falling over it. If she noticed the roughness of his hand she made no sign, in the moment of discovery that he wore no wedding band, as she also did not. A sudden, almost imperceptible tightening of her grip finally brought the words he needed.

"I'm sorry, sisters, but I have to find someone before we get moving. Have a–"

"Someone?" said Cinya, holding his eyes and increasing the pressure on his fingers.

"Yes.... A lady."

"A lady," she echoed, her coquettish smile fading with the realization that she might be trespassing on the claim of a priestess who outranked her. Then the smile returned, and she tugged him closer to speak in his ear above the rising crowd noise. "Well, if you can't find her, come back. Iris and I will look after you. You can come to the convent with us." He felt her slip something inside the sash-wrapped fold of his jacket.

"All right ... thank you," he managed, and was on the move again.

The column of Citadel citizens and their servants had grown substantially. Prosperous-looking men and women of the clergy and the merchant class subtly or not-so-subtly preened and posed as they chatted and waited. A troop of silver-clad guards was formed up in front, followed by a percussion band preparing to play the only kind of music agreeable to ZAH–according to the Messengers–followed by those on foot who passed the event staff's scrutiny, followed by the carriage-borne most-high, who would arrive last and leave first. Jenna did not seem to be among the walkers, so she had to be in one of the carriages. He tried to get close enough for her to recognize him, but when the various household guards eyed him suspiciously, he retreated toward the front of the column, thinking to station himself in her path.

With a sudden drum roll, the crowd noise fell and the massive double doors swung inward on rollers, revealing the open paradeway and expectant spectators craning over the barricades beyond the still-lowered iron portcullis. A cadence issued from the drums and cymbals and the Citadel Guard contingent and band began to move together at a strolling pace, drawing the celebrants through the portal behind them. The portcullis began noisily to rise from the pavement.

From Citadel Square beyond, a great cheer and clamor erupted, insured by the black-uniformed Error Police whom the townspeople could see among themselves and the plain-clothed ones they could be sure were also moving about. Stout wagons with barred windows waited at the periphery for those who suffered a failure of enthusiasm or respect.

The townspeople were mostly alien creatures to the elite, and frightening to some, so the celebrants drew closer together and spoke and laughed nervously at first, but under the cloudless sky a genuine party atmosphere began to develop. Townspeople knew better than to step off the low curbs into the paradeway up the middle of the square, but as they stood behind the barricades with children on shoulders, their enjoyment of the spectacle became real, and the mood of the walkers lightened in response. At the outside of the column, not far behind the band, Ronnie began to bump fists with some of the children and their parents and some of those Citadelians around him took his example. He grinned as he found himself bumping with young Jak while Owlly and Nel and Brod smiled and nodded their support; he'd gone no more than a few paces beyond when he turned back to see that the smiles had faded but were quickly restored. Not smiling at all was Scarface Tom, who glared at him in disbelief from a few rows back. Ronnie pretended not to have noticed him; maybe his neighborhood nemesis would conclude he was seeing things.

At the end of the square the column turned left toward the bridge. Ronnie's height enabled him to look back across most of the heads to the line of carriages at the rear, but he could discern no familiar faces at their windows. It was too far, he told himself, and anyway, the elites were too dignified to lean from carriage windows to wave at crowds.

At the bridgehead the band veered out of line and stationed itself to one side to give cadence to the Citadel Guard troops who continued forward, sweeping the common folk from the bridge and securing its far end. The celebrants continued onto the bridge, spreading out with an air of liberation after the encroaching throng of townspeople.

Ronnie moved to the middle of the flow and turned to let it sweep around him, ignoring the curious or irritated glances of others, intent on not missing that one face in the crowd of more than two thousand, oblivious to the beauty and desirability of many other women, even the ones who contrived to brush against him unnecessarily.

She must be in the carriages, he concluded, and found a spot with the gawkers near where the celebrities and the most-high would dismount and then walk between rows of Citadel Guardsmen to a roped-off enclosure at the center of the bridge.

First came glamorous young men and women in fancy dress and jewels, and Ronnie anxiously peered past each one for the figures yet to emerge into the sunlight. Then came those wearing the satin- or fur-trimmed outer robes of the high clergy, mostly worn open to reveal opulent brocade dresses and suits. One of these he recognized by

Jenna's description: Grotius, the enormously fat chief of the Ministry for the Suppression of Error–the Error Police–who had confronted Jenna at Firstportage and accompanied her to the Citadel, and who now settled into an eight-man sedan chair for the short ride. Ronnie's heart thudded as he waited the excruciating seconds for Jenna to step out, but out came only an elegant, slender young man, wearing on a gold chain around his neck a diamond the size of Ronnie's thumb.

Finally came the Messengers–near-mythic personages who communed with ZAH himself and conveyed his commands to the people, according to the Teachings. Ronnie knew there were eleven of them and he now counted ten large black coaches and, at the end of the queue, a huge gold one, whose eight matched white horses were actually led from the front by two liveried men on foot as another on the seat ceremonially held the loose reins. This ship of the road surely carried the one Messenger identified by the god as the enforcer of his will: the all-powerful, the Sword of ZAH.

As the four-horse teams and black coaches began to turn through their half-circle at the bridgehead and offload their passengers, amid variously perfunctory or enthusiastic applause and cheers, Ronnie consciously engaged his memory to absorb as much as he could of the information and gossip emanating from the people around him. *This* Messenger's clan dominated such-and-such a ministry, *that* Messenger's clan another. *This* Messenger owned half of the property in Shopping Street, *that* one the other half. *This* Messenger was married to so-and-so but consorting with someone whose name made listeners gasp, *that* one was celibate. *This* one had ascended through blackmail, *that* one through murder.

As the line of coaches shortened, people became more circumspect, whether out of respect, or fear.

"That's Lord Mortimer," said a priestess to her teenage children of an ordinary-looking fellow disembarking without fuss. "His clan have had the Treasury and the Ministry of Instruction since the time of the Cleansing. He's responsible for deciding who will be allowed to learn reading and writing in service of the priesthood, making sure that doesn't lead to error. It's a difficult job. His niece is Censor.

Censor. Ronnie had heard that epithet, but he didn't know it referred to a woman. It was she, then, who was responsible for the wagonloads of books that periodically issued from the Citadel gate to make a ceremonial circuit of the square and then head down Woodmaker Street to the crematorium to be burned, in a ritual of extirpation of esoteric knowledge. The first time he'd seen the spectacle, he was stricken by the reaction of the people on the sidewalks, which was to extend a hand as if warding off evil and rapidly and repeatedly make the Z-sign in the air until the wagon was safely past. Some brave teenagers, challenged by their friends, darted into the street to spit on the piles of books. Once, when a fat encyclopedia had fallen to the street and opened to a picture of the Colosseum of Rome, Ronnie had been heartbroken to see it kicked around before being retrieved by an attendant in thick gloves and thrown back on the pile, knowing that such pictures were among the last evidence of the existence of a great and ancient city that was now a giant crater.

His reverie ended when the door of the second-to-last coach was opened, and a hush fell over the crowd.

"Sula," someone whispered. Not "Lord Sula," or "Lady Sula," or "Messenger Sula"–just "Sula." Deputy to the Sword of ZAH, de facto chief, through her clansmen, of the ministries of War and Error: Sula.

From the shadowed interior of the coach emerged the long-fingered hand to the footman, then the elegantly booted foot to the step, then the black-hooded head through the doorway, then, as she alighted and lowered the hood, the pale face and dark red lips of the most remarkable person Ronnie had ever seen, seeming a mature and commanding woman but with the taut face and straight black hair and slender body of youth. He couldn't have said whether she was twenty-five or forty, or what her heritage might have been, but she was beautiful.

Belated applause erupted as the onlookers got over momentary paralysis to endorse her dramatic entrance and seek to ingratiate themselves. As two handsome young men climbed from the carriage and stationed themselves behind her shoulders, she scanned the crowd as if gaging the enthusiasm of its individual constituents. The volume of applause and shouts increased in response. At one point in her survey she stopped, turned almost imperceptibly, and spoke to the man who'd leaned forward to receive her command. Following her gaze, the man looked at someone in the crowd and spoke in Sula's ear. Instantly the volume increased further in that part of the crowd.

Ronnie was mesmerized. He'd never seen anyone instill such a mixture of fear and adoration in a crowd, never imagined the power of such a combination, or thought he hadn't. Then he smiled to realize he *had* seen and imagined it– she'd cultivated the vampire queen look he'd once come to know through words and images in the Firstportage library, perhaps the same words and images that had instructed Sula, who would have had access to old books and magazines growing up, like other high clergy. He was contemplating her successful adoption of the persona and admiring the jeweled circlet about her head, from which a small, diamond-formed "Z" dangled onto her forehead, when, to his utter shock, he realized her eyes had stopped on *him*.

He glanced to left and right and back to glimpse what could only have been a slight smirk on Sula's lips. He realized he wasn't applauding, so he started, but as she half-turned to speak to her other retainer and her eyes briefly left him, he melted into the crowd and took up station some distance away, feeling like it wasn't far enough.

Sula's coach pulled away and all turned their attention to the remarkable last vehicle. The crowd was allowed to become a little impatient as attendants took final positions and as the two liveried guides shortened their hold on the tasseled ropes attached to the two lead geldings' bridles. Then a soft drum roll emanated from the band, the guides spoke to their charges and tugged on the leads, and the coach began to move.

It was enormous to his eyes—an iron- wheeled and footed

behemoth, whose height had dictated the height of the main gate's opening upon its construction–and it made a tremendous racket as it drew nigh. When it stopped, so did the band, with a flourish.

"The *gold*," murmured a nearby man to no one in particular, shaking his head in wonder. Indeed, the coach wasn't just covered with powdered-gold paint, it was entirely fitted out with the cast or hammered metal–from the tack hardware to the lamps to the decorative trim. It was a lot of gold to see in one place, to be sure, but according to what Ronnie had been taught of the priesthood's economy, it was surely a mere fraction of its hoard. His father had said the secret of the priesthood's success was not just the fear it instilled, or the desire of many people to ascend and to elevate their families in its hierarchy, but its practice of permitting the people to own property and to freely trade among themselves, facilitated by gold and lesser coin convertible to it as the market dictated. It had taken no great economic thinker to design this system; rather it had arisen organically after the Cleansing. The Chaplin's genius had been to leave it alone, and to tax it. And where did the gold come from? From the entire ruined world over which ZAH had given his priests dominion and which only their licensed "miners" were allowed to work, digging in the walls and back yards of abandoned homes in the Forbidden Zones and in the rubble of former businesses, for anything of value not prohibited by law and especially for coins, gems, and for gold like that on display now.

With its big spoked wheels the golden coach was so tall that a staircase with a landing had to be brought for its passengers. When it was in place, the Lord Chamberlain of the Council of Messengers ascended, opened the door, and backed down a couple of steps. After a moment, to the cheers of the crowd and the consternation of Ronnie, a very unprepossessing man slipped out onto the landing: short, doughy, an uncertain-looking man of about sixty, whose main purpose could be imagined to be bearing about ZAH's realm the bejeweled, too-big, Z-surmounted crown that sat precariously on his head, and the sheathed sword that dangled from his waist almost to the ground.

"Lord Endo ... the Sword," intoned a middle-aged priest nearby to his skeptical-faced daughter or girlfriend.

"Really?" she responded, too loudly. "He looks so ..."

"He's the most powerful man on Earth," he assured her forcefully before she could say anything foolish, glancing at and through Ronnie.

"If you say ...," she began in retort, but stopped as another figure emerged onto the landing beside Endo. "Now him, 1 could believe," she shouted over the intensified applause, for before the adoring crowd stood a truly striking specimen–tall, robust, silver-haired, intelligent-eyed.

"Him?" sneered the priest, as Ronnie edged closer for whatever intelligence he could gain. "That's Magnus, the new ambassador. He's not even a Messenger."

"Well, he should be," she asserted, which caused the priest to look about nervously again, before his need to impress the young woman–definitely a girlfriend, Ronnie decided–overcame discretion.

"So some people say," he said conspiratorially, "but his enemies keep him from the Council because they fear what he might one day become."

"Which is?"

"Sword of ZAH."

"Wow!" said the girlfriend, drawing the priest's hand around her waist to her belly. "It's all so exciting!"

Lord Endo and his guest were soon down the stairs and on the move, preceded by the band. Seeing that troops were now preparing to seal the west end of the bridge, Ronnie went with an air of privilege to find a spot at its north side near the dignitaries' enclosure, overlooking the *Wind* at the quay some three hundred paces away. He'd been forced to conclude that Jenna was not in the crowd–left in a rich house to babysit, perhaps–but he scanned it once more before turning his attention to the *Wind.*

What a magnificent vessel it was! –with it extendable topmasts reputedly the largest sail-powered yacht able to pass under the Husson's pre-Cleansing bridges, up to this point, and supposedly preserved by ZAH at one of the great estates for the use of his priesthood. Today, still moored facing upriver, it was a beehive of activity as last-minute cargo and passengers were brought aboard and equipment was checked and rechecked. Then, as the Citadel elite on the bridge and the townspeople strung out on the river roads watched, and as the sun rose to its zenith, all came into readiness and activity ceased. White-uniformed crewmembers stood at the ship's stern facing the bridge and civilian passengers—some of them women with hoods up against the midday sun—sat or stood forward.

On a dais set at the north side of the bridge, the Sword spoke some barely audible words, performed a ritual borrowed from some ancient religion—involving smoke from a metal pot and water sprinkled in the direction of the *Wind*—and introduced Lord Magnus.

Unexpectedly, this man's powerfully spoken words seized Ronnie's full attention, for in his account of the history of the age of ZAH, he asserted that the Teachings left behind by the Chaplin and his early followers hinted at the notion of progress—eventual progress, under ZAH's supervision, out of an age of mere obedience and into one of reasoned choice. Of course, he said, almost as if to assuage the consternation his words were sure to have caused in his black-robed listeners—the entire world had to first be brought to a state of abject submission to ZAH's will, to calm restless spirits, before that age could dawn. That was the mission on which he embarked.

Ronnie left his place at the rail and tried to get closer to the speaker, but he was blocked by the guards and the press of people around the dignitaries' enclosure. He looked past others at the faces of those standing before the dais and saw not a few frozen smiles beneath fearful eyes, and got an idea why it might be important in some circles to distance this man from the Citadel. For the coming age he spoke of could only be a threat to the status quo, to the power and privilege and wealth of those who already had it.

Two faces were not so conflicted, however. One belonged to Lady

Sula, who stared at the speaker from a few feet away with utter contempt, the other to a high priestess who stood at the side of the dais and beamed at him with pride. Looking at the tall woman, Ronnie felt a tug of recognition, even though he was sure that, with her intelligent face and abundant salt-and-pepper hair, he had never seen her before. Perhaps she was Magnus's wife.

Soon the ambassador finished his remarks and waved his farewell to the crowd as an upholstered sedan chair was brought for him. A guard formed around it, the band began to play and parted the crowd with its advance, and he was carried through the cheering elites and off the bridge, down onto the river road and to the quay where the *Wind* stood waiting for him.

As the crowd on the bridge watched at the distance, he was ceremonially welcomed by the captain and crew and then by other passengers, spending some moments in the embrace of a woman in a hooded, rose-colored garment, her back to the bridge, and Ronnie concluded the tall priestess at the dais had not been his wife after all.

On the bridge a curious social dynamic, which had been covertly in play all morning, was suddenly overt. The party was almost over, and the time to cultivate alliances or arrange assignations was growing short. Ronnie had to keep on the move to avoid awkward conversations that might reveal his trespass and distract him from his purpose, but that didn't keep women and girls and a couple of men from thrusting their cards at him or slipping them inside his jacket, even after being told he was "with a lady."

Another cheer went up at the rail and Ronnie pushed his way closer to see the ship's departure past others' shoulders. It had been unmoored at the bow and was being pulled away from the quay by two sixteen-oared tugboats. Soon the current gained purchase and began slowly and majestically to swing it into the river. Once it was perpendicular to the quay and straining to be free it was unmoored at the stern and a minimum of sail set to continue its reorientation before the northwesterly breeze and move it toward midriver. As it neared the center of the bridge, Magnus and several of the other passengers came to the bow to return the salute of those above. Ronnie's eyes were drawn to the woman in rose behind Magnus, who now reached up to lower her hood and to smile and wave at the crowd. It was Jenna.

"JENNA! JEN–" Ronnie tried to shout in panicked disbelief over the cheering of the well-wishers, convulsing with the pain in his still-mending ribcage. Desperately he clawed his way to the rail to glimpse the top of her head as it passed out of sight more than forty yards below. "JEN–!"

He spun and crashed through outraged Citadelians to the opposite rail, just as those inside the enclosure were making the transition at a more dignified pace.

"JE–" came his aborted cry, but her attention seemed to be on someone a few feet away within the enclosure, to whom she threw a kiss.

Within seconds the *Wind* started to pick up speed as one mainsail was raised to give the vessel positive steerage in the estuary's ebbing current. Frantically, Ronnie looked around for someone to stop it, bring it back, then summoned all his love and breath and desperation.

"JEN-NAAA!" he cried in full voice, holding his ribs, but she and Magnus gave final waves and turned to look downriver.

The people around Ronnie had backed away from him as if he were having a fit. Inside the enclosure, the tall priestess and her entourage had also heard his last cry and seen him collapse against the barrier. Still staring at him, the priestess turned her head and spoke to a man who nodded and moved toward him, passing the guards and dipping under the heavy purple rope strung from one bridge rail to the other.

Suddenly Ronnie wrenched himself erect and ripped his way through to the less-populated part of the bridge, where people were now engaged in conversation, and sprinted toward the bridgehead. Slowing momentarily to avoid alarming the guards there, he descended stairs to the river road passing under the bridge's first span and resumed running.

At the bridge rail the priestess watched him as her servants, sensing her sudden preoccupation, prevented others from disturbing her. She saw him shed his outer robe to the ground and run at full speed past surprised townspeople and carts and warehouses and boat docks, all the way to a stone breakwater sheltering a small harbor. He ran and scrambled and leapt his way to the very end, where, for a few seconds, he was even with the *Wind,* now raising more sail at midriver. He leaned on his knees and panted for a moment, then stood, reared back, and, as the watching priestess put her own fist to her heart, emitted a cry that could faintly be heard at the bridge and brought Ronnie to his knees.

"JEN-NAAAAaaa!"

On the *Wind,* leaning against the bow rail beside Magnus, Jenna turned her head slightly, as if she'd heard a whisper or felt the tug of memory. She listened for a moment, but there was only the sound of the bow cleaving the water as the ship listed to port and picked up speed. Turning back to link arms with Magnus and rest her head against his shoulder, she looked forward, toward the Great Ruin and the open sea beyond.

12 - Childhood's End

When the doorbell sounded in early evening, Nel and Jak looked up expectantly from their showroom duties and Owlly and Brod stepped from the workshop wiping their hands. Insipient smiles died. Standing inside the door without his fine robe and with a tear in the knee of his new trousers, head down, Ronnie radiated failure and defeat. After a moment, without looking up, he headed for the stairs and slowly descended. No one spoke. Shaking her head, Nel resumed adding and subtracting numbers at her desk and the others soon followed her example.

The next afternoon Owlly went halfway down the stairs to make sure Ronnie hadn't hung himself, and, finding him in bed facing the wall, crept back up.

The day after that, at midmorning, Ronnie appeared in the workshop and asked in a soft voice, "What needs doing?"

Owlly, hands on hips, looked around and suggested, "The ministry's chairs? They're ready for their front legs." Ronnie nodded and began setting up for the job.

At lunch he was practically speechless, and, despite not having eaten in two days, ate little before going back to work in the shop. Only at supper did the story come out of him. It was Brod's girlfriend Suki, long since made aware of the secret of Jenna, who pulled it out.

"So, Ronnie," chirped the black-haired pixie, to warning glances from the others, "what happened at the bridge? Did you find her?"

Despite their own hesitation to ask, the others looked at Ronnie's lowered head, waiting.

"Yes," he answered.

"And? What happened?"

After a long pause of reliving, he summarized: "She left."

"You mean she just walked away?"

"*Sailed* away ... on the *Wind.*"

Owlly took over. "Ronnie, you mean she was a passenger on the *Wind of ZAH?* Well, did you speak to her? What did she say?"

"I saw her from the bridge. I waved and called to her, but she didn't respond.... She was with Magnus. "

"Magnus? The ambassador? What do you mean, 'with' him?"

"They embraced—like lovers."

Nel joined in: "You mean they kissed?"

"No, just hugged when he went aboard, but I could tell."

Now Nel became agitated. "Ronnie, Ronnie ..., *we* were watching from the river road. The bridge was packed with people, all yelling and waving their arms. How can you be sure she saw you?"

"When the ship came out on the other side, she waved right where I was standing and blew a kiss, but not at me."

Nel shook her head slowly. "I don't know, Ronnie; that's not—"

"Besides," Ronnie interrupted, going on to tell about calling from the jetty, which explained the discarded robe and torn trousers even if he recounted without drama. When he concluded with the part about Jenna starting to respond to his call but instead snuggling up to Magnus, with her head on his shoulder, all were silent.

One by one they resumed eating, the chink of pre-Cleansing stainless on china the only sound. Finally, the irrepressible Suki broke the silence.

"You know, Ronnie," she began to more looks, "there's a million other girls who'd like to be with you.... My sister, for instance."

The others looked for some kind of outburst or protest or breakdown, but Ronnie only said, "Yeah? Which one?"

One was fourteen and had an open crush on him, the other seventeen and the busy new mother of priestblood twins.

"Both!" chirped Suki. "*Together*, if you want!"

Eating and breathing stopped at the table. Ronnie did his best to raise one corner of his mouth in a smile. "We'll see."

Breathing resumed, then eating, somebody chuckled softly, and the worst was over.

At dawn, Ronnie drew his arm under the pillow and gazed at the footprints on the dusty floor. As in the past, when he'd neglected to clean his living area for a few days, he could see evidence of numerous visitors, and he knew his adoptive family had once again conducted secret affairs in his absence. Irritably he got up and swept the dust away, then set about tidying the rest of his domain, all the while mumbling to himself that they'd probably been waiting for him to get over his Jenna-sickness–one way or another–and settle down.

Under the bed where he'd kicked them, he discovered the clothes he'd worn at the bridge. When he pulled them and the stone-scuffed new boots out, he also discovered the numerous cards that had been thrust at him or slipped into the fold of his jacket and which had fallen to the floor when he'd distractedly untied his sash. He collected them and sat on the side of the bed to look at them.

They were hand-lettered, some in the same fine hand even as they identified different women and men; one from the latter category had an impromptu pornographic drawing added to it. Some of these Citadelians might not have been able to read their own cards, he knew, and might have expected him to have to go to a licensed readwriter to have the marks deciphered, but he had no difficulty, except with putting names to faces. Most hadn't spoken their names anyway, or asked his, in the short time before he'd repeatedly made a break to find his "lady," but at least one had: Cinya. He flipped through to find her card and stared at it for a long time, thinking about what Suki had said about a million girls, and about how childish he'd been to pin all his hopes on a first love. For his own sanity, and for the work that needed to be done, he had to put away childhood, as Jenna apparently had done.

First things first, though.

13 - Gate Crasher

Uncle? ..." began Ronnie, as he and Owlly shopped for lumber down Woodmaker Street at the roofed yard set hard against the wall.

"Yeah?" said Owlly distractedly, comparing maple boards

"I was invited to the convent ... and I was thinking to stay on the other side tomorrow and meet Brod at the job the next morning. Would that be all right? I'll stay off the street."

Owlly stopped his inspection and regarded his adoptive son. "Of course," he said, then, "You wanna talk about anything?... ask any questions?"

"No, I'll be fine."

"You can talk to Nel too, you know."

"I know."

"Well, enjoy. And *give* enjoyment, if you want to be invited back.

Owlly had been secretly delighted, not just to see Ronnie moving on from first-love-heartbreak, but because his absence for a whole night would present an opportunity to take care of long-put-off business. Once back at the shop he'd given a message to his younger son, had him repeat it back twice, and sent him on his rounds. Now, as daylight dwindled on the second evening, he prepared for the arrivals.

They came on foot, some entering by the front door as last-minute customers and others by the side gate and unlocked back door—sixteen in all, many bearing parcels. As darkness fell, they were all comfortably seated in the showroom around a low table with one small candle on it, exchanging pleasantries and inquiries about family over tea and biscuits served by Owlly and Nel and only then getting down to business–the business of heresy and rebellion, and Ronnie.

Finally, the biscuits gone and the tea cooled, Owlly spoke up.

"Well," he said, picking up the candle, "shall we?

The flame cast eerie shadows as he led the others to the stairs at the side of the showroom and descended. Reaching the smooth concrete of the original pre-Cleansing structure, he raised the candle toward the first windows to make sure Jak had closed the curtains before joining his mother in the living quarters above. The circle of light preceded and shadows darted as he moved between stacks of lumber, semi-finished furniture pieces, past shelves of paint, glue, odd tools, bins of hardware, bolts of fabric and leather, household items, then on into Ronnie's neat living area–defined by a raised platform–and finally, at the end of the long room, to a stand of stout shelving anchored to the wall, on which were stored numerous and mostly fragmentary examples of pre-Cleansing woodcraft, only occasionally taken down and studied for design inspiration.

Taking a position before the left-side section and handing the candle off, he grasped a heavily laden, hip-high shelf with both hands and lifted. It rotated a couple of inches off its supports with a muffled rasp from somewhere behind and the section swung inward, through the back wall. Owlly retrieved the candle, studied its flame as it fluttered slightly in the opening, and started down the rough steps beyond–ten feet deep, fifteen, twenty, onto a landing and through an opening anciently chiseled in a concrete wall, and into the open space beyond. He walked forward a few paces and prepared to light the lamp set on a round table, as the others began to file in behind.

"*Wait,*" said a voice from the shadows ahead, and though the single word was uttered calmly, its effect was not calming; fright and consternation erupted as the visitors shouted and fell back upon themselves in the semi-dark, tripping over feet and furniture and stacks of books, drawing knives or lifting parcels protectively or preparing to flee back up the stairs.

"Wait, Uncle," said the voice. "I haven't seen anyone's face yet."

"Ronnie?" said Owlly incredulously, now beginning to make out a standing figure as he continued to shield the others from the candlelight with his body and they in turn shielded themselves with hands and parcels. "What are you *doing* here?"

"Forcing you all to decide.... Now. Tonight."

"Decide *what?"*

"Whether to have me in your circle, or let me leave to find my own people, or kill me to keep your secret." He stepped forward to reveal that he was already dressed for travel, wearing country clothes and with his pack and axe on his back, its cover off. To general alarm, he reached to push the deadly instrument up with his left hand and sweep it out with his right to lay it heavily on the table, where its blade glinted in the candlelight.

"My father and I made this axe when I was fourteen.... The last thing I used it for was to kill an army scout so more than thirty Freethinkers could get away to the mountains. You can use it on me if you don't trust me."

No one spoke. The candle flame moved infinitesimally in an air current from somewhere. Finally a shoe scuffed on concrete and a figure moved into the light at the table. It was Patty Pubkeeper.

"Hi, Ronnie."

"Mistress," he nodded, somehow unsurprised.

Then came Brod, then a man whom he recognized as the operator of a readwriting kiosk within the Citadel, then a man he knew as some sort of attendant at the crematorium, then an aged sub-priestess he'd once seen in conversation with Nel in a distant street, then two or three others he thought he'd never seen before. The others remained in the shadows.

Seeing there would be no further votes of confidence for the moment, Patty untied the sash from around her waist and held it out to Owlly.

"Let Brod do it," he said, understanding, and she handed it off.

Brod came around the table and pulled out a chair. "Take off the pack and sit down," he said with an authority Ronnie hadn't heard before, but when the blindfold went over his eyes and Brod said "I should probably be tying this around your neck!" he sensed amusement.

Soon the brighter light of the oil lamp filtered through the blindfold. The axe was drawn to the other side of the table, chairs scraped, and Ronnie waited. He started as an open hand slammed the table to his right.

"*Listen,* you arrogant little fuck!" growled the man's voice that went with the heavy hand, "I don't care if you killed the fucking Sword of Zah himself! You had no right to endanger Owlly's family and the rest of us without an invitation. Who fuck do you think you are?"

It was a rhetorical question, one of many in different voices and volumes concerning his sanity, maturity, common sense, credentials, honesty, commitment, discretion, courage, and intellect. Eventually there was a pause for an answer, but Ronnie didn't like the question, so he didn't answer it.

"I *said,*" repeated the woman's voice, "who were the members of this Firstportage circle you claim? Was it unitary or cellular? If you can't tell us something we can check out, then you must be lying, or exaggerating."

Ronnie remained silent and still.

"They're probably all dead now anyway. You won't be betraying them. Just give us the names."

Nothing.

"Well, did you have a library?... Did you teach the young?"

Ronnie thought about that for a moment, then, "Yes. I taught math and history."

"From books?" asked a new male voice. "Where are they now?

Did your library survive?"

"It belongs to the Circle."

"Your circle is *dead.* We *told* you. Give us the library or some useful information or there's no use having you. You're just dead weight—a liability."

"Not yet. Not till I find my people ... or don't find them."

"Boy?" demanded the first voice with another hand-slam, "do you understand you're in danger of losing your head here?"

"Yes, sir."

Suddenly the woman interrogator started speaking to the slammer in German, as if it were a secret code-language that no one could understand, which, since the end of learning and of travel after the Cleansing, was mostly true. Ronnie listened for a moment, then interrupted.

"Auf jeden Fall," he said, *"wir brauchen die eigentlichen Bücher nicht. Ich habe sie hier drin."* He tapped his temple, signifying that the actual books weren't needed because he had them in his head.

Patty took over in the surprised and suspicious silence. "What do you mean, Ronnie? You remember books? How many books? What books?"

"Well, I didn't really understand Krylov's Theory, so I couldn't explain that, and I have trouble retaining languages that I haven't heard spoken, and I sometimes forget fiction unless I read it aloud ... but yeah, I remember. Maybe five hundred? Not word for word, of course, but ..."

"Bullshit," said a gravelly new voice to derisive snorts and laughter. Ronnie turned his head to the new speaker.

"No, sir," he said, then, "I think you must be the man from the crematorium.... You picked up a book in the street a few months ago. An encyclopedia—on its way to be burned, I thought, but there it sits in a stack by the entrance, unburned. If you look up ancient Rome, you'll see a picture of the Colosseum—top right. I couldn't read anything from the sidewalk that day, but I can tell you about the Colosseum—or the

Roman world—if you want to test me."

He sensed the others looking to one another uncertainly, and went on. "My parents always told me I had a good memory, that I should use it to help the Circle, so I try to remember what I read and hear and see, when it seems important.... Like on the bridge."

"What do you mean, 'on the bridge'?" asked a skeptic.

"Show them, Ronnie," encouraged Owlly.

Ronnie was still for a moment, then put his elbows on the table and his head in his hands in concentration, and commenced in a droning low voice. "I dressed up and went to look for a friend at the sailing of the *Wind of ZAH.* At first, I was mostly thinking about her, but I remember things like the guards not challenging me because I looked and acted like I belonged.... In the crowd, I was close up with hundreds of people—heard them say each other's names or pet names or titles, listened to their gossip and jokes and business talk and sex talk and politics. Remembered their voices and expressions and clothes and manners and the way they were treated by others. Heard what they said about the Messengers and the Sword—who went by close enough to touch, by the way."

"Like what, Ronnie?" said Owlly. "Give us an example."

Ronnie raised his head as if he were looking beyond them through the blindfold. "A tall, dark-skinned high priest told a much-younger woman—he called her 'Cherry' and she called him 'Nibbles'—that Lord Magnus was being sent on his mission by his enemies to get him away from the Citadel, because some people wanted to make him Sword of ZAH. Later, when Magnus was giving a speech, two women were watching the Messenger called Sula and gossiping about how she had sex with her bodyguards but never let them ... finish. I watched Sula and saw how much she hated Magnus, especially when he talked about free choice and—"

"What?" said an unfamiliar voice from the shadows. "What did he say about free choice?"

"That Zah meant for people to have free choice—once their spirits were calmed. I think that's the best way to summarize it. He said it's suggested by some of the Chaplin's original writings."

This set off an excited round of murmuring debate, and then more questions that didn't dwindle until the oil-depleted lamp had dimmed and flickered and been replaced by another one. In the end it was clear that a sixteen-year-old boy with audacity and a sponge-like memory had succeeded in collecting more intelligence about the hidden culture of the Citadel elite, in one day, than many could in a lifetime. And he'd done this while mooning over a girl. Such a talent could be useful.

Finally, those who chose not yet to be seen by Ronnie trooped with a couple of the others up the stairs and left in ones and twos–prepared as always with bribe money and explanations for their presence in the nighttime streets, in case they encountered police.

In the secret place, the blindfold came off and Ronnie found himself sitting with Owlly and another man as Patty and Brod puttered about the misshapen space with the other lamp, now refilled.

"Ronnie, this is BeeBee from the crematorium." The older man stuck out his fist and Ronnie met it with his own.

"It's short for 'Bookburner'," said the gravelly voice. "You can call me 'Bee'."

"Happy to meet you, sir," Ronnie responded, amused at the irony.

"Do you wanna look around?" asked Owlly. "Or did you already?"

"I didn't want to disturb anything yet."

"Just *us*?" asked Bee with a straight face.

"Sorry to put everyone on the spot like that."

"Well, it worked, I think," said Owlly, getting up from his chair. "Come on."

He picked up the lamp and led Ronnie around the space, which was almost as big as the furniture showroom up the stairs. Farthest away from the entry point, it was a great jumble of smashed pieces and contents of the office building that must once have stood above it, appearing to block the space from side to side and up to the high ceiling.

"What was this, do you suppose?" asked Ronnie.

"A parking garage, we think," said Owlly, "for cars.... The building above was demolished when the wall was created, the floor collapsed and the debris fell in, but left this little space. That's the theory, anyway. The story is that one of my predecessors was trying to create a passage into the Citadel and discovered this instead, so he made it a library. It has ventilation from somewhere, and it never gets wet."

Ronnie looked around at the tables and many shelves of books and at more stacked on the floor—many more books than he'd ever seen in one place. He was awestruck.

"It's a lot of books, Uncle—just for the twenty of you?"

"Oh no," replied Owlly, "many more, but nobody knows how many."

"Why not?"

"Our structure is cellular, and cells don't share information about their membership, and individual cell members may have cells of their own, which they also don't normally talk about. But we all share books and ideas."

He raised the lamp toward the entry, where the departed had left their parcels. "That's what *those* are: books brought for exchange. After the fright you gave us tonight, I think the others decided to finish their business another time."

"Again, Uncle—

"Don't worry about it, son. What's done is done. Now the only thing to do is decide whether to make you a library keeper and teacher, or kill you."

Ronnie turned back to Owlly with a smile, only to realize he'd been serious.

"This circle has survived for generations, because it's careful—and ruthless in its defense. In my own time, four members of this very cell have been executed because they became compromised and didn't have the courage to take their own lives—people we loved. Two others committed suicide last year during the pogrom, to break the connection to the rest of us.... Get the picture?"

"Yes, Uncle. I understand."

"Still wanna join up?"

"Yes."

"Well, then, we've just got to decide on a job for you.... Maybe one where your people-skills and good memory can be put to use."

"I'm at your command, Uncle, but ..."

"What?"

In answer, Ronnie extracted from his pocket a bound packet of the sort of social and business cards favored by the Citadel elites, each one an invitation to intimacy with a member of the ruling class.

"Can I make a suggestion?" he said.

14 - Transitions

Years 107-109 of the Age of Obedience

Sister Cinya had been the first. He'd gone to the four-story convent one evening after a job, given his name and Cinya's card to a woman in the lobby, and gone back out to wait on the busy sidewalk, as befitted his workman's dress and toolbox. When she came out onto the porch, flanked by her sidekick Iris, she initially overlooked him, until Iris nudged and pointed.

"Ronnie?" Cinya called uncertainly.

He turned and met her surprise with a sardonic smile, then strolled closer to look up at her at the top of a short flight of stairs.

"You look ... *different*," she remarked, noticing his Citadel work badge.

"I *am* different."

"So you're a ...," she studied the tools protruding from his wooden toolbox, "a *carpenter?"*

"Furniture and cabinet maker."

"I *thought* your hand was a little *rough*, for our crowd. What were you doing on the bridge?"

"Trespassing. You gonna have me arrested?"

"That depends," she said, pretending to consider. "What are you doing *here?"*

"Looking for work. Got anything that needs my attention?"

Cinya was amused, and liked the calm, confident way he looked at her. She put her head on one side. "Maybe. Are you a hard worker?"

"I *aspire* to be. It's just that ..."

"What?"

"I'm ... *inexperienced* ... in need of *training*."

Cinya and Iris shared a look of mischievous delight, then openly appraised Ronnie's long workman's body and the face that was in the process of maturing into something extraordinary.

"Don't worry," said the nineteen-year-old sub-priestess of ZAH, "we'll take care of that."

And so they had, with dedication and the help of several others over the three days that he was a virtual captive in the convent, with priestesses skipping their duties or hurrying home from their jobs or feigning illness to experience his youthful exuberance and an expertise that grew by the hour.

Once he'd learned the basics and then a few specialties, he'd practiced them with a vengeance, for his mission and his pleasure and to forever erase the memory of the inconstant Jenna and the one tender-hot night they'd had. By the time Owlly came asking for him on the third evening, he'd been taken over by more senior priestesses—to the helpless chagrin of Cinya and Iris and the other more junior ones—and was becoming educated in the sexual politics of the Citadel.

Priestesses of inferior rank yielded to their superiors, as he'd already learned, but even these did not exercise their legal right to the seed of an unmarried commoner without restraint, for to do so smacked of unseemly desperation. He could decline invitations or simply discourage them by implying dedication to a higher-ranking lover.

This was what had sent him rifling again through the cards given him on the bridge, for memory told him that some of the hands that had thrust them into his jacket belonged to priestesses of high rank indeed. Their elegant cards, unlike others, were often "trysting cards," giving only a post office box number or readwriter's kiosk, designed to keep jealous husbands in the dark. It was especially in *their* beds and company that he would learn the secrets of the priesthood and its fortress.

Before two years had passed, Ronnie could pick and choose his lovers and lifestyle, but mostly chose to sleep in his own narrow bed and to help tend the library. He'd fathered several children—who were never discussed or shown to him—and turned down numerous offers of luxurious Citadel accommodations, and even of marriage, always telling himself that the mission required him to be unattached. He'd accumulated many "gifts"—rings from patron's fingers and bracelets from their wrists and gold and silver coin—and this booty now resided hidden partly in the debris-fall in the library and partly in the cemetery, where it could be recovered by the family in the event access to the library was lost.

Other gifts came in the form of the clothes he wore, and these sometimes caused problems, for though he still wore work clothes most of the time, he couldn't offend his patrons by shunning their offerings of fine garments. Being seen in them between the shop and the Citadel gate was one thing, but being seen at Patty's in snakeskin boots and leather pants and shirtsleeve rolled to reveal thick gold bracelet was quite another. Especially when it came to his nemesis, Tom Stonecarver.

Ronnie had been forbidden to again challenge the peace between woodworker and stoneworker by trying to penetrate Redline Alley, but that hadn't stopped him from seeking retribution for the beating he'd taken there. Once he'd felt sufficiently recovered from his injuries, he'd first sought permission from "Mom" and "Dad," as he'd been invited to call them, then gone after the dinner hour one evening to the head of the alley, across the street from Patty's, and stared down it until he attracted everyone's notice.

"SCAARRFAAACE!" he yelled in his pasture-spanning country voice, just once, which was still enough to sting his ribcage a bit.

Activity in the alley ceased, and a few minutes later Tom exited his building with an entourage and headed Ronnie's way at a deliberate pace. When he arrived to stand face-to-face a few feet away, the others began to fan out around Ronnie, even as woodworkers who'd been moving about the area began to collect in the street behind him.

"You think you're gonna need all these people?" he asked calmly, and Tom raised a hand to stay the others.

They fought. They fought by the unspoken rules of such challenge fights that no eyes or teeth or balls be taken and no weapons used, except for the hard sidewalk and curb, the lamppost, the crunching wheels and clomping hooves of passing vehicles, and the sharp brick corners of the buildings on either side of the alley. They fought for five minutes, ten, fifteen, until finally they were separated by adults when they'd fallen into a desperate clutch and police were spotted down the street.

Then they'd fought again, and again, across the seasons and always without a clear victor. When Ronnie began occasionally showing up at Patty's in fancy clothes and other signs of a favor that the mutilated Tom would never know from desirable women, the friction escalated.

"Hey, priestfucker!" he'd called across Patty's one time, "how many dicks you suck today?"

"Listen, Face, I'm not prejudiced or anything," Ronnie called back reasonably, "but why are you so preoccupied with *dicks?"* And they were out the door again, followed by a beer-toting audience.

And so it went, until the Toolmaker Square incident.

It happened while the Citadel police force was momentarily depleted and stretched thin during an unscheduled army drive on a group of villages across the river to the east, where a Christian cabal had allegedly been discovered. The usual killing and pillaging had taken only a few days, but the torturing and raping and the dividing of spoils had dragged the operation out for two weeks. That had been long enough for bands of young toughs, and a few other town-dwellers, to get up the nerve to begin harassing and robbing clergy and merchants and defacing public property. One evening in Toolmaker Square, as the midsummer sun was going down, that had taken the form of a group of masked young people spraying bladders of pig's blood across the large, ridiculously flattering portrait of the Sword of ZAH that was draped down the front of the precinct audience house, where citizens were called to receive instructions whenever ZAH deemed it necessary, according to the priests. Ronnie had been returning home with a canvas satchel of new chisels and a large, freshly sharpened saw, when he'd witnessed the band at their work and seen them set upon by a squad of reserve police.

The police might have been second-rate, but they were armed with short swords and long batons and quickly cornered much of the band on the steps of the precinct house, as other pedestrians and a lamplighter fled. Suddenly the band's apparent leader, whose voice and physique and fighting style Ronnie could not mistake, ran at them, shouting and squirting his blood-bladder to give the others a moment to escape. The police rebounded and some began to poke and pummel him with their batons as others tried to get at him with swords. The hooded figure wrestled one of the batons away and fought back but began to wither before multiple blows. The swordsmen pushed to finish him before darkness fell.

Suddenly a policeman at the rear shrieked as his sword arm was nearly severed by Ronnie's viciously hacking saw. Two more swordsmen were struck before they could reorient themselves and panic seized all. They fell back before Ronnie's and the masked man's shouts and blows and then fled at the reappearance across the small square of the other vandals.

Ronnie caught the injured figure around the waist as he began to sag and helped him to stumble toward his friends. Halfway across the square he relinquished his burden to other arms and started to return the saw to the satchel slung on his back as the light dwindled.

"You should maybe split up and lose the masks," he said, "and not go straight home—they might try to follow."

The sagging figure looked up at him with a misshapen eye. "Do what he says," he ordered the others in his familiar voice, then nodded to Ronnie before turning and being helped into the darkness.

Ronnie and Tom never fought after the Toolmaker Square incident, but they continued publicly to insult each other for form's sake. The bile had gone out of their rivalry, though, and with it the thuggish militancy in Tom's demeanor. Patty Pubkeeper's daughter Polly saw the change before others and swooped in with the attention and affection Tom had never expected to know, and within months they were married and Tom was doting on Polly's two-year-old priestblood daughter, Lolly. Now it was Ronnie's turn to look enviously over his beer at Tom in a corner at Patty's with the child on his lap, her little hands on his cheeks, gazing adoringly at him, oblivious to his disfigurement. Ronnie could only smile ruefully at the irony—the fearsome Scarface become a loving family man and the aspiring family man become a cynical and lonely whore.

15 - Lady Rosamund

"Ah! —yes! —just! —like! —that!" stuttered Lady Rosamund as she maneuvered the young man between her legs into just the right position and pace. Ronnie swelled anew, not in real passion but from the thrill of power he'd taught himself to substitute for it. Again he let his mind meld with that of his mistress, saw himself through her eyes, exulted in his own enslavement, in his own callous manipulation. But just as she was about to climax again, he looked down at her edge-of-orgasm expression with disgust and growled, "Noooaahh!"

The priestess's eyes fluttered open in irritation as he struggled from her grip on his ass and rolled to put his bare feet down on the antique rug spread before the fireplace. After a few seconds she closed her lubricant-smeared legs and moved beside him, her arm across his broad back.

"What's wrong, honey?" she cooed with motherly concern.

"You always *do* this to me," he said through gritted teeth. "You just *use* me. You don't hear a word I *say!*"

"No, baby," she soothed, sliding her hand across a slick thigh toward his deflating cock. "You know you're very special to me."

"Then why won't you *help* me?"

"Whaddayou need, baby," she said against his shoulder. "Wanna do something kinky?... Need some money?"

He pushed her hand away. "Stop it. You know what I mean."

Now she sat back on her heels in feigned impatience. "*That* again?... We've talked about this."

"I know," he pouted, "but we never *do* anything."

"Don't you like being with me? Am I not good to you?... Generous?"

"Of course, but you know I want to better myself. Learn how to work in your world, so I don't have to make furniture the rest of my life ... or ..."

"I *want* to help you, Ronnie ... when I can find an *opportunity*. But I can't bring you into my ministry or my social circle. If my husband finds out about you, he might have you killed, along with your family. And you don't have the skills for office work anyway. You don't even read or write."

"Then *teach* me, Zahdammit! I'm not stupid!"

She slid to a position between his knees to looked into his face. "Of *course* you're not stupid. You're a very smart boy. It just takes time to find the right place for you." She started to take his cock into her mouth again but he stopped her.

"Help me understand how things work and I'll find my own place," he proposed.

"What do you mean?"

"You're a fucking deputy minister, for Zah's sake! You probably know how the whole government works. Just explain it to me so I can understand how to make myself useful."

"Well, each part is different. I don't–"

"So explain how *your* department works! What does a property department even *do?"*

Lady Rosamund, high priestess of ZAH and chief of the Property Department of the Error Ministry, considered. She didn't like the interruption of her pleasuring, but it was a small price to pay for the company of this extraordinarily adept and malleable young lover. Besides, his ambitions would come to nothing. Most of the Citadel's power was in the hands of older men, and they resented the unmarried boys who'd overstayed their welcome in the beds of childless priestesses to become the full-grown playthings of older women who no longer had legal claim to them, many of whom were married and could only enjoy them in hideaways.

Sometimes, illicit lovers could be paraded before friends in small gatherings, but otherwise they were a secret to be closely kept. Their only way up was through marriage into the priesthood or the bureaucracy or the ranks of priesthood-favored merchants, but that was rare for young men who hadn't started as children on an approved path to favor. Still, he could dream, and in his harmless dreams become even more beholden to her.

"My department," she began, "manages all the property that comes into the ministry's hands through its operations, and some property belonging to individuals. Buildings and farms and mines and boats and many other things. A lot of this property generates revenue and ... Do you understand 'revenue'? – money coming in?"

"Like when I sell my furniture and get paid?"

"That's right," she smiled, now taking him lightly in hand without resistance. "This revenue goes toward the government's expenses, like the army and police and all the people working in offices...." She began to knead him erect again, her well-practiced thumb just below the head of his cock.

"How does the ministry get the property," he asked earnestly, ignoring her ministrations.

"Some of the government's property was given by ZAH to the Chaplin after the Cleansing, some was left by will or accepted in payment of fines and such. Those properties are managed by the Interior Ministry. The Error Ministry manages property seized from enemies of the state.

"Whaddayou mean, 'enemies'?"

"Heretics," she said. "Freethinkers, Christians, Bobists, Eggists, other degenerates." She reached for the pillow that had been under her hips and placed it behind Ronnie. "Here, lie back."

"How do you catch heretics?" he asked, complying. "Don't they hide?"

The deputy minister dribbled spittle on Ronnie's belly to reliquify the dried lubricant that had seeped from her aging vagina and used it to work him to full erection. Then she put her mouth on him. Ronnie reached for her, held her head with both hands for a moment, feeling the facelift scars in front of her ears with the tips of his fingers, then pushed her back so she could answer him.

"Don't they hide?" he repeated.

"A lot of rich people are secret heretics," she said, resuming her kneading, "but they're left alone because they're useful. If they cease to be useful, or if the Citadel needs extra money for something, then they're exposed, and their property comes into *my* hands." She climbed atop him and worked him into herself. As she started to move, she slid her fingers between the shaved, shrunken labia to stroke herself.

Ronnie watched her use him until her eyes closed and her mouth opened, then asked, "When a lot are exposed at once, it must be a lot of work for your department. I mean ... do you have any warning? How—"

"Shut up ..."

"I mean, how do you know when—"

She clamped her hand over his mouth.

"Because ..." she panted with exasperation as she let Ronnie's reddened cock slip from her and moved up to straddle his inclined face and finish against his obedient tongue. "I! ... know! ... *everythiiiing!*"

"'Everything,'" repeated Ronnie to the three who'd been designated to hear his intelligence: Owlly, Big Jon the table-slammer, and Sister Lilum, who still wore the grey robe of a sub-priestess even after a long career as a records clerk at the treasury.

"I think that means," he went on, "I *hope* that means, that she has to be kept informed of the leadership's long-term strategy, so her department is prepared—prepared to deal with the property-management consequences of attacks on Freethinkers."

"Or anyone painted as a heretic," added Jon.

"Yeah."

"And what of the other woman?" inquired Lilum. "Her subordinate?"

"Sister Janelle," said Ronnie with a twinge of guilt. "Well, she's been ... *dispossessed,* I think you'd say. Of *me.* If I see her again, it'll have to be kept from Rosamund.

"Agreed," nodded Lilum.

In the thoughtful lull that followed, Ronnie considered poor, deluded, deceived Janelle, the plain, 24-year-old sub-priestess who worked in the secretarial pool outside Rosamund's office suite. She'd only wanted a baby and borrowed Ronnie from another woman for the purpose, but then she'd fallen in love and asked him to marry her. Ronnie's immediate purpose had been to find out what secrets her job made her privy to, but he's made the mistake of enjoying her kindness and self-deprecating humor and actually trying to please her, despite her foolish devotion to Zah and her conviction of the goodness of both the god and his representatives. As rare and desirable as an offer of marriage into the priesthood was, he had to get out of it and move onward and upward, and he'd done so by allowing himself to be observed by Lady Rosamund. The hook was set with one long and knowing look across the department's dining room; he became hers, and woe was due to any lesser woman who would interfere. A heartbroken Janelle could only accept her loss and exchange rueful glances with her "fiancé" on his rare visits to the ministry.

"Still," said Sister Lilum, bringing him back to the round table in the hidden library, "she has a reason to be disgruntled now, and that might make her useful in future. Keep that in mind."

"Yes, ma'am."

"Well," said Owlly, looking at the others and preparing to rise, "shall we adjourn?"

"I think I'll read for a while," said Lilum. "Ronnie, could you come for me in an hour or so?"

"Of course, sister," he answered, knowing that this was the only place she could safely indulge her passion for books, since she lived under observation in an elder's convent. As he was about to pass through the rough portal, he looked back and was amused to see her gazing into a book of poetry, knowing also, from the way he'd seen books disarranged in the past, that she'd probably soon head for the shelf of yellowed and fragile novels of passion-filled romance.

Climbing the stairs quietly, he envied her.

16 – Club Scarface

WHAT?" yelled Brod over the driving beat from the bandstand, as thrusting and stomping bodies crowded nearby and wall torches flickered.

"I *said*," Ronnie yelled back across the table, "*what the fuck are we doing?*"

"We're dancing and getting drunk," responded newly married and new-father-to-a-priestchild Brod. "*You* are, anyway.... What's up, brother? Aren't you having fun?"

Ronnie raised his glass again and drained it before looking around skeptically. He was at Scarface, the new establishment which had been Patty Pubkeeper's gift to her daughter and son-in-law and which the authorities had surprisingly allowed to be opened in the Smithville district, several blocks south of Patty's. It was the third such music and dance venue opened or converted in recent months, and he was disturbed that he hadn't learned of the policy shift before it was implemented. At the moment it was a madhouse of young people at their instruments and on the drum-like wooden floor, trying to invent a style to test the limits of the new freedom.

The new freedom. It was troubling. The priesthood didn't do *anything* out of concern for the people's wishes; now, all of a sudden, three such popular establishments were operating outside the wall and more were on the way. Why?

It was supposed to have been a simple neighborhood pub called Polly's, with the fearsome Tom very much in the background, but the sociable Polly had overcome her secretly shy husband's doubts by leading him about the mixed neighborhood of smiths, tanners, saddlers, hardware dealers, cartwrights, undertakers and others, to get support for their enterprise. At first the various opinion-makers and shot-callers had been hostile toward Tom, but his new wife had taught him manners and self-confidence and he overcame first their revulsion and then their resistance. Then, before conversion of the one-time hardware store had gone far, people had appeared from the mayor's office to suggest the change. Patty had approved, in order to curry favor with authorities for the sake of cover, and Tom had become a celebrity as Scarface, with whom everyone now claimed acquaintance.

Tonight Ronnie had danced for a straight hour to the percussive music that, once let loose, had derived over one winter from the combining of the somber fare meant to accompany processions and ceremonies with the syncopated tapping and banging of exuberant street kids. At one point, a band member had shouted out mere gibberish to go with his drumbeats and the crowd had thrilled at the newness of it. Song lyrics, like public speeches, were forbidden as potentially subversive, as everyone knew, but these yelps and wails came exhilaratingly close.

Ronnie watched new mother Suki and her friends on the dance floor as another beer appeared before him. He took a sip and leaned again to Brod.

"I feel distracted," he said.

"What?"

"*Distracted*–like I'm forgetting something important. Maybe that's the point of this."

"This what?"

"*This*," said Ronnie, gesturing around.

"Whaddayou mean?"

"Think about it. If I'm hearing a lot about the Citadel's plans, and I didn't know *this* was coming, what does that mean? The place that's most hidden from us is the Error Ministry, and if this new policy came from there, what does that mean?"

"Whaddayou *think* it means?"

Ronnie took another sip and looked around before replying. "Look," he said, leaning forward, "I'm having fun, you're having fun, we're all having fun, but we're not *talking*, which means we're not plotting rebellion. Plus, we're collected together, where we can be observed. I think we have to be worried about spies."

"More than usual?"

"I think so. These new places mix strangers together, so it would be easier to insert someone."

"Yeah.... Listen, Ron, you said 'plotting rebellion'.... What's on your mind."

"Well, that's what our lives have to be about, right? Not just surviving from one generation to the next. I feel like if we don't do something in *our* generation, the will to act may fade away completely. The priesthood has ruled for more than a century. It's not shrinking, it's expanding, trying to rule the whole world. I'm hearing rumors about new missions departing south and west next Spring. Big missions. Expensive. Which could mean a new pogrom to raise the money for them.... We should be thinking about getting more weapons and training—looking for an opportunity *now*—not just to *survive*, but to *overcome*. The priesthood's power will be broken by *us*—here where it resides—or not at all."

"You're drunk, you know," Brod observed.

"Or not drunk enough," said Ronnie, upending his cup again and thinking how much more cautious Brod was now that he was responsible for Suki and her adorable priestchild.

"Let's join the girls," he said.

In a moment he was lost in the beat, all thought of armed rebellion put aside.

17 - Lady Clare

Spring, year 109

To Ronnie's immense relief, Lady Rosamund's husband had accused her of having an affair. Indignant, she'd threatened to divorce him, but he was a functionary of the Council of Messengers and she didn't want to lose the connection. She'd had to curb her appetite, though, farming Ronnie out to a couple of her lower-status friends to keep him occupied, making available to them the secret trysting spot above a boutique on Shopping Street in the same block as his tailor, whom he now often visited. One of the women worked for the State Ministry and Ronnie was mightily conflicted about eliciting information from her. He wanted to know about the objects and destination and progress of Lord Magnus's now-two-year-old mission—whose details were a state secret—but he desperately wanted *not* to hear anything about Jenna. As it turned out, the unpredictable and duplicative courier traffic indicated that after sojourning at Zahist colonies on what must have been the Mediterranean coast of the former country of Spain, and at the Nile delta, safe passage had been arranged and the party had disembarked within a day's sail of the still-mysteriously-poisoned ruin of Istanbul, to proceed along the route of what history books told Ronnie was the ancient Silk Road. The party was reported to have arrived eight months ago at the wrecked but partially repopulated city of Xi'an in China, the seat of a warlord whose name the State woman couldn't pronounce. Despite his earlier resolve, Ronnie had gone straight from State's bed to the secret library, to open a large world atlas on the table under the lamp and run his finger along the route the party had taken, imagining all the wondrous sights Jenna must have seen, the people she must have met and even learned to talk to, with her charisma and her facility for language. When Ronnie realized the generous nature of his thoughts he drew back for a moment, trying to cling to his sense of martyrdom, but he couldn't sustain it. He smiled ruefully to himself. How could she *not* have taken advantage of the opportunity offered her at the ambassador's side—an opportunity to be a part of history, perhaps even to participate in shaping it. He'd been childish to be so hurt and aggrieved, and it was past time to forgive Jenna and wish her success and happiness—even if it had to be in the arms of another. After all, it wasn't as if he was saving himself for her—not as if he wouldn't try to work the next well-situated woman to walk through the door.

"Good morning, my lady," said Ronnie on a fine, late-spring day, hearing the doorbell and coming out of the shop to find a high priestess moving about among recently completed and offered furniture pieces, her status signaled by the satin-trimmed black robe, the two bodyguards left on the front porch, and the fine carriage and horses standing at the curb. He recognized her before she turned around, from her height and bearing and full head of salt-and-pepper hair, which she'd lowered her hood to reveal. She was the priestess from the bridge whom he'd thought might be Magnus's wife, before he'd seen the affection with which the ambassador treated Jenna.

"I'm afraid the master and mistress are out at the moment, ma'am, but if I may assist you ..."

She turned to regard him. Her expression was neutral, but her gaze was steady and appraising, automatically taking note of the two tattoo strokes on his left earlobe. When it went on wordlessly beyond a certain point, he drew the usual conclusion, gave her a slight smile, and waited.

Despite his experience of mature women, he was a little surprised. This one seemed too dignified to want to be with a man as young as himself—or rather *to be seen to be* with one so young. Maybe that was why she'd come so early in the day. Unmarried younger clergywomen, with legitimate claim, had no need of discretion, and in early days he'd taken a few to his narrow bed in the basement or serviced them against stacks of lumber at the bottom of the stairs, but older ones wanted to maintain a certain decorum in public, and this woman was even older than Rosamund.

Important, too, by what he'd seen on the bridge two years ago, and by the look of her now. Perhaps important enough to devote some time to. He let his smile grow bolder.

She chuckled. At least he thought it was a chuckle, but as it was simultaneous with a turning away and a clearing of the throat, he couldn't be sure. It certainly wasn't the response he'd come to expect. His smile faded.

"Is there something ...?" he said to her back as she ran her fingers over the surface of a narrow side table inlaid with a geometric pattern.

"You made a box," she said cryptically.

"A box, ma'am?"

"A box, for a lady—a lap desk, you called it. With a bird on the lid."

He didn't answer. His armpits moistened slightly.

"You are Ronnie, are you not?"

"Yes, ma'am—Rondak, by birth."

"Rondak—like the mountains?"

"I think so, ma'am."

"You think so? Who gave it to you?"

"My parents."

"Their names?"

"Bern and Marta Woodmaker," he said, hoping she didn't notice the slight hesitation.

"Why don't you ask them?"

"They're passed on, ma'am."

"Passed ..." Her fingers stopped moving and for a long moment she became perfectly still. When she spoke again her voice was strained.

"So now you create things in wood, like your father."

"And my mother. She taught me to do inlay." He stepped near to indicate the tabletop she was touching. "Like this. It's the most complicated thing I've done—meant to display a vase here in the middle."

"Very fine. Artistic ..."

"Thank you, ma'am," he said, and waited again.

"So," she said finally, turning to face him and becoming businesslike, "we must talk about this bird. Where did you get the idea? ... for the image, I mean."

"A bird, ma'am? Well, I ... "

Ronnie's throat constricted and he shifted from one foot to the other, unable to close his mind's eye to the image.

It was a Great White Heron, a bird not native to the valley of the Husson, and which he could never have seen in nature. Worse, in his unwelcome vision it was displayed in full color, standing on one leg among reeds, just as he'd seen it reproduced from a painting done more than three centuries past by John James Audubon—in a book. He had the sickening feeling that this woman had seen the book too—probably had it open on a table in the dungeon where she kept her instruments of torture.

"I ..."

The doorbell sounded and Ronnie turned with relief to see one of the bodyguards enter while the other politely detained Owlly and Nel on the porch. The priestess made a sign and the guard stepped aside to let them pass.

"Lady Clare!" effused Owlly as he approached. "It's an honor to have you in our shop again. It's been a long time."

"Yes. How are you, Master Owlly?" she said, extending her hand, which Owlly raised to his forehead. "And Mistress Nel, isn't it?" she said, giving her hand again and receiving a small curtsey and murmured greeting.

"And you've met Ronnie?" asked Owlly.

She gave her hand, and as Ronnie raised it, he was returned to a state of confusion by the intensity that passed through her fingers.

"He's been showing me some things," she said, letting him go and turning. "This side table is especially lovely."

"That's Ronnie's own work. The rest of us are in awe of his ability to create designs."

"Well, I'll have it, I think–for my entry hall."

"Of course, my lady. That will be an honor for us, to know one of our pieces is so prominent in your home. Shall I have it delivered this afternoon?"

"No, I'll take it now, if you can secure it on top of my carriage. Ronnie, too. He can help install it." She turned to her guard, still loitering inside the front door. "Bear, make sure Mistress Nel is paid, then help with the table and join me next door at the cradlemaker's." The big man nodded.

"My lady, wouldn't you like my boy Brod to help too?" asked Owlly as the priestess prepared to leave. "He's just down the street at the lumber yard. We can offer you some tea while we get him."

"No, Ronnie will do. I have something else I want to show him."

"I see," he said, starting to walk with the already moving priestess toward the open door, wondering if she had another motive for having Ronnie alone. "Well, Thank you again, my lady."

"Good day, Master Owlly, Mistress."

Twenty minutes later, Lady Clare came out of the cradle shop with her two guards and stopped in her tracks on the sidewalk at the sight of Ronnie placidly sitting cross-legged on the overturned and padded and lashed-down table on the roof of the carriage. She came closer and looked up at him with amusement. "Don't you like riding in carriages, boy?"

“Ma’am?”

“Get down from there,” she said, taking Bear’s hand and mounting the retractable steps to sit facing forward. Ronnie clambered down and was brusquely motioned in to sit opposite her. Once the cab was buttoned up and the guards had taken positions by the driver, that man spoke to his horses and moved the reins and they pulled gently away from the curb.

Ronnie sat erect with his hands on top of his thighs and politely directed his attention out the open window, feeling the priestess’s eyes on him. The carriage made a couple of turns to get turned back toward the Citadel main gate.

“How old are you, Ronnie? Precisely.”

Now he looked at her. “Nineteen years and three weeks, ma’am.”

“And still unmarried? Why?”

“I guess I like my solitude too much.”

“Oh, really ... Solitude ... Do you get much of that? a handsome boy like you?”

“Well, I do my duty, ma’am, when I’m asked.”

“So I’ve heard,” she muttered, and looked out the window.

Ronnie did the same.

He felt like a puppet on a string, being jerked this way by courtesy, that way by sarcasm, the other way by flattery, yet another by implied threat. It dawned on him that this woman might be of the Ministry of Error, practiced at keeping a suspect off balance. For the first time, he let his eyes move to study the inside of the carriage and realized it was not just elegant and substantial, but armored, probably heavy and perhaps pulled by four or more horses on the open road. Though covered here and there with leather and cloth, he could see that sandwiched between the cab’s forming ribs and its wooden shell was some sort of metal mesh, shiny, its openings smaller than his fingertips—small enough to prevent an arrow or lance penetrating from the outside or a prisoner from escaping, once the shutters were raised and locked and the doors secured.

Why hadn't Owlly or Nel tried to warn him? They were afraid, that's why, and the guards' presence had prevented them taking a chance. Owlly's attempt to delay and send Brod along had surely been an attempt to protect him from a dangerous isolation.

So I've heard, she'd said about his commitment to duty. She must know about his particular attention to lovers with access to sensitive information, like the Treasury bureaucrat for whom he'd made the lap desk, with its drawers and compartments for writing instruments and materials. He glanced to find her eyes humorlessly fixed on him and quickly looked out the window again.

In ominous silence they passed through the Citadel main gate without slowing, then up and up the hill, the horses' effort audible inside the cab, into as area of great tree-shrouded and walled mansions, some of which may once have been commercial structures. Guards saw them coming and smoothly opened and closed the iron gates as the carriage passed. Servants were already coming out of the many-chimneyed pre-Cleansing red brick house as it crunched to a stop on gravel. A man approached the carriage to extend the steps, another opened the door, and a third, wearing a dark uniform suit, waited attentively at the bottom of the steps.

"Cornelius," Clare said to him once she'd alighted with her passenger following, "this is Ronnie. Help him bring this table into the entry. Gently. Let him direct you."

"Yes, ma'am," he said, then, turning, "We're at your service, young man."

"Well, it's a little heavy ...," said Ronnie. "Since we have plenty of hands, if I could have one man on top with me and four more below?"

"Jojo," snapped Cornelius to an eager-looking teenager. "Up top!"

Once on the carriage roof Ronnie unrolled the end of the pad on which the table rested and draped it over the rear luggage rail. Then he and Jojo lifted the six-foot-long,

two-foot-wide piece onto the rail and maneuvered it over and down to the waiting hands.

"Don't set it in the gravel, please. If we could take it onto the porch to turn it over ..."

Once he was down to participate in that operation, he'd had to move back to give place to those who came closer to inspect the new acquisition. It glowed in the late-morning sun, its subtle colors varied with wood type and grain, its complex design mesmerizing.

One by one the servants became aware of their presumption and stepped back, glancing apologetically at their mistress.

"Beg pardon, ma'am," offered Cornelius.

"It's his own work," she said with a confusing note of pride in her voice. "Ronnie's own work."

"It's ..." said Cornelius, looking at it again, "beautiful."

"Well, Ronnie, there you have it, from a connois– from a good judge of fine things: beautiful."

Ronnie could only smile awkwardly and nod.

Inside the foyer a handsome cabriole-legged mahogany side table, looking to be contemporary with the house, was consigned to storage or to use elsewhere and the new piece installed in its place, with a vase of flowers set on the center medallion. The helpers again took a moment to admire it and then excused themselves. Only Bear the bodyguard remained.

"Come," said Clare, giving Bear a gesture of dismissal and turning toward the interior of the house. She led Ronnie first into a mammoth hall flanked by two unlit fireplaces and sunlit rooms beyond on either side, then up a broad staircase covered by a patterned carpet. Having learned something of the manners of the elite, or at least the manners that the elite expected of others, he did not gawk or comment on anything–not the many silver candelabra or the paintings on the walls or the fine furniture or the architecture. But he was amazed. He ached to be allowed to study the design and construction of furniture pieces he suspected were pre-Cleansing, possibly even mined from the forbidden zones. And the art! –how could pieces that many Zahist zealots would consider as subversive as books be displayed so openly?

Not just the acceptable images of family and of figures from Zahist history, but of angels and demons from the age of heresy and other canvases which contained no figures at all—just swirls and shapes of color that alternately provoked thoughtfulness or thoughtless passion, states held by the Teachings to weaken one's commitment to obedience. He could barely keep his eyes on the priestess's back as she mounted to the landing.

He assumed, despite his earlier misreading of signals, that she was taking him to her bedroom. When she paused to let a loitering servant girl take the black robe from her shoulders, to reveal a soft grey summer dress and a still-attractive body, he was sure.

But he was wrong again. She led him not into a bedroom but into a suite of rooms mostly devoid of furniture and with painters' drop-cloths on the hardwood floor, then into a well-lighted room where some large object sat covered in the middle.

"Pull that off," she ordered, and Ronnie stepped forward to draw back the canvas from what turned out to be a desk.

Not just any desk, but a masterpiece, which Ronnie guessed, by what he remembered from a book in the Firstportage library, was in the Art Deco style, probably made in the 1920s or 1930s.

"Zah's ba—" he started to mutter.

"That's what I said, sort of. The miners found it on the long island, beyond the ruin."

"May I?" he asked.

"Of course. This is what I wanted to show you."

He stepped up and ran his fingers over the scarred, honey-colored top, which had a band of inlay near the edge on three sides, seeing and feeling the delamination and splitting. Stooping, he noticed the same problem in the geometric design inlaid in the front and sides. Pushing sideways on the top's edge, he felt a wobble.

"Do you think you could copy it?" asked Clare.

"Copy it? You mean the whole desk?"

"Yes. Use it as a model for a new one."

Ronnie looked dubious. "My lady, I'm not sure *anyone* could do that. It would mean inventing and making new tools and techniques, and then all you would have would be a copy, instead of someone's original creation. No, you should restore it, not copy it."

"Really? You could do that?"

"Me? Well, yes, I think I could ... if the drawers still work."

He went to the other side and slid out the middle drawer, which was empty. He inspected the mechanism, pushed levers on both sides, and pulled the drawer completely out. He worked the action, pronounced it of highest quality and serviceable, and put it back in. Then, with the priestess watching him closely, he pulled out the right-side drawer—and froze.

Nearly filling up the shallow space, like a fat black snake waiting in ambush, was a book. And not just any book, Ronnie realized, but a Christian bible, the book of one of the peoples who had most offended ZAH and brought on the Cleansing by presuming to understand and teach that which he had not invited them even to ponder.

Too late, in Clare's eyes, he recoiled from the desk as if just realizing what the object was. From a yard away he stared at it, met Clare's eyes for a moment, then looked again and pointed.

She came around the desk and looked in the drawer, and then at him. "Do you know what that is?"

"It's a book—isn't it?"

"Have you seen books before?"

"The priests show them to little kids, to warn them, and I've seen them in the street, going to be burned."

"Shall we look at it?"

He backed another step, shaking his head. "Best not, ma'am. It's forbidden."

She studied him for a moment. "Aren't you curious? ... Take it out."

He stared at her, and realization dawned: This was a set-up.

"I can't, ma'am," he said. "It's ... "

"Forbidden. Yes, you said that. Listen, Ronnie ... Look at me! ... I am a high priestess of ZAH, and nothing bad can happen while you're with me. Understand? Now quit being a baby. Take it out."

He stared at her for a moment, stepped forward to contemplate the instrument of his damnation, then reached and curled his fingers under it and lifted it out.

It was bound in black leather and heavy—and upside down. He began to rotate it so the cross on its cover would be upright and the spine would fall naturally into his left palm, then stopped and contrived awkwardly to set it on the desktop and step back again. Clare watched his every move.

"Open it," she commanded.

He hesitated, then stepped up and with two thumbs and exquisite care, folded the cover back away from himself.

Impatiently, Clare reoriented it on the desk, turned a couple of pages, and tapped.

"Do you know what these marks mean?"

"No, ma'am."

"This is a bible—property of a Christian family—and this is a record of births and deaths and marriages over about ... sixty years, it looks like. A pretty big family, and rich, I'd say...."

Ronnie stared until she turned the page, and then was transfixed by a beautiful image—of sunlight breaking through clouds to illuminate calm waters. Not a printed image, but a finely detailed painting, somewhat soiled and tattered by many hands. Then she turned another page, Ronnie's eyes fell on the oversized words at the top, and before he could stop himself, his lips moved soundlessly: *In the beginning ..."*

Lady Clare smiled inwardly and closed the book.

"Madam?" said Cornelius from the doorway, glancing with barely disguised concern at the book on the desktop and at the startled boy standing over it and then at his mistress.

"It's all right, Corny, we'll be right there."

Ronnie fretted: now there were *two* witnesses to his heresy.

"You have good table manners, Ronnie," said the priestess to her young guest, who'd been surprised to find himself led not to the torture chamber but to a round table on the terrace covered in white and set with pre-Cleansing china, silver, and crystal. "I commend your parents or your lady friends or whoever taught you. You don't eat that way at Patty's Pub, I'm told."

Ronnie was no longer nervous. it was clear he was in a trap, and that, with guards sprinkled around the grounds, there was no way out for the moment. Might as well enjoy lunch.

"At Patty's," he said, about to take another bite of lamb, "you have to bring your own utensils, if you're dining."

"Really?" she responded, amused. "Well, that's only practical, I guess, if your customers are poor enough to covet the house flatware. Tell me, though, do you see yourself ever rising above all that?"

"Above all what, ma'am?"

"Above Woodmaker Street. Above just getting by and being respectable. Above needing handouts."

That didn't sit well. Thanks to "handouts," he was already surely the richest nineteen-year-old in the neighborhood, able to help his family and his Circle and save up for the struggles to come, but he was still sensitive about being labeled "priestfucker," even in such subtle terms. He put down his fork and pushed his plate away.

"Oh, don't be so thin-skinned," said Clare scornfully. "It's beneath people like us."

People like us?

"I simply mean, can you see yourself one day being part of *this* world, she continued, gesturing to their surroundings. "Not as a servant or visitor, but as a member?"

"Well," he answered with a sardonic smile, "not this far up the hill, maybe."

"You'd be surprised ... surprised how many handsome young

cocksmen have ingratiated themselves with the ruling elite–married into it, even. But it's not done just through the women. Men hold most of the power; to elevate yourself you must somehow be of service to *them.* And I don't mean in the bedroom."

"What do you mean by 'of service', then. What service could I provide that would make me so popular?"

"You could spy for us."

Ronnie's mouth opened slightly and remained that way as he tried to process her blunt words and formulate a response.

"*Please,*" she said with sudden harshness, raising a hand to forestall him, "don't insult me with coyness. I know what you are, Ronnie; I can feel it in my bones. And you know I know. One word from me and these men will drag you away and start cutting pieces off until you beg to tell them every secret you've had since childhood. So don't play with me. Understand?"

"Yes."

"Then pay close attention," she said, leaning toward him. "*What you are* can either get you tortured to death over the next few days, or be the foundation for a brilliant career, leading to riches and social position and ultimately power, if that's what you want. You just have to help us identify our enemies among the populace. And that doesn't have to include your own friends and family. By helping us, you'll protect them. We just need help to identify enough of the Freethinker underground that we can eliminate it surgically–without destroying the city's economy. When that's done, you can join us on the hill–as high up as your talents and ambition will take you."

A long silence ensued, during which the birds in the trees were the loudest sound, then, "Can I have a few days to think about it?"

The priestess sat back suddenly, anger suffusing her face. "I told you not to play with me. *No,* you cannot have a few days to warn your friends. Either you start talking to *our* interrogators waiting in the house–right now–or you're given over to the not-so-gentle ones at the Black Tower. Make up your mind."

Ronnie studied the woman's face for a glimmer of irresolution or sympathy or mercy but found none. He toyed with his napkin and silverware for a moment then looked across the lawn to the back wall, where two guards stood beside a rose bed. The two out of earshot, at either end of the broad terrace, stared at him. He let the images come to him–of his parents, brother Bo, Jenna and her family, all the others he'd known throughout his life, and even shadows of the hundreds or thousands whose faces he didn't know but who must be there, waiting, depending on him. Finally he sat erect, patted his mouth with the cloth and placed it beside his plate, and consigned himself to oblivion.

"I want to thank you for appreciating my work," he said, "and for giving me lunch. I hope you'll find someone to fix your desk. Tell them not to use steam on the inlay."

She stared in disbelief, shook her head slowly, and resignedly looked an order to Bear over Ronnie's shoulder. Instantly the big man was there to haul him to his feet, the other man arriving to take his other arm and drag him over the toppled chair.

"Be careful, boys," the priestess said mildly, looking out over the garden. "He's got a meat knife in his shirt. Don't let him hurt himself before time. And if he changes his mind before you reach the Tower, bring him back."

Bear turned and, without preliminary, buried his huge fist in Ronnie's solar plexis, driving the breath out of him and buckling his knees. The knife was found and tossed on the table and the gasping, gulping boy was dragged around the corner of the house. Waiting there was the armored carriage with shutters now closed and two more guards at the door, four horses in harness to transport six big men on business rather darker than shopping.

Once all were sealed in and the carriage under way, Ronnie tried to regain his senses and figure out how to kill himself without the knife. Trying to provoke these disciplined men to do it would be useless, as they were in complete control of him, one on either side holding his arms and two facing, watching his every labored breath. If he cried out, they would just beat him unconscious, in which state he'd waste even more time. No, he could only hope there might be a place in the Tower from which he might leap, a sharp edge on which he might cut himself, or a bar or fixture from which he might hang himself, if they left him with any clothes or bedding from which to fashion a noose. Whatever he was going to do, he had to do it quickly, before names and locations started spilling out of him.

He felt the carriage reach open space and knew it was almost at its destination. He would be very calm, docile. In transferring him to the Error Police, his escort might relax its guard and he could run himself into a wall headfirst, entangle himself on something and break his own neck, or grab and ingest something that would strangle him—maybe the work-badge still pinned to his shirt. He willed himself to placidity, even as he coiled inside.

The carriage turned widely into a narrow passage, moved a short distance, and braked abruptly. Outside, the jailers called to one another lightheartedly, as if their trade was candied fruits and souvenirs instead of pain, humiliation, and death. The door opened and his guards roughly pushed him through it to sprawl on the pavement of the intake bay next to a stone wall. The carriage started moving again before he was restrained and, seeing his chance, he lurched to position himself so that his neck might be broken under the iron-rimmed wheel, feeling, in that last moment, relief.

Faster than his mind could process what his eyes saw under the carriage, instinct made him jerk back. The wheels spun by in front of his face and moved the carriage away, and before him was not the prisoner-intake bay of the Black Tower but the end of an alley giving onto a scene he saw nearly every day: the small plaza that lay before the pedestrian gate not a hundred yards from his home. The candied-fruit- and souvenir-selling "jailers" were in fact innocent hawkers of those goods, and the "prisoner-intake bay" was merely the back of a restaurant.

He began to gather himself to stand, only to realize how drained and shaky he was. He moved to lean against the wall and drew his knees up. In a moment he put his elbows on his knees and his hands to shield his eyes and quietly wept.

18 - The Clans

What did it mean? After an hour of walking about the Citadel, and another spent in a chair before the cold fireplace of the love nest on Shopping Street, he still couldn't figure it out. It was a puzzle for which he had not enough pieces.

When he'd stopped crying in the alley and resumed thinking, his first impulse had been to defy expectations. But what had Clare's expectations been? Whether she believed him a Freethinker or not, surely her expectation would have been that he would rush through Woodmaker Gate and tell Owlly and Nel all that had transpired. And what purpose of hers would *that* have served? To sow fear and chaos? Why? To cause their circle to panic and reveal its membership and connections to other circles? and those circles to still more? without the blood and bother incident to arresting and torturing a bunch of mere suspects? That would have taken a prepositioned army of watchers, a thought that made Ronnie realize he'd probably been followed from the alley. Too late to worry about that now.

Could it have been a mere afternoon's entertainment for a bored sadist? or, if real, somehow a signal or test for an informant already within the circle? or a ploy to alter the dynamic within the circle or between the Citadel and Freethinkers in some inscrutable way? or among Freethinker circles or political cliques within the Citadel? Was the approach to him even a Citadel operation? or Clare's own? If her own, was she now giving him time to come to his senses and change sides?

Had seeing the Audubon bird and learning of his attentions to important women prompted her to test him? or give him a warning? Why would she do that? Who was she, to do *that?*

And what was his duty now? As always to protect his adoptive family and the other Freethinkers, and, as his parents had taught him, to protect freethought itself from extermination. Did he do that best by reporting the mornings events and possibly setting loose a destructive paranoia? or by trying to interpret and respond to them according to his own best judgement?

Freethought had survived the Cleansing in the same way humanity had survived the plagues: by gathering itself into smaller and smaller units and dealing ruthlessly with trespassers. Only after the world had reached a tenuous stability had communities and then Freethinkers reached out to one another. But the experience of near-extermination had imprinted on Freethinkers the importance of keeping secrets, so that even a century and more after the Cleansing, they were kept, even from one's own loved ones and fellow circle members, until they *needed* to be shared.

For Ronnie, the question was whether this secret needed to be shared–just yet.

It was late afternoon by the time he climbed the steps again, ringing the bell with the opening of the door. The entire family had contrived to be about: Owlly and Nel and Jak dealing with half a dozen customers in the showroom, Brod sticking his head out of the shop, and Suki coming to the loft rail with daughter in arms to meet his eyes with concern.

Making his way back to Woodmaker Gate, he'd mentally practiced a nonchalance he didn't feel, getting ready to tell the first outright lies he'd ever told his family, convincing himself it was the right thing to do under the circumstance. Now he was relieved to have the buffer of customers in the store and even more relieved when Owlly was the first to speak.

"Your delivery's in the shop, Ronnie," he said, pointing with his thumb. "Nice piece."

"What? Oh, thanks ... sorry I wasn't here."

"No problem," Owlly said, returning to his conversation with an arm-in-arm pair of men looking at sofas.

Brod wasn't so casual, accosting him inside the shop door. "So?"

"So, what, you pervert."

"What happened—with Clare?"

"You mean did I screw her?"

"No, dummy. I mean did you *talk* to her?"

"Yeah, about *this*," he answered, making his way to the large object in the corner. He immediately looked in all the drawers to find them empty, then began to inspect the peeling laminate to make sure none had been knocked off. Brod stooped to join him. "It's a beautiful piece, isn't it."

"Yeah," said Brod with some impatience. "So you don't even know who she is, do you?"

"No, I'm waiting for you to tell me, and also why I didn't already know about her. Who is she? *What* is she?"

"If you don't know, maybe that means somebody else is working her. I'd better let Mom and Dad tell you."

Dinner was strained, with everyone studiously avoiding the subject of the high priestess and instead talking about the day's sales and new orders and about the affairs of family and especially about the excruciatingly cute baby girl named Madi, who gazed at her mother from a rocking crib set beside her chair and occasionally received a touch of her mother's hand. Finally, with Brod and Jak cleaning up and Suki installing herself in a comfortable chair to feed her baby, Owlly gave a sign and he and Nel and Ronnie adjourned to the dim showroom to draw chairs close together till their knees almost touched.

"So why do I get the feeling this lady is important?" Ronnie began.

"What do you know about her?" asked Nel.

"She's the lady on the bridge I described two years ago—the one who seemed so proud of Magnus when he spoke. I thought she was his wife, until ..."

"She's his sister, not wife."

Ronnie nodded in understanding. "The Censor."

"So you do know ..." said Owlly.

"I mentioned it at the time ... Someone in the crowd said Magnus's sister was the Censor, but I didn't know it was her. I haven't seen her since."

"She's very private," said Nel, "but very important."

"How so? And why haven't we spoken of her?"

"She's spoken of elsewhere," said Owlly. "You haven't needed to be party to those conversations. That may change now. As for why she's so important ... Nelly?"

Nel gathered herself and leaned forward. "It goes all the way back to the first days. As we were all taught, the Chaplin had eleven grandchildren, who came to lead eleven clans, with lots of intermarriage and subgroups over the years but remaining distinguishable, with different natures and power centers and so on. Clare is of the Ruthian clan, descended from granddaughter Ruth, who organized the first Zahist schools and decided what could be taught. She also handled the family's money, and because she and her descendants did that well, her clan developed a reputation for propriety that has survived. That's why Ruthians still run the Treasury, as well as the Ministry of Instruction, with de facto control over State.

"In the current era," Nel continued, "the clan is called Mortimerian, after the Messenger Mortimer, who is Clare's uncle. If he were to die, the clan would probably elect Magnus as its head-of-family, but only because Clare's husband is dead and Clare herself would decline. Her husband and two children were assassinated long ago and she's led a withdrawn life ever since—doesn't socialize much, doesn't take lovers—that we know of—but she's still influential, even though her only official title is Censor."

"So she's the head book-burner," observed Ronnie.

"Yes, but there's more to it. Owl?"

Owlly took over. "There's a tension between education and enforced ignorance.... The Citadel's bureaucrats and officers have to be literate and numerate in order to function, but nobody can be allowed to learn enough to threaten the priesthood's power. That line is policed by the censor. She determines what sort and how much of the old world's knowledge is allowed to be taught–throughout Zahdom–and she controls access to the physical materials."

"Physical ...?"

"Books, of course, but books themselves refer to other sources of information that were once common–pictures, films, electrical things ... They all go through her. We don't know how much survives."

"Well, can't we find out? Maybe we can divert something.... How do things get to her?"

"Ordinary people find things and turn them over to police or priests, and some comes from discoveries of secret libraries, but most comes through the Depot."

"You mean the big place where the traders pick up their goods?"

"Yes. It was once a kind of market, where hundreds of sellers displayed their merchandise to thousands of buyers. Now it's the place where the miners of the forbidden zones bring what they've found. It's inspected and sorted; some is destroyed on the spot, some put into storage, some distributed to privileged people or sold to Citadel merchants and to the traders–the kinds of things we were used to seeing sold at Firstportage, or that we buy now in the hardware stores."

Owlly paused to make sure Ronnie was comprehending.

"So," Ronnie said after a moment, "all these things are collected by the miners from old world sites, put on boats and wagons, and–"

"Wait a minute," Owlly interjected, "let me clarify. The miners themselves are specialized, and controlled by separate ministries, which in practice means they're loyal to certain clans. The Instruction Ministry's people are part of the Mortimerian clan and loyal to Clare personally. Others are loyal to the Treasury and to the ministries of Commerce and Interior. Miners are supposed to relinquish materials outside their areas of responsibility, to the appropriate crews. We've always assumed there's some misdirection and theft–if you're a book miner and you find a cache of gold or jewels, it's gotta be hard to turn it over to the treasury–but it must work, 'cause we don't hear much about big clashes or scandals.... It probably helps that clan loyalty and peer pressure are so strong, and that the penalty for infraction is decapitation on the spot–by your own clansmen."

"You didn't mention Error," said Ronnie. "What do they get?"

"Nothing, really, which we've heard over the years makes them crazy jealous. It was the Chaplin himself who placed the Censor's office in the Ministry of Instruction, but Error believes it rightfully belongs with them, and they may even have killed in the past trying to get it."

"You mean the assassinations?"

"Yeah, but Clare rode out that storm. Now their only responsibility on the sites is to insure the miners' obedience to Zah, which they deeply resent. It does give Error opportunities to spy on everybody else's business, however."

"And War?"

"That's ...," began Owlly, and stopped. He sat back and looked at his wife. "What do you think, dear? Should we wait?"

Nel thought so long that Ronnie had to break the silence.

"Wait for what?"

"I say it's time," said Nel, "We'll square it with the others later."

"Go ahead, then."

Nel leaned forward again and spoke low, even though the three were alone in the near dark.

"Weapons," she murmured, "discovered by Interior Ministry miners in the zones or by the army during its operations. There's always tension between the two ministries about their possession, and since War is a virtual branch of Error, that's a dispute with potentially dangerous consequences."

"Weapons," Ronnie murmured back, "You mean like swords and lances and such?"

"No. Like guns and tanks and airplanes."

"What?... Are you serious?" Ronnie had seen pictures of tanks and airplanes and he'd once found a rusty gun with some old bones in the woods, but he hadn't envisioned such things as part of the world they lived in. "How can that be?" he demanded.

"People in this part of the world often had guns in their homes or vehicles, and the soldiers and police had them, so they're discovered sometimes. Regardless of who finds them, they're supposed to be turned over to Interior, and *they* are *very* secretive about where they're kept—whether nearby or far away. As for the other things, they were just abandoned by the dying. They don't work, of course, and maybe never could again, but they're cataloged and protected—just in case.

"But," asked Ronnie in a mere whisper, "if they *have* guns, why don't they *use* them?"

"Don't need to," answered Owlly. "The people are under control without them. They probably see that if guns were ever reintroduced, rebels might get ahold of some and become a serious threat."

"Makes sense, I guess.... It makes you realize that any uprising would have to be unexpected and successful on the first try. That the idea?"

Owlly and Nel slowly sat back without answering. Eventually Nel leaned forward again.

"I think we've crossed enough red lines for one night, Ronnie. It's late and we need to talk to the others. But let's get back to Clare for a minute. You should know that there is a faction among us, a small faction, that believes the Mortimerian clan is a liberalizing force within the priesthood, subtly at war with the Sulan, which controls Error and War. This faction received a big boost two years ago, from *you,* when you gave that detailed account of Magnus's speech on the bridge—and the reaction of the crowd and especially of Sula herself. So learning more about Clare is of great importance, and you must seize any opportunity to get close to her. Time will tell if she is enemy or friend."

∆ ∆ ∆

Time, thought Ronnie as sleep approached; if Clare was a friend, and if the old-fashioned hell she'd put him through contained any message for him and the other Freethinkers, it was that there wasn't much of it left.

19 - Something in the Air

Weapons. Now Ronnie saw them everywhere he looked: in the chisel in his hand and the saw on the wall, in table legs and kitchen knives and hammers and axes, at the hardware store in crowbars and pitchforks and rope and wire and screwdrivers and myriad skull-crushing metal items, at the farrier's in iron horseshoes to be swung at rope-end or in canvas bag, at the boat chandler's in oars and netting and marlinspikes, on the street in loose bricks or broken bits of paving stone to be thrown or tied in net as bludgeon, at the housewares store in iron pots and fire tongs, at the tailor's in long scissors, at the butchers in head-rending cleavers, and at the fuel store and the ancient petroleum tanks south of the city in ingredients for incendiaries. In fact, as his preoccupation grew, he realized that every person in every location and walk of life had access to deadly weapons. Recognizing and preparing to use them was simply a matter of mindset.

Learning that the priesthood possessed old-world weapons—somewhere—had concentrated Ronnie's mind. He'd quickly dismissed the idea of finding and trying to steal them, when nobody even knew how to use them, as likely merely to provoke the authorities to bring them into use themselves.

That—in his daily-developing conception of military tactics and strategy—left only *preemption.* Somehow, someday, Freethinkers and whatever allies they could find had to coalesce on short notice, take to hand makeshift weapons they'd already identified and practiced with, and take power before guns could be brought to the fight. The fact that a rebellion, probably beginning with less than one thousand inexperienced attackers, would immediately confront hundreds of city police, then about two thousand well-equipped and led Citadel Guard troops, then about six thousand Citadel-based regular army troops—after they'd been issued their arms at the armory—then thousands more arriving from outlying posts, had to be looked at as merely the obstacle to be overcome. To conceive otherwise was to admit defeat and perhaps consign freedom of conscience to oblivion.

Something was in the air and there was no time to waste. The circles were already aware, thanks largely to *his* intelligence, of the possibility of a new pogrom to help finance evangelizing missions of conquest, and signs of preparations abounded. Over the winter, military contracts to blacksmiths, uniform and boot makers, wagon builders, horse and mule dealers and others, had quietly increased, and blacksmiths and fletchers in particular had also been drafted to work behind the wall in the armory's own fabrication shops. Friends among them reported growing stocks of swords, lances, bows, and other war-waging materiel, some of it submerged in barrels of oil for preservation until needed.

At the precinct halls around the city, where Zah's latest instructions were periodically passed to the people and where violators were required to present themselves to be chastised by finger-waving and punishment-imposing priests, delinquent men and boys we're being taken away for military training in ever-greater numbers, to the point that the drunkards and the homeless in doorways and alleys were becoming increasingly scarce. Likewise, the main jail was reported to be releasing prisoners directly into the army, to be broken by sadistic drill sergeants and taught to kill or summarily hung to create cell space for new arrivals.

Nor were he and his friends invulnerable to the draft; one whose family ran the lumber yard and another who sold wooden toys in the street had lately been called. Business owners and expert craftsmen like himself always expected not to be inducted, especially if they could afford to bribe district officials and priests, but anything could happen. One thing was sure: Ronnie could not allow himself to be drafted; the outrageous idea that was starting to germinate in his mind required that he not be separated from his circle. He would do what he had to do to remain on the scene and to learn all he could.

"That! –that! –that! –that!" went Lady Rosamund as usual, holding onto the headboard of the bed in the Shopping Street hideaway as Ronnie drove her home. She'd responded with alacrity and by uniformed government courier to his readwriter-penned note about needing to say goodbye because he might be drafted, and now he was doing his best to remind her what she would be missing if she allowed that to happen.

"I'll fix it," she said in a motherly way a few minutes later, cradling his head against her now-becalmed heart.

"Thank you," he mumbled with faux-guilelessness, "but if my brothers and our friend Tom get drafted, I'll have to volunteer anyway. I can't let them go without me."

"What are their names?" she countered with mock weariness.

"Brod and Jak Woodmaker, at Owlly's, and Tom Stonecarver, at the club Scarface."

"I've heard of that place," she said doubtfully. "I don't think–"

"And ..." he interrupted, throwing the dice again.

Rosamund took ahold of his thick hair with both hands and raised his face from her. "What, you bad boy!"

He grinned sheepishly. "If something happens, can I stay here for a couple of days?"

"You know you're not permitted inside the wall overnight."

"Nobody needs to know–not even my family. I won't leave the apartment, I promise." He rested his chin on her chest.

"I don't know," she replied. "I may not be in the city myself. There's going to be an operation."

"Then just tell me the day now.... I don't want to get killed from being in the wrong place at the wrong time."

Rosamund looked at him for a long moment and in such a way that he wondered if she saw through him and just didn't care.

"Equinox," she said finally.

"What?"

"The autumn equinox. Do you know what that is?"

He shook his head, lying.

"The day when the length of day and night are equal– in about ... one hundred thirty days. Do you understand?"

"I think so."

"So? ... Happy now?"

"Yes, ma'am," he smiled, and resumed kissing her wrinkled breasts.

"Master Baladur!" cried Ronnie a few days later as he strode across the traders' common toward the familiar old van and the familiar old man in the now-worn, broad-brimmed hat.

"Yes?" said the man, turning from his attentions to his mules, and Ronnie was taken aback. The trader, so robust and vital three and a half years before, was now shrunken and wizened and wore old-world wire-framed glasses over lightly glazed eyes. Ronnie, suddenly feeling himself disrespectfully big and strong before his one-time savior, spontaneously diminished himself in stature and voice.

"Master Baladur," he repeated more softly, and seeing he wasn't recognized, continued, "It's Ronnie ... son of Bern and Marta ... from Firstportage? It's been–"

"Ronnie?" came a woman's voice; and he looked up to the van door to see a very pregnant woman.

"That you, Rae?" he smiled. "You look ... different."

"Feel different, too," she smiled back, stroking her belly. "How've you–"

"Ronnie?" said the old man urgently, stepping close and putting a hand on his shoulder to peer at him. "Ronnie?"

"Yes, Baladur, it's me."

"Ronnie? But you're all grown up! You were just a boy! How ...?"

"I grew up, Baladur, thanks to you and your family. If not for you I might still be standing at the side of the road in the rain."

"Offering your axe for a ride," the old man chuckled, now pleased with himself to have remembered.

"That's right. I still have it, by the way, with the cover your daughter made. Keeping it sharp for a special job."

Baladur grinned, mostly toothlessly. "Ronnie, Ronnie where've you been?"

Ronnie raised the toolbox he carried—now mostly for camouflage—and showed the owl logo branded on its side.

Baladur frowned; his daughter saved him.

"Owlly's, right?" she said. "You remember, Dad, the furniture shop in Woodmaker Street?"

"Owlly's. Of course," he muttered, still frowning.

Ronnie's attention was drawn by the glimpse in his side vision of a large figure striding purposefully at him. He turned to confront or make explanation to the man just as he faltered in step and broke into a slight smile, his most ebullient expression.

"Hey, Chatter," said Ronnie, extending his hand for an old-fashioned grasp. The big man took it firmly but to Ronnie's amusement used it to hold himself at a distance, as if defending against a possible embrace. "It's good to see you."

"Yeah," said Rae's ironically nicknamed husband, then he awkwardly broke contact and stood with his hands on his hips.

"Honey," said Rae to him, "if you'll make a fire, we'll fix some tea and catch up. Can you stay awhile, Ronnie?"

"Actually," he said, looking around to all, "if you permit me, I have a better idea."

△ △ △

"Good," pronounced Chatterbox, the first one to speak.

The others were still at work on the rich lamb stew and raisin- filled bread and the wine that Ronnie had walked the hundred yards to Trader's Inn to order brought and served picnic-style. To his relief, Baladur, seated on feed sacks with his big hat now on the blanket beside him, was managing the specially cut-up lamb and vegetables and warm bread much better than he might have the alternative of roast haunch of venison that he'd planned to order, and Rae and Chatter were soaking up the last of the stew with the last of the bread. He wondered how long it had been since they'd had such a meal.

They'd set the earthenware bowls aside and continued to sip from their cups–infrequently in Rae's case–speaking of Ronnie's adoptive family and of his work and city life and the onerous necessity which they shared of dealing with Citadel bureaucracy and of the girlfriend from Firstportage–a subject quickly abandoned–when finally the subject of travels north came up.

"You know, Baladur," said Ronnie, "I'd almost given up looking for you here. Most of the others had either not seen you or didn't want to say, and the ones who did speak had seen you west, towards the new settlements. Don't you go north anymore?"

"North," said the old man, frowning again, perhaps trying to remember how much Ronnie was to be trusted. "Don't go that way so much anymore." he raised his chin toward the Black Tower looming not far away. "Too many of *them.*"

Ronnie studied him for a moment, thinking. "Do you ever consider settling in the city?" he asked. "I could help with that, you know. Lots of good places for you right in my own neighborhood–work, too, if you want it. You wouldn't have to go back out at all. Any of you."

The trader looked at him at length, and momentarily stirred. "You're a good boy, Ronnie ... son of Bern and Marta," he said, "but my place is on the road, with ... with ..." He faltered to a stop.

"Dad," said his daughter softly, glancing at her husband, "why don't you have a rest now, while we tidy up." Chatter was immediately at

Baladur's side to gently take the wine cup from his hand and pass it to his wife. Ronnie stood as the old man allowed himself to be helped to his feet and onto the wagon. Chatter followed him into the van and returned in a few minutes and sat again by his wife on the blanket. Ronnie broke the silence.

"Your mother, Rae?"

"Dead. Two winters past. Dad cries sometimes when he's reminded."

"I'm sorry."

"Not your fault. Seeing you just jogged a memory, that's all."

Ronnie had noticed something amiss when he first spotted the van. Paint was faded, tack was worn, a couple of wheel spokes were missing, no 'official business" pennant flew, and the animals were thin and weary- looking. Nor were Baladur, Rae, and Chatter in better condition. He was just glad he'd come to see them in his mended work clothes instead of the fancy gear he sometimes wore.

"Do you want to tell me what happened?"

Rae knew he meant not just how her mother had died, but how the family had so obviously fallen on hard times. She moved from leaning against a sack of feed to sitting on her heels with her belly cradled in her hands.

"It was right after the first snow," she began, "Mom suddenly developed a rash on her throat and a fever, and we couldn't make her better. Townspeople shunned us, but outside Cataract Village a man was friendly and offered to sell Dad an old book of remedies—potions made from things we could find in the woods or the market. Dad bought it, and right away the local police arrested the three of us for having it—said they'd suspected us of heresy for years—took us to jail and left Mom alone in the van. Dad traded all our goods to the police and the local priest for our freedom, but it was too late. Mom was dead by the time we got back to her. They'd even taken the blanket off her....

"We didn't have money for a proper service," she continued, "and others were afraid to help ... so we buried her at the side of the road....

Then ... a few days later ... we buried the baby boy ... I'd been carrying.... That's why Dad won't come in off the road—continuing the life is his way of being with Mom and little Salam—till the end."

Ronnie nodded and looked for a while at the ruined remnants of looping roadways nearby and across the former city park that now hosted traders having business at the nearby Depot, the gargantuan building where miners of the Forbidden Zones brought their discoveries. Vans and open wagons and hobbled draft animals dotted the landscape, but nobody seemed to be paying particular attention to the picnickers. He looked back to the others, then took to his knees to move and settle closer. "If you wouldn't mind," he said, "my people have a little ritual—a way of remembering and honoring the dead in private. It's just a holding of hands and a speaking of names, but—"

Rae extended her hands to Ronnie and to her husband, who extended his in turn to Ronnie. "We share the custom, Ronnie. Go ahead, speak the names."

Ronnie closed his eyes and said, "Mother Hemma, and little Salam; we remember."

"Mother Hemma, and little Salam; we remember," the others said, and were silent.

When they broke, and to cover for her husband while he wiped away sudden tears, Rae said, "That's a mountain custom, isn't it?"

"I think so," said Ronnie, sitting back, "but it's been adopted by certain others."

"Freethinkers, you mean."

"Yes," he said, studying her. They'd never been so direct before—never uttered the word. "Do you run across them in your travels?"

"You don't have a sense of them so much in the new settlements, and to the north everyone is still so cautious. It's hard to tell."

"How far north have you been since we last saw each other?"

She thought for a moment. "Maybe three days ride north of the falls. Couple years ago. Why?"

"Did you ever hear of people from Firstportage living up that way?"

"No. But nobody knows who's in the deep woods. Troops stay out, mostly, but they still guard the Message Stone.... You know about that?"

"Yeah.... Is there still no way to leave messages, then?"

"Not safely. Not that we hear of."

"Well ... "Ronnie murmured with a hint of hopelessness, looking away.

"They *be* there, Ronnie," said Chatter, uncharacteristically. "Somewhere *deep*, near *water* and *rough ground. Don't give up!"*

Ronnie looked at him and smiled. It was the longest speech he'd ever heard from the big man. "I won't, Chatter," he said. "Thanks."

The ice broken, and trust once again prevailing, Ronnie proceeded to collect as much further intelligence as he could from the accommodating but increasingly curious couple, regarding the stationing and movement of troops and materiel, the politics and the mood in the settlements, rumors on the road. Finally, aware that his own life-saving secret could be wasted if he was arrested or killed, he was ready to give back. He resumed sitting on his heels and glanced around before speaking.

"I was so glad to see you today," he began, a little nervously, "because lately I've been wondering ... If you knew there was going to be another big pogrom, and when, would you be able to make use of that information discretely? ... Would you ... *want* to?

There–he'd let the tiger out of the bag, with no way to get it back in.

Rae and Chatter both looked at Ronnie for a long time before sharing a silent communication between themselves, then Rae answered. "In theory, yes, and yes. There are certain traders, and certain people in certain towns, who might be able to make use of such information, but two things come to mind. First, the reliability of the information, and second, the difficulty of us of moving around effectively to spread it."

"Why the difficulty?"

"Because we're poor, as you can probably see; our loads nowadays consist mostly of consignment and credit items. We can't take time to hang around anywhere long enough to pass the word safely."

"Let's assume for a moment that you're *not* so poor. What do you mean about reliability?"

"Well, I mean, what's the source?"

Ronnie hesitated. How much to reveal? Despite his good intentions, it might take only one downstream failure of security to rebound through the traders and himself and turn good intentions and the entire Freethinker enterprise into a pile of ashes. He had to make the torture-interrogators' job as difficult as possible.

"This is where everyone will have to exercise their own judgement," he said carefully. "I can only say that *I* believe *my* source, you can only tell others that *you* believe *your* source, and others down the line will have to judge *their* sources–and whether it's worth taking a chance that the information is wrong."

"And what about us being broke?"

In response, Ronnie glanced around and then turned down the front waistband of his work pants to reveal three small slots from which he worked three heavy coins. He held them close in his palm to avoid flashing their telltale color to onlookers.

"My father gave these to me just before we got separated, more than three years ago. I carry them in case I suddenly have to become a fugitive, but now I'll be happy to see them used to help our people, if your father approves. There's only one condition. You have to go north *first*–and spread the word as far as you dare. You can send the message elsewhere by others, but I need the assurance that you'll be the ones to carry it toward the mountains.

Once again, Chatter made a few words count. "What's the message?" he asked.

"Let's make it simple and memorable," answered Ronnie. "Tell them, 'Beware the autumn equinox.'"

20 - Draft Dodging II

Duty had compelled Ronnie to pass the information gained from Lady Rosamund to his controllers; friendship and his own developing strategic vision had led him to share it with Baladur's family, so that Freethinkers in the villages and countryside and mountain hamlets might have a better chance of saving themselves. Now he would indulge an instinct and follow his own judgement again—with Lady Clare.

He'd sent notice of intent to make delivery and, when it wasn't refused, loaded Clare's desk in the shop's cart, rented a horse—Owlly's shop being unlicensed to own military-capable animals—and headed through the main gate and up the hill. At Clare's gatehouse a guard joined him on the wide seat and directed him not to the main entrance but to a more utilitarian one at the side of the house. Cornelius appeared as if by magic, leading a band of servants, and the heavy desk was duly taken down and carried through the house and up the main staircase, to its place in the freshly painted and tidied room where it would reside. Everyone stood back to admire it for a moment, then Cornelius and the guard moved in such a way as to let Ronnie know he was to leave.

"If it's all right, sir," he said quickly, "I've left some drawings in the desk drawer.... Some ideas for finishing up the room. Perhaps Lady Clare would like to see them? or if not, you could just discard them."

Cornelius looked at him for a moment, dismissed the servants, walked around to remove the large folio and plop it on the desktop, and began looking through the loose sheets with a disdainful air. Soon he was looking back at previous drawings and comparing one to another.

"Wait here," he ordered, gathering the sheets into the folder and walking out, leaving the guard watching him.

This guard was one of those who'd taken him on the worse carriage ride of his life, but at the moment he didn't seem hostile. He merely observed Ronnie as he stepped off the dimensions of the room and then stood at the window with his hands behind his back.

Suddenly a small missile of a squealing child came hurtling into the room to slam into Ronnie's leg.

"Ooff!" said Ronnie in mock distress.

From the hallway came theatrically heavy steps and a familiar voice. "Where is the little monster? I know he came this way. Is he in *here?*" Sounds of opening and closing of doors and knocking of walls. "No, he must be down *here*.... Stu, have you seen a little monster? About *this* big? With a big nose?"

"No, ma'am," said the guard stoically, "don't think he coulda slipped by me."

"Let's just have a look," said Clare, handing Ronnie's folio off to the guard and entering the room with elaborate stealth to search noisily in the closets as the child tittered behind Ronnie's leg. "Ronnie, have you seen any small monsters around here?"

"No, ma'am. I thought I did for a second, but he disappeared."

"He does that sometimes. Let me just check back *here*." And with that the shrieking and giggling fugitive was captured in mid-flight and swept up.

Once in arms, the boy calmed down and took an interest in the stranger over Clare's shoulder as she walked around the desk, studying it. Somewhere under three years old, in Ronnie's estimation, he had blue eyes and reddish-brown hair and a happy expression, and bore only the slightest resemblance to the brown-eyed, once-black-haired woman who held him.

"Monser," said the boy, pointing.

"Well," said Clare, "he could be a *secret* monster, like you, but we know him as Rondak. Ronnie, this is Zander."

"Hello, Zander."

"Ronnie can make beautiful things with his hands, so we call him 'master'. Can you say 'Master Rondak?'"

"Masseronak," said the boy, to Ronnie's delight. It was the first time anyone had honored his work by calling him 'master.'

"Stu," said Clare, "would you take this little monster back to his cage?"

"Ma'am?" said the guard with obvious discomfort.

"I'll be all right ... just ..." she made shooing gestures, but the man wouldn't comply.

"Ronnie, my bodyguard refuses to leave me alone with you. If you let him search you first, maybe he'll go."

"Of course," said Ronnie, and as Clare turned away with the child, the disgruntled man put the folio on the desk and patted him down, then took the boy and left. Ronnie had no doubt he'd soon be back on station within earshot of his mistress's cry for help, if he left at all.

He'd somehow known she wouldn't explain the reason for his terror ride, so he wasn't surprised when she went straight back to admiring his restoration job and asking how it was done. Then she opened the folio to a drawing of the desk in its setting with other additions to the room.

"Explain," she ordered, and Ronnie complied, describing his vision for the suite of rooms of what he took to be a private apartment under preparation.

"This is my idea," he said, "for an additional low piece behind the desk between the windows, and for banks of shelves and cabinets on either side between the windows and the corners of the room, all made to match the style of the desk. I've drawn alternative arrangements of cabinets and open shelves."

"And this?" she asked of a different sheet.

"Well, I take the room next door to be planned as a sitting room, and if that's so, I thought a similar wall arrangement might be good there, but with a different theme."

"Birds."

"Yes, ma'am. you've seen the only bird inlay I've done so far, and I thought, if you liked that one, I could do a whole series on the cabinet doors. You could choose the birds—maybe from the ones that visit here. In fact, I could draw them up here, if you like, and make them at the shop."

Watching Clare in profile, he was gratified to catch a slight smirk, guessing from it that somewhere in this house was a contraband copy of Audubon's book for him to use as reference.

"The shop's pretty busy, but if we don't all get drafted, we should be able to complete this much by end of summer. Then there's bedroom furniture and such to consider."

"Drafted?" she queried. "What do you mean?"

"Well, it's just pub-talk, but they say guys are being taken for the army. If my brothers have to go, or our associate Tom has to go, the work will have to be put off."

"Don't your foster parents have connections?"

"The usual ones, I guess, and I mentioned it to a friend of my own."

"One of your lady friends."

Ronnie didn't answer.

"You can't trust them, you know," said Clare, and when he still didn't respond, she turned her head and raised her chin: "Stu!"

The man was at the door in three seconds, glaring at Ronnie.

"Tell Cornelius to join us."

"Yes, ma'am," he said, looking disappointed. Cornelius took all of thirty seconds: "Ma'am?"

"Ronnie is going to be doing some work in these rooms, Corny. Give him daytime access when he needs it, a chair, whatever else he needs. Also, he's going to give you three names, besides his own. These four are required for local duties and are to be exempt from military service. See to it."

"Yes, ma'am."

"We need him here in the city," she said, inscrutably glancing to Ronnie as she turned for the door. "He's got important work to do."

21 - Lakes of Blood

The Priesthood of ZAH had ruled the known world for over a century, ever since the aged Chaplin and his sect moved its base from the village now known as Mount of ZAH, down the river Husson, to the already-fortified but plague-decimated city called All-Boney, supposedly after the skeletal appearance of some of its blasted-but-still-standing buildings. Once special squads had exterminated or driven away troublesome survivors and been themselves killed, and after all the bodies had been processed into ash at the mammoth plague-era crematorium, and after the priesthood had formalized its doctrine and disciplined its members, and after it had brought its third generation to adulthood, it became unstoppable. Bickering villages, towns, religions, and ideologies fell before it as it offered power to the ambitious through blood-connection to others of their kind, and to the Chaplin himself, to whom ZAH had entrusted the sword that was now enshrined in the inner sanctum of the Palace of Messengers. In the fertile environment of ignorance, fear, desperation, and general chaos, it had so far outcompeted every rival with which it had come into contact, identifying in each place a coterie of self-interested men and women who would jump at the chance to become founding members of a new ruling class, empowered to command others with the weapon of a religion whose only commandment was obedience to its own priesthood, and to exterminate those who would not be commanded. Over the last fifty years it had spread colonists and conquered settlements as far north as the great river that emptied the lakes, west to the great river that emptied the plains, south to Land's End, and east past the coastal ruins and the great ocean to coasts and seas and rivers of the old world. While doing so, according to Ronnie's State Ministry source, it had learned of the only other re-emerging center of power in the bomb-and-plague-ravaged world—that of the warlord Zheng, in faraway China. Lord Magnus's unarmed mission to this aborning empire was not intended to conquer, but to co-opt, selling the warlord and his inner circle on the virtues of the Zahist enterprise and melding the two powers, so that, together, they could get on with the business of subjugating the rest of the world without undue fuss. Once this was accomplished and Zahism entrenched worldwide, it might be impossible to kill even by cutting its heart out, but for now there was still a chance, for the heart of the all-devouring beast beat within the Citadel, vulnerable.

Midsummer, year 109

"Don't you *see*, Dad?" asked Ronnie, exasperated, as he and Owlly placed a table in the back yard for sanding. "In the whole world, we're the only ones who *can* do it."

"Of course I *see*, boy," replied Owlly, uncharacteristically defensive, "but we have to be *practical*. We can't just go running up the hill with hammers and pitchforks, twenty or thirty of us, and overthrow the most powerful force in the world. We must work out a grand strategy, raise funds, network with other circles in other towns, get the people riled up, figure out how to bring a larger force to bear.... Maybe in two years ..."

"Two months," said Ronnie calmly.

"What?"

"I think, if we don't act at the equinox, we may never have another chance."

"Ronnie," said Owlly patiently, "your information about that helps us to *survive* the pogrom, so we can *fight another day*, but there's no way we can be ready to mount an attack in two months. Even if we decided to use at-hand weapons, we still have so many steps ..."

"So we skip them."

"What are you talking about?"

"Look," said Ronnie, pacing in the yard to put his thoughts together, then stopping, "the Citadel City network is the largest in the world, and it has survived intact for generations. Right? That means–if we can assume we're not in fact infiltrated and *allowed* to survive by the priesthood–that we've perfected security. But circles and networks in other places are not accustomed to such complexity, and in a lot of cases we'd still have to identify the right people to talk to. So I say we don't try to engage them in the rebellion in advance. If we do that, any one of those village circles could not only expose and compromise themselves and get themselves killed but start a torture-chain that could bring us all down. No ... we act on our own ... suddenly ... with no visible preparation and with as many people as we can muster ... and with a plan to pull in allies the moment the attack starts."

He paused to look at Owlly at the other end of the unvarnished table.

The older man studied him for a long time. "You make a good point," he said finally, "about the integrity of the outlying circles. But how do you see a force as small as the one you're suggesting being able to defeat the army and the guard?"

"I've got an idea."

"It's called a *'coup d'état'* in the old books," said red-hooded Ronnie to the four men and two women seated on rocks and chunks of broken concrete at the old storm drain below Bil's Rigwash, the six distinguished, one from another, by the color or design of their own hoods. Beneath the million-starred sky he raised his voice only enough to be heard over the rustling river a few paces away, speaking in a monotone and in a lower register than natural, to further disguise himself. "It's a French term, but everybody used it. It means 'stroke of state,' and it refers to the sudden, violent overthrow of government by a small force. It usually involved stealthy pre-positioning of multiple small groups, and then a coordinated strike on the main elements of state power–in our case the Council of Messengers, the Guard, the Ministries of War and Error, and the Treasury–plus the armory. If we succeeded in capturing the Sword and the other Messengers, and in temporarily trapping the others in place, and we cut them all off from their money ... we'd be in a position to dictate terms."

"Dictate terms?" said a tall, lanky man scornfully. "Why not just *kill* them all?"

"Because we'd lose leverage over the army and Guard. If this pogrom is like the last one, the Guard will follow the army out to invest nearby settlements, to allow the army to extend its reach. But they'll both return when they hear of our attack, and if we're not holding hostages by then, there'll be no reason for the field generals to hesitate in forcing the gates and wiping us out."

Ronnie paused as this point was quietly debated by the others, all of whom, except for Owlly and the tall man, were strangers to him. The tall one, called "Candystripe" after his diagonally striped head cover, was certainly Bil Rigwasher himself, whom he'd seen and heard talking familiarly to Baladur when he'd arrived at the city on the trader's rig, more than three years past. Somehow it didn't surprise him that a friend of Baladur's was a Freethinker, and an important one.

The group was comprised of the military-planning delegates for several circles and small networks, and Ronnie was there because Owlly had convinced them that a certain young man, who had studied military history and tactics since he was a boy, had something worthwhile to contribute. Hooded and nameless like the others, he invited skepticism, but his ideas had enlivened debate, and now, as he listened to the woman in the star-emblazoned dark blue hood expanding on the necessity of exterminating Zahism in order to be free, he was moved to speak again.

"I disagree, ma'am. May I?"

She reluctantly gestured for him to speak.

"Part of my understanding of our creed is that all must be free to hold and practice their own beliefs, as long as they don't try to force those beliefs on others. If that's truly what we're about, then we can't be creating a future in which people are *prohibited* from believing in Zah. That wouldn't be possible anyway, for a lot of people who've grown up knowing nothing else. No, we don't have to *kill* Zahism or Zahists, we just have to take away their *political power*–without it the religion will die on its own after a generation or two."

"And how do we do that, young man?" she responded with poorly disguised disdain. Ronnie looked around at the dim shapes, their heads turned toward him, their eyes shadowed, some behind spectacle lenses. The woman's "young man" had unexpectedly threatened his confidence before these important people, reminding him that he was just a village-raised, book-learned dreamer, perhaps even a mortal danger to the enterprise on which they were all embarked–if he expressed his opinion, if it was acted upon, and if it resulted in failure.

"We capture the elites," he said, taking the plunge, "take away their lives–money, power, position–then offer some of it back in exchange for accepting and facilitating our new order."

Except for a derisive snort from the woman, there was no response. Finally a portly man in a checkered hood leaned forward and spoke: "Explain."

"It's in the history books. Lots of the great empires came into being not by exterminating their enemies but by capturing their leaders and showing them the chopping block, then letting them and their families live and keep some of what they had, as vassals. Sometimes conquest wasn't even violent. The greatest empire ever was that of Britain, a small island that controlled much of the world through such vassals, like in India, where individual princes chose to give up absolute power in order to keep their wealth and status. We could do that in miniature."

He stopped and looked around. "Shall I go on?" The portly man made a small gesture.

"So far, our intelligence indicates," Ronnie said, refraining from mentioning that much of it was his own contribution, "that on Equinox Day, the Messengers and other dignitaries will review departing troops from the stand in Chaplin Square. Unarmed army troops will first form up on the parade ground near their barracks, march by units to the armory, enter and be locked into the entry courtyard, pass one at a time through a heavy revolving door into the building, receive their weapons , pass through the other revolving door into the exit courtyard, be released by units under Citadel Guard supervision to march to the square for review, and then pass out the main gate into Citadel Square and on to their destinations. The reason for this protocol, we know, is to prevent armed army troops from outnumbering Guard troops inside the wall, which might invite trouble.

"Now, our spies have identified a flaw in this system.... In a separate walled space at the side of the armory are the loading dock doors and two worker entrances on opposite sides of them, one east for the armorers and guards and such and the other west for office workers. The east door is armored, but the one into the offices appears breachable. We're told that in the paymaster's office, at the end of the corridor, is a counter and another breachable door that was recently added so workers could come through to receive their pay. The building is lightly guarded when the army is away, externally by the Citadel Guard, so a small band should be able to rush the side gate, break these two office doors, and open the big loading doors from the inside for a larger party. Then we could arm ourselves with real weapons, gather more for the other parties, and join the fight up the hill."

He looked around again. "Do I understand all that right, so far?" The others rotated their heads to the portly man.

"Go on," he said.

"Okay," said Ronnie. "So that addresses one of the targets in my scenario. The Guard Tower, the Treasury, and the War and Error Ministries I'll skip for now because initially we wouldn't have to occupy these, just briefly trap everyone inside, maybe by blocking the exits or the interior stairs and threatening to fire the buildings. That leaves only the main target, the Messengers and the other elites, who, fortunately, are going to tie themselves up on a big red bow for us."

"At the breakfast," said the second woman, her excitement barely concealed by a caramel-colored hood printed with cavorting ponies.

"Yes, ma'am, at the breakfast conference. Since we can't do anything until the army is at least half a day's fast march away, and since we can't hope to round up everyone from their guarded homes and offices, we wait for them to come together on the morning after. By then, couriers and birds will have arrived with reports of overnight activity and they'll all meet for breakfast to discuss developments. Best of all, they're going to have breakfast in a hall served directly by the main kitchen, which is adjacent to the delivery docks. That's how our main force will get in."

The group could restrain itself no longer and erupted in urgently murmured debate, variously addressing each other as "Checkers" or "Stars" or "Ponies" and so on. Ronnie sat back, for the moment excluded by his elders. He was gratified to hear support and committed the objections to memory until he could digest and reply to them. Twice he heard mention of "the colonel," both times to see the portly man make an admonishing gesture to the speaker, and he wondered if this was the source of some of the new information Owlly had prepared him with, especially the details of the breakfast.

Was "the colonel" just a nickname, he wondered.

The portly man quieted down first and leaned back; the others took his cue.

"Okay," he said to Ronnie. "In your vision, what happens next? The armory is robbed, the ministries are blockaded, the elites are captured–presumably all at the same time–then what?"

"Well, it might be best to have the armory attack start a few minutes before the others, if what I hear about Citadel Guard numbers is accurate."

"What's your understanding?"

"That a large part of the Guard will exit the city after the army and occupy nearby villages and roads, until the army starts returning. If that's true, then the city will be undermanned and the armory attack might serve to draw some of the Guard troops and police away from the palace during the breakfast, making our task there easier."

"Say that's true," said the portly man, "and it all happens as you hope, then what? How does it lead to the bloodless triumph of freethought over Zahist tyranny?"

"It doesn't."

"It doesn't?"

"No, sir. It leads through lakes of blood and piles of severed heads to a place where people are free to believe as they choose. Where–"

"Lakes of blood? Piles of–"

"Sir," Ronnie interrupted with calm conviction, "we have to destroy the tyranny of the priesthood in a matter of hours, not by taking a few square feet here and there or scaring a few people, but by creating utter terror and defeat in the minds of its principals. Once the actions start, we must behave like a pack of rabid wolves, growling and yelling and screaming, killing anyone who fails to flee or yield, getting rebellious types in the town to follow up with attacks on priests and police and symbols of authority. At the palace, we have to slaughter kitchen workers who don't get out of the way fast enough, waiters, guards, then start on the lesser bureaucrats and aides. By the time we get to the Messengers and ministers, they have to *believe*, and to have *given up hope*. Then we give a little back to them."

Stunned silence prevailed for a while, as six scholarly Freethinkers, probably none of them warriors, processed what had just come out of the mouth of one they'd thought to be a very smart and well-spoken–but perhaps too-nice–boy.

"But ... the *innocent* ..." ventured a young-voiced man in silver mask.

"We'll grieve for them later," countered Ronnie. "Until our terms have been met, we can't reveal our humanity. In other words, we must make ourselves into the kinds of creatures the elites will recognize–and fear. Otherwise, we'll fail to establish control of the situation.

"What do you mean by 'terms'?" asked portly man.

"The way I see it, sir," said Ronnie, leaning forward again, "we must have a public ceremony–on the steps of the palace, right away, before the army can be brought back–where Lord Endo and the others disavow divine authority and Zah's sword is broken. The very next step has to be about money."

"How so?"

"In addition to the Messengers, who are usually heads of their respective clans, we'll be in control of the largest hoard of gold and other valuables on Earth, as far as we know. We'll be in position to impoverish or enrich at will. We'll use that power–and the Messengers' written orders–to stop the army outside the city. Among the clans and military and bureaucrats and the rich, we'll offer, to the first to cross over, the ranks and properties of the slow-to-decide, as the Romans and others did throughout history. To everyone who doesn't oppose us, we'll offer continued employment or a comfortable retirement–to the younger soldiers, maybe free transport to the frontier towns and a cash bonus. All that should co-opt the opposition until we've had time to work out the next steps. One thing is certain, though: apart from the Priesthood of ZAH and its allies, there's only one other group capable of running this world–that's us and our allies, whoever they turn out to be. We'll have to form a council to dictate government policy until the people are better prepared to handle things. Maybe a few years, or a generation." Ronnie stopped and looked around for opposition.

"Or two," said portly man, and all nodded.

In the secret history of Freethought, passed down orally since the Chaplin's time, there was no report of rebellion carefully planned and executed specifically to effect overthrow of the Priesthood of ZAH, only of outbursts and spontaneous uprisings in response to new outrages of oppression, or to discovery of cells. In normal times, discovery might lead to the death of dozens or even hundreds, sometimes comprising entire village circles or multi-village networks, but even then the first thought was not of fighting back, but of surviving, which, as the years accumulated, came to seem the sensible choice. The Freethinkers' inculcated penchant for pre-arranged flight into the wilderness at the first sign of exposure and of suicide at the prospect of capture and torture, and the plague-fearing government's practice of burning dead bodies without taking time to identify them, made it work, in a grotesque way, and thought of revolution faded into unreality. Now, suddenly, for seven men and women talking out the details of rebellion and its aftermath by a river beneath a canopy of stars, it was become real.

The rebellion was alive, and it lived in *them*.

22 - The Armory

Ronnie could feel the Earth relentlessly turning, moving through its orbit to the day of reckoning. The summer solstice—a time of ancient pagan rituals now noisily and mandatorily and inaccurately celebrated as the anniversary of the Chaplin's ascent of the Mount—had come and gone. The days were growing shorter, the nights longer.

Less than eighty days till the autumn equinox. Across Citadel City the inhabitants variously lived or died, embraced family life and friendship or shunned them, worked at occupations to which inclination or duty or force compelled them, brought goods to market or shopped there for them, rushed between fancy shops accumulating packages, attended parties at the palace or in elegant mansions or in not-so-elegant venues outside the wall, and in low voices and private places planned industrial-scale theft and murder in the name of the god ZAH—or plotted rebellion against all the name represented.

Ronnie's coup plan had been adopted and this gave him hope of participating in the all-important attack on the palace, but it was not to be. The mysterious "Colonel" would lead that team, it was said, and Ronnie had not been selected for it. Instead, he would be part of the force attacking the armory, under command of one already elected but not yet identified to him. In the meantime he had to divide his time and his life into even more compartments than it already was, sometimes in the same day being furniture maker, reference librarian, meeting planner, attack planner, martial-arts instructor, secret lover, and diplomat-spy, In the latter role he'd sought the paid assistance of

Scarface habitues Keera and Jane, whose presence on his two arms had gotten him into several of the new clubs more effectively than showing up alone or in a pack of fighting-age strangers could ever have done.

"Evening, citizen," he might begin to an owner or doorman as the girls smiled guilelessly and money changed hands as needed, "I'm Ronnie from Woodmaker Street. My friends and I were wondering if we'd be welcome here," to which the reply was usually something like, "Of course, Ronnie, let me find you a spot." It didn't hurt that the girls, Ronnie's age and already liberated by their status as mothers of priestblood children, were shameless and enthusiastic man-magnets, who soon had the local males trying to ingratiate themselves with their escort, instead of ejecting him. Soon he was laughing and trading shots of the newly legalized and heavily taxed distilled liquor and learning about the personalities and the dynamics of whatever subculture he found himself in: builders, taxi drivers and carters, market traders, household servants, livestock breeders and dealers, fishermen and women and other river folk, farmers, artisans, garment makers, office workers, caterers, florists, morticians, smiths and farriers, and all the others who made the city run, usually without raising their heads or their voices. Then there were the gangs, often the underemployed and posturing youth of certain occupations but sometimes geographically based and engaged in activities just short of what would bring the police down on them, like drug-dealing and "protection."

In each case Ronnie endeavored—even through an occasional alcohol haze—to catalog grievances and understand motivations and identify shot-callers and triggers, and to contemplate how disparate groups might suddenly, on the very day of rebellion, be brought into common cause against the forces of the priesthood.

Sometimes the responsibilities of day and night clashed.

"You stink," said little Zander late one morning, wriggling on Ronnie's knee as they both studied the cutting pattern Ronnie had been drawing on stiff brown paper laid atop the art deco desk, Audubon's Birds of America nearby, open to the picture of an owl.

"*You* stink," replied Ronnie distractedly, at a loss as to how to place the next line.

"You stink *more*."

Ronnie realized the boy wasn't speaking metaphorically and leaned back in the upholstered chair. Maybe he did stink. He was, after all, still a little hung over from the previous night's work. He laid his pencil down and moved to stand up. In the corridor, a female bodyguard, sensing movement, looked past the doorframe to see if he might be preparing to murder her young charge.

"Let's get some fresh air," said Ronnie, lifting the boy over his head onto his shoulders and heading for the terrace door. The guard entered the room and watched to make sure he stooped and didn't bash Zander's head on the way out, and then watched them through the glass.

Ronnie stepped to the rail and contemplated a scene he'd contrived to study several times on his visits to Lady Clare's house, usually leaving his work on the glass-topped terrace table and feigning the air of the artist awaiting inspiration while visualizing the battle to come.

The house sat on a knoll on the south side of the long hill, not far down from the palace, and afforded the best view anyone could hope to have of the targets. Its facade and second-floor terrace faced southeast, across the Tangle and toward the bridge, in an area where many one-time commercial structures had burned or been taken down for paving materials, leaving open ground around fewer structures. Clare had taken him to her end of the terrace and shown him that, if he looked around the corner, he could see the shattered Egg, the Palace, and the Guard Tower further up the hill; from the right end, one saw, first, brother Magnus's house over the side wall, where Clare was attending some ceremony at the school there, then the town dwindling west into farmland and beyond to rolling hills and vast forests. Spread out across the middle, from left to right, were the river docks built on grounded barges and identified by boat masts visible above roadside trees, the river pylons that once supported the mighty bridge feeding the looping Tangle, the slightly lopsided remaining bridge, the twin plazas within and without the wall at the main gate to the south, the pedestrian gate to Woodmaker Street, and the armory just inside the wall a little further west. The row of high-rise barracks housing the army was blocked from this side by the house itself, but the upper floors of the Black Tower, which contained the ministries of War and Error and the reputed torture chambers, loomed over the roof, seeming ready to fall upon it. Coal smoke from the steam plant that powered its elevators and ventilation fans cast a slight pall over the scene.

Clutching Ronnie's hair with one hand, Zander pointed with the other. "Sojures," he said. Ronnie followed the gesture and determined that he must be pointing at the sword practice going on, in Clare's absence from the house, in open ground between the carriage house and the front wall, featuring Kemal, Clare's horse guard captain, and a half dozen luckless trainees.

"That's right," he said distractedly, knowing one of Zander's teachers must have taught him the new word.

As he admired Kemal's technique with the wooden saber, he compared it to what he'd seen two days before, when he and Brod had bluffed their way to the belfry of one of the only Christian churches to remain standing in the city, a structure that owed its survival to its location—overlooking the army's training ground—and to its having become a brothel, the red lantern in the belfry at night driving recently virgin young soldiers to excel and win special passes to it. From that rare vantage, observing troops training near their high-rise barracks with *their* wooden swords, he'd been stricken by the apparent brutality with which—and *for* which—they were being driven to fight by hectoring instructors. Even as individuals fell into submission, others continued to hack and stab at them, and Ronnie concluded that the exercise was meant to extinguish any troublesome humanity the young conscripts might feel toward those whom their superiors had identified as heretics, which also explained why they were kept isolated from other citizens, even at leisure. The big church-brothel was just one of the establishments along Swan Street that served the young men exclusively–and the common soldiers were indeed all male, for their training made females unsafe among them.

Even at Warlaw, the soldiers-only head-banger joint that was the only such establishment within the Citadel itself, the patrons were all male and the women they consorted with all professionals–or almost so. Some masochistic Citadel adventuresses attended, and the doormen had been quite enthusiastic about having Keera and Jane, but on the one occasion the three had tried to get in, Ronnie–with his too-long hair and civilized manner–had been rebuffed. He'd barely been able to extract the nervous girls and get them back into a cab.

On the terrace, as Zander pulled his hair unconsciously in coordination with Kemal's attacks, Ronnie shifted his gaze to the armory, a flat-roofed, four-story, one-time warehouse with slit windows, set just inside the great wall and surrounded on three sides by a shorter, later wall that connected with the big one. It was a secure-looking structure, but he knew that intelligence from someone among the conscripted metalworkers employed there continued to support the plan his elders had approved, of rushing the loading-dock gate or going over the lower side wall to gain access to the office suite where the vulnerable door in the paymaster's office gave access to the rest of the building. The biggest question remaining was where, in the vicinity of the armory, to congregate more than two hundred fighters, in the hours before the morning attack–a question he understood had already been answered for the other teams and targets. It was a problem he and the others had been working on, with the leading idea so far being to infiltrate the fighters one at a time over the wall or through the gates with counterfeit passes and then to occupy a precinct audience house near the armory, securing or killing the priest and staff who lived there along with anyone who arrived early the next morning. But Ronnie saw so many ways for this to go wrong, and he tried to come up with a better solution.

In the secret library he'd studied precious pre-Cleansing maps of the city and drawn up a version with the wall and other major changes shown. Then with toolbox in hand he'd walked the streets nearest the armory and still not found a better gathering spot than the precinct house, or a safer way to get so many fighters into the Citadel. But he wasn't ready to give up; staring at the map, he'd wished he could see through its surface to what lay beneath.

He'd never stopped thinking about the walk-in storm drains, and how the surface watercourses that guided runoff to them were often rust-stained downstream from the iron-saturated great wall. With Owlly and Nel's permission, he'd taken his enthusiastic 17-year-old brother-in-bond Jak, and his dog Junior, on a rowboat-borne survey of drains, both pretending to fish or to ogle dock-side vessels as they rowed and coasted all the way from the drain below Bil's Rigwash to a reed-hidden old boat ramp north of the bridge, where they'd hauled the borrowed boat out and arranged with a carter passing on the river road to return it to its owner for the deposit. Most drains they'd seen, some underneath docks, had been smaller and sewage-emitting–surprising in an era when most Citadel waste was picked up after midnight by a mysterious tribe of cloaked and shuffling figures called the Dead after some ancient legend, fear of whom helped mothers get their children in at night. Others were too far north to give access to the right area or adjacent to busy or guarded places where ingress by a large group might have raised alarm. One came out of an embankment just feet south of the boat ramp and was secluded enough, but it appeared to drain an area south of the wall and rising to the western hills. With little hope he'd hoisted Jak up into the great pipe's mouth from the rock-strewn riverbank and been relieved to see the grin grow across his face as he inspected the old concrete. *Rust,* Jak had said, *lots of rust.* They'd rushed home to assemble a pack for the excursion: gloves and a hat to avoid scrapes and a change of clothes for later, a lantern with extra fuel, matches kept dry in the document tube that had once held Ronnie's fake travel pass, and a small broom from the kitchen to frighten or ward off rats. At sundown they'd returned with Owlly and Nel's fearful yet prideful blessing and Jak had begun his scouting of a subterranean world that post-Cleansing taboos had made unexplored for generations. Now, looking down from Lady Clare's terrace and aware that Jak hadn't returned home by morning, Ronnie tried to guess where in the jumble below he could be, and if he needed rescuing yet. For the next few hours he'd try to put his little brother out of mind and work on other problems.

"Bass," said Zander, pointing again.

"What?" Ronnie looked in the direction indicated, a few blocks northwest of the armory, but saw nothing noteworthy. Then, when the boy moved his pointing finger around, he realized he was following a swooping flock of small birds in the distance.

"Bass," he repeated, as the terrace door opened behind.

"*Bats*, he means ... don't you, monster?"

"Milady," said Ronnie in greeting, as the boy reached to be taken and Clare complained about how heavy he was. Below, the practicing bodyguards had already disappeared.

"Bats?" he inquired.

"Bass," said Zander.

Clare pointed with her chin. "Those are birds–swallows–but in the early evening they dart about for insects like bats. In warm weather the actual bats come out of there at twilight and the birds leave."

"Come out of *there*, ma'am? Don't they live in the hills? In caves and such?"

"Usually, but during the Cleansing they settled in an abandoned church."

He was confused. He hadn't seen any bats in the old church's rafters, nor did he know of any other church within the Citadel. "Do you mean the place on Swan?" he asked, and immediately regretted doing so when he saw the look of distaste on her face.

"Definitely not," she said. "No self-respecting bat would enter such an establishment; they like peace and quiet. She shifted her burden and pointed. "See it? ... Just there, near the western wall. Overgrown."

Ronnie stared at what had appeared to be a hillock until he could discern the shape of a gray, peak-roofed building covered by shrubs and small trees.

"A church, ma'am? ... "You mean ..."

"A Christian church, yes," she said with some impatience in her voice. "It would have been torn down like all the others, but the ancestors kept it as a bat roost—they eat mosquitos."

"It must be quite a sight inside."

"Probably, but no one may see it; it's forbidden."

"I see," said Ronnie, contemplating the distant ruin as another puzzle-piece slid into place.

A moment of companionable silence went by, then Clare's demeanor changed, as if she'd caught herself in indiscretion or untoward familiarity. Zander frowned at her uncertainly.

"*So,*" she said like the paying customer she was, "how goes the work?"

Ronnie took his hands from the rail and straightened up to face her, once again jarred by her rapid mood change and still wondering if she had some purpose in keeping him off balance, or if she suffered from what the medical reference in the secret library described as *schizophrenia.*

"Almost finished here, ma'am. Adjustments are done in the Deco room and I'm working on the last pattern for the bird room. I'll finish the doors at the shop and install them in about three weeks."

"Good. Cornelius will pay you when you come back." She looked ready to say more but came out only with "Goodbye," then headed for the open door, Zander looking back over her shoulder and Bear awaiting her within. When the door was closed behind her, Ronnie turned back for a last look at the city before returning to his drawing.

A half-mile away, from the rooftop of the 44-story Error Building, a gimlet eye studied him through a tripod-mounted telescope, recently recovered from a house near the Great Ruin.

"You say she only comes out on *this* terrace when *this* boy is in the house?" the black-robed woman inquired of the men standing at a respectful distance, watching her every move.

A balding man leaned forward, his pate glistening with perspiration. "That's been the pattern, ma'am. Three times in thirteen days. Twice she came when he was working at a table on the terrace, today he was there with the child when she came."

"'Working at a table,' you say. Writing?"

"More like drawing, ma'am. Perhaps he–"

"Who is he? Lover?"

"A workman of some kind, we think," said a less-frightened man. "Our file suggests she's celibate."

The woman straightened up to gaze over the telescope toward the house. Something about the boy ...

"Find out," she ordered. "Right now." The man bowed slightly.

"Yes, Lady Sula."

23 - The Church

And then I got to like a square room with a manhole cover up a ladder and another pipe from the side and I saw the rust again but not the straight one and I turned there and—" Jak paused the minimum time required to take a breath, then, "smaller rooms and pipes came from the left side but there was no rust and then one had rust but I went straight and the next one—" another breath, "had rust but the next one not so much so I went back and—" another breath, "went up bent over and the little pipes came from both sides and the light started—"

"Light?" mumbled Ronnie incredulously.

"and the pipe got smaller and I got tired and hit my head on a ladder and went up it and listened till there was no traffic or voices and pushed the cover up just a little and—" a final breath, "and *there it was!"*

"There *what* was?"

"The armory! Well, the boot shop a block up Armory Road. I went *past* the armory."

Standing at the foot of the basement stairs from which Jak was giving his exuberant report, Ronnie burst out laughing and gathered his little brother off the steps into a twirling bear hug as Junior, who'd come down behind him, caught the mood and barked excitedly.

"Good job, brother!" he cried, then stopped suddenly. "Are you all right?" He moved to brush Jak's hat off. "Your head?"

Jak held his hat on. "I'm fi—"

"Rat bites? Cuts?" the Dead?

"No, Ronnie. I'm fine. Really. The rats run away."

Ronnie calmed himself and grinned. "Do you realize how important this is?"

"I think so."

"As long as the followers of Zah are afraid of such places, they're left to us, and now we have a secret portal right into their back yard.... Let's tell Mom and Dad!"

"And Brod?"

"He's not a party yet–need to know–unless Mom and Dad say different. He and Suki can watch the showroom while we talk."

"Tell about the light, son," said Owlly at the kitchen table.

"In bright daylight, enough light comes in some places to find your way without the lantern. Other places, seems like they got covered up. But once you know the way ..."

"How many turns, then," asked his mother.

"Just two. Big pipe to medium to small."

"How small?"

Jak got up from the table and stooped over. "This small."

Discussion ensued about whether a large group of armed fighters could congregate in and deploy from such a small space, then Nel raised a not-so-obvious issue.

"They might be afraid, you know," she commented.

"Afraid?" said her husband.

"Not afraid to fight ... afraid to go in the pipe ... the old fears ..."

The others thought about that for a moment, about how everyone–Freethinker and Zahist alike–was taught in childhood to fear sources of disease, like dead bodies and rats and dark tunnels into the earth where death dwelled.

"Good point," said Ronnie finally. "Another reason we need time for the operation–a full day or more. Time to wait out rain showers, time to coax the fearful and move with cumbersome weapons, time to gather and prepare. The pipes give us a safer way in, but we still need a big space to deploy from. We have the precinct house, but I might have a better idea. If you approve, I need to check it out right now, before sundown."

Walking up Armory Road with toolboxes and backpacks slung and Citadel work badges displayed, Ronnie and Jak were dismayed to see, at each intersection, that the pre-Cleansing manhole covers had been covered by mortar-set bricks even where the curbside drains were still functional. But a block further west, as the road approached the wall, the bricks yielded to much-repaired original roadway and the covers were still exposed. When the boot shop appeared on an opposite corner the two contrived to wait for traffic to clop past and then to cross the intersection diagonally in order to look at the cover in the middle. It was made of steel and had narrow slots on either side by which it might be lifted.

"Looks secure," Jak said in passing.

"Looks heavy," said Ronnie, by way of complement.

"Little bit, yeah."

They turned and moved one street over and turned west again. A block ahead a wild growth of shrubs and trees pushing against a rusty wrought-iron fence marked the old church. When they got to the cross street on which it fronted, they saw that the roadway ceased to be marked by signs of carriage traffic and greenery grew from cracks. Ahead on the right, where the iron fence stopped, an original man-high masonry wall began and continued forty paces or so until it was crushed under the iron-seeping great wall, and on the left a row of worn-looking townhouses turned their backs on the church and the evil it represented by means of another wall. Straight ahead, in the middle of the disused street, partially obscured by a bush, was a steel manhole cover. Regarding it side by side, the two boys casually touched knuckles in silent celebration. Now they needed to find out if there was good reason to crawl this far past their target.

They idly loitered as if waiting to be picked up at the end of a day's work, contriving to study the church through the rusty fence and vegetation. It appeared to be constructed of stone or concrete and covered about four times the ground of the structure in which they lived on Woodmaker Street. Doors and windows were bricked up except for painted-over clerestory lights and a round stained-glass window high above the main entrance that was mostly covered by rotting grey boards. The small section left exposed revealed several holes, perhaps made by projectiles during the Cleansing.

"Maybe that's the bats' way out," said Jak, raising his chin.

"Yeah," said Ronnie, impatient now. "If we're not out of here in the next two hours, we're going to find out. Let's keep moving–over the back wall."

The boys stood facing each other at the wall, as if in conversation, Jak surveying the scene over Ronnie's shoulder. "Go," he said softly, and Ronnie set his toolbox on the top of the wall and scrambled over. He retrieved the box, took Jak's toolbox and the backpack in which Junior was patiently riding as he had since his puppyhood, and Jak followed.

They leaned against the inside of the wall among shrubs and listened for shouts of alarm or warning but heard nothing untoward. Looking around, they found themselves in a surreal jumble of tombstones, many toppled or set askew by the trees that had reached maturity among them over the last century.

"Better and better," said Ronnie as Jak nodded, both knowing how loth the enemy was to enter cemeteries.

Ronnie had half-expected to find a community of homeless or at least a fugitive from the law, but when he stood and scanned the acre of graveyard and the back of the church beyond a vine-choked low fence he discerned no such presence. He was surprised to see an intact stained-glass window to match the one in front, its survival perhaps due to its orientation facing the great wall, beyond which it could not be seen once its original boards had fallen away. He studied it but couldn't make out its design through the glare of the lowering sun.

Through the open low gate and up a flight of stairs the rear entrance was well-bricked like the front, but the small basement windows to either side near the ground looked less carefully done.

"You check that side," said Ronnie, pointing. "I'll look over here."

Jak lifted Junior out of the backpack into his arms, gently clamped his muzzle closed, looked him in the eyes and made a shushing noise to quiet him, then set him down and started inspecting the basement windows. Within minutes he'd found a particularly sloppy mortar job, gone to work with the prybar from his toolbox, and forced the intact but shrunken and warped window beyond. He peered inside, Ronnie and Junior at his shoulders, but could make out only irregular shapes about a large room. Reversing position, he lowered himself legs-first, and dropped–noisily.

"Shit!"

"What's wrong?" whispered Ronnie ungently as Junior whimpered beside him.

"I stepped ... Ohshit!ohshit!ohshit!it's a body! Help me out!"

Ronnie grabbed his little brother's hands, but instead of pulling him out he held him still. "Jak ... Jak ... *Look* at me!... You said a *body*. You mean a *dead* body?"

"Pull me! Pull ..." Looking into Ronnie's eyes, he calmed a little. "Yeah ... Well, a *skeleton* ... I stepped on the *skull*."

"Did it try to bite you?"

"What?"

"Bite you or pull you down to the underworld?"

"Well, not yet, I guess," said Jak, trying to smile through embarrassment.

"Then push it out of the way with your feet so I can come in."

A minute later the boys stood side by side in perfect stillness as their eyes adjusted and their ears strained at the slightest sound. The dark shapes resolved, and the two spontaneously grasped hands. Jak trembled slightly.

"How many do you think?" Ronnie said hoarsely.... "Jak! Concentrate! How many do you think?"

"Hundred, maybe," Jak said softly.

"Then half the space we need already, and this is just one room. Once we clear–"

"What?"

"Listen, we're gonna be bringing a bunch of strangers here. We don't know how they'll act if they see this. We're just gonna have to come back and clear it all away.... Understand?"

Jak stared at him in disbelief for a moment, then looked again over the insect-and-rat-cleaned-and-gnawed bones of adults and children still partly covered by moth-eaten scraps of clothing, many clutching each other in death, the means of death revealed by the bullet holes in skulls, the spent cartridges littering the floor under a thick layer of fine dust, the dropped drinking cups, and the large bowl and ladle on a table at the far end of the room. He stopped trembling and let go of Ronnie's hand. "Yes," he answered more steadily, "I understand."

"Good.... Okay, listen.... We have to get out of here for now. Why don't you go out and see what's over the wall on the other side–and if there's a manhole cover there too. Hand me the lantern down and I'll take a look upstairs and come right back. Okay?"

"Yeah."

Once Jak had been boosted out the window and had handed the lighted lantern back in, Ronnie made his way through the scattered remains of what he assumed to be Christians, among the most accursed of Zah, according to the priests. Whether their end had been by their own hands or the hands of some mob, he could not take time to consider. He found a stairway and ascended, the lantern's light bringing strange shadows to life, the air growing thick with a pungent odor, his every deliberate step raising a cloud of dust and leaving perhaps the first footprints in a century. At the top of the stairs, a broad dark corridor ran from the rear entrance around the stairwell and past open doors of what might have been offices, to a blank wall toward the front. At the corners of this wall a faint light glimmered through twin passages. Ronnie set the lantern on the floor and padded softly toward it. The wall divided the office area from the sanctuary of the church, and when Ronnie eased through the right-side passage and around one end of it he found himself on a broad dais, facing a sight out of a dream—or a nightmare.

Faint, colored light, coming from somewhere above, dimly illuminated the scene. Before him, a large space was divided into three sections, lower-ceilinged at the sides beyond twin rows of narrow columns and vaulted across the middle. Down the center aisle and overlaying the pews on both sides to an impossible height were stalagmites of pale guano, and above, brown and thick in their thousands, were their creators.

A soft shudder went through the sanctuary, and through Ronnie. He stood perfectly still until the creatures settled again and then began to look around. He had to know how sensitive to intrusion the bats were, how disturbed they might be by the smell of two hundred nervous fighters in the basement or the sound of their voices and movements penetrating walls and floors to hypersensitive ears, knowing that any change in the bats pattern of comings and goings, caused by these disturbances, might draw attention.

All the furniture and fittings on the dais and the wall behind had been smashed, he noted. When, with head down, he slowly moved down a short flight of steps and into the right-side gallery, he saw that the same had befallen statuary and inscriptions in alcoves there. Once he reached the closed front doors, he raised his eyes and found the source of light: the round window at the back that overlooked a loft where singers might have stood. It appeared once to have been painted over on the inside with grey paint, but now great sheets of it hung down, exposing enough of the image that he could guess it depicted Jesus Christ, speaking from a hilltop.

He admired the window's craftsmanship and beauty for a few seconds, then raised his eyes further to see that images had once also adorned the vaulted ceiling, and that there had been an attempt to obscure these as well. He cast his mind back to the day and saw loyal church members frantically concealing the images that had become so abhorrent to others, painting the window and lower parts of the ceiling with rollers on long poles. They'd been overtaken before they could set up to paint the higher part. A mob had attacked the church and driven its members to the basement; some of the attackers had gotten into the space between the roof and ceiling and kicked the smooth lath-and-stucco surface to hanging shreds, exposing many dark and dry surfaces from which bats could perch.

Or, the members could have perpetrated the destruction themselves, for reasons he couldn't even guess. When it came to the madness of the Cleansing, one explanation was as likely as another.

He moved on around through the other side-gallery and returned to the dais without alarming the bats and was soon out the basement window and helping Jak to replace the bricks and clear away the loose mortar from the ground.

"What was the other side like?" Ronnie asked as they worked.

"More space, like maybe a parking lot. A wall, but with gates–trash bins outside. Couldn't see any manhole covers without going over.... We could check it tomorrow.

Whadju see upstairs?... Ronnie?"

"I wanna go *now,* Jak, before the sun gets any lower."

"Whaddaya mean?"

"Look, I'm pretty big. If I can show that *I* can get through this far–right now–it'll give the others confidence."

"That's dangerous, Ronnie. The pipes could go a different direction from here."

"We're only one street over from the line you were on. If I get downhill and find I can't turn right, I'll come back and stay here tonight. Okay?"

"I dunno ..."

"How long did it take you to get back from where you stopped?"

"Maybe an hour?"

"So maybe I can do it in two from here. Just–"

"*You* may have to go on your *knees* at first. Hard to handle the lantern like that."

"That's why I'm not taking it," said Ronnie, taking his dagger from his pack and strapping it at his back, "and why I have to go *right now.*"

Jak stared at him. "That's–"

"Crazy? Maybe, but only half as crazy as *you* going where *nobody's* been in a century. He gathered the attentively listening Junior to his chest and stood up. "C'mon, no more talk, now. Hold your pack open."

Jak did as bid and soon had Junior once again riding on his back. Both boys found the valuable pre-Cleansing claw-hammers in their toolboxes and stuck them in their belts. In a moment they were over the wall and stooping behind the bush that nearly obscured the manhole cover. Quickly now they inserted their hammers' claws in the two slots from opposite sides and lifted slowly, conscious that a careless noise might be noted by someone on the other side of the streetside wall just a few feet away.

A coordinated jerk broke the seal that undisturbed time had created and the cover was moved just enough. Without delay Ronnie swung his feet onto the ladder bolted to the side, scanned the sky for any sign of rain, and spoke low to his anxious brother. "I'll leave my pack in the pipe here, so I'll know where to stop if I have to come back. You go home and get me a change of clothes–and boots–and wait for me at the river. Okay, Brother?"

"I'll be there, Ronnie, I promise."

"I know you will–you and that big rat of a dog."

He rubbed the side of Junior's face and squeezed Jak's shoulder. "Cover me up, now."

24 - The Dying Begins

Late-afternoon light ricocheted its way into the narrow tube as Ronnie made his was down the hill, stopping occasionally to listen to carriage traffic and voices above. Rats scurried before him and into side pipes descending from curbside drains and then returned after he'd passed.

At first he moved almost doubled over, taking short, rapid steps and trying not to scrape-anything. Soon his back and leg burned and he put his gloved hands down and moved like an ape, perspiring heavily and grunting with each forward lurch. By the time the light had gone, he was on his hands and knees and longing to reach the larger pipe.

He tried to imagine what the passage would be like for a big, 45-year-old grocer or seamstress who had not only never been underground but who wasn't accustomed to strenuous physical activity or to pain. He slowed to what he estimated to be a sustainable pace for such a person, then let his mind drift to other matters.

Lady Clare still mystified him. One moment she was familiar and almost affectionate, the next cold and dismissive, like today, when he'd been left to walk down the hill with his pack on his back and his wood-sided folio under his arm even though a trap that had just brought a servant with parcels stood ready in the drive and could easily have been ordered to take him to Woodmaker Gate, as it had been a couple of times before. Then, when the iron gate was closed behind, he'd started walking in a mild state of unease only to be offered a ride by a man whose company exacerbated that state.

"Workin'?" asked the youngish, compact, leather-jacketed man once Ronnie had taken the bench opposite and set his pack and folio down.

"Yes, sir. Thank you for the ride, sir."

The man waited with an encouraging half-smile for Ronnie to say more before going on.

"No 'sirs' for me, little brother" he said. "I'm just somebody's errand boy, workin' up the road from Clare's.... What's she got you doin'?"

A little tingle started at the back of Ronnie's head, but the man's open expression was compelling. "I do cabinet work—well, my family, that is."

"Oh yeah?... Big job?"

"Nah ... one more day, I think."

"So ... all done tomorrow?"

"Nah ... gotta build some stuff first ... 'bout three weeks, reckon.... Your boss got work?"

The man ignored the question. Instead, he rubbed his fingers together in a timeless gesture and said through his fixed smile, "Must be good money, though. You like money? ... lots of money?"

Oh, thought Ronnie. He glanced past the man out the window to see whether he'd make it to the bottom of the hill before being propositioned and put on an uncomprehending expression. "Da gives me enough fer beer. That's all I need."

"Yeah," said the man, eyes twinkling, "but did you ever want to be rich—have your own brewery, maybe?"

Rich? Was this strange man soliciting merely sex?... or something else entirely.

"Seem like a lot a bother, bein' rich," he replied. "All the stuff ta keep mind of ... people follerin' y'around like puppies. I like things quiet."

"You might be surprised. What if—"

"Here we are, sir," interrupted Ronnie, scooting up to look out the window. "Gotta go inna hardware store onna corner."

The man's smile disappeared for an instant and then reappeared as he rapped on the carriage roof and the driver pulled over. "I'll wait for you," he said, "take you home."

"Oh no, sir," said Ronnie, opening the door to climb down. "It's not far now. Thanks again."

"Well," said the half-smiling man, extending a fist through the window as Ronnie closed the door and began to turn away, "good luck."

Courtesy compelled Ronnie to step back and meet the proffered fist with his own, and in that instant, he saw the smiling man's eyes fleetingly leave his own to look at the brass Citadel work badge pinned to his shirt, and at the number stamped on it.

In the darkness, Ronnie briefly reached into a side-pipe he'd known would be there, pleased to have discovered that the reflected sound of his labored breathing changed where there was an opening. As he continued on, his mind turned to the intelligence coming to the military council through its members, now often imparted to him by Owlly even when it broke protocol to do so. Though no one person knew the full details of the sources reporting to each cell, it was obvious that some such assets were employed within the Citadel, perhaps as servants, cooks, day-laborers, waiters, craftspeople and the like. The things they reported were often seemingly innocuous in themselves, but as the day approached, they began to assemble themselves into a great, if still-shadowed, beast.

Underlying the changing mood of the city was the rumor, aborning in the markets and pubs and other gathering places, that Zahdom was under threat from some new enemy–a fearsome enemy being hidden from the populace even as it approached the horizon. How else to explain, the reasoning went, the increasing conscription and the moving of troops and supplies in and out of the city, the feverish training with wooden swords and shields on the training field and the equally feverish banging together of metal ones at the armory, the increasing tension in the faces and manner of those most likely to have their fingers on the pulse of the Citadel. But Ronnie saw something even more ominous: Citadel City-born conscripts mostly being sent to distant towns, and soldiers from those same towns replacing them in the Citadel. After hearing secondhand the reports of spies who'd talked to soldiers and after getting drunk with a couple of those who'd ventured beyond the wall to Scarface, he'd come to the chilling conclusion that soldiers were being systematically removed from among their own people and sent among strangers to dull their sense of empathy for those they'd soon be called upon to attack. To Ronnie it portended callousness, cruelty, extermination.

"Yes," he murmured in satisfaction at reaching an intersection he'd heard before feeling. In the square space joining small pipe to medium, he sat back to check his aching knees. His heavy work pants were holed, his skin broken and bleeding, but everything was still working. Again he took a moment to consider how the middle-aged grocer or seamstress would feel after such a passage.

He pulled himself up by a ladder that surely led to a sealed manhole cover, then released it and started down the capacious thoroughfare to his right, able to stay afoot bent over for the two minutes it took to reach the next intersection. He stopped to take his bearings—being careful not to lose them by turning carelessly—and concluded he was within yards of the armory, and that the smaller pipe to the right was the one Jak had taken an additional block west. He'd now crossed his little brother's path and was in the home stretch.

He was elated, not just to have established, in one day, a route of ingress to the Citadel and a vital mustering place for the armory attack force, but at the general progress toward the overthrow of the priesthood. From what Owlly had told him and Brod and Nel in secret, several hundred men and women were at that moment quietly preparing and training with their chosen weapons within their own families and cells, anticipating the day when they would come together with others of their kind, on a few hours' notice, to receive their assignments in a life-or-death struggle that could change the course of history. Of the major elements of the coup plan, only the nature of the attack on the Palace of Messengers remained in question. A gathering place had been established for the assault team but there was disagreement about whether spies should infiltrate the venue of the breakfast to appraise the situation and give a last-minute execution signal, or if that posed so great a risk of exposure that it was safer to attack without such intelligence. Owlly had said that Checkers—the portly man with the mask of black and white squares—and Candystripe, whose mask featured diagonal streaks of color and whom Ronnie knew to be Bil Rigwasher, favored the former course, but that others—allies and admirers of the mysterious "Colonel"—favored the latter. A decision was ...

Ronnie froze in his tracks, his musings suddenly replaced by the conviction that someone—or something—was in the pipe with him. Whatever it was had stopped when he did, listening. Then there it was again! A light step, the faint scrape of nails on concrete. Too big for a rat. A barefoot child? A raccoon? A bear or wolf? A rabid raccoon might only kill him a few painful weeks from now; a threatened or hungry bear or wolf might kill him right now. He drew his knife and prepared to fight.

An indecipherable sound came from just a few feet in front of him in the blackness—a waving or writhing or swishing. Then, just as he was conjuring an image of what kind of awful creature could create such a sound—a familiar whimper.

"Junior?" said Ronnie softly, putting the knife away. "That you, boy?" and the nervously wagging dog was upon him, licking his face while simultaneously wetting his lap when he sat down crossways in the pipe.

"*You* are a *good boy!"* he said with a face rub. "*Yes,* you *are! You* are the *bravest dog in* the *world!"* And so on until the courageous animal's fear subsided.

Ronnie had always marveled at Junior's ability to find any of the family members, anywhere they'd walked in the city, with the simple command to do so, but this time it was hard to figure. Only Jak's scent was in this part of the pipe, so if Jak had been the one to lift him into the pipe, what command had he given? Find Jak? Ronnie didn't want to confuse him with the same command, which might lead him uphill, so he chose a safer one.

Holding the dog's face close to his own, he murmured, "Junior–find Dad," and set him on his downhill side with his legs already in motion.

The dog raced ahead and Ronnie abandoned caution to follow. Soon he found himself in another square space with a ladder. Junior's feet still sounded somewhere, and he was pretty sure this was the turning he'd made, but ...

"Junior?" he called into the emptiness to his left and received a high-pitched bark in reply. Now he entered the final pipe and strode with just his head lowered. After a few minutes a curious sound stopped him and he strained to identify it. The river.

"Jak?" he called once, then again louder.

"Ronnie?" came the distant reply, but not from his brother. Elation turned to foreboding at the tenor of the voice.

"I'm coming, Dad," he shouted, and quickened his pace. Ahead, a faint light appeared and Junior came back to lead him toward it. As he approached, Owlly stood with the small lantern in one hand and welcomed him with an embrace.

"You all right, son?"

"Fine, Dad. What's wrong? Where's Jak?"

"Spreading the word."

"What word?"

"That the dying has begun.

25 - Checkers

"Don't get too close," Nel admonished at first light as Ronnie slipped his toolbox strap over his head. "They'll be watching the spectators."

"I'll be careful."

"And if you get compromised and can't get away," said Owlly, "don't hesitate." *To slit your own throat,* he meant. "Once they lay hands on you and get you in the wagon, it'll be too late.... Understand, son?"

"I know what to do, Dad," Ronnie assured him, a bit offended. To make his point he drew his newly sharpened dagger and made a gesture with it before returning it to his back. Nel burst into tears. Ronnie moved to embrace her as Owlly stood by stoically.

"Don't worry, Mom," he said, patting her back. "I'll be back before lunchtime."

Striding through Woodmaker Gate with the usual wave, he glanced to see if the guards paid any special attention and was relieved when they did not. In the square beyond, he boarded a three-team omnibus and sat with his toolbox on his lap as it made its stop-and-go way around the lower environs of the inner city. The bus soon buzzed with the news.

"What's going on?" he asked a woman sitting next to him with a big bundle in her lap.

"They say a man went crazy and killed a buncha' people last night—with a axe or sumpin."

"Really? Whereabouts?"

"Up past the water gate, summers."

Ronnie craned like other passengers after the bus passed a plain gate through which a constant procession of mule-drawn tankers carried river water to private customers and hilltop reservoirs overnight and continued toward an area of ancient houses and later commercial structures, some of both repurposed into stables and carriage houses. When the volume of voices rose suddenly, he stood with others to peer at police redirecting traffic and barricades in the street two blocks beyond.

"Everybody sit down, please," shouted the attendant. "We're movin' over one street for a few blocks. Sit down, please. Nothin' ta see."

After the bus turned west, with every passenger straining for a look out the right side, Ronnie rang the bell and dismounted at the next corner. He walked back and looked up the street to the crowd gathered at the barricade and at the narrow, three-story brick building on the right side, a block away. The scene was brightly lit in the morning sun and, as he watched, a man appeared at the building's belly-high roof parapet to regard the police and spectators below and then disappear. Even at the distance Ronnie recognized the man's portly shape and posture: Checkers.

He lowered his sight and found the excuse for being in the area that had to be his first stop: a decorator's shop that showed some of Owlly's furniture in its displays, set on the left side of the street and just half a block from the surrounded building. The shop's double doors stood open but most of the staff seemed to be out in the street with other gawkers. Ronnie strolled down and sidled through the loose crowd, up beside an elegant-looking middle-aged man.

"Master Julyen?"

The man turned and would have looked down his nose at Ronnie if Ronnie hadn't in fact been a little taller than he.

"Ronnie!" he exclaimed, throwing an arm across shoulders and hugging sideways, hip to hip. "What brings you, handsome boy?"

"Just came to see how the new-style chairs were selling.... What's going on here?"

Julyen became serious and motioned down and across the street with his clean-shaven chin. "Freethinkers, they're saying, but you know ..."

"Locals?"

"It's Balz the Barber—has that hair salon—men on one floor, women another, apprentices—lives above with his family."

"You know him?"

"Just in passing. We're on a shop-owners' committee together, but he's pretty reserved ... never gave any sign."

"The priests say heretics are crafty, devious—say it's in their blood."

"So they say," said Julyen in an unguardedly sarcastic tone, then an instinct of self-preservation surfaced. "Well, they know best, I'm sure."

Ronnie studied the crowd. A lot of people were sitting down on the pavement; some wandered off as others arrived.

"What's the holdup?" he asked. "What's everybody waiting for?"

"The finale, of course."

"What's that?"

"The last act, like in a play on stage, where all the main players come out and everything is revealed and the story is complete. Have you ever seen such a thing?"

"You mean like at the precinct house?"

Julyen glanced at him pityingly and didn't answer. "Yesterday, near sundown, a bunch of Error Police showed up," he said instead. "Scared the whole neighborhood. They say when they went for Balz he took fright and fled upstairs, taking a couple of hostages—priests. That's why they don't attack. The first time he came to the roof he had a big cleaver—like for cutting meat? —told the police to stay back or he'd kill the priests?"

"Why don't they just shoot 'im?"

"Word is the whole family are heretics and spies, and they're all upstairs with the hostages—the wife, two sons, two daughters. He's not alone. An arrow or two might only make him angry. Heretics don't feel pain like normal people, they say."

Wrong again, thought Ronnie, just as "they" were wrong about the number of family members on the third floor. It had been Checker's fourteen-year-old son Tofer who'd brought word last night, knocking softly but persistently on the back door until Junior barked once and led Owlly through the kitchen to open it. Owlly had been about to send Jak back out to wait for Ronnie to emerge from the drain, but the boy's news, delivered with stoical courage despite its message of failure and death, caused him instead to send Jak to warn others in *their* circle. Checker's emotionless boy would not accept refuge or help to escape the city until he'd taken his father's message to all members of *his* circle, and to the council members whom he served as courier and knew by sight; he left to complete his rounds with nothing more than a flask of water, a little food, a handful of silver coins, and the knowledge that he had a place, if he chose to return. Ronnie knew this new brother-in-bond could now be anywhere, except in his own home.

"Is that him?" asked Ronnie, pointing to Checkers as he came into view again and appeared to be checking all sides of his building.

"Yes," said Julyen, his sad tone revealing more than "in passing" acquaintance.

When Checkers again stopped at the street-side parapet to scan the people below, Ronnie felt an inexplicable tug.

"It looks like he's looking for someone, doesn't it." mused Julyen beside him. "I wonder who."

Me, Ronnie realized, *or someone like me*. Someone of his secret world whose appearance on the scene would signify that his son and his message had gotten through, someone to bear witness to the others of what must now happen.

"Let's get closer," he said, taking Julyen's hand and coaxing him into motion, but Julyen could take only two hesitant steps before freezing up.

"Best not," he said. "The police ..."

Ronnie half-turned to assure him, saw how pale he'd suddenly become. Despite his earlier carefree manner, the decorator was afraid.

"I wanna see," said Ronnie like an impatient child, breaking the connection. "Talk to you later, okay?"

"Please be careful, Ronnie. Don't attract attention."

"I know. I won't."

He moved with excruciatingly slow haste, determined to get to where Checkers might see him before he again left the roof, willing him to scan back in his direction one more time. As he passed a narrow alley and slipped through the thickening crowd, he took from his pocket a scarf that Nel had given him before he left the house and tied it around his neck. It was made from the same scarlet cloth as the mask Checkers had seen him wearing that night beside the river.

He pressed forward until he was only a few bodies away from the police cordon strung between the police vehicles standing across the street from the ground floor barber shop and the structures adjacent to it on either side. The vehicles were of course black with black horses—suggesting the abyss, doom—and carried black "Z"-symbols on the armored doors in a flat paint that was only distinguishable at certain angles. Within the cordon, bracketed by the two or three hundred spectators without it, were several mostly black-leather-clad Error police and about thirty uniformed paramilitary troops, armed with swords and short lances and a few axes, accompanied by several archers with bows strung but slung on shoulders.

The Error men had been milling about and chatting, but when Checkers came to the parapet they directed their attention to him. Or rather most of them did. A few watched the crowd, especially that part of it the barber was looking at.

With admirable calm Checkers scanned the spectators, dwelling on some faces and then moving on. Ronnie knew he might be disguising his interest in certain people by wasting time on others, and perhaps trying as well to imagine a bare-faced man or woman before him as someone he'd only seen masked. He wasn't distracted from his search when a senior officer climbed to the roof of a carriage and resumed rotely assuring him that they just wanted to have a talk at the ministry, that his family would not be molested, and that the two priests should be released unharmed as a goodwill gesture. Some of the crowd seemed to think it sheer arrogance to ignore this reasonable request.

"HERETIC!" someone shouted at his intractableness, and soon the deadly accusation was being chanted up and down the street. Spectators seated on the pavement began to stand and join in.

"HERETIC!" shouted Ronnie over and over as the questing eyes neared him, but when finally they fell and dwelled on him, he went silent and raised his composed visage. The snarling faces and rising din faded as the two regarded each other. Ronnie put two fingers through the scarf knotted at his neck and tugged it up an inch, as if he would pull it over his face. Checkers gave the tiniest nod, even as his eyes moved on and Ronnie resumed chanting.

Finally, with a look, Checkers acknowledged the plain-clothed officer for the first time and that man raised his hands for silence. The chanting dwindled away.

"So?" said the officer, looking up. "What's it going to be, Balz?"

"What about my wife and children?" asked the barber.

"What about them?"

"You won't hurt them?"

"Of course not. Why should we hurt them?"

"They say you torture whole families. Kill them."

"That's a heretic lie!" declared the Error man as the crowd murmured. He glanced at the captain of archers who in turn signaled his men on a nearby rooftop to unsling their bows; this troublemaker would not be allowed to confuse the people, hostages or not.

Checkers raised a hand in surrender. "All right, all right," he said. "I'll just make sure they're safe, then I'll join you."

"Sure," said the Error man with a barely disguised smirk that was imitated by some of his colleagues on the ground. "Go ahead. We'll be right here."

Checkers disappeared from the parapet. Error men at the shop's open front doors began to look inside expectantly.

In the crowd a certain unease prevailed now, engendered by the barber's remark about murdered families. Five minutes went by, ten. Suddenly there was movement on the roof again and all eyes went there. The barber was doing something below the parapet wall. Then he stood, and the crowd erupted in a cacophony of gasps, shouts and screams.

He was covered in blood. Not just specks or splashes of it but great smears, as if he'd anointed himself with handfuls of the blood of the beloved family he'd just saved from the torture-inquisitors, with one stroke each to the back of the neck with the cleaver. To make his message clear, he raised the red-stained instrument to more outbursts and looked momentarily at Ronnie, who with sudden tears in his eyes nodded and stuck fist to heart in sympathy and salute. Then Checkers tossed the cleaver aside and with exquisite casualness lifted one knee onto the parapet and rolled over it as if he were rolling into bed. The rope he'd secured around his neck let him fall halfway to the sidewalk before jerking him upright with a snap loud enough to be heard over the cries of astonishment, and he hung with twitching feet and elongated neck and open eyes.

With everyone else, the Error commander on top of the carriage stared for a moment in disbelief, then surged into action. "GO-GO-GO!" he bellowed to the men who'd scattered away from the toppling body and a dozen or more of them rushed inside and up the stairs. Unable to look at Checker's corpse anymore, Ronnie concentrated for several minutes on the doorway and thus saw, in the shop's shadowed interior, the two hostage priests in their black robes being led down the stairs unbound and apparently unharmed. The Error commander saw them too and quickly moved through the doorway to quietly stop his men and have the priests taken back up the stairs, to the vocal displeasure of the older one. A minute later, the sound of brief struggle and muffled cry barely rose above the murmuring of the crowd, and then died away. The Error men somberly descended the stairs and came out shaking their heads to report to their leader under the crowd's eyes. Soon they dispersed to the barricades to tell the people to return to their homes and businesses and incidentally to lay foundation for the rumors to come.

"Whaddyu find, officer?" asked one breathless spectator near Ronnie.

"Are the priests okay?" another.

"Whattabout the family?" another. "Is it true that ..."

The craggy-faced, seen-it-all plainclothed officer looked for a moment as if he would break down, until an old woman put her hand on his shoulder and quietly asked what he'd seen.

"Horrible things," he said, head down. "Priests hacked to pieces, family members ..."

Ronnie started to back away through the crowd as the lies rolled.

"... sexual ... disgusting ... pieces of missing children ... devil worship ... cannibalism ... books ..."

He surreptitiously drew his dagger and held it against his forearm as a precaution as he turned with his toolbox to make his way into the clear and was just about to return it to its sheath when the glimpse of a figure in his side-vision stayed his hand.

"Hey, boy!" said the leather-jacketed man as he approached, the fake smile coming only fleetingly this time and never in sync with the eyes. "I thought that was you! Whatchu doin' here?"

"Hey," said Ronnie, his mind working furiously.

"I asked what you're doing here."

"Whatchu mean?"

"What-are-you-doing-here? You a friend of the barber?"

"Who?"

"Come with me," the man ordered, taking Ronnie by the upper arm and steering him into the dead-end alley and behind a trash cart even as Ronnie concealed the dagger in the folds of his full shirt sleeve. A uniformed guard who'd been on the smiley man's heels took up station nearer the head of the alley, alternatively scanning the street and behind himself, hand on sword hilt.

"Don't play with me, boy," said smiley-man from a few inches away, his hands wrapped in Ronnie's shirt front. "I saw what you did–your little gesture. You're Freethinker, aren't you–you and–"

He spasmed into speechless rigidity as the blade was forcefully pushed into his heart from under his arm. Ronnie glanced to see the guard watching the street, wrenched the blade around inside a bit and pulled it out. The man stood motionless, eyes down, blinking, not prepared to accept the reality of the situation. Before he could collapse, Ronnie stooped and set the toolbox down and slipped toward the guard, who'd become distracted as the crowd responded to some development down the street. He was a tall and robust young man, whose armored torso and head left little room for a strike to the heart or throat. As he started to turn back to the alley, desperate instinct guided Ronnie's hands.

"Oh, shit!" exclaimed the guard just as Ronnie seized him by the collar of his backplate with his left hand and, with his right, drove the long thin blade into his anus to savage internal organs and genitals that were protected from frontal assault but left vulnerable in back so he could sit. The guard's entire body jerked away from the searing pain and he fell hard on his back. Ronnie went in to find his throat, but the guard had drawn his sword even as he fell and slashed wildly with it behind his head.

Ronnie jumped back, the flashing blade tearing his sleeve. It suddenly came to him that he couldn't allow himself even to be injured or let anything else happen to draw attention. He could neither die wearing a work badge and carrying a toolbox that would lead back to Owlly's, nor fail to silence this witness. He had to win.

Holding Ronnie at bay, the guard scrambled to his feet and turned his head to shout over his shoulder.

"*Fight me*, you fuckin' coward!" challenged Ronnie, striking the sword with his knife and jumping back as it was thrust at him and returning to parry again as the guard tried again to collect himself to shout.

"C'mon, recruit! You've got a fuckin' *sword!* I've only got this little *knife!* Did they train you with the *girls?* C'mon, just stick me *once*, so I can tell my friends I was in a *fight!* C'mon ..."

Suddenly the guard seemed to get a message from his hemorrhaging guts and put his hand to his balls as if that might stanch the adrenaline-driven pulses of blood soaking his loose trousers and boots. He looked up at Ronnie in wonder, knowing he was mortally wounded and that no amount of help could save him now.

Ronnie grinned. The guard's face contorted in helpless rage and he charged, without finesse but with great swipes of his sword that threatened to turn him around, his strength and coordination failing.

Ronnie lunged repeatedly, only to fall back farther and farther into the alley, past the crumpled body of smiley-man and shielded from view by the trash cart. Finally the guard just stopped and looked down at himself. His sword tip came to rest on the ground.

"I'm fucked," he murmured.

"Yes," said Ronnie, with a little kindness now. "Why don't you sit down."

"Yeah ... "The guard slowly slumped to his knees, breaking his descent with the sword.

Ronnie couldn't wait for him to bleed out. Without rancor, he stepped behind to draw his head back and slit his throat, then, before he'd even fallen over and stopped gurgling, he moved to wipe the knife on smiley-man's pants and put it away, retrieve his toolbox, and head for the street.

Most of the crowd had lingered for the theatrical bringing out of the remains, but in the other direction, Julyen and his people had retreated inside. Glancing into his shop as he went by, Ronnie saw the normally ebullient decorator sitting bent over in a chair with his hands covering his face. He passed on.

Lady Sula, her back-yard telescope still trained on the scene at the hairdresser's, missed Ronnie's part, but she was well pleased with the denouement.

"Perfect," she said to herself as most of the police vehicles and troops began to disperse, leaving a token force to guard the building and the barber's still-dangling body. She reached to turn knobs to center and enlarge the dead man's face, its open eyes on her.

"Perfect," she repeated.

After a moment she stepped back from the instrument and gestured for a man standing at a respectful distance among her retainers and guards to take a look.

"Now don't fail me," she said evenly when he'd done so and turned back to her, her eyes unblinking.

"Never, milady," said the colonel.

26 - The Bakery

On arriving home, Ronnie had made his report of the Balz family's sacrifice to his own staring and horror-stricken family, but he hadn't told them or anyone else about smiley-man and the Error Ministry guard, and neither had the Ministry.

Their reason was obvious—they didn't want the public to know they could be bested—*his* was more complex. He knew that this greatest chance in the history of Zahdom could be lost from trepidation, and that trepidation could take root and flourish from the smallest seed, so he decided not to plant it. Instead, *he* would be the one to judge the danger he represented to the Circle and the rebellion. *He* would be the one to balance that danger against the service he could provide. Only thus could he be sure of being in the fight to avenge Checkers and the other hundreds of thousands who'd been murdered since the Chaplin came down from the Mount of ZAH.

The dying has begun, Owlly had said, but he'd been wrong. There'd been no apparent contagion. The Balz family's friends, neighbors, and customers hadn't even been taken to the Tower for the expected bowel-loosening "mild" interrogation, much less the harsher sort featuring beating, suffocation, strangulation, eye-gouging, testicle-and-nipple crushing, vivisection, and, inevitably, rape, the last sometimes performed by Minister Grotius himself, though few men and boys had survived to tell that sordid tale.

Young Tofer returned two days after carrying his father's warning to the others and took refuge in the secret library. He could have gone to ground elsewhere, but he seemed to be carrying out some sort of unspoken mandate, or to have a special affinity for Ronnie, who recognized early on that he was a peculiar kid and treated him accordingly.

Tofer didn't speak unless necessary, and he didn't often make eye contact or express emotions overtly—at least not in the ways of ordinary people. Nor did he appear to feel pain or discomfort. When he gave his soft but persistent knock on the back door after completing his rounds, he was haggard and bruised but seemed oblivious to his own condition. When straight alcohol was applied to his scrapes and scratches, he flinched from the physical contact, but did not wince or cry out. What he did do—with great dedication—was arrange things.

Given the freedom of the library and a supply of lamp oil, he first rearranged the books by color, then by size, then by size within color, then by color within size. At first, they'd been afraid he'd use the solitude to kill himself in latent grief; now they were more afraid he'd run out of possible book arrangements.

The boy's return had brought great relief because, after the death of Checkers, who'd been de facto head of the military committee, it became apparent that neither Owlly, nor possibly any other member of the committee, had the ability to get members together without great risk of exposure. Even though Ronnie thought he recognized Bil Rigwasher in the lanky tall man, and Owlly suspected the identity of one of the women, they couldn't be sure. Membership was by anonymous invitation, and the real identities and locations of all the members had been known only to Checkers—and to the 14-year-old boy who attracted sympathy or scorn but never suspicion, the son Checkers had saved in order to save the rebellion. Now he was the only sure link between its most vital elements.

"Tofer?" began Ronnie four nights after Checkers's death, and after a Circle meeting had dispersed from the library. "Did you hear what we talked about tonight?"

The boy looked up from the comic book he'd been reading in the far corner and fastened his eyes on a point somewhere to Ronnie's right. Ronnie also looked-away.

"Some," he said flatly.

"Could you tell we were trying to figure out what to do, now that we can't talk to your dad anymore?"

"Yeah."

"Owlly and Nel and Brod and Suki and Jak and all these people that were here tonight are trying to do what your mom and dad wanted to do. Do you understand?"

"Yeah."

"The problem is, we need to do it together with your dad's friends, but now we've lost contact with them. We don't know who they are."

He waited to see if Tofer would work it out, then went on. "Do you know everybody? All the people in your dad's secret circle?"

He waited for an answer. And waited. He waited so long that he gave up and tried a different tack. "Can you–"

"There's two," said Tofer to the garage wall behind Ronnie's head. "One, two."

"Two what? People?"

"No."

"Two circles?"

"Yeah. Two circles–one, two. Big and little."

Big and little circles?

"How many people in the little one?"

"Five. One, two, three, four, five." The military committee. He only counted the number of people he had to take messages to, excluding his own father.

"How many in the big one?"

This seemed more problematic. Tofer made faces and kept changing his eyes' resting place. Maybe it wasn't always the same number.

"How many last time?"

"Thirty-four. One, two, ..."

Ronnie stayed his own hand before he could raise it and let Tofer finish in his own way.

Thirty-four. He thought about that for a moment. "Is one of them called 'the Colonel'?"

Tofer gave his frustrated look again. "What about 'the baker'?"

"Yeah."

Contact. "Is he a real baker? With a shop?"

"Yeah."

"Where is it?"

Tofer pointed vaguely toward the top of the hill.

"Could you take me there tomorrow? Me and Brod?"

"Yeah."

On an overcast morning just forty-five days from the autumn equinox, Brod urged Daisy, the rented mare, to pull the shop's cart on through the Citadel main gate as Ronnie and Tofer rode in back, appearing to brace a large, laid-out wardrobe cabinet with their feet. The guards had officiously looked inside the empty cabinet but paid scant attention to the boys themselves, who all wore Citadel work badges—Tofer's borrowed from Jak and worn in place of his Citadel resident's pin.

Everything looked normal as Brod followed Tofer's pointing to steer Daisy to an area on the northeast shoulder of the hill that featured businesses serving the government quarter and the prosperous neighborhoods nearby. People there seemed to be going about their affairs as if the world were not about to explode and to end for some of them. Even the cops were relaxed.

"Whaddaya think?" said Brod over his shoulder.

"I think, if there's an ambush," said Ronnie, "these people don't know about it."

"They wouldn't, probably."

"True."

Ronnie looked across at the boy, whose eyes repeatedly glanced forward and then down.

"Tofer?" he said.

"Yeah."

"Don't point anymore, okay?"

"Yeah."

"Just tell me—are we getting close?"

Tofer started to point but stopped himself. "Yeah," he said.

Ronnie studied the street ahead.

"Is it the yellow brick building on the right?"

"No. "

"The red brick one on the left?"

"Yeah."

"Okay," he said, then to Brod: "I think this is close enough, brother. From here you can turn at the corner if there's trouble."

Brod pulled to the curb by the side of a beer warehouse. Ronnie dismounted and beckoned Tofer to join him on the sidewalk next to the cart. With Brod watching for watchers, he spoke low.

"Okay, Tofer. We're going to go in the bakery like regular customers—wait in line if there's a line, side by side. Do you know why?"

Ronnie looked down at the sidewalk while Tofer thought about this.

"Friends," said the boy.

"That's right. We want the baker to see we're friends, so he'll talk to me. Ready?"

"Yeah."

He looked up at Brod. "If there's a party, don't hang around for the fireworks," he said, handing over his and Tofer's work badges for safekeeping.

"And you—" said Brod, "if there's a party, make sure you serve your guest before yourself." Kill Tofer before himself, he meant.

Ronnie grinned. "You know I would never forget proper etiquette, brother. Let's just hope there's no party!"

Brod smiled ruefully as the two walked away. Then he climbed down, pretended for a minute to be interested in the horse and her tackle, and assumed a position leaning against the curb side of the wagon from where he could observe the bakery over the wardrobe.

The bakery was pretty big, Ronnie realized as they approached, with elaborate samples behind expensive glass panes and customers passing in and out and a wonderful aroma wreathing it. Inside, there was not just one line of waiting customers, but three, with a painted sign over each depicting its specialty. He was trying to make up his mind which one to get in when he realized he was being stared at by a woman serving one of the lines. He gestured for Tofer to follow and got in the woman's line, even as she gained control of herself and looked away to the customer in front of her. A girl with dark braids came through swinging doors, saw Tofer, and bobbled the tray of rolls she was carrying. At Ronnie's side, Tofer bounced on his heels at seeing her.

The girl went to a stand-up desk where a grey-bearded man worked. She spoke quietly, he looked over her shoulder at Tofer, and then he and Ronnie locked eyes as he spoke to the girl and she went back through the doors.

Ronnie could well imagine the turmoil filling the man's mind. Tofer, at the moment the most dangerous 14-year-old in the entire movement, had brought a stranger among them. If he was the *wrong kind* of stranger, it threatened death for their circle and beyond.

The man came from behind his workstation and relieved the woman serving the line. She took his place and pretended to do something at the desk, her eyes nervously darting to Ronnie and Tofer and to the front door every time someone entered.

"May I help you, young man?" said the grey-bearded man finally, as the two advanced to the counter and Tofer moved from one foot to the other faster and faster.

"Yes, sir, good morning, sir," said Ronnie in his most relaxed tone. "My friend Master Checkers sent me," he said, hoping the barber was known by such name in his own circle. “Said I was to pick up a parcel of raisin bread?”

The baker looked at him as if trying to place the special order. He glanced at the momentarily still and listening Tofer, at the other waiting customers, and back at the unblinking young stranger.

“Let’s take a look in the back, shall we?” he said, then, over his shoulder, “Daughter, would you take over here?” and to Ronnie, “C’mon.”

Ronnie gestured to Tofer and went around the end of the counter and followed the baker through the swinging doors. He was immediately stricken by the size of the skylit space beyond, with numerous antique ovens and racks of bread and pastries, a yellow delivery van standing at a loading dock through a wide rear portal, and a dozen or more white-clad workers moving about industriously. Several of these tried and failed to hide their interest in him.

“This way, please,” said the baker. “Let’s look in the ready-room.”

The old man strode to put his left hand on another wide, metal-sheathed swinging door. As he pushed through straight ahead and Ronnie followed with Tofer on his heels, the hackles went up on the back of his neck. Instinct and childhood lessons of capture-avoidance took over.

In a blur, he caught sight of a piece of clothing through the hinge-side gap and spontaneously rammed the door with a lowered left shoulder. Grunts and cries erupted from the other side and a violent push-back sent him reeling toward a small corner beside the door. His outstretched left hand grabbed and pulled Tofer into the corner behind him as the door swung shut and he swept his dagger out before him. The baker spun around, open mouthed.

“Stand back!” Ronnie said forcefully but not loudly to the three young men who confronted him with various tools of the baking trade, including a long cake knife. Courageously if unskillfully, the knife-bearer tried to engage, only to get Ronnie’s boot in his belly. The other two advanced with makeshift cudgels.

"Stand back!" said Ronnie again, moving the knife to a position between his own throat and Tofer's, just behind his left shoulder. "I'll kill us both!"

The men hesitated, glancing at the baker. The old man stepped and put a restraining hand on the knife-wielder's forearm. A burly, black-haired man cracked the door and looked in and Ronnie moved the knife closer to the wincing Tofer's throat in response.

"Stay out!" ordered the baker and the door closed. Then to Ronnie: "Please don't hurt the boy."

"I won't let him be captured!"

"*Captured?* Tofer's part of our f*amily*. He belongs with *us*." Ronnie didn't change his posture. "What do you want here?" asked the old man.

"To talk to the baker."

"So talk."

"I'm not talking to a bunch of people. Just one."

The baker nodded, understanding. "Step outside, boys," he said to the three men. "Let me hear what he has to say. Don't let the customers see anything unusual."

Ronnie stayed on guard as the men reluctantly filed close by out the door to join their co-workers gathered beyond, some armed with big ladles and dough-smeared paddles and other unlikely weapons. Then he moved himself and Tofer toward the back of the room.

"You go by the door," he ordered the old man, and when he'd complied, he lowered the knife to his side and turned to the boy, who had kept his hands half raised as if in alarm through the stressful moments of tension and physical contact.

"Tofer, I'm sorry I pushed you," said Ronnie. "I got scared for a second. I'm just trying to do what your dad would want.... Are you okay?"

The boy didn't answer.

"Are you mad at me?"

"No," said Tofer after a few seconds.

"And you're okay, then?"

"Yeah."

"Good.... Put your hands down.

"Yeah."

"It's okay, Tofer," said the baker. "You can put your hands back down now." Slowly the boy lowered his hands and started moving from one foot to the other. "Do you need to pee?"

"Yeah."

"Give him the big metal bowl on the rack behind you," said the baker. Ronnie retrieved it while keeping the others in his side vision and handed it to Tofer.

"Take it in the corner," said the baker, "and leave it there when you're finished. Okay, son?"

"Yeah," said Tofer, turning away. Ronnie let him go.

"So, young man," said the old man, "what brings you here?"

"Tofer's family are ... lost, as I'm sure you've heard," said Ronnie. "Some connections were lost with them. I'm trying to restore them—so we can carry on."

The old man regarded him for a long time. Tofer came closer again and waited.

"And why do you come to me?"

"I was in a meeting a few weeks ago—someone mentioned 'the baker' like a person of consequence and Checkers shushed him. I asked Tofer, after he'd brought warning. He understood what needed to be done."

"A *meeting*, you say," the baker repeated with ill-disguised skepticism. "You're a member of the committee?"

"A visitor, actually."

"Ah, yes. The kid with the ideas. The military history buff."

"Yes," said Ronnie, suddenly realizing it was likely not Checkers who led this circle, but the elderly man standing before him. Checkers had been merely his delegate, albeit one who'd been acknowledged as committee head by its members. "Why didn't you go to the committee members first, if you had Tofer's help. Ever read about 'chain of command' in your books?"

Ronnie shrugged. "We made a judgement call. Your cell seems to be the source of some vital elements of the plan—so's ours. We had to be stitched together—fast.... And we wanted to give you a chance to select a replacement for Checkers before the next meeting. He would want that, don't you think?"

"There's a meeting scheduled? You have contact with all the members?"

"No," said Ronnie, gesturing toward Tofer with his head, "but he does. That's why he's not leaving my side until the committee has met and adopted new methods of communication. Then he can stay out of sight for the next few weeks—until the day."

"Listen, son, you can't keep Tofer *prisoner.* We're his *people;* he belongs with *us.* He can take one of us to talk to the others."

"*You* listen, Master Baker—Checkers sent his son to my family first, to call one of us to witness his honorable end, which I did with my own eyes. Then the son returns to us for refuge after completing his mission. We have kept him safe and will continue to keep him safe and hidden until the day, then return him to you.... And besides," he added, glancing sideways, "maybe Checkers sent him to us because he was concerned you'd let sentiment get in the way of doing the necessary, if he was in danger of capture.... You have to honor his judgement in this."

"Maybe," conceded the old man at length, looking at the head-down but listening boy.

A thoughtful silence ensued, then Ronnie half-turned: "Tofer?"

"Yeah."

"You told me there were two circles: big and little. Remember?"

"Yeah."

"You showed me the big one; now I need you to show me the little one. Will you stay with me a few more days? help me find the little one?"

When Tofer didn't answer, the old man spoke: "Would you rather be with us, son? with Bren?"

The boy screwed up his face in frustration, then decided.

"Dad said help Brown's circle," he said.

"That's me," said Ronnie to the old man, with a little smile. "Now I see why he came back to us after he'd made his rounds; his dad told him to." Then, thoughtfully, "Do you have contact will all the members of your own circle? or do you need Tofer for that?"

"No, we'll manage," said the baker resignedly.

"Okay, listen ... Are you familiar with the meeting place that I was invited to three weeks ago?"

"Yes."

"What if the message for the committee members is to meet there tomorrow night? An hour after sundown?"

"That sounds all right. It's called 'the dairy,' by the way, that location."

"Thank you.... Now, can you get me out of here in one piece?"

"One thing–your circle knows *us* now, but we don't know *your* circle. How do we communicate?"

"Correction, Master Baker–*I* know you, but that doesn't mean I'll be spreading everybody's secrets around unnecessarily, even to my own leader. If you settle on a protocol for contacting me tomorrow night, I'll come to hear your message for the others. But I have an idea ...

A few minutes later, the baker had stepped out first in order to calm the loiterers and send them back to their duties. When Ronnie and Tofer came out, the girl they'd seen up front came irresistibly to Tofer, and Ronnie had been amused to see how they interacted, both looking away as the girl did most of the talking, but with Tofer being more voluble and permitting the girl to lightly touch his forearm in a way he hadn't seen. He could imagine them being childhood playmates and was glad to know Tofer had such a friend. *Bren,* he supposed.

With Owlly's approval he'd secured a circle-connected cab and gone with Tofer to deliver meeting summons to the other four committee members, with varying degrees of drama. The skeptical-voiced woman whom he guessed was "Stars" had come to the service entrance of a Citadel house to receive Tofer's message without comment, barely glancing at Ronnie, while the proprietor of a government-contract print shop within the Citadel had—in the voice if not the gentle manner of Silver—lambasted him for taking advantage of Tofer's misfortune to usurp the role of messenger to which the committee had not appointed him.

The printer had been correct, of course; he *was* usurping that role. Whether he was doing so because *somebody* had to take over from Tofer, or in quest of more power for *himself*, was something he wasn't inclined to dwell upon.

The third committee member, whom he took to be Ponies, was merely surprised and a little scared to be confronted at her wedding-planner service, but the last was positively delighted. Bil Rigwasher, after inquiring after Tofer's safety and well-being, had actually *embraced* Ronnie, figuratively and literally, as the logical choice—since he'd already attended a meeting without bringing the Error Police down on them *and* was capable in his own right, as well as conveniently mobile, with his Citadel work badge and carpenter's toolbox.

Following protocol, neither had mentioned that they'd seen each other before—two years past when Ronnie entered the city on Baladur's rig—or spoken of parties not present. There'd be plenty of time for reminiscing—*after* the revolution.

27 - Bats and Mosquitos

Forty-three days before the Autumn Equinox

At a table under a window in the workshop, Ronnie sat wielding an antique carving knife, looted from some forbidden-zone hobby shop by the miners, on the image of a mallard duck laid on a wooden cutting board. One by one the pieces of similarly looted heavy paper were liberated from the whole to later be positioned on sheets of fine veneer for cutting. The duck was the second-to-last image for Clare's guest apartment and he was anxious to finish the job, if only to give the appearance of normal operations. Plus, though he couldn't have explained why, he felt compelled to see her one last time before becoming instrumental in the destruction of her world and the building of one that she might not survive to know.

His mind boiled with questions, scenarios, to-do lists. First on his mind was what protocol for summoning the messenger he would suggest for Owlly to put forward that night. Suddenly he stopped cutting and put down his blade.

"I'll be right back," he announced to Owlly and Brod working nearby and went out.

On the street he hunched his shoulders slightly against the chilling drizzle and headed down Woodmaker Street toward the square. When he reached it he turned right and then right again up an alley to a public toilet, paid his penny and went in.

It was not a facility for sensitive gentlefolk, with mismatched fixtures and broken tiles and little light, but it did offer a little privacy in the form of a row of cubicles against the back wall. On market days, when the place was crowded with country people of both sexes and all ages and the occasional trysting couple, it was hard to secure a cubicle, but not today. Ronnie went in one and looked around, went in the next, and worked his way to the last one, where he first inspected the fixture for hazards and then closed the door and sat down.

On the inside of the door was painted a large Jesus-cross, which surprised him. There was always talk of secret Christians and practitioners of other pre-Cleasing religions—and new ones too—but this was so indiscrete and provocative. No Freethinker would attract attention in such a way, and he wondered if the image was not the work of the Error Police. The absence of Freethinkers with paint-pens was also apparent from the few "words" underlying or overlying other graffiti, difficult to make out as words and just as difficult to comprehend but obviously meant to shock with their violence, vulgarity, and revelations about the sexual habits of this person or that. Less obscure was a drawing of a crowned man lifting his elaborate robes to ecstatically lower himself onto a big sword—presumably Lord Endo sitting on the Sword of ZAH.

Amused and strangely heartened by this blasphemy, Ronnie stood and found a spot convenient to himself but unsuitable for graffiti, in the corner where the back and side walls met. He drew his dagger, held it near the tip like a pen, and scratched a small five-pointed star into the paint. Then he headed back to the shop.

"Clear, Dad?" he inquired as he entered the workshop and grabbed a towel to dry himself from the rain, making sure there were no strangers about to overhear. Brod was gone.

"Clear," mumbled Owlly as he carved gracefully on a chair leg held in a vise. "What's up?"

"I think I've got a good spot for the committee members to leave signals for the messenger, if they need to."

Owlly laid his tool down and gave Ronnie his attention. "Tell me."

A few minutes later it was decided: that night, at "the dairy," Owlly would suggest to the members that any of them who needed the messenger could send someone to write the single digit identifying such member below the star on the wall of the public toilet; urgency could be signaled by circling the number. The spot would be checked daily.

"There's something else, Dad," Ronnie said after the messaging protocol was settled. "I think you should propose yourself as committee leader, if you're not satisfied with Checkers's replacement."

"Me?"

"Why not?"

"Well," said Owlly, shaking his head. "I'm no great military leader, son."

"Maybe you aren't, maybe you are. We don't know, do we? Besides, unless the baker sends another Checkers, who's going to do it?... Just propose yourself as *manager* of the committee's affairs."

"Well, I–"

"If somebody doesn't take a strong hand, everybody will start relying on this Colonel guy, and he's not even a member. That's the other thing: if the committee is going to rely on the information and help of a Citadel traitor, everybody needs to know his story.

"That's not–"

"And another thing, Dad–the mustering places should be kept secret. If the members insist on knowing, suggest they designate one member to check out each place and report.... Also–"

Ronnie stopped, seeing Owlly frown.

"I'm sorry, Dad," he said. "I've got too many things banging around in my head."

"Don't be sorry, son. I'm just sorry you're not old enough to be accepted in my place on the committee. You'd be better than me."

Ronnie was momentarily speechless, then embarrassed. "Dad, I didn't mean to–"

"Don't worry about it. And don't be modest. You've got a good head for this stuff. You just keep talking to me about it. I'll pretend they're my idea and take all the credit."

"Okay. Good idea."

At midday, Ronnie and Suki, young Tofer's two favorite people in the family, went underground to share lunch with him and found him engaged in a new project. Whereas before he had busied himself with rearranging books or looking at maps and diagrams or reading what he could, now he was digging.

Tofer himself was nowhere to be seen in the lamplight, but a waist-high pile of debris at the far end of the space led the visitors to a pair of wriggling boots sticking at head height out of the wall of broken masonry and metal that once comprised the building and contents. They watched for a few minutes by the light of a candle perched on a steel beam at Tofer's shoulder as he loosened small chunks with his bare hands–and a steel bar he's liberated–and pushed them out with his feet.

"Hey, Tofer," said Suki finally, and the boots stilled, "whatcha doin'?"

"Looking for the air." came the muffled reply.

Ronnie understood. They'd always known that fresh air was coming from somewhere, and that it entered the space right where Tofer was digging, but trying to penetrate to its source had always seemed a daunting and not especially useful task. Now Ronnie realized that what the job had always needed was an energetically obsessive boy with nothing better to do and lots of time to do it.

"Come out and have some lunch with us, Tof," he called.

The boy looked longingly at the face he was working for a moment before relenting. "Okay," he said, and squirmed out with his candle to stand before them.

"You are one dirty boy," observed Suki, looking him up and down.

"In fact, you may be the dirtiest boy I've ever seen."

Tofer looked pleased at this superlative and the visitors could see he was actually having a good time.

"Can I dust you off, T," asked Ronnie.

"Yeah," said the boy, and Ronnie went to work.

Tofer's hands were scraped and bleeding, his nails broken. He let Suki wash them, along with his face, in a bowl of water on a side table, then poured the water in his waste bucket to take away. They sat down to eat from a basket of meat-and-vegetable-filled pasties that Nel had prepared.

"If you're going to be digging, we'll try to get you upstairs for a bath every night," Ronnie said to Tofer. "But not tonight. Is that okay?"

"Yeah."

"If Mom and Dad say what you're doing is okay, I'll bring you some gloves and tools and–"

"Yeah."

"But I think they'll say no digging after dark, when everything gets quiet. The neighbors might hear through the ground, you know?"

"Yeah."

"We just have to figure out how to get the debris to the dump without drawing attention," Ronnie mused, looking at the pile Tofer had created just since breakfast. "You're digging pretty fast." He took another bite.

In the late afternoon Jak walked Daisy from the nearby stable and hitched her to the cart. The three boys loaded up with cleaning materials and camouflage furniture pieces and headed at a leisurely pace for the main gate, where they were waved in with a glance. Contriving to first pass the armory for the opportunity to study their target, they rose further up the hill, turning unnecessarily a couple of times to gage activity in the area and finally arriving at the overgrown dead-end street adjacent to the church's graveyard. Ronnie and Brod casually surveyed nearby traffic and checked the windows and doorways of nearby buildings and gave Jak the okay to turn up the left side of the street. He drove over low bushes almost to the foot of the great wall and made a U-turn, coming to a stop next to the graveyard's wall. With a last look to see if they'd come to anyone's notice, the older boys stood and threw their bundles and backpacks and brooms over the wall into the pile of trash on the other side. They sat down, studied what they could see for a moment, then stood again and rolled smoothly over the wall to a soft crunch. Jak urged the mare away and kept going.

The boys gathered themselves and their gear while still covered by the sound of the horse and cart and moved through the low gateway to the back of the church. As Ronnie inspected the window opening for signs of disturbance, Brod looked around.

"Wanna explore?" asked Ronnie.

"Yeah, let's."

The two put down their burdens and passed back through the gate to wander among the tombstones. Most were overgrown and tangled with trash that had been thrown over the wall over decades and had to be cleared for the finely-cut inscriptions to be read.

"John David McCarthan, Emeritus Professor of Literature, Beloved Father and Grandfather," read Brod quietly.

"Deaconess Caroline Miller, Dearest Wife and Mother, Friend to All," read Ronnie.

"Baby Sara, Abiding with the Angels," said Brod, then: "This is kind of like our custom, isn't it? Speaking the names aloud, with respect."

"Yeah, but they didn't have to be secretive about it. In fact, from what I've read and heard, they had big ceremonies to honor the dead, with the dead right there among them, laid out."

"Guess they weren't so afraid of dead things as now," said Brod.

"Guess not.... Well, shall we get started?"

∆ ∆ ∆

The boys stood side by side against the back wall, looking quietly. After a while, Ronnie raised an arm and pointed to the front. "There's a big bowl with a ladle in it on that table, and lots of these around," he nudged a dust-covered foam cup with his foot, inches from a man's grimacing skull, "so Jak and I were thinking at least some drank poison." He fished in his pocket and brought out a grey-green object. "There are also a lot of these. It's a bullet holder, and some of the skulls have holes in them, so they were either shot, or shot themselves. There are no guns, so if they shot themselves, then whoever found them collected all the guns."

"Yeah," said Brod hoarsely, not yet trusting his voice to say more.

"Let's go see the bats, before it gets too dark."

The two stepped through the obstacle course of bones and personal belongings into the basement corridor and up the broad stairway. At the landing they laid down their materials and Ronnie led to the wall at the end, where faint light beckoned.

"I think it's time for the bats to wake up," he said low, "so let's just step around this wall and look for a few minutes, then come back." Brod nodded.

Soon they stood at the front of the dais, looking up. "Amazing," whispered Brod, as some of the mouse-size creatures began to unfurl their wings. The scene faded toward darkness.

"We better go now," Ronnie whispered back, motioning his brother to precede him. They stepped into the short passage and were about to step out of it when Brod ran solidly into a body—an upright one.

"Zah's balls!" he exclaimed tightly, frantically searching for the knife inside his shirt as he and the other recoiled from each other.

"Don't kill me, brother!" said Jak urgently, "It's only me!"

"Be still!" said Ronnie, and all froze in place, listening for bat-panic. After a minute they retreated to the corridor and Ronnie opened a couple of office doors to let in the remaining light from the dirty windows.

"Tryin' ta give me a heart attack, little brother?" Brod said affectionately. "I almost pissed myself."

"Sorry, I–"

"How'd you get back so fast?" asked Ronnie. "We weren't expecting you for another hour."

"I know the way now–no need for light." He held up a knotted bandana. "I blindfolded myself."

The older boys chuckled at the audacity. "Brilliant," said Ronnie. "We can tell the others about it when the time comes–build up their confidence–right after we scare them with the news that they have to go underground to get to the fight."

"I'll have to see how fast *I* can go, so we have a range," said Brod.

"That'll give us a range for different size young people, but we have to estimate for older ones too," said Ronnie. "Maybe Slammer Jon will try it. He's almost fifty and as tall as you and me."

"Yeah."

"Okay," said Ronnie, "down to business. We're going to bed down right here on the floor and start when the city wakes up to cover our noise. So let's get on these brooms."

It was almost dark by the time the boys had cleared part of the corridor of a century's worth of dust and droppings and sat down on the choir loft stairs to talk but then abruptly stopped, listening.

"Is that the bats?" asked Jak.

"Let's go see!" said Ronnie, jumping up to ascend the stairs. When he reached the top, he eased out against the back wall and the others took up positions next to him. Directly in front of them, more heard and felt than clearly seen, was a boiling black cloud of bats, filling the entire sanctuary from the edge of the loft to the stained-glass window at the front and from colonnade to colonnade. Eventually a single bat flew through the hole in the window and was followed by another and then another, until the creatures formed a thin black stream that depleted the swarm second by second. When it was gone, the church grew quiet again.

“Awesome,” said Jak.

Ronnie led the way downstairs, found his backpack mostly by feel, and took out a long, thin candle and matches. “We’d better close the office doors,” he said, and it was done.

He lit the candle and set it in a holder on the end post of the stairs. “Pick a spot,” he said, and everyone set about unrolling their bedding and settling in for the night, with water bottles at hand and a piss-bucket in the corner.

At first no one could sleep. Lying on the floor of the mustering place for the attack on the armory—the first act in the first coordinated attack on the Priesthood of ZAH in its 109-year-long history—the poignant reality of the undertaking was upon them. Each entertained private thoughts: of the battle itself, of its aftermath—win or lose— of a world long dreamed of and hoped for but also troubling to contemplate, and of their loved ones. For Ronnie a thought of Jenna insinuated itself, but he shook his head and drove it away. Instead he thought of bats, and as sleep came, he was already dreaming of how they had formed themselves into a disciplined troop and gained inspiration and momentum from each other and then suddenly poured out onto the battlefield in an irresistible mass, in search of the blood-sucking mosquito, the world’s most useless and destructive creature.

In his aborning dream, the mosquitos were man-size and wore black robes.

28 - The Colonel's Dilemma

Forty-two days from Equinox

A cloudy morning offered little light, even at the six-o'clock bell, but it was enough for their grim task. As it turned out, human skeletons numbering more than a hundred weren't very heavy and didn't take up much space when stacked. But they'd taken their time-with them.

After a breakfast of bread and fruit and water, an exploration of the other rooms on the two floors had located three useful things: overflow space for those fighters who wouldn't fit in the big meeting room, a cache of folded choir robes, and a game room where the bones could be laid.

A sagging table with a short net in the middle had been turned up against the game-room wall and the armloads of robes taken into the meeting room and piled on the table next to the poison bowl. The boys surveyed their task.

"I think we have enough robes that we can keep what looks like families together, if you want," said Ronnie. "Somehow that seems important right now."

"'Cause this is history," said Brod. "We have to live it as honorably as we can ... for ourselves and our children."

The others regarded their normally ineloquent older brother.

Ronnie asked, "How do we honor *them,* then?"

Brod looked over the remains and moved to take hands and make a circle with the others.

"We remember these unknown," he said simply, "beloved of the people of Professor McCarthan, Deaconess Miller, and ..."

"Baby Sara," provided Ronnie.

"Baby Sara."

Ronnie looked to Jak and helped him as they all recited together, "These unknown, beloved of the people of Professor McCarthan, Deaconess Miller, and Baby Sara. We remember."

When they had let go hands, Brod took a robe from the stack, selected a nearby cluster of bones, spread the robe on the floor beside it, and prepared to transfer the remains. The others joined to lift them awkwardly onto the robe, together with a handbag, a stuffed bear, a storybook, and other nearby items. The robe was tucked around and lifted at its ends to be set aside and the next laid out. In this way the remains were wrapped with increasing efficiency and placed side by side to be moved to the game room. By late afternoon, having stopped many times to examine the dead's effects before wrapping and moving them, and having swept up an enormous amount of dust and droppings, the boys were finished. Outside, a steady rain fell.

Sitting on the table from which the big bowl had been removed and looking at his filthy co-workers, Ronnie said, "I think we should leave by the pipes."

"It's raining," observed Brod.

"That's why we should do it—so we can see what it's like. We don't want to drown a couple hundred people because we didn't know how much water there would be if it was raining when we launched the rebellion. Besides, we look like chimney sweeps, not cabinet makers. We'll attract attention."

"Good point," said Brod, then, turning, "What say you, little brother?"

"Let's do it. We can rinse off along the way.

∆ ∆ ∆

Three hours later they were home, undrowned. Nel and Suki had prepared enough hot water for all the boys including Tofer to have a bath and by the time they were done a cauldron of venison stew stood bubbling on the stove. A mood of accomplishment pervaded the company, but Owlly's absence was acutely felt. Even though only Ronnie knew exactly where he was and what he was doing, he was assumed to be on a mission of great importance that might keep him out all night. So when he lightly knocked on his own back door some time after midnight and entered with his own air of accomplishment, those who'd waited up for him were elated. Seemingly against all odds and despite the loss of Checkers, the rebellion was still on schedule. It was so impossibly exciting that it worried Ronnie a little bit.

In her palace apartment up the hill, Lady Sula looked up from her couch at the tall, steel-grey-haired man standing before her. "You don't know?" she inquired, the timbre of her voice causing two guards lounging against the wall to stand forward a step and rest off-hand on sword pommel, in case they were ordered to kill the hapless retainer where he stood. The man sensed the movement, fought to control his bowels, and went on.

"Well, of course I know *approximately*, milady," he said with transparently false assurance. "It's just that there's a lot of dark riverbank between where she launches and where she appears again.... And sometimes she simply abandons the boat and reappears in town.... And sometimes—"

"Spare me your excuses, Colonel," she said, looking away in boredom. "I'm not interested in the many ways you've failed me. I'm just waiting to hear about a success big enough to justify the two years we've spent on your operation."

The colonel's mind raced over his accomplishments as he tried to formulate a defense—back to the beginning.

He'd never been a very *popular* army officer, with either superiors or subordinates, but he'd made himself useful by the violent rapaciousness of his operations against those accused of freethought and other blasphemies. Many a property or valuable bauble had passed through his hands into those of senior officers and priests, many of their previous owners had died, many an enemy had been painted with the suspicion of heresy at the behest of powerful people. He'd been paid with modest commissions and the freedom to embezzle funds and operate as he chose, but it had been his slut of a wife who'd put him on the road to high position and real fortune.

A whore when he married her, she'd remained one even after bearing him two brats, spending more time in the beds of priests and officers who outranked him than in his. When an Error Ministry high priest had demanded that he release her to become his own wife and threatened to ruin him if he didn't give in, the wife had brokered a deal agreeable to all. The priest had taken her proposal to Grotius, Grotius had taken it to his kinswoman Sula, and the foundations of a great lie began to be laid.

First, rumors were put about that the colonel's reputation as a heretic-hunter was fabricated to cover his own heretical inclinations and activities, and that, far from exterminating entire Freethinker communities, he'd actually facilitated such perfect evacuations of them to the forests that they'd never been found. Then came the Springfield affair.

In the once-again-thriving town three day's march to the southeast, some forty members of a fugitive Freethinker circle had been encountered in such a way that they couldn't simply be let go. More than half of them had been slaughtered before the colonel could save the rest by having his own loyal sergeants murder two of his junior officers. The rest of the fugitives made it into the forest and several ended up in Citadel City, where they eventually found others of their kind and spread the legend of the self-sacrificing Colonel. Details of the affair inevitably leaked out and the colonel was subjected to a much-gossiped-about court-martial, whereupon another junior officer and-two common soldiers who'd been expected to testify against him mysteriously disappeared.

The charges had been dropped on condition that he resign and—though it wasn't discussed openly—give up his wife and children, after which he embarked on a downward spiral that soon found him ensconced in a grain-alcohol-shooter bar, where he appeared to be trying to drink himself to death.

It was all sham, of course, the supposed witnesses killed to add authenticity, just as the two priests would later be killed at Checkers's, but to a Freethinker spy who tracked him down at the bar, it seemed heroic. When the spy had finally made his judgement and revealed himself, the colonel had fallen into his arms and wept, as if corning home after an arduous journey.

The circle that took him in was happy to have someone who'd been part of the Citadel establishment—especially a former military commander with Freethinker credentials. When talk of rebellion started, he was perfectly positioned to participate in its planning, if only as an adviser to Nuyen, the woman who became his circle's delegate to the new military committee. When he made himself her lover, his position was secure.

Not useful or powerful enough, however. Nuyen was very good at adhering to security protocols, and he hadn't been able to find out where the committee met or the identities of its members—with one exception. As Sula stared at him with distaste, he grasped at its lifeline.

"With respect, milady," he said, "I would remind you it was my idea to cause the man Balz to eliminate himself. That removed the best military planner from the committee and henceforth my suggestions, advanced by Nuyen, should no longer be dismissed."

Sula sneered. "That's only useful if Balz's replacement is someone less troublesome and if you can now discover the rebels' assembly points, so they can be trapped and exterminated without public spectacle, if necessary. You'd better pray to ZAH that tonight's committee meeting moved in your favor.... Now get out."

"Yes, milady," said the colonel, stifling whatever he'd been about to say and backing out of the room.

The two guards passed him off to more guards in the outer room and closed the heavy double doors behind him, then turned back to await their mistress's command.

Sula drew a leg onto the sofa and leaned back against the pillows, thinking, moving the chess pieces in her mind: the rebels, the army, that bitch Clare. The candles in the chandelier flickered slightly as a wind gust made its way in through the ancient ventilation ducts. After a while her gaze shifted from the empty space in front of her to the two guards.

"I want to see you," she said, and the young men began methodically to shed their weapons and armor and underclothes.

When they were naked, they stood expressionless and still while she studied them. Knowing what she liked to see and what she liked to believe about her own desirability, they competed to arouse themselves with their minds alone.

Sula put her hand through the folds of her robe and massaged herself for a few minutes. Then she stood and turned for her bedchamber.

"Come," she ordered.

29 - The Quickening

Thirty-five days out

Across Citadel City, secret activity quickened. Families and circles, knowing defeat meant miserable and humiliating death, prepared to fight with household implements or other objects that would not give away their intended purpose if discovered ahead of time, practicing as much as they could without alerting neighbors and police. The need for discretion was reinforced in younger children and many were put to such work as sewing long weapons bags and knee pads–for use in the pipes–and in fletching arrows. Young Jak and three of his smallish friends were tasked to begin transferring weapons to the church, pairs of boys slinging the heavy bags between themselves to move repeatedly through the pipes at night, dropping them quietly over the wall into the trash at the church in the hours after the Dead made their rounds.

At the armory, the smiths banged away at sword and lance and armor, apparently trying to stay ahead of the "recruiters" who now searched the shooter bars and street corners and game rooms and jails with ever-greater urgency for yet more bodies to put into uniform, seemingly unconcerned about the low quality of their finds. Down in the basement a small contingent of army troops inevitably lounged, talking about women and adventures past and future and the incompetence of their officers and the uselessness of their jobs, since the armory had never been attacked before and surely never would be.

In the secret library, Ronnie worked on the map he'd started some time before, while Tofer dug. Based on a city map in the real-estate section of a local newspaper from 2027, it now included not only the great wall and other major changes to the city center now known as the Citadel, but the features on all sides, including Owlly's shop, the stable and lumber yard and pub just down the street, and the forbidding cemetery with its periodically smoke-belching crematorium a few blocks beyond. Widening his vision, he took mental note of the home of Lady Clare—that enigma whom he might see for the last time in a few days—of the assault teams' assembly points and targets, and of the military committee's meeting places: "the dairy," "the boathouse," "the grocer's," and "the bootmaker's"—none of which matched the names they'd been given. He thought, as he worked in pencil and then pen, of what he'd heard of the dissension that had descended upon the committee in recent days, of the new assertiveness and influence of the woman known as "Stars," whose circle had found the Colonel and who championed his positions—especially that the assembly locations should be revealed and openly discussed, that the attack should commence without any last-minute scouting that might expose the coup-makers, and, most recently, that the Colonel should lead the attack on the palace himself—all ideas opposed by Owlly and the new woman known as "Flame," who'd replaced Checkers.

In the third-floor home on Toolmaker Square, above the club Scarface, Polli quietly spoke to her husband Tom—in the hours before the evening crowds came—about things he'd known instinctively all along but never required to know explicitly: Polly, her mother, and many of their friends and relatives, were Freethinkers—not just the casually open-minded sort, but the militant, coup-plotting kind—and they were all about to face mortal danger, endangering those about them in turn. Now they needed Tom and his friends—old and new—to be prepared to fight too, not just to confront soldiers and police but to sow chaos at the right time, to keep the priests' forces off-balance. The bond between husband and wife was strengthened by the shared secret and the importance of the task, and Tom set about priming various friends and acquaintances without giving them more information than they needed.

On her guest-apartment terrace, Clare paced, papers in hand. She often came to the empty rooms when she thought of Ronnie, and what she could learn of his activities, tracing the geometric designs he'd made in the cabinets with her long fingers. She could scarcely believe what she was hearing from her uncle Mortimer and from her spies, of a corrupt Council majority's continued support for Sula's plan for a new, revenue-raising pogrom, of the inexorable movement toward a fork in the road of history, the danger faced by all, not least herself. And now this: a smuggled report from across the seas concerning the progress of the two-year-old diplomatic mission.

She looked again at the once-tightly-rolled pages and marveled at the news of her brother Magnus, of his faraway hosts and the world they were creating, and of a certain young woman.

And at the Black Tower, looking through the telescope at her pacing enemy, Sula seethed and demanded to know why Lady Clare was still alive.

30 – Trading Proofs

Thirty-four days out

Zah's balls!" exclaimed Ronnie upon opening the library door to take Tofer his breakfast. At first his mind couldn't comprehend what he was seeing, and it couldn't tell him whether to retreat and give warning or go toward the danger.

He backed up a few steps and set the tray on the table near his bed, then dashed down the steps, leaving the door open. Diffused morning sunlight filled the space, which now seemed otherworldly and shabby.

"Tofer?" he called, not too loudly. "Tofer?"

Nothing. He turned and took the stairs three at a time and ran to the foot of the basement stairs. "Mom! Come quick!" he called, knowing she was already puttering about the showroom above.

Footsteps hurried. "What is it?!"

"Tofer's broken through and he's gone! I'm going to look for him. Be ready for trouble!"

"Goodgod!" she said–the closest thing to vulgarity he'd ever heard from her. "Be careful!"

He grabbed the dagger from under his pillow and the work badge from the bedside table and rushed to close the disguised door behind and clatter back down the stairs. Stepping through the chiseled opening, he paused.

"Tofer?" he said, listening. Now he could see a burned-down candle fluttering uselessly on the nearby table. At the far end of the space, the sunlit debris pile had grown substantially since yesterday evening. Obviously Tofer had forgotten or ignored the "no nighttime digging" rule.

At the hole, he peered in, half-expecting to see a curious Citadelian looking back. He could only see about fifteen feet to where the tunnel took a turn to the left. At the turning a small lamp set on a chunk of concrete still burned.

"Tofer?"

Listening again, he could hear the distant sound of horses clopping and iron wheels rolling on brick and of peoples' voices. He slid his dagger into its sewn-in sheath, put his badge in his pocket, and climbed in.

It was a Tofer-size tunnel, and Ronnie struggled to make progress. After a few feet he stopped fighting it and relaxed. He took a deep breath, made himself small as he let it out, and gained a few inches, then did it again. Behind him he heard the camouflaged door open and felt the breeze that made the open-flame lamp flicker.

"It's me, Ron," said Brod calmly. "Dad and Suki are going in to look for him. Mom's minding the store. Jak's on his way down. You wanna wait for 'im?"

"No," said Ronnie over his shoulder. "I think I can get through. Anything unusual on our street?"

"Negative."

He resumed worming his way through, making the turn and starting up an incline. Eventually he realized he'd passed into the heavy steel cage of some sort of small industrial vehicle. Squashed into this on one side as he continued to rise toward the light was an automobile, its strong plastic and fiber passenger compartment filled with dirt and debris but still maintaining a recognizable shape. He crawled through what must have been the driver's window and headed for the opening at the passenger side, then stopped short and lay still for a moment, listening, and slowly raised his head.

The tunnel had fortuitously opened into a blind alley rather than someone's back yard, knee-high above ground and partly overgrown with shrubs and weeds like all but the manicured parts of the wall. Looking through leaves, Ronnie saw trash bins on either side, so there was definitely traffic, however infrequently. At the end of the alley stood a slender, solitary figure, hands at sides. Ronnie spoke over his shoulder again.

"I see 'im," he said low, "at the end of the alley. If I can get 'im, I'll send 'im back this way and close up from the outside."

"Got it," Brod acknowledged. "What about you?"

"I've got my badge. I'll come back normal."

"Okay."

In two more minutes he'd eased his way out to the ground, which was littered with material from the tunnel. He moved quickly to one side to dust himself off and then sauntered up the alley, willing Tofer not to wander off.

When he came up beside him—not too close—he spoke casually.

"Hey, Tof," he said, studying the morning street scene that the boy was so absorbed by. There was no answer. After a minute he saw Owlly and Suki approaching on the other side of the street and subtly waived them off. They changed course to a bus stop bench and pretended to wait.

"Whatchu doin' out here?"

"Goin' home," said Tofer after several seconds.

Ronnie waited for people to pass, then, "You miss your family."

"Yeah.

"We all miss 'em, but they're not there anymore. You understand that, don't you."

"Yeah," said Tofer after a long pause.

"We all have to make a new family now—a big one—with Bren and her family and me and Suki in mine, and all the others. But we can't do it for a few more markets."

"Yeah."

"If you come back and stay with us, I promise we'll get out more. Then in a few markets we can go wherever we want. Would that be okay?"

"Yeah."

"We're worried that somebody might see you out here on foot and try to hurt you.... Can we go back now?"

"Yeah."

"C'mon,' said Ronnie, and turned back toward the wall. Tofer hesitated a moment before following.

Halfway down the alley a man came out with a basket of trash and lifted the wooden lid of the bin to empty it in. For a moment he looked at the boys with adult disapproval and seemed prepared to interrogate them, but Ronnie couldn't afford to accommodate him just then. He transformed himself on the fly into a teen predator, adopting a hunch-shouldered posture and purposeful gait and unblinking glare that caused the man to finish his task and scurry inside before the young hoodlums could reach him. The boys passed on to the wall, Ronnie looking back to make sure they were attracting no attention from pedestrians on the sidewalk.

"Brod's waiting for you," he said, ushering Tofer into the bush-shrouded car window. The slender boy snaked in, moving much more freely than *he* had. Once his feet were in, Ronnie hurriedly filled the opening with most of the dislodged debris and kicked aside the rest. He turned to survey the alley, dusted himself again, and headed for the street to cross over and sit on the bench near Owlly and Suki.

"How's it look, Dad?"

"Normal, to me," said Owlly. "What happened?"

"Homesick, seems like.... Too much time alone."

"Poor thing," said Suki.

"What about the tunnel?"

"It's brilliant. I'm already thinking it may be the way to come into the Citadel on certain jobs. Opens into an active alley, so not a good way to move a lot of people quickly, but still ..."

"You close it up?"

"Yeah, but if we're actually gonna use it we'll have to enlarge it and disguise the exit better ... more foliage, maybe."

"So let's get to it," said Owlly, getting to his feet.

Ronnie went his own way in order to pass out the main gate and check the public restroom for a summons. It was market day, and the country vendors who'd taken their positions the night before were just opening for business even as others arrived to set up. The restroom had a line already, but a quarter to the attendant put Ronnie next up for the last stall. There he saw, in the designated spot, for the first time, a summons from Flame, whom he knew was to be found at the bakery.

Eight bells had not rung yet, so he cleaned up, told Owlly where he was going, made some quick suggestions about the tunnel, and set off on foot, through the nearby gate to Woodmaker Square and then most of the way by bus. Upon entering the bakery he took a position in the corner near the entrance, as if waiting for someone. The woman the baker had called "daughter" noticed immediately, motioned for the girl Bren to take over her position, and gestured with her head for him to follow. Passing through the swinging doors, she made eye contact with a man wheeling a cart of pastries and led Ronnie into the same room he was in before. Nobody behind the door this time.

The woman turned and the two regarded each other. She was of medium age and quite striking, her thick brown hair swept back from her face under a scarf, her grey eyes intelligent and serious. Ronnie waited patiently, turned slightly to the door. Soon it swung open and the baker entered, followed by the young man Ronnie had kicked in the gut on his last visit.

Good morning, Ronnie," said the older man, extending his hand for an old-fashioned grasp. "Tofer doin' okay?"

"Good morning, Master Baker," said Ronnie with a firm grip, keeping his eye on the younger man. "Yes, he's fine."

"Good, good," nodded the baker, glancing at the man and woman but not yet introducing them. "Listen, Ronnie ... time is getting short, and we've become stuck in disagreement," he said. "I propose to break protocol to get moving again. Are you agreeable to talking a bit?"

Talking a bit? This was not a casual question or an insignificant matter. "Talking," with those not of one's own circle, even "a bit," went against generations of training and the very survival instinct that kept Freethinkers alive. Just forming the military committee to do it on urgent matters had been a momentous achievement of diplomacy.

"Why me?" asked Ronnie. I'm just the messenger."

"Because you're not 'just the messenger,' *are* you? You're the kid in the red mask who impressed everyone with military knowledge. And now you've become the only person in the city besides Tofer who knows where to find everyone, and so far, you haven't betrayed us. Talking with you doesn't make us more vulnerable than we already are. So what say you?"

"What do you have in mind?"

The baker turned to the woman: "Daughter?"

"Hello, Ronnie," she said, extending her hand. "I'm Katren. I also have another name ..."

"Flame," said Ronnie.

"Yes. Good." She gestured at the younger man. "This is my husband, Verjil."

"Hello, sir," said Ronnie, spontaneously using an honorific upon learning he was the older Katren's husband. "Sorry about kicking you last time."

The other extended his hand with a self-deprecating smile, showing his good teeth. "S'okay, Ronnie. Taught me a lesson. And call me Verjil."

"Verjil. Thank you."

"Here's the situation," said Katren, "if you don't already know.... The committee has divided into two factions, and you and we are in a position to resolve one issue right away—before a meeting scheduled for tomorrow night—if you agree."

"Go on."

"Okay ..., said Katren, raising her hands to shape the problem in space like a ball of dough. "The members want to be assured that the two assembly points are appropriate to their purpose, but there's disagreement about whether everyone needs to know everything about them. Brown, Candystripe, and I," she said, including herself with Owlly and Bil Rigwasher, "believe it should be adequate for the two circles—the ones that *have* the two locations—to inspect each other's and report to the committee. Stars, Ponies, and Silver insist on knowing everything. Since you may already know our location ... Can you guess?"

"This bakery, I'd say."

"Of course. So since you already know *our* location, the smallest possible expansion of knowledge would be for us to know *yours*. Do you agree?"

"Yes," said Ronnie with secret satisfaction, having earlier suggested this very thing to Owlly.

"So ... we propose to give you a tour—right now—and for you to take one of us to your location. Then tomorrow night we'll both present our reports—as a fait accompli. You know that term?"

"Yes. Accomplished fact."

"Indeed. The others may be upset that the decision was taken without them, but it will be done, and it may break a logjam that we don't have time for. You agree?"

"Absolutely," said Ronnie with conviction. "One problem, though ... I can't commit without consulting my leader, so if you're going to show me more right now, there's a chance you won't get reciprocity, at least not right away."

Katren looked to her father and husband for a few seconds, then back to Ronnie. "That's acceptable.... Now, Dad and I have things to do. Verjil's going to show you around, and he'll be the one to come to you later, if your leader approves. All clear? Any questions? Comments?"

"No—not now."

"Thank you, Ronnie," said Katren, shaking hands again even as she moved toward the door. Her father was more relaxed, taking Ronnie's hand in both of his and grinning. "This is kinda thrilling, ain't it?"

Ronnie broke into a grin himself. "It *is,* sir! Everything seems possible, suddenly."

The baker patted him on the shoulder. "Well," he said, "see you at the Bastille."

"À la Bastille alors," replied Ronnie, to the baker's amusement.

So began a sometimes sphincter-tightening tour and demonstration of Assembly Point "P"—for Palace. Twenty or more pairs of eyes stole glances of the stranger as he was walked around the large skylight-illuminated open space, containing multiple wood- or charcoal-fired ovens, preparation tables, many-shelved carts, potentially deadly implements everywhere. At the charcoal bin serving one of the ovens, Verjil kicked the containment wall at a certain point and a small, disguised door popped open.

"C'mon," he said, stooping to enter. Inside were low shelves full of weapons—purpose-made and make-do.

"We have three spots like this, and plenty of less-secure space that could be used in the final days."

"How many are you able to arm?"

"Between what will already be here and what people bring at the last minute—at least three hundred."

"And how will they arrive and deploy?"

Verjil showed his teeth in the dim hiding place. "Let's take a ride."

More eyes followed the two as they headed for the loading dock, where a dozen yellow vans in two sizes were alongside with two- and four-horse teams waiting patiently. Men and women took empty wicker trays out and put full ones in through the vans' side doors. A boy and a girl Bren's age passed among the horses, feeding them some kind of treat, probably ensuring their enthusiasm for completing their rounds and returning for another one.

Verjil led Ronnie down the steps and across the alleyway into what might once have been a skating rink or bowling alley or some such but was now a big stable and a storage place for idle bread vans. At least ten were lined up and another was just getting a fresh two-horse team hitched to it.

"That's our ride," said Verjil. "Climb aboard.

As Verjil took the reins and maneuvered the van out into the alley and thence onto a street heading toward the river, he laid the assembly-and-deployment plan out to Ronnie at his side. The bakery operated twenty-seven vans, which began flowing out of the alley at six bells, supplying shops and individual customers across the city and even outside the wall on special order, though the traffic jam at the gates made this impractical most of the time. The point was that the yellow vans were a normal part of the cityscape and that no one would notice if each one, after going out on deliveries, returned with more than empty bread trays. Fighters thus picked up and assembled at the bakery throughout the day before, would, by morning, have plenty of time to rest and eat a simple meal, organize and arm themselves, and receive final instructions.

On the day, the shop would be open as usual for early customers, and the usual early deliveries would be made, but as nine bells approached, several vans would be loaded with fighters—the vans' suspensions rigged to disguise the extra weight—and driven four blocks to the kitchen loading docks at the back of the palace. The main body would stream out of the bakery at a jog at around nine on a yet-to-be-determined signal: as soon as their approach was noticed by guards or workers at the palace, the fighters already at the dock in the parked vans would exit to secure entry through the kitchen into the dining room where the dignitaries would by then be assembled. That's where and when the rebellion would succeed or fail.

"Brilliant," said Ronnie in awe, as Verjil completed his scene-building. "It makes me acutely aware of one thing ..."

"Which is?"

"You and your circle are totally committed. It's obvious that all of your people at the bakery are members—"

"Have been for generations.'

"and that you've all accepted that this is a fight to the death. Others might be able to hide and get home if the attack fails, but not you. You'll be totally exposed. I salute you all, and I'm proud to be in this with you."

Verjil grinned. "So you like the plan so far?"

"Yeah. So tell me the rest—the treasury and the ministries."

"Got your diaper on?" asked Verjil.

"What?"

Verjil gestured forward with his head and there, looming ever taller, was the headquarters of the Ministry for the Suppression of Error—the Black Tower.

"You're not ... "

"Why not? Call it an inoculation against fear, like they did for disease in the old days. By the way, take off your badge."

Looking at the epicenter of so much evil, Ronnie remembered his first day in the city, when Trader Baladur, suspecting the sixteen-year-old village boy had some secret business beyond the great wall, had contrived to put him on foot at the gate to handle his rig's mules. Leading them past armed guards and through the opening, Ronnie had found himself briefly but fully inside the Citadel and looking up the hill to the Palace and the Blessing House beyond it, where resided—until he could rescue her—his beloved Jenna. He'd smiled when he realized what Baladur had done to help him lose his fear of the Citadel, and now he smiled to realize Verjil was doing the same.

"Okay," said Ronnie, putting his badge in his pocket, "what do I need to know?"

"Hey, Chubs," called Verjil to a short and fat but in-charge-looking dock foreman. "Remember me?"

"Whathell you doin' here, this time 'a day?" said the foreman as he came out onto the dock and up to the side of the van. He spoke across Ronnie, ignoring him.

"Tryin' ta catch *you*, maybe. You change shifts on me?"

"Well, I ... Seriously, Verj, whatchu doin' here?"

"Seriously tryin' ta collect my ten dollars on the turtle race, but ... I also need your empties. We're runnin' short."

"Oh. Okay. Well, you know where they are ..."

"And the ten?"

The foreman adopted a sheepish look.

"Look, Verj," he said, "things have been a little—"

"Chubs, Chubs," interrupted Verjil. "Let me help you out here.... You get your guys to load as many empties as will fit, while I show my man the lobby, and we'll call it even."

"The lobby?... You know how much trouble I'll be in if you're caught there?"

"You know how much I want that ten dollars?"

"Okay, okay. Just *go*. But if you're busted, I'm sayin' you went on your own."

"Deal," he said, then to Ronnie, "C'mon."

The two climbed down and headed through roll-up doors as an attendant watched the rig and the foreman gave orders for the bakery's empty bread trays to be gathered and loaded. Behind them, across from the loading dock and beyond a carriage house, the Black Tower's steam-generating plant emitted a narrow plume of coal smoke.

They passed into a broad, plain corridor, lit by wall-mounted lanterns even as sunlight entered through windows at either end.

Directly across the corridor was the large, gated opening of what Verjil had warned him would be a freight elevator, its car big enough to accommodate the van they'd arrived in, less the horses. Turning left and passing a janitor's cart outside a door, they grabbed a dust mop and a push broom and kept walking; other building workers ignored them. As they approached a double door, Verjil made a slight gesture and Ronnie glanced through glass panes to see stairs ascending and descending. A little further on Verjil hesitated at a broad metal door and spoke over his shoulder.

"Look at the floor," he said. "No eye contact unless someone speaks to you."

He turned the knob and stepped through with the slight awkwardness of a minion cowed by his surroundings. Ronnie followed. A few steps in, Verjil stopped and turned back, his broom resting on the floor.

"We'll take one minute here," he said low. "Look over my shoulder as we talk."

They were at the side of a large, granite-floored space, thirty feet tall, decorated, like the service corridor, by lighted wall lamps despite the abundant sunlight streaming through the tinted-glass wall to the left. Men and women carrying cases with handles entered and departed as, beyond the glass, carriages came and went under the eyes of several elaborately uniformed guards. To the right, two men behind a counter waved on or stopped to vet the new arrivals. Most of these then passed into a stairwell and started up, but a few moved to a bank of openings and waited.

"Two passenger elevators are operational now," said Verjil, "plus the freight elevator, but there's not enough steam to run them all at once, and none of them will work if the steam plant is disabled. Only the bottom five or six floors are used, plus the top three."

"Are there really basements, as people say?

"Oh, yeah, several of them. But only the first two are used–for a security detail ... and the detention center."

"Why is that?"

"There's always been a serious taboo about discussing it. It's sure that this building, and many others, once had below-ground access, but not now. As for the why, there'll be plenty of time to discover that, after the revolution.

"Not many guards—none inside."

"It's complacency," said Verjil. "The Ministry's too arrogant to believe it would ever be attacked; it's never happened before.... Your minute's up; let's go."

"One second," said Ronnie, frozen in place. Outside, the guards came to attention as three large government carriages pulled up in caravan and began disgorging black-clad bodyguards wearing short swords. These seemed intent not on anything happening in the lobby but on establishing a human corridor from the middle carriage to the door. Verjil half-turned with his dust mop to watch as the curiosity of others in the lobby gave cover. One of the men behind the counter rushed to evict passengers from a newly arrived elevator car and to hold it. Outside, the middle carriage's steps were extended and a slender figure in a satin-trimmed black robe emerged.

"It's Sula," breathed Ronnie.

"Su—" stammered Verjil. "How do you know?"

"I've seen her, face to face, two years ago."

As Ronnie spoke, three or four guards entered and began shooing gawkers away. One came their way and the two dropped their eyes and moved toward the service corridor door with their broom and mop. As Sula strode through the front door, glancing around, her eyes fell on Ronnie's distinctive cheek and jaw, lingered as he passed out of sight, and looked away with a fleeting sense of recognition.

"Zah's balls, Ronnie!" said Verjil tightly as the loaded van pulled back onto the street. "That woman scares me, and I've never even *seen* her before. How did *you*?"

"I'll have to talk to my superiors before I tell you any more, but look, Verj, I'm completely convinced by what you've already shown me and I'm gonna tell Brown so. I don't need to see the Treasury; you can tell me about it. Let's go right to the next step: drop me at the main gate, give me 'til, say, eight bells tonight, and meet me at a club called Scarface. You know it?"

"I've heard of it ... on Toolmaker Square, right?"

"Right. Wear nice clothes, but not too fancy; sit at the back of the bar, facing the dance floor, and be prepared to spend the night."

"Got it."

"Great. You wanna tell me about the Treasury as we ride?"

"Yeah. Okay, to start with, the Treasury has only one way in or out ..."

"Hello, stranger," shouted Scarface regular Keera over the driving music as she and Jane bracketed Verjil at the bar. "May we sit with you?"

Verjil, a little embarrassed, raised his ringed finger and shouted back, "Sorry, ladies–I'm married."

"Oh, honey," pouted Keera of the wild black hair, leaning and drawing his upper arm to nestle between her ample breasts, "please don't play hard to get. It hurt's our feelings."

"We don't bite," said Jane of the blond ponytail, giving similar treatment to his right arm with her small but confident ones, "unless you ask nice."

"Just let me whisper something in your ear," coaxed Keera. "I promise you'll like it."

"Well, I ... "

Keera's lips brushed his left ear. Her breath was warm and moist as she said, "There's a door behind you. Straight through it is another door to the alley. Somebody's waiting for you in a cab with an appaloosa mare in harness."- She nibbled his ear. "Got it, sugar?"

Verjil's awkward half-smile remained plastered on his face for a moment, then he turned his head slightly and said, "That sounds nice. I'll be looking forward to it." Keera smiled and let him have his arm back as she got up. Jane pinched his right bicep and winked before following her friend back toward the dance floor.

Verjil finished his beer and headed for the alley.

As soon as he exited the club and entered the cab's open door it pulled away, it's driver not even looking at him. In the dark interior Ronnie unshaded a small wall lamp to reveal himself and offered his hand.

"Hope the girls didn't jerk you around too much," he said. "They like to play."

"I felt like a mouse in cat-claws."

"Good," Ronnie chuckled. "I'll pass along the compliment.... Now," he said, handing over a small backpack and a bundle, "take off your clothes and put these on."

Verjil inspected the heavy work clothes and scuffed boots in his lap and began disrobing.

It was middle of the next morning by the time Verjil returned to the bakery. He went in the front door, the sooner to see his wife, and glimpsed a mere two seconds of worry on her face before she looked up from serving a customer and was transformed by the smile on his own. Her brow cleared, ten years fell away, and she uncharacteristically made some remark to her customer that brought a laugh. Soon she and her father were in the storeroom and hearing an amazing story, of a reed-choked riverbank and a gape-mouthed dark tunnel whose throat grew ever smaller until finally delivering the two to a bat-inhabited pre-Cleansing Christian church a mere three blocks from the armory, of Ronnie keeping him distracted during the passage with alternately fascinating and surprising descriptions of the dignitaries he'd seen on the bridge two years earlier, and of a stroll past the open side gate of the armory and the gatehouse occupied by two Citadel Guardsmen, who represented legal control of the weapons by the council of Messengers, and two soldiers, who represented actual control, all of them already bored-looking at nine bells of the morning. Katren and her father were thoughtfully thrilled by the account.

The audience that night at "the boathouse"—actually the hayloft of a westside barn—was less rapt, more annoyed. Denied the details and simply told by the "landlords" of the two assembly points that they had inspected each other's facilities and found them more than satisfactory, Ponies had changed her vote and the others had grumblingly accepted the fait accompli.

Controversy reigned anew, however, when Brown revealed that his young guest of a few weeks earlier knew all the Messengers and even the Sword himself by sight, and when Flame suggested that his inclusion in the palace assault team would ensure that anyone who tried to doff robes and escape the Colonel's eye in the anticipated chaos would be caught. Stars raged about the insult this represented to the brave turncoat, while others repeated the argument that the history of the triumph of freethought over tyranny needed to feature the sons and daughters of generations of painful sacrifice, not an alcoholic convert, however much appreciated.

Hearing this news from Nuyen when he called at her home later, the colonel stormed out in feigned outrage and went to the palace. Sula received his intelligence in the broad, torch-lit marble corridor of the residence wing, accompanied by half a dozen bodyguards, not even deigning to invite him into her private apartment. His report constituted her second disappointment of the night, and it could not be borne. When the colonel had nervously ended it, she mildly turned to regard her other disappointment over the shoulder of another: a new young guard. The incontinent pup, despite being given clear instructions by the more experienced men, had this very night taken his own pleasure of her without permission, and then crowed about it.

"You. Come here," she ordered, and when the young man complied, casually said, "Seize him. Hold him still."

Nearby guards instantly did so, to their recent colleague's dismay.

She reached to the waist of one of these, drew his dagger, and, before the ill-disciplined youngster had even gotten a few hearty screams out, had the bloody instruments of his crime in her hand, showing them to the colonel. Down the corridor, servants and at least one Messenger came out to investigate as the frenzied and disbelieving screams continued, but, seeing it was Sula's show, retreated inside.

"This is how it will begin," she said as the offal dripped on the marble, "if you fail to neutralize the one in the red mask. Understand?"

"Yes, milady."

"Good. You may keep this as a reminder," she said, handing it over and wiping her hand on her lavender lounging robe.

"Thank you, milady. I'll find him."

31 - Watching the Watchers

Thirty-one days out

"Ohfuck!" exclaimed the man to himself just before impact, jerking his eyes away from the oncoming face a fraction too late.

"*Sorry*, sir!" said Ronnie, clutching a leather tool-satchel to his chest with one hand as he reached to steady the man who'd stepped in front of him with the other. "You okay?"

"Yes, I'm–" mumbled the man, keeping his head down. "Yeah. S'cuse me."

The two disengaged and went on their way, the man to continue his aimless wandering about the intersection–two doors east of Owlly's on Woodmaker Street–and Ronnie to return home.

Ronnie returning home? thought the man. How could that be? The boy had never *left* his home and place of business–at least not in the past few hours. According to the first-shift watcher, he'd come out at first light and gone down the street to the lumber yard with a large and empty old screw-top plastic jar and come back with a full one. Since then only customers seemed to have come and gone. Now the man, wandering from his watch-station past a building corner while looking down the street where he *expected* to see his target, had instead crashed *into him* coming from the *opposite* direction. How could that be?

And what to do now? *No way* could he file a report that he'd seen a subject return to a place he'd never left, especially if the subject was someone of importance. *Was* he? –this *kid?*

Rumor said no. Rumor said a detective had flagged him a couple weeks earlier and then had to back off, but not before getting the kid's work-badge number. Then the detective had gotten himself stabbed to death while on another job. Others had spent a good ten minutes mourning their colleague–he of the irritating half-smile–before rifling his workstation for keepsakes and incidentally finding the unfiled report revealing the cabinetmaker's identity and connection to Lady Clare. Recognizing its value at a time of intense interest from on high in anything to do with Clare, the finder had pocketed the report while others were dividing up the agent's allegedly heretic-produced collection of pornography and presented the subject's identification as the product of his own work.

He must have been disappointed in the response, the watcher figured. A small crew of low-level operatives like himself had been assigned to the subject with the simplest of briefs: follow him until he returned to Clare's house, then immediately report this occurrence to a certain constantly manned small office in the palace complex not far up the hill. That was it; no in-depth reports, no vantage point rented or coerced in a nearby building, no multi-agent teams constantly rotating eyes and faces to lessen the chance of the subject spotting anyone. Just three junior guys disguised as homeless and taking shifts as proprietors of the temporarily disused side entrance of a building at the corner, and of the bundles of personal effects too measly even to attract the attention of the real homeless. The watcher also rejected, after a few seconds, the idea of telling his superiors he may have exposed himself and should be replaced. How would *that* look. *No way, man!* Besides, he hadn't really compromised himself–had he?

Ronnie entered the shop without looking back, but he was unsettled by the encounter. The rough-dressed man had looked surprised to see him, as if he'd seen a ghost, which some people still claimed to do even knowing it could get them into trouble with the priests. But it wasn't that—it was the awkwardness with which he'd looked away—embarrassment, almost.

He scanned the shop to see Nel wrapping some fabric swatches for two women he'd assisted before and Suki's head behind the terrace rail as she probably sat nursing her child; the sound of sawing emanated from the back. He greeted the women as he passed up the center aisle to enter the workshop and put his satchel on a worktable. Owlly and Brod glanced up from their work and would have returned to it had Ronnie not held Owlly's eyes a moment longer than necessary as he turned back to the showroom. Brod stopped sawing a table leg held in a vise but resumed as Ronnie gave him a "keep-going" roll of the finger.

Ronnie lifted a furniture cloth from a hook and moved randomly about the shop until Nel got the message and walked the gossiping women to the door. Ronnie held it for them, smiling.

"What's up?" asked Nel as the door closed.

"I want to show you something," said Ronnie. "Let's step back a little."

Ronnie had seen his own abode from the outside enough to know they wouldn't be visible on a sunny day if they stood back from the display window. As Owlly joined them and took up position, Ronnie pointed.

"The bank on the opposite corner?" he prompted.

"Yeah?"

"Back from the corner of the building, almost out of sight—a guy sitting in the doorway?"

Just then Brod stepped from the shop, saw in hand. "Everything all right?" he asked. Above him, his wife stood with her child in arms.

"Probably," said Ronnie. "Can you give us some random carpentry noises for a few minutes, brother?"

"Okay," said Brod, disappearing.

"The guy in the doorway?" Ronnie repeated.

"Yeah?" Owlly acknowledged. "What about him?"

Ronnie described the encounter, then, "It felt like he recognized me, but tried to hide it. And like he was very surprised to see me—at least see me corning from that direction."

"Ah ...,' murmured Nel, "I get it."

"Get what?" asked her husband.

"Ronnie left by the tunnel this morning. A watcher would have expected him to still be here, but now he shows up corning from the other direction. Surprise!"

Owlly looked out the window and nodded slightly. In his doorway, the man sat on the low landing, his legs akimbo across two steps, a begging-bowl on the pavement near his foot. As they watched, he leaned back against the closed door, his eyes half closed but seemingly looking down the street toward them. Once, when a low carriage stopped at the corner and blocked his view, he got up and wandered for a moment, then sat back down.

"I think that door's normally in use during the day," observed Ronnie, and all were quiet for a while.

"Could you be wrong, Ronnie?" asked Nel, after twice watching the man scoop donations out of his bowl and put them in his pocket.

"Sure, but—"

"*Wait,*" said Owlly, staring intently down Woodmaker Street through traffic. There, coming toward them, was the bane of all no-bribe-paying, doorway-squatting, lowlife, so-called rough sleepers—the uniformed beat cop. His cross-draw short sword was sheathed, but his long truncheon was deployed, and he slapped it against his boot with each step. At the bank's main entrance he paused and looked in proprietorially but did not mount the steps.

As he approached the curb the officer glanced right toward the pedestrian gate, then left, and stopped, looking over his shoulder. He remained that way so long that he must have been shocked into immobility at the effrontery of the beggar, who had chosen to drop his head and feign invisibility instead of quickly gathering his belongings and fleeing the scene. When the cop finally turned and presented his back to the three observers, he was in full bully mode. His shoulders hunched and his back grew wider and he loomed over the unfortunate beggar, booted feet planted wide before him and truncheon held low in both hand across his body. But the scene didn't play out as usual.

Only someone staring at the cop's back as intently as Ronnie, Nel, and Owlly were doing could have understood what happened next. In an instant, the man shrank to his normal size and beyond, his head jerked back an inch as if he'd received a mild slap, and he took a small step back. He lowered his weapon behind his leg and brought his feet together momentarily as if corning to attention, then casually stepped away south and out of sight. The beggar leaned his head back against the door and resumed his half-lidded vigilance.

"Mother?" said Owlly mildly.

"Yes, dear?"

"I think we should break out the new biscuits, just in case."

Wordlessly, Nel made her way through the displayed furniture and soon returned. She held out her hand to reveal what looked like seven large beans, which in fact were the cured stomachs of tiny birds, tied off and resin-sealed to secure the poison within.

Owlly took one in his fingers and held it up. "You understand, Ronnie," he said low, "this is just a precaution. If you bite down by accident, spit it out and wipe inside your mouth with a cloth–quickly. He tucked the "biscuit" into his cheek then watched as Ronnie and Nel did the same.

On the balcony, Suki's baby, perhaps suddenly held too tightly by her mother, began to cry.

Briefly explained the situation, Brod and Suki and Jak did what was expected of any adult Freethinker. Jak took on the added responsibility of keeping a dose of poison for Tofer, tucked into his other cheek.

For the sake of the watcher, the day had to go on as usual. Customers came and went, carpentry noises emanated from the workshop, Jak and Brod and Owlly separately ran errands, and in late afternoon Brod and Ronnie loaded a fine new conference table into the wagon–upside down and sticking out past the gate–while Jak went to the livery stable for Daisy. When Ronnie drove away alone to deliver the table to the tax office near the Error Ministry and the beggar was observed to follow, they learned two things: one, Ronnie was his one-and-only target, and two, he was himself working alone—otherwise a fresh face that Ronnie didn't know would have tailed him.

The rebellion couldn't be postponed just because someone was under suspicion, and Ronnie's errand had had to serve yet another purpose—to confuse any watchers during the reactivation of Tofer.

"Think about it, Dad," Ronnie had said, practicing to speak naturally with a foreign object in his mouth. "That day at Checkers's, the Error agents told the crowd the barber had killed his whole family, when they knew they were missing the corpse of a 14-year-old boy. Why? I'd say because they didn't want to seem less than perfect—to have left a loose end. And if they were going to maintain that fiction, they couldn't contradict it with a wanted poster or a bulletin to the city police. That means the city police may not even be looking for Tofer. He may be as safe out there as me—as of today, I mean. Besides, what's the alternative? Today's signal from Stars was posted after the noon bell, so it requests the messenger no later than tomorrow morning. We need Tofer before that, and the tunnel's ready for him.

Owlly couldn't argue with that. Inspecting Tofer and Jak's work that morning, he'd found the tunnel enlarged, carpeted with blankets, and with an exit camouflaged by a thick bush transplanted from the side of the wall that loomed over the back yard. Ronnie had made a successful daytime test of it, and it was as ready as it was going to be.

"Okay, son," said Owlly, "but talk to him carefully. Make sure he's ready."

When Tofer had been told he was needed again, he'd been so excited at the prospect of resuming his rounds that he'd wet his pants. Once he'd been cleaned up and Owlly had assured himself that he was up to the task and understood some new protocols, he was off, with Owlly himself plugging the hole behind him.

In the meantime, Ronnie was on *his* rounds, delivering the heavy table and installing it in a small conference room with the help of the tax office's workers, parking to stroll with his toolbox past a sidewalk cafe where some of his patrons took tea–in the hope of garnering some silver to top up the rebellion's coffers while further confusing the watcher–and unhitching his mare so she could enjoy a change of diet at the Traders' Meadow. There he wandered politely among the vans–which weren't supposed to be open for business inside the Citadel–standing at a respectful distance from the families' mobile homes unless invited closer, introducing himself and talking about the state of the roads and weather and the nature of life at the frontiers of Zahdom. He desperately wanted to ask about Baladur and Rae and Chatter but knew that might compromise them, since a watcher might come after him and demand to know what he'd talked about.

After managing to buy a collection of antique hinges tied together with string, Ronnie made a noise and called the mare by name and she raised her head, but then decided to have just a few more bites of grass, so he maneuvered among droppings to retrieve her and hitch her up again. Heading for home, he gazed up the hill and wondered how Tofer was doing on his rounds.

In the Citadel's industrial northwestern quadrant, the Colonel sat sour-faced on a blanket in bushes from which he'd earlier driven a couple of drunks, his saddled horse left with his man around the corner. He'd never done anything so undignified in his adult life, but the image of his own genitalia being shown to the next retainer who disappointed Sula–while he bled to death unattended in a corner as the young guard had been left to do–kept him focused on his task. That task, now that he'd gotten Nuyen to call for the messenger and for a committee meeting, was to spot that messenger among all the customers entering her establishment and follow him to learn his identity.

Nuyen was maddening, seemingly enamored of him but still not letting her guard down. He attributed her self-discipline to a life-lesson hard-learned. From what he'd been able to gather, she'd married for love outside her Freethinker community and later suffered as her husband refused to let her educate their children and then abused her with impunity, the threat of revealing her secret always implicit. When he sought to divorce her and take the children and the lighting company they'd built together—an incidentally to expose her circle—she'd enlisted the help of members of that circle to bludgeon him to death in an apparent robbery while she was in a public place, securing the circle and the company even as she let her husband's family have the already ruined children and adopted a solitary and celebrate lifestyle herself. While shunned by some gentle "readers" as a ruthless killer after that, it had later been this very quality that had put her on the military committee and now accounted for her infuriating adherence to protocol, which kept him at a distance when she was expecting secret contact.

She *had* let one musing thought escape her lips, though, and that had sent him to hide in the bushes.

"Same person, I think," she'd said, when they'd briefly spoken about sending for the messenger to set up a meeting that both he and the young man in the red mask could attend. Red Mask had spoken with "a droning voice, artificially deep," she'd said, but he'd been tall and well-built like the dark-haired new messenger, from whom she'd so far heard only a few words. Otherwise, there wasn't much to identify him.

The colonel sighed deeply, remembering the days when he'd had myriad nameless non-coms and junior officers to handle such mundane chores. For now he had to make do with the ex-drinking-buddy sergeant who tended the horses around the corner, but it wouldn't be long before he had a couple of stars on the shoulder boards of an elegant new uniform and an adjutant to carry out his discreetly murmured orders.

He just had to make sure that the precocious Red Mask, who now claimed to be able to identify all the messengers including the Sword, did not participate in the palace attack, and that he, the mature man of destiny, not only participate in it, but lead it.

The afternoon wore on. Servants and homemakers came and went, often entering empty-handed or with empty jugs and exiting burdened with bundles of candles and full jugs of lamp oil. In mid-afternoon a young teenager came down the sidewalk with a peculiar stiff gait and went in empty-handed and came out the same way, but he was too young and slender to be the one. Then, not ten minutes later, a dark-haired, robust young man parked a taxicab nearby and ambled over to the door. He didn't have the presence of a military genius, the colonel mused, but he did fit the physical description, and when he came out empty-handed and Nuyen followed within seconds to head for her house next door, the identity was confirmed; surely she wouldn't have left her shop if she hadn't already met the messenger and conveyed her request for a meet.

As soon as the cabbie pulled away and established a direction, the colonel hurried around the corner and mounted his horse to follow, leaving the sergeant to catch up. When he brought the cab into sight, he slowed down.

The cabbie picked up and delivered fare after fare, and the colonel thought how convenient it was for the messenger to work as a cabbie, a profession where one was often legitimately employed to convey messages. Plus, any of the fares could have been a Freethinker agent. If he'd been a dozen agile trackers instead of one not-so-agile one, he'd have followed and documented each passenger, but Sula insisted he continue to conduct himself like the shunned loner he was supposed to be instead of the chief of some elaborate official operation. So be it. For now he would follow the messenger into his lair and stand point over it for Sula's goons, and his genitals would be saved.

Trouble was, this guy didn't seem to be such a big deal. The colonel knew Sula now feared that Red Mask was some sort of palace insider, or someone in the social circle of one or more of the Messengers—in other words, someone who couldn't be tolerated to remain alive—but when in late afternoon the cabbie stopped taking all fares except those headed toward the Cheapside Gate in the northwest, and when he surrendered his rig at a ramshackle depot, and when he was met in the street by a pregnant wife and two clinging youngsters and led laughing down an alley to a low-roofed hovel, he didn't seem like anyone to be feared. But didn't that speak to the special skill that Freethinkers had been honing for generations? – the ability to hide in plain sight?

What now? If he informed Sula and she had the cabbie arrested, he'd probably be consigned to the Error inquisitors. As a field officer he'd never attended a Black Tower torture session, as some did for entertainment, but he'd heard the stories. Suspected heretics were often required to watch their family members brutalized and killed before being tortured themselves–sometimes flayed alive–all while being asked to read some document or other. Many turned out to be so fanatically dedicated to their creed that they died insisting they didn't know how to read.

And what if he was wrong? The thought made the colonel's balls seek refuge inside his body. Sula wouldn't like having her time wasted.

At the head of the alley of hovels the colonel shifted in his saddle and made a decision. Two nights hence, while he and Red Mask were both at the meeting, the sergeant would pay a drunken visit to the hovel on some pretext. If the cabbie was at home, it would prove he wasn't Red Mask, even if he could still be the messenger. That way, Sula couldn't hold him responsible for misleading her.

The colonel gave his instructions, made sure the sergeant fixed the right alley and the right door in his mind, and reined his horse for Nuyen's, to see if he could learn anything new at her supper table or in her bed.

In Tofer's tunnel Ronnie lay comfortably on his stomach with his chin propped on his hands, looking out through leaves. Before him was the alley between two rows of single-story businesses, with four trash bins on one side and three on the other. At the end of the alley pedestrians hurried by, increasing as the sun dipped below the horizon, dwindling quickly as the light faded and streetlights began to be lit.

Still no Tofer, but it wasn't quite time, Ronnie assured himself. After a few more minutes he rolled on his side and spoke behind.

"Jak," he said quietly, and waited.

"I'm here," said Jak after a few seconds. "Anything?"

"Not yet. Still a little early. Time to close the curtain, though."

"Got it," said Jak, and Ronnie knew a dark cloth was being draped over the library-side opening to insure no candlelight escaped.

No streetlamp directly lighted the alley, but nearby ones kept the street dimly visible even as night fell. Despite himself, Ronnie grew tense as the minutes passed and all he could discern was cross-traffic.

Had Tofer really understood his instructions? He was supposed to wait for nightfall to enter the dark alley, so that anyone following him might reasonably conclude he'd gone into one of the seven doors, instead of through a wall forty feet tall and sometimes as wide at its base. But had he really understood all that? Ronnie knew he wasn't stupid, and that he was courageous, but his mind was a mystery, and one couldn't be sure about its processes.

A silhouette appeared against the faint light of the street, not posed in stillness but marching stiffly. It came closer, then took a position ten paces away against the building past the last trash bin and looked back up the alley. Ronnie watched the alley entrance as well. One minute, two.

"Ready, Tof?" he murmured around the poison packets in his mouth.

"Yeah."

"C'mon," he said. "Headfirst and keep going." Then he retreated into a wide spot the boys had created. Tofer was in and past him in a flash. Ronnie regained the opening, made sure the camouflage still looked right, and turned to crawl back down.

"All good, Tof?" he said once he'd emerged, removing one of the packets from his cheek and passing it to Jak.

"Yeah, all good," deadpanned Tofer, in his version of high spirits.

All good, but not all complete: Candystripe resided *outside* the wall on the north river road, and it was too early to tell if Tofer could safely pass Citadel gate security to get to him, so he'd go by bus in the morning. In the meantime, the boys joined the others for a congenial supper, followed as usual by an airing of concerns that, even within the family, adhered to security protocols. The boys washed up and Ronnie took a solitary turn about the darkened showroom. Standing back from the window as before, he studied the beggars' doorway station and other places from which a watcher might have a good view of the shop, but saw no one suspicious among the few dimly lighted pedestrians.

Owlly had said at the table that at sundown the watcher had gathered his bundles with an air of someone getting off work. He hadn't seemed to hand off to anyone else–just gathered his things and, without another look at the shop, headed for Woodmaker Gate and perhaps a waiting official vehicle or taxi to take him to his own hearth and supper, or more likely to his cot and institutional meatloaf.

A question posed itself as Ronnie was about to turn to his own bed: If the watcher only watched during the hours his subject could legally be within the Citadel, which of the subject's Citadel-only activities was he looking at, or waiting for?

32 - Origin Myth

Twenty-nine days out

As Ronnie pulled on the skiff's oars, he watched the river's dim western bank for other departing boats. Owlly sat sideways in the stern and looked upriver for traffic. Under a partly cloudy night sky, they could see little of the riverbanks themselves but kept orientation by the small lighthouse near the ferry landing where they'd offloaded their small craft and camouflage fishing gear, by the faint lights of homes and businesses on both sides of the river, and by the streetlights of the city on a hill a few miles downriver. Occasionally Ronnie stopped rowing and the two listened for oarsplash over the soft murmur of the river.

For this special occasion they were headed to "the bootmaker's," the military committee's least-used and therefore most-secure meeting place, an anonymous shack in an anonymous field on an anonymous farm somewhere on the several miles of river between the confluence of the Muak and Husson rivers and the-bridge, reachable by boat in the slow current of late summer from any point within two miles of the Muak ferry crossing.

The special occasion was the second attendance by a non-member ever, and the first attendance by a former member of the enemy camp. The purpose was to finally decide on command of the force being assembled to attack the palace and seize the Messengers. When Owlly had met with the committee the previous night and then reported that Red Mask was required for the following night, and that the Colonel would be in attendance, too—unmasked—Ronnie was surprised, but not concerned about being able to slip the watcher to make the meeting safely. Just the day before, he'd learned through a contact at the bank that the beggar had been on station only a couple of days and then confirmed he was his only target when he lured him away from his post—so Tofer could get to the bus stop unobserved—by going to the market with Jak and then sending Jak into the public restroom to check for signals. Not only had the watcher been observed to follow the pair down Woodmaker Street to the square, but he also remained fastened on Ronnie when Jak left him for a few minutes. The solution was therefore obvious: leave home and return by the tunnel unobserved, even if that meant he'd have to wait until sunrise after the committee meeting in order to pass the gate security and get back to the tunnel.

As for the committee's reasons for commanding his presence, that wasn't so obvious, and Owlly was unforthcoming, so he just tried to ready himself for any questions he might be asked regarding preparations for the attack on the armory, continuing to order his thoughts even as he pulled closer to the eastern bank of the river.

"Just drift awhile now, son," murmured Owlly. "Stay close, but don't get tangled."

Owlly commenced to stare in the direction of the city, and Ronnie surmised he was waiting to see a particular alignment of streetlights going up the hill beyond the wall.

"Get ready," he said, now turning to look for something else on the near bank. "Get ready ... Okay. Pull hard! Don't look—I'll guide you."

Ronnie felt himself skirting a wooded bank but kept his eyes on Owlly's form.

"Bear to port ... mudflat coming up ... contact!"

△ △ △

They'd masked up and arrived first, as befitted the "manager-chairman" of the committee. Then as they puttered about the shack by lamplight, making sure all was in order and that the farmer had left hot water for tea on the small stove and honey and milk on the rough sideboard, the others followed, some by water, others by the east river road. Ronnie offered each a steaming earthenware mug then stood aside as the principals engaged in unrevealing small talk. They were eight in all: Owlly as "Brown," the committee's agreed leader; Katren as "Flame," who'd replaced her honorably dead kinsman "Checkers;" Bil Rigwasher as "Candystripe;" the former prostitute and now wedding and party planner Rosa as "Ponies;" Bundy the printer as "Silver;" Nuyen the candlemaker as "Stars;" Ronnie himself as "Red;" and finally "The Colonel," who by consensus was never called anything else.

When Nuyen entered with the colonel and Ronnie served him a mug of tea, the hackles went up on the back of his neck. He was momentarily disconcerted, sure he was reacting not to an inner danger-sensor but to the man's uncovered face and appraising eyes and the knowledge that, no matter how many Freethinkers he'd saved toward the end, he'd surely killed many to become a colonel in the army of Zah. Nevertheless, he'd try to respect the man's eventual change of heart and his commitment to righting the wrongs he'd committed.

"Colonel," said Owlly as Brown, motioning the visitor to a chair next to his own. "Red, on my other side, please.... Everybody?" All sat down in the mismatched chairs with their mugs and gave their attention to the chairman.

"Call to order," said Brown. "First order of business: Colonel, I want to thank you on behalf of the committee members for your contributions thus far, and for being here tonight." The colonel nodded. "Red, thank you for coming as well." another nod, then back to the other man in his distinctive owlish way. "Colonel, I will start by telling you that we try to keep these meetings short, for obvious reasons, and that we mean no disrespect by our haste." He waited for another nod. "Also, I want to make sure you understand you're unmasked because we all had to become familiar with your history months ago, whereas *we* are meant to be unknown even to each other." Another nod.

"Now, with the members' permission, I'll summarize our situation and the reason we're meeting." Nods all around. "Very well ..."

Brown took a breath. "In less than a month's time, we and a few hundred of our brethren are going to overthrow the tyranny of Zahism and replace it with freedom of conscience–and all that follows from that. To accomplish this, we're going to perform a coup on the main elements of Zahist power while the army and part of the Guard are away on a pogrom. The attackers will gather at two main locations on the night before the attack. At about nine bells the next morning one group will attack the armory and another the Palace, the Error Ministry, the Guard's Tower, and the Treasury. Once the armory attackers arm themselves and load whatever they can, they'll arm and fight with the second group until all objectives are secure. While all this is going on, anti-government elements within the populace will be provoked to sow chaos–to prevent government forces from organizing a counterattack and to keep the army and Guard out of the city while certain political events are taking place, which we don't need to go into tonight.

"Now, we've come to an impasse regarding battle commanders," he continued. "I'm confident the committee will approve a man I've recommended for the armory, but we're not close to unanimity on command of the palace group, and we need to decide tonight. Some favor *you*, Colonel, and others favor a man in Flame's circle who has been instrumental in making arrangements for the palace attack thus far. Last night we selected Candystripe to articulate the case for that man, and Stars to advance yours. Both speakers may engage you directly, and we'll have open discussion after.... Now, do I have everyone's permission to start with Candy?" All nodded. "Candy, you have the floor."

Tall, lanky Bil Rigwasher leaned forward on his forearms with his big, bony hands clasped and looked into the colonel's face. What he saw was a man in his forties, tall and erect but with a slight paunch, dark hair going grey, handsome in a way recently corrupted by alcohol but nevertheless possessed of a commanding presence, and inscrutable.

"Colonel," he said, "before I make my case, I'd like to know how well educated you are, especially about political theory and about history–pre-Cleansing history. I mean, obviously you had to be able to read and write to perform your duties, but were you ever able to study such matters privately?"

"Well, certain books came into my hands ..."

"For instance, if I mention Napoleon?"

The colonel brightened. "Yes, of course. The great general."

"And Plato?"

"I don't ..."

"What about Romulus? King David? Mandela? Churchill? John Locke? Lincoln? Hitler? Jeffer–"

"Hitler!" said the colonel, grasping, "and the one before ..."

"Lincoln?"

"No! Church ..."

"Churchill?"

"Yes. They fought each other in a big war."

"Do you know what justification Hitler gave his people for going to war? How he motivated them?"

"Well ... no, I don't recall."

"All right. I ask these things not to embarrass you, but to gauge your familiarity with ideas with names like 'foundation myth' or 'origin myth', and the idea that a successful, long-lasting political state has to be based on a compelling story about how and why and by whom it was founded."

Candystripe broadened his audience to all present. "Once the first generations are gone, it becomes easier to modify or perfect or falsify the story, and then we can't be sure who did what or if things happened at all, so we call it *myth.* If the myth is embarrassing or shameful, the people will not cohere around it and the state will fail. If it inspires pride and loyalty, it will survive, at least until a more powerful state—or one with a more compelling mythology—replaces it. The origin myth is such an important element in the creation and survival of the state that in the writings of the philosopher Plato, a long time ago, it's referred to as the 'Noble Lie,' and he defended political leaders making up whatever origin story they needed to fit the accepted facts and win the people's allegiance." He paused to take a sip of tea.

"The Priesthood's foundation or origin myth," he continued, "is that a god called Zah brought destruction upon humanity for its arrogance in seeking to understand him or commune with him, then gave it one last chance: obey or die. The god gave all power to one man and his descendants and then it was *they* who had to be obeyed, and through them he gave a set of instructions about how to live, including how to spread the lineage of the first holder of the god's power—the Chaplin—so everyone could aspire to be connected by blood or marriage to the first family, the essential first step to achieving social position and wealth.

"Now, we don't know for sure that *any* of the stories about the Chaplin are true, but that's a powerful story—and it *worked.* Not because it was inspirational, necessarily, but because it imposed order in a time of chaos—farmers could farm, traders could trade, and so on. But it always relied upon murder, and that reliance can only grow in future. This world once had *nine billion people* in it, maybe thousands of times more than now, and it's growing again, faster than the priesthood will be able to keep up with. But it will try, even if it has to bring back the old weapons and kill millions to keep the world in the state of ignorance in which it thrives.

"But things are about to change. The Priesthood of ZAH is about to be overthrown by a collection of seemingly ordinary people—tradespeople and businesspeople, mostly. But these people are not ordinary at all. They're the progeny and the beneficiaries of generations of sacrifice, who've fled pogrom after pogrom and seen their friends and loved ones slaughtered time and time again, all to preserve *knowledge* and the ideal of *freedom of conscience.* These are the people and the noble ends upon which the new order must be seen to be founded, and every one of the leading characters in the founding drama must have impeccable credentials, meaning not only that they be brave and fight well and be of good character, but that they embody the sacrifices of the past century. This will give us a foundation story that we don't have to fabricate or embellish, and it'll only grow in power as the people come to understand what we've preserved for them.

"Now, no one doubts, Colonel, that you bring to the fight something we desperately need: military expertise and experience. But your presence, if too prominent, also confuses the history were trying to write. Some will take it as a sign that the new order is just a variation on an old theme, not a clean break with the past. So I want to urge you, Colonel, to withdraw your candidacy for command of the Palace group, and to accept the role of adviser to one who not only has superior leadership skills but who better represents, unambiguously, Freethinker ideals.

"One last thing, sir. I'm not suggesting you be erased from history—truth be told, we'd probably all like to be regarded as heroes one day—but I do suggest that history will treat you more kindly if you display self-effacing modesty right now. Step to the side, let the old-line Freethinkers take center stage, and wait for your role to be discovered and honored as it deserves."

Candystripe leaned back, put his big hands in his lap, and nodded to Brown. Others looked like they would speak but held their tongues as the chairman raised a hand.

"Hold your comments, please. Stars? Your response?" Nuyen composed herself: taking a sip of lukewarm tea, placing her splay-fingered hands on the tabletop, and leaning forward slightly. But before she could utter a word she was stopped by the colonel's hand on her forearm.

"May I, ma'am?" he asked.

She looked askance at him for several seconds. "Are you sure?"

"Yes."

She looked to the chairman. "I yield to the colonel to respond."

Brown rotated his owl head around. "Any objection?" he asked, then, "Go ahead, Colonel."

The colonel scanned the disembodied eyes fixed on him and came to rest on the pair framed by the snug, diagonally striped hood.

"Sir, that was one of the most amazing things I've ever heard," he began. "Thank you for making so clear to me how important it is to the Freethinker community to effect the overthrow of the Priesthood of ZAH with *propriety*." Candystripe nodded, a little uncertainly.

"So important is it, in fact," he continued, "that you've wasted a century, and countless lives, imagining how to do it with propriety instead of actually *doing it!* So my response to you, sir, is ... *bullshit!*

The little room erupted in cacophony. Chairs scraped and toppled, fists slammed the table, the hanging lamp swayed after a thrusting head hit it.

"Bullshit? –" echoed Silver in incredulous, rising outrage.

"Colonel, those 'countless lives' must be–" began Flame.

"Listen, you! My grandfather died trying to–" blurted Ponies.

"Colonel, I don't think–" cautioned Stars, half standing with one restraining hand on his shoulder and the other warding off attack.

"Well–" was all Candystripe could get out.

"Order! Let's have order!" demanded Brown, coming to his feet and rapping a knuckle.

As the din grew and then began to subside, only the colonel and Red remained calm, looking at each other. The colonel knew his sergeant must by then be on his way to the cabbie's door in Cheapside, drunkenly swinging a lantern and calling out a woman's name, but he already knew he would find the young man at home. *That one* kept his various parts in constant motion and had, he was pretty sure, brown eyes. This one had dark eyelashes but his eyes were blue, and he sat with an air of calm self-possession.

Ronnie, for his part, was perversely amused. The colonel had gotten an even bigger reaction out of this conservative group than he had with his own first-visit talk of lakes of blood and piles of severed heads.

"Order," Owlly said again, less urgently. "Everybody, sit down. Please."

Eventually all were seated again. Some sulked. Others glared.

"Colonel," said the chairman, "I assume you have more to say?"

"I do, yes. Thank you." He looked to Candystripe. "I speak from frustration, sir. In truth, I understand and honor everything you said, but it represents an *ideal,* not the *reality* facing us. The fact is that such niceties will be meaningless if we don't *win.* If we don't win, we may be so thoroughly annihilated that there aren't even any fugitives to carry the story of our heroism into the woods for future generations. If we don't *win,* then that century of sacrifice you talk about will be for *nothing.* Even *I* know that Napoleon couldn't have spread his legal system if he didn't *win* first.

"Right now you need a *killer*—one who's experienced at inspiring and leading others to kill. When the attack starts, there can't be the slightest hesitation. The commotion in the kitchen will alert the Citadel Guards on duty as well as the personal bodyguards of the dignitaries. If we don't overwhelm them all in a matter of seconds, we'll fail. We've got to burst out of the kitchen and drive right through to the exits and secure them. Then we turn back, while our people are still coming in, and kill every bodyguard and Guardsman and anybody else who doesn't immediately yield. I can lead our people through that. *Then,* when it's *over,* and we have the Messengers and the others in *custody,* *then* we can start massaging the story for the history books. I don't have to be in them *at all;* I just want to crush the Priesthood—and atone for the wrongs I've done in its name."

After a few seconds the committee members began to look one to another. Finally, Ponies made a gesture to the chairman.

"Colonel, are you finished for now?" asked Brown.

"Yes."

"Go ahead, Ponies."

"Stars!" she began, startling the woman who'd expected questions to be directed to the colonel. "What have you shared with the colonel about our plans for the palace?"

"Well, I ...," stuttered Stars defensively.

"Because some of his words sound a lot like words uttered once before in this committee."

"Well, as I say ... I mean ... of course, he's had to be given certain ..."

Ponies, the one-time cold-hearted prostitute, shook her head at the other woman's infatuation-induced indiscretion.

"Let's move on," said the chairman. "Flame, you had something?"

"I'm a recent arrival here. As I understand it, Colonel, your unique contribution has been to help us understand the mood of the army, its psychology, what will motivate its commanders to stop its return to the city and negotiate.... What makes you think you're also uniquely qualified to lead the Palace attack?"

"Look, madam," said the colonel as if to a thick-headed child, pretending he didn't already know about Red Mask's claim to know the Messengers, "I've *been* in that very *room*–for awards ceremonies–I *know* the layout, I've *seen* the Messengers, *with my own eyes.* I won't be fumbling around like someone at a party he wasn't invited to."

"Neither will the other proposed commander." Flame looked to the others, and to Brown. "May I?" she inquired of the group.

Brown looked around. "Without identification?" The others nodded. "Go ahead."

"There are other people here tonight who've been in those rooms," said Flame, referring to herself and to Rosa, who'd planned two weddings there. "That's why your information is merely cumulative concerning the target venue. And as far as being able to lead the attack, I suggest that the man I propose has the advantage there because the fighters are already loyal to him and accustomed to him. Lastly, you're not the only one who can identify the Messengers. So even if you elect to stay behind and help from the rear, we'll still be covered there."

The colonel seethed. This woman wasn't just challenging his fitness to command the attack, she was trying to demote him to headquarters-bound flunky! And getting nods from the others! After all the trouble he'd gone to!

First, by selectively sparing elements of three different Freethinker communities and ensuring that they'd make it to safety in the Citadel to tell the tale, he'd created a legend for himself as their selfless savior. Then he'd allowed himself to be humiliated, robbed of his family, and driven from the army. Then he'd planted himself to be saved from a drunkard's death and nursed back to health and given purpose by the admiring and soon love-struck Nuyen. Then he'd obtained Sula's leave to familiarize himself with the banqueting wing of the palace. Then, when these steps failed to add up to being offered command of the Palace attack over the objections of the respected Checkers, he'd killed Checkers, or rather forced him to kill himself. But now this new woman was making herself as big an obstacle as Checkers had. It was infuriating!

With all eyes on him, the colonel desperately cast about for a way to leave the meeting with some prize–any prize–to assuage Sula's deadly impatience.

"Ma'am, I am a soldier in this army," he said in a chastened tone. "I will do whatever is asked of me. I'm not going to sulk if I don't get my way. But if you're going to send me to the rear, at least let me help vet the people you're putting in my place. For instance, on the descriptions of the Messengers–if I could hear them, I could confirm their accuracy for you."

That generated a lot of looking from eyehole to eyehole. "It's not a bad idea," advanced Silver.

"Any objection?" asked Brown, and when there was none, he lowered his eyes and asked, "If any of you able to identify the Messengers is prepared to accommodate, speak out."

"I'll do it," said Ronnie in his Red Mask voice.

"Carry on."

Red scooted to the edge of his chair, looked down at the tabletop for a few seconds, then raised his head and spoke.

"There was a ceremonial occasion—outdoors. I stood about forty feet away. A string of VIPs arrived in carriages. Starting with Grotius, people in the crowd said their names and exchanged gossip about them...." He paused, said "Excuse me," and moved to place his elbows on the table and his face in his hands, covering his eyes.

"The first Messenger was ..."

And so began a remarkable few minutes that felt like it could have been stretched to hours, if not purposely abbreviated. Only Owlly and his circle had ever seen this feat of recall before and all were silent as Red's words streamed out in a monotone with barely a pause for breath. His descriptions conjured not just the physical but the emotional aspect of each Messenger—his or her state of mind, as it were, manifested in a way of moving or looking, how the Messenger treated or was treated by companions, retainers, and the crowd. Each description was frustratingly short, for the occasion, but so vivid that there was no room for doubt that it was accurate. When it was over, Red raised his head and looked around.

"Is that enough for now?" he asked.

All eyes moved to the colonel, who, despite himself, was moved to admiration. He struggled to remember his task.

"You mentioned Grotius, but didn't describe him," he said to Red. "Was he alone in his carriage?"

"No, a young man was with him, but walked as Grotius was carried in a palanquin."

"And the young man? What was striking about him?"

"He was unusually good-looking, but I think you're asking about the diamond."

"The diamond?" asked Flame as the colonel nodded.

"He wore a diamond on a chain around his neck," said Red, demonstrating with the end of his thumb. "That big."

The colonel nodded again. "At the bridge, two years ago, for the departure of the *Wind of ZAH*."

"Yes," said Red.

The colonel looked around and to the chairman. "I was there, too, and can confirm everything he says," he said, leaving out that he was at the back of the crowd, present on the bridge with his wife only because she'd arranged an invitation through one of her lovers, and that he knew about the thumb-size diamond only because people in the crowd talked about it.

"So," he continued, adopting an air of chagrin, "however much I want to be in the front of the fight, it appears I may not be as indispensable to it as I thought. Therefore, I await your instructions."

There it was. Nothing more to be said. The chairman looked around for further comments or questions, but there were none. His eyes came to rest on Red, who, after a moment, gave a tiny shake of the head.

"If the committee members require," said Brown finally, "we can have the colonel and Red wait outside while we discuss this further, but let me state a position and see if we have consensus.

"Time is short," he said, "and many people are established in their roles and that applies to Red here, as you all know. He's been instrumental in planning and preparing for the armory operation and shouldn't be moved if it can be helped, in my opinion.... Now, if the colonel will accept the role of field adviser to the commander proposed by Flame, and if Flame feels herself in a position to decide without further consultation with her candidate, we can vote now. First of all, Colonel, would you accept such a role?"

"I would."

"Then Flame, it'll be most efficient if we know your position first: send them out so we can talk more, reject any combat role for the colonel and transfer Red to identify the Messengers, or approve the arrangement I just described, subject to an interview with both commanders tomorrow.

All eyes went to Flame, whose intense brown eyes showed the seriousness with which she took her responsibility. She briefly thought of her friend, the martyr Balz, of what he would have done, and hoped her decision would bring credit to his memory. She raised her hand.

"Approve," she said.

"All in favor?" said the chairman. He waited until four more hands were in the air, then raised his own. "Passed unanimously. Thank you, Colonel; thank you Red. Any further *urgent* business? None? Good. Meet again tomorrow as arranged. This meeting is–" he rapped a knuckle on the table, "adjourned."

The committee members dispersed at five-minute intervals. In the rowboat carrying Nuyen and the colonel back to a spot on the west bank where a carriage waited, silence reigned. Nuyen was subdued by her failure to get her protege appointed to lead the Palace attack, but the colonel was secretly elated. He'd kept himself in a position to influence the execution of the attack, he'd assured that he was the only one on the Palace team who could identify the Messengers, and, in a most gratifying twist, he had learned that the precocious Red Mask was a member of the Citadel elite *and* found a way to identify him. After all, how many tall, dark-haired, blue-eyed, late-teen guests could there have been on the bridge that day, "close enough to touch" the Sword himself?

Where was the VIP guest list? he wondered.

33 - Mining for Gold

Twenty-six days out

Rebellion was expensive, even such as this, where obvious changes of routine were to be avoided. Families still needed to eat while taking time for training and secret meetings. They still needed to buy common items that could be used as weapons: axes, long knives, hoes for bending and modifying into lances, bows and always more arrows, the purchases spread out over many weeks. And, perhaps most expensively, cash had to be accumulated for potential use on the day, to motivate town troublemakers or bribe enemy commanders.

Ronnie's contributions became more and more important just as his time to generate income became scarcer. The payment from Lady Clare in a few days would help, but he needed more. When he saw a familiar Error Ministry messenger come through the shop door, he sensed his chance for a big payday.

Lady Rosamund had not summoned him in nearly a month, busy, presumably, with helping to plan the systematic robbery and torture-execution of anyone not in favor with the Priesthood who could plausibly be accused of heresy during the coming operation. Now she had an hour and wanted him. He listened to the verbatim, droned-out message, looked away a moment, and replied.

"Tell Lady Rosamund that I won't be able to make it today," he said. "I have an appointment with a lady."

The messenger, one of that tribe born and trained not to react to the message itself or engage with the sender or recipient, broke character and looked at Ronnie a few seconds to gauge if he might be insane or joking. Seeing he was neither, he resumed his professional demeanor, repeated the message, and left.

Half an hour later, an Error Ministry carriage with the almost-invisible flat-black Z-symbol on the door clattered down the street and stopped in front of the showroom. Ronnie tongued the poison-packet into his cheek and came out of the workshop to investigate.

A big man in livery barged in, banging the door and causing Nel and several customers to look up.

"*You*," he said to Ronnie, advancing, "come with me."

"I can't right now, Momo," said Ronnie. "I told the messenger I had–"

"I said come with me–now."

Ronnie hesitated a couple of heartbeats and started to turn. "Lemme get my badge."

"You don't get in the fucking carriage right now, I'm ripping your head off, you little shit."

"What's wrong?"

"You tell me," said the gorilla, taking his elbow. "C'mon."

"I can't say, milady," said Ronnie to a highly agitated Rosamund in the Shopping Street love nest. "You know that. I never talked about *you* and I can't talk about *her*. It wouldn't be gentlemanly."

"*Gentlemanly?*" she said with incredulous exasperation. You think you're a *gentleman?* Why, you're nothing but–" She stopped in surprise, seeing that Ronnie was about to be hurt by her insult, however truthful.

"I take it back," she said. "You've always been discrete." Then, "It's

Clare, isn't it? You're fucking Clare."

"What are you talking about?"

"You think I don't know you go to her house sometimes? You think—"

"I'm doin' a job for her."

"I'll *bet* you are. Getting that old crone off is probably a lot of work."

"I. am. not. fucking. Lady. Clare. And what's a 'crone,' anyway?"

"It's a ... never mind. Don't change the subject!"

"It don't sound flattering."

"Is she high clergy? Does she outrank me? Is she married? What's her clan?"

"C'mon, Rosie, let's—"

"Don't call me that! You're just a ..." She stopped again, recalibrating.

"Ronnie," she said more softly, "Ronnie ... just tell me what's wrong." She stood close and drew his hips into light contact with hers. "I thought you liked being with me. Liked the nice things I gave you."

"Of course, milady," he said, allowing himself to swell slightly, "but you don't *help* me."

"What do you mean? Don't I give you money? Nice clothes? Keep you out of the army?"

"Yes, and I'm grateful, but ..."

"But what?" she asked, taking half a step back to rest against the back of the sofa and drawing him along.

"I'm almost twenty," he said distractedly.

"Yes," she breathed in his ear as he leaned his weight into her. "At your most beautiful."

"Soon nobody will want me, though. Not like now. I have to make my way." He moved against her through her clothes.

"Make your way, baby?" He let her cup his balls below his hardening cock.

"I wanted to learn how to be in *your* world, but you never helped me. You just wanted to fuck and send me back through the gate!"

"Don't you like to fuck me?" she asked, unfastening his pants to let them drop and gathering up her dress above her lace boots. She was bare and freshly shaven for the occasion– and he couldn't help wondering what her husband thought of that–if he ever saw it.

He wrapped a hand across the back of her neck to brace, held his cock with the other to smear her juices about, and buried himself in one slow thrust. She made a guttural sound like the first gulp of spring water after a desert crossing and started to spasm against him: He communed and worked with her like no lover she'd known to ascend and fall back from the heights and finally, when she was just about to cry out, he withdrew and angrily pushed her grasping hands away.

"Don't–" he said.

"Ronnie–Ronnie," she stuttered urgently. "Just–just– just–"

"No! We're not doing it *any more*!" he said, pulling his pants up and buckling his belt. I gotta go."

"Wait! You can't ..." she cried, then, "Just tell me, Ronnie–what's she promised you?"

Keeping her at bay with one hand, he said, "She's helping me with a down payment on my own shop. Here–in the Citadel. Now ..." He turned to go, but she grabbed his sleeve.

"How much?"

"What?"

"How much has she promised you?"

"A hundred ounces of gold."

"*A hundred–!* Ronnie, you can't believe that! These women ..."

He moved to turn down the front waistband of his pants and push an overlapping panel aside to reveal three large coins in their slots. "She already gave me ten ... I carry some ..."

"Give them back!"

"I can't do that! Besides ..."

"Give them back! *I'll* give them to you!"

"You? ... I don't believe you! You're just trying to get me in trouble with her!"

"No! I promise, and ..." she impulsively pulled a ring from her finger and thrust it at him. "Here!"

He marveled at it: gold with a large blue stone among diamonds, surely the one-time property of some pre-Cleansing plutocrat or plutocrat's mistress.

"Rosie—I mean milady ... I don't know ... I've already ..."

"You don't really *like* her, do you?" she asked plaintively, past scolding him for his familiarity.

"She's old," he mused, still looking at the ring as if deciding whether to give it back, "but ..."

"I'll have Momo bring you the gold this afternoon," she said in desperation. "Just say you'll let me be the only one to take care of you—help you get what you want.... Just say it!"

In the afternoon, Momo entered the showroom with an air of resignation. He didn't bang the door this time. Nel looked up from her standing desk and thumbed him toward the workshop.

When he entered, all three men looked up—Jak was at the square, checking for signals from the committee members—and Ronnie laid aside the brush he was just about to dip in a pot of varnish.

"In private?" asked Momo.

"Here's okay," said Ronnie.

Momo hesitated, as if in disbelief at what he was about to do, then unbuttoned his uniform tunic and shirt, reached inside to unfasten a slim canvas moneybelt from around his waist and pull it out, and tossed it on Ronnie's worktable with a clunk. In growing disgust he pulled out a second belt and a third and a fourth and tossed them until they lay on the table like a ball of snakes next to the inlaid image of a quail taking flight.

The retainer glared at his boss's suddenly very expensive plaything as he buttoned up and pulled his jacket straight, then raised an index finger and sighted along it.

"I'll be watching you," he said.

Ronnie followed him to the front door and watched as he climbed to sit beside the driver. When the carriage had pulled away, he looked back toward the square through the obscuring front glass, observed the beggar at his post for a minute, and wondered how he'd interpreted the day's comings and goings, which had surely had him scrambling. He would have the ministry carriage's number to check on and would presumably make the connection to Lady Rosamund, but that shouldn't be a problem, assuming they drew the usual conclusion regarding a handsome young man and a rich priestess.

Besides, Ronnie sensed their interest lay elsewhere.

34 - Assassin's Bolt

Twenty-three days out, and a beautiful late-summer morning. In their secret meeting places, Freethinker circles finished selecting squad and platoon leaders from among their own. At the company level the military committee had already chosen Flame's husband Verjil to lead the Palace attack and Slammer Jon, from Ronnie's own circle, to lead the armory one.

When Ronnie and Brod first learned of Slammer Jon's appointment, they were skeptical, until Owlly shared a secret known to only a few: in his youth, the table-thumping but otherwise genial Jon had been the notorious highwayman called Priestbane, so-named for his skill in relieving traveling clergy of their valuables and in extracting ransoms, killing freely in early days to encourage compliance in later ones. When he and his band finally retired from road to city and the attacks dwindled, the Priesthood claimed to have killed them all, but lingering fear of him was the reason clergy never traveled without military escort thereafter. Verjil was the logical choice for the Palace group because he was the most charismatic and respected combat-age member of the largest circle in the city—a circle which more than others had inculcated belief in the inevitability of revolution and trained for it. The Colonel would be his field adviser.

The boys had been told Slammer Jon's secret because Ronnie was to be his adjutant and Brod one of his platoon leaders. When these platoon leaders were finally brought together, it was an occasion for surprise and amusement as well as confirmation and bonding, as young and mid-life men and women found themselves in as assemblage of fellow Freethinkers the like of which none had ever known, because, since the rise of the Priesthood of ZAH and the murderous suppression of its competitors, none such had been attempted.

This morning Ronnie was loading the last job that might interfere with his military duties: the installation of the Audubon-inspired doors on the cabinets in Lady Clare's guest apartment, the intended occupant of which had never been revealed to him. After that, the only activity taking place in the workshop, that wasn't simply for show, would be their part of final attack preparations.

He'd sent notice of delivery by messenger the previous afternoon, and now, as Jak helped him secure everything and hitch up Daisy, he felt a certain melancholy. The hours he'd spent at Clare's house had been the most satisfying of his young career. Sitting alone at the Art Deco desk he'd restored or at the worktable on the terrace, a sheaf of paper and drawing instruments at hand, Audubon's forbidden Birds of America open nearby for inspiration, little Zander sometimes watching, he'd started by making fine copies but finished by creating original art. The three or four mere "copies" he'd kept back; the sixteen pieces of art now lay wrapped in blankets in two rope-handled boxes in the bed of the cart.

As he urged Daisy out onto the street and crossed the intersection, he observed that the watcher was ostentatiously counting the coins in his begging bowl, but he had no doubt the man would be on the move to commandeer a cab as soon as the corner of the bank building blocked him from view. No matter. Delivering a job to Lady Clare was an ordinary piece of business, not the sort of thing to attract the interest of the Error Police, even if they had other reasons for being interested in her. He couldn't dismiss the proximity of Smiley Man to her house the last time he'd been there, nor the fact of the Citadel-related surveillance on himself, but he couldn't see how the two fit together, unless the Error Police had suddenly taken an interest in the sexual habits and improprieties of the elite Citadel women who were his patrons, and mistakenly took the celibate Lady Clare to be in that pantheon.

The gate opened as he drew near the tree-shrouded mansion and the guards waved him through with a greeting. Forewarned by some mysterious means as usual, Cornelius and his crew of eager young men were waiting as he pulled up to the service entrance.

"Good morning, Cornelius," he said, setting the brake.

"Master Ronnie," returned the house's majordomo, continuing his mistress's practice of honoring the mastery of his craft, even if he was technically still an apprentice. "So today's the big day?"

"The big day, yes," said Ronnie. "It'll take me a couple of hours to install and adjust the doors and that will be it." He spoke with enthusiasm though he felt sadness.

"Shall we, then?" said Cornelius, putting the boys to unloading the boxes with a glance.

Someone must have monitored his progress, for no sooner had he put his tools away and wiped his hands and stepped back to get the full effect of the installation, than Clare walked in with Cornelius, a servant girl trailing and her bodyguard Bear keeping an eye from the hallway.

"Milady," he said, and fell silent as she stopped before the first image.

A wave of panic assailed him. Clare had seen the drawings from which the panels were to be made and had surely noted the variation from the style of Audubon, but she hadn't explicitly approved them. Would she now erupt in reprimand? Ronnie's mouth grew dry and his armpits moist. By the time she'd come to the last panel he was a self-doubting wreck.

Finally, after an eon, she turned her head, smiled, and nodded. "Well done, Master Rondak."

Sweet relief and confirmation. "Thank you, ma'am," he said, resuming normal breathing.

She turned infinitesimally toward Cornelius with a tiny nod and that man left. Returning her attention to the image of a falcon just tucking into a dive, she began to Ronnie, "How ...?"

"Ma'am?" he said, stepping beside her.

"How can you capture the *energy* in the bird so?"

"Ah ... I fear sounding foolish, ma'am."

She simply waited.

"Well, I put myself in the *mind* of the bird. Try to feel its *mood.*"

"The bird's *mood,*" she repeated with a twinkle.

"Yes, ma'am. Whether the bird is startled by a threat, or pining for a mate, or nurturing young, or focused on prey—like here—I imagine myself as the bird and try to portray that feeling."

"And the three-dimensionality?"

Dangerous ground, said a voice in the back of Ronnie's mind. How would an illiterate cabinetmaker know anything about *dimensions?*

"The depth, ma'am?" he asked anyway. She nodded. "Well, if you notice, the things beyond the bird are rendered with softer lines and darker shading than the things in front. It tricks the mind."

"Like da Vinci."

No way was he going to respond to *that* provocation. Instead he just stared at his falcon until Clare gave up toying with him and moved her attention to another panel.

As Ronnie relaxed again, he became aware that the room was slowly becoming populated with members of the household staff—chamber attendants and butlers and secretaries and others including kitchen workers who'd doffed their aprons and even a few bodyguards—and he realized Clare had had Cornelius invite them to see his work. They entered deferentially, singly or in small groups, and gazed raptly or studied critically according to their nature, sharing impressions quietly and stealing glances at their mistress and Ronnie.

"Your first art show," said Clare, leaning toward him. "Enjoy." And with that she stepped away toward an apparently mesmerized serving girl and asked, "What do you think of this one, Bitsy?"

The girl couldn't take her eyes away as she replied.

"I hardly know what to say, ma'am. It's so ..."

Ronnie missed the rest, as others took the opportunity to speak to him and to bump fists in congratulations. One matronly woman who might have been one of Zander's teachers impulsively embraced him with tears in her eyes.

As he tried graciously to accept the staff's praise and to respond to questions, his eyes were continually drawn in fascination to Lady Clare as she moved about the room. She challenged every prejudice that Freethinkers as a group maintained about the clergy. He marveled at how easily the lower-status members of what must be her own clan spoke to her, not merely listening and responding mechanically but offering their own opinions in a lively fashion. Some even *touched* her, like the schoolteacher who appraised one panel standing arm-in-arm with her. He couldn't imagine Sula or any of the high priestesses he'd met being so congenial with their inferiors. It just wasn't done.

Despite the relaxed atmosphere, the bodyguards remained vigilant. Three or four besides Bear had filtered in with the staff, perhaps thinking such a gathering, even unscheduled as it was, was the perfect opportunity for a traitor-assassin to strike. Nor was their vigilance unreasonable, given that Clare's husband and two children had long ago been murdered in an apparent attempt to weaken or extinguish her line, and that only she stood in the way of someone's dark plan. Looking about, Ronnie thought he understood another reason why she was moved to treat staff like family: she kept actual close relatives away for their safety and the safety of the clan and created a surrogate family in their stead.

Across the room, Clare met Ronnie's eyes and gestured with her head toward the terrace doors. Her guards saw the gesture too and began subtly to extricate her and make a path. Ronnie excused himself and followed. When he'd passed through the glass-paned double doors the guards closed them behind, staying themselves inside. Cornelius positioned himself near the room's entrance; the assembled staff, sensing the changed dynamic, began to filter past him down the hallway, still murmuring pleasurably to each other. Some of the guards followed them out to take up station in other rooms with access to the long terrace. Outside, Lady Clare and Ronnie commenced to slowly stroll up and down, falling into step, turning in unison at each end, Ronnie nearest the rail with his hands elapsed behind.

"OUT OF THE WAY!" yelled Lady Sula's guards as they virtually trampled Minister Grotius's slower-moving party on their way to the roof's edge, forty-three floors and a half-mile away. In their midst, the self-presumptive heir to the Sword of ZAH strode with head thrust forward and teeth clenched in rage that it had taken more than two hours to locate her and get her to the Ministry after the cabinetmaker arrived at Clare's house, then to find that the Black Tower steam plant's charge had been depleted in lifting the four-hundred-pound Grotius and all his guards and attendants from his luxurious second-floor apartment to the penthouse in the freight elevator. Maddeningly, the "express elevator" carrying Sula and her party had inched to a stop at the thirty-first floor and the guards had had to take turns carrying her up the stairs on their backs. Once on the roof and passing the waddling grotesque of an Error Minister on her way to the waiting telescope, she resolved to have him pushed over the parapet—once she'd seen Clare die.

"There's a change in the air," said Clare, turning at the end of a lap.

"Yes, ma'am. Summer's almost over."

"I mean in our lives."

"Ma'am?"

She walked on without speaking, gathering her thoughts. She wanted to ask him questions—so many questions—but knew he'd have no option but to lie or play dumb; that would be a disservice to them both. Besides, how much can you safely ask of, or say to, someone subject at any moment to torture-interrogation? Are you and they made safer by the *speaking?* or the *not* speaking?

She looked up at the house's rank of chimneys silhouetted against the cotton-ball clouds. "This house has stood, in various guises, for about two-hundred-fifty years," she said. "Can you guess why it survived, while so many others were destroyed, after the Cleansing?"

"Lots of fireplaces," he replied in good humor.

"Exactly. And radiators, although those were only put back in service recently.... A house built for one era survived into another, and then another, because it was *adaptable.... People* survive radical change the same way—not reflexively denying and resisting it but anticipating it and riding it to a new place. Same goes for those times when you expect change that doesn't come. You must survive, adjust to setback, and go on.... First, you must survive."

"What about honor?" said Ronnie, more from instinct than reason. What, after all, were they talking about?

"SHUT UP!" yelled Sula through the back-yard telescope. "Just step to the rail and die!" She violently jerked the instrument to search for the carriage but became frustrated. "WHERE ARE THEY?"

"Your permission ... "said a man, who took over, quickly found what she was looking for, and stepped back. "You can only see the horses and driver through the trees, milady, but they're in position."

She peered for a moment, then, "Back to Clare!" and the man again found her target.

"Honor?" said Lady Clare. "That's a problem, isn't it? How to survive *and* live honorably ... I think ... maybe ... it's the sum of our lives—not the moment—that's most important ... that—"

The door opened and a familiar object issued in a blur to slam into Ronnie's legs. "Oofff!" he said as expected, before upending Zander and holding him out to Clare by his feet.

"How do you tell which end is up on this thing?" he asked. "Is this it?... Hello?" he said to the feet, to giggles from below.

Clare gathered the boy to herself right-side-up and held him on her right hip. He raised an arm and pointed into the distance.

"The child!" exulted Sula at the distant glass. "Yes! He likes to look at the view!... No! Not *that* way!"

"Come here, Ronnie," said Clare, heading with Zander to the end of the terrace, which gave a view uphill to the palace. "If you look at what I can see from here, you might suppose I can tell exactly what's going on at any moment, but I can't. Neither can you. Neither can anyone. One thing you can be sure of is that you never know *exactly* what's going on, because you can't get in the minds of all the participants. Things are not black or white–always grey–especially for people of conscience. Your vision must be attuned to the nuances of grey. And another thing ..."

She started to move to the streetside rail in response to Zander's persistent pointing.

"you can never predict where you'll find friends and allies in life, so keep your mind open."

"Yeesss," breathed Sula, caressing the eyepiece.

"Sounds like advice from my father," said Ronnie, laying his hands on the rail a couple feet away from the priestess and noting his own cart and mare below, standing with a groom in the driveway, ready for his departure. Down the street past Clare to the right, a fine light carriage, as if having stopped to pick up a passenger at a nearby gate, eased away from the curb and rolled down the street behind two large grey geldings. Zander had seen it and pointed, but Clare was preoccupied.

"Your father?" she said, obviously delighted by his small observation. "How do you remember him?"

Ronnie looked away from the carriage to the cloud shadows moving across the farmland to the south.

"As a child I thought of him as stern but kind and loving, but I like an adult's description I heard later: 'quietly charismatic.'"

"Yes," said Clare softly, her eyes also in the distance but not seeing farmland.

The carriage stopped beyond the wall and Ronnie's eyes fell to it. At the same moment Clare turned sideways to the rail with Zander in her arms.

"Ronnie ... I–"

"LADY CLARE!" called a well-dressed woman from the window of the carriage now standing some thirty paces away, and time slowed down. As the priestess uncertainly turned back to the rail and began to raise her free left hand in greeting, Ronnie's mind was trying to process what he was seeing: a dark curtain hung lengthwise within the carriage's shadowed interior, something protruding from it beyond the waving woman.

"Now ... just ... die," murmured Sula prayerfully.

In the same instant, the crossbow launched its bolt and Ronnie moved.

"ARCHER!" he yelled as he lunged toward Clare and the boy, instinctively wrapping his arms around both at mid-body and driving and twisting with them so that they fell as one upon himself. Clare screamed, Zander filled his lungs for a wail, and several terrace doors crashed open at the same time. Behind the sudden din, Ronnie could hear the geldings' hoofbeats on the street.

"GET 'IM!" one bodyguard shouted.

"KILL 'IM!" another.

"TAKE 'IS HANDS!" another.

"STOMP 'IM!" another.

"ARCHER! ARCHER! ARCHER!" yelled Ronnie through the blows. "IN THE STREET! THE CARRIAGE!"

"DON'T HURT HIM!" yelled Clare, shielding him with one arm as she clutched the now-wailing Zander with the other. A trickle of blood wet the side of her neck.

Finally the message got through and Bear stepped over the bodies to the rail to see the two horses carrying the carriage away at a gallop.

"YOU!" he shouted to the young groom below, who was already looking up in alarm. "HORSES AND ARMS! NOW!"

Rising unsteadily, Ronnie grabbed Bear's arm. "My cart! It's standing below! Let's go!"

Bear glared for two seconds, and turned, pointing. "You and you, go with him!" Then to Cornelius, hovering nearby. "Fetch the doctor."

Ronnie tumbled down the main staircase between the two guards to avoid being attacked by others filling the house and grounds. Racing out the front door, he first went to the agitated horse's head, so she'd know who was commanding her.

"Be brave, girl!" he said, then jumped aboard as the others knelt in the bed and he put leather to Daisy's back with a shout.

The mare started in sudden consternation but lurched forward. By the time she reached the flung-open gate she was running faster than she had since she was a yearling. Skidding onto the street and heading downhill, Ronnie put his hand on the brake to keep the now-heavily-laden cart from overrunning her if she faltered.

The carriage had disappeared, but as they galloped out of a slight dip and were immediately faced with a fork in the road, they caught sight of it below. Ronnie reined Daisy to a stop.

"What doin'?" demanded the older of the two guards, quickly standing with his hand on his short sword's hilt.

"We need a man here to give directions!"

"Right!" said the guard, understanding and motioning the other man off.

Ronnie urged the traumatized Daisy back to a very sloppy gallop that scattered pedestrians and other vehicles and threatened to throw the two out of the cart, but they again caught sight of the carriage with the grey horses. It had slowed, perhaps thinking itself in the clear, but now it picked up speed. Ronnie could see where it was headed: to the warren of old houses and businesses on narrow streets near the great wall, north of the trader's meadow. It would be difficult to maneuver a carriage and two there, but easy for the passengers to dismount and get away on foot. He pressed Daisy harder and it looked for a time like they were catching up, then the valiant mare reached her limit.

She'd been running as hard as she could on a brick-surfaced roadway, ears back, mouth foaming, sides heaving with audible breath, her stride becoming more and more awkward. A couple of times she'd misstepped, bobbed her head almost to the ground, and recovered. But not this time. Her front hooves came down on the brick too soon or too late and her legbones shattered with an awful sound. She went down helplessly; the cart ran into and over her and violently upended to smash down ahead of her, throwing Ronnie and the guard even farther down the street.

In the darkness, someone screamed over and over, pausing only to raggedly draw breath. Eventually the darkness lifted and Ronnie found himself lying in the street with pedestrians trying to help him as vehicles slowed to gawk at the crash site. Sitting up with assistance, he saw the immobile guard surrounded by another group, and then, turning, the tangled and terrified and screaming Daisy, whose flashing hooves and protruding sharp bones kept away those who would comfort her. He struggled to his knees, then his feet, and reached for his dagger. Not there, because he didn't wear it at Lady Clare's. Against insistence that he sit back down, he stumbled to the group surrounding the other man and pushed through. Without checking if he was dead or alive, he found and withdrew the guard's dagger. The onlookers fell back as he made his way to Daisy. He found the safest approach, sprawled across her flailing head until he could get ahold of her bridle, and lifted her head to give her the only relief he could, cutting deeply from the corner of her jaw to and through her windpipe to the other side. Blood came from the arteries in great pulses and sprayed out her nose and mouth with each labored breath. He lay across her as she quieted, then rested.

Shouting men arrived ahorse and some left again as he pointed toward the old town into which the assassins' carriage had fled. Others helped him to his feet and sat him on a curb. Soon they brought the other guard and sat him down too, his head scraped and bleeding. Ronnie wiped the borrowed dagger on his own pants and handed it back. The man looked at it, trying to understand its significance.

Citadel Guard paramilitary police arrived and attempted to rearrange everyone, to no particular purpose, but found themselves reduced to crowd and traffic control by Bear, who'd returned from setting several of his men to bribe, threaten, or cajole the denizens of Old Town for any information about the disappeared carriage-and-two.

From the east-facing parapet of the Black Tower, Sula watched the downhill scene with troubled eyes. She'd shouted in triumph when Clare went down out of sight, but then grown silent as her enemy had been lifted from the cabinetmaker's arms and hustled inside. She hadn't looked like a woman with a crossbow bolt buried in her throat.

Some of the sycophants who'd been on the roof minutes before had now melted away, including Grotius. Sula wasn't surprised. Clare's death would have cemented her own power, even if everyone knew its author, but a failed attempt demonstrated only incompetence, the kind no one wanted to be associated with. She had to get ahead of the repercussions. "Make sure everything's cleaned up," she ordered a trembling subaltern over her shoulder. "Everyone in the carriage and chop-shop: 'killed resisting arrest in the investigation'; the watchers on the boy and their immediate superior: 'embezzlement.'"

"What about the Guard, ma'am?" ventured the man. "They would have juris– Yes, ma'am. Right away, ma'am."

As Ronnie sat with his aching head in his hands and the injured bodyguard lay back next to him, Clare's armored carriage rolled up and stopped in front of him. He struggled to his feet to greet his patron but was instead confronted with Cornelius, who beckoned him inside.

"How is she, Corney?" he inquired as he took his seat and the carriage pulled away.

"Lady Clare instructed me to make sure you were all right and to see you home safely," said the uncharacteristically businesslike older man.

"Yes, thank you–but is she–"

"Lady Clare further instructed me to thank you for your services and tell you they will not be required again."

"Okay," said Ronnie uncertainly. "But–"

"She instructed me further to say that you are ..." he looked away, discomfited, "*forbidden* ... from ever coming to the house again–that payment for your services and compensation for your losses will be brought to you."

Ronnie was dumbfounded. He sat with his mouth open for a minute as the carriage passed through the main gate and turned onto Woodmaker Street. "Corney ... am I suspected?" he asked.

"Finally," Cornelius drew himself up to say, "Lady Clare instructed me to ask if you understand and will abide by her wishes."

When no answer came, he asked again, "Master Rondak?"

"Understand, no" said Ronnie flatly. "Abide ... yes, of course."

They rode the first traffic-slowed block in silence. When they'd passed the intersection and pulled up in front of Owlly's, Ronnie reached for the door handle, but Cornelius grabbed his forearm to stay him. When Ronnie looked in the dignified majordomo's face for an explanation, he saw incipient tears.

"Corney?" he said softly, and waited.

"She's very dear to us, Ronnie," said the older man hoarsely.

"I know," said Ronnie. "I'm so glad she wasn't seriously hurt."

"The bolt ..."

"Yes," said Ronnie, "it nicked her neck."

Cornelius looked at him hopelessly. "The *bolt* ..."

"What?" said Ronnie with foreboding.

"It was *poisoned!*"

35 - Chains of Acquaintance

Sula doubled down. Encouraged by the rumors of Clare's impending death and with everyone knowing what that would mean for her own ascendancy, she claimed center stage, haranguing the Council of Messengers about lawlessness in the city, calling for an investigation of the inept Citadel Guard, and, with theatrical reluctance, supporting the suggestion of an ally that martial law be declared, which would have put the army in direct control of the Citadel for the first time in its history. The Council-controlled Citadel Guard had been so slow to react, she claimed, that it had fallen to a contingent of Error police, controlled by herself through Grotius and that day performing some duty in Old Town, to pursue and confront the assassins, who had resisted so fanatically that all had had to be slain.

Few of the elites bought it, of course. The nature and dynamics of the situation were in fact pretty well understood: The Sulan clan and Clare's Mortimerian had been at odds for generations, the authoritarian former one resenting the respect and moral authority accorded to the latter. In the current era this had resulted not only in the assassination of Clare's husband and children but in the elevation to the Council of relative mediocrities like Endo, the Sword, from a neutral clan, and Clare's uncle, Mortimer, a competent but lackluster placeholder. Sula's real achievement had been in so far preventing the rise to the Council of Clare herself or her even-more-threatening brother, Magnus, who, thanks to her machinations, was presently on the other side of the world.

With Clare out of the picture, those who presently hindered Sula's rise to ultimate power would have no champion, and many such were now positioning themselves for that eventuality. At the moment, that meant giving lip-service to Sula's proposals while finding reason to delay implementation. In response, Sula stoked the fires of fear of an unknown enemy just over the horizon: an enemy unlike any that the forces of ZAH had ever faced, one that called for the strengthening of—and loosening of constraints on—an army formed to destroy small bands of heretics, that was now called upon to face a vast army of them. As the equinox neared, talk of the shameful "army gap" was aloft in all the pubs and markets.

Ronnie spent a day in self-doubt and chagrin over the role he's unwittingly played in the attack on Clare, which was confirmed by the disappearance of the watchers, now that his movements were no longer of interest to the assassins. He should have told Owlly and Nel about the two encounters with Smily Man and acted on their counsel, just as he should have told them about his approach to the trader Baladur. But he couldn't undo that mistake, and there was no time for self-flagellation, so he got back to work.

Work included once again making the rounds of the clubs with Keera and Jane, mining for intelligence and gossip. At Scarface he had Tom and Polli to guide him to possible sources and identify possible spies. By now the pace of military preparations was such that it could no longer be hidden, and the effort to do so ceased. But still no one, even when drunk, claimed to know the exact day when the army would depart to confront the mysterious enemy, ever more horrific in description. Knowing that day with certainty became Ronnie's most important job.

Lady Rosamund expected her money's worth, and Ronnie gave it to her—four afternoons in the first week after she'd sent him one hundred gold coins in several designs but all containing one troy ounce of the precious metal. He wondered if she'd embezzled them to keep him, but it really didn't matter. As long as he made himself indispensable to her, he knew she'd tell him of any change in the inception day, so that he could retire to a safe place to wait for her.

But Ronnie wasn't the only one with an interest in Lady Rosamund.

The two watchers from Woodmaker Street and their immediate superior had first been gagged–to stifle their annoying claims of innocence–and then garroted–right in their office in front of their colleagues–on "evidence" of embezzlement, and an ambitious detective–temporarily jumped up to deputy inspector duties and immediately calling himself "inspector"–had been charged with cleansing the record they'd created.

In doing so he'd come across the report of a certain afternoon when an official Error Ministry carriage had taken the subject Ronnie to an apparent assignation with Lady Rosamund–high priestess and chief of the Ministry's property department, who worked in the same building as the inspector–apparent, that is, if the final kisses in the doorway before Rosamund left meant what they usually did. The inspector, who was jealous of Rosamund because of the lucrative position she held by virtue of her skillful misdirection of funds away from the Council and Treasury and directly into Ministry operations–which enriched the army at the expense of the Guard–decided to flesh out the skeletal record, for whatever advantage might accrue to him.

"Thank you for taking time to see me, milady," he said to the section chief when he was finally admitted to her office. "I know how busy you must be."

"Not at all, Inspector. How can I help?"

"Well, as you know, ma'am, one of our responsibilities is to monitor contacts between Ministry functionaries with security clearance and members of the general public. That way we're always in a position to protect our people if anything comes up with regard to the citizen."

"Makes sense," said Rosamund, with a foreboding she strived not to show.

"Now, I should preface my questions with the assurance that our first concern is for the security of the Ministry. We don't automatically share our intelligence with other branches, and in fact the matter may not need to go farther than *me*." *I won't tell your husband at the Council,* he might have said*, if you cooperate.*

"I see."

"It's about the young man Rondak, your lover." Rosamund managed to remain perfectly still.

"You know the one," said the inspector mildly; "you've been with him four times this week."

My God, thought the priestess, *they've been following me! Or Ronnie. How long? How much do they know? What's wrong?*

"Yes, that sounds right," she said.

The man nodded slightly, congratulating her on having made the choice not to deny. "Good," he said. "So, when your relationship with him is not about sex, what's it about?"

"How do you mean?"

"Well, one doesn't usually have sex continuously. One rests and talks. What do you talk about?"

"Oh," she began, looking around and back to the policeman, "inconsequentialities, mostly. Amusing things that happened–in his shop, in the market, on the street."

"In the office?"

"No," she lied, "he knows I want to forget about the office when we're together, and he accommodates. When we're between, he amuses me."

"Between?"

"Well, to paraphrase *you,* Inspector," she replied, "one doesn't usually rest and talk continuously, one has sex."

The policeman smiled slightly as expected, then, "What does he think about your work?"

"Well, as I said," she answered, shifting in her chair, "We don't really–"

"What does he think you do?"

"He thinks I keep track of the Ministry's tables and chairs."

"Intelligent?"

"Intelligent?" she echoed. "No, I wouldn't say so. Rather simple, really, though he has a good sense of humor."

"Does he hide things from you?"

"Hide ...? What do you mean?"

"I mean, if something momentous was happening in his life, would you know?"

"Oh, of course," she replied confidently. "He loves to tell me about his small adventures and successes.

"What has he told you about Lady Clare?"

"Clare?" said the priestess, getting a bad feeling. "Only that she bought some of his furniture and he took it to her house."

"The assassination attempt happened four days ago; you've seen him, what, twice since then?"

"Yes."

"And did he speak of Clare?"

"No."

"So, if I told you that before she was struck, she'd been engaged in a lengthy and serious conversation with Ronnie at her house, that at the crucial moment she was *saved* by Ronnie, that he then initiated a pursuit of the assassins in a pony cart, that the rig crashed not two blocks from here, killing the pony and injuring Ronnie–would that surprise you, Lady Rosamund?"

She sat with her mouth open, until she could make it mutter, "He said he'd been in a fight; I thought it was sexy."

"So, Lady Rosamund, can you see now that we may have a problem?"

"Yes, Inspector," she said with sudden deference. "Of course, anything I can do ... I mean ... *Can you help me?*""

Ah, the magic words. The ones that turned the tables, put him in control.

"I'll do my best, milady, or course. For now, I think it's best if we keep this between the two of us. Do you agree.? ... Good.'"

ZAH save me! thought Rosamund. She'd told the boy the inception date for the operation! She'd told him! She couldn't get over her foolishness. And now she was to continue her affair as if nothing was wrong, while the inspector took the list of names of other women she'd given him and tried to determine where and how he'd entered the life of the Citadel, and just what might have been revealed to him.

This is it! exulted the inspector, clutching the three names in his hand as he left the building. *The break I've been waiting for.* But it had to be artfully handled, lest some ambitious colleague take it away from him.

First he'd confront and terrify Rosamund's friends in sensitive government positions outside the Error Ministry—with whom he didn't have to be so polite—then he'd return to the Tower and speak with poor Janelle, the homely girl in the secretarial pool who'd hoped to marry and make babies with Ronnie but who'd surely been a mere steppingstone to someone more important, like Rosamund. Then, when he had the entire chain of acquaintance figured out, he'd find a way to get the information directly to the one person who'd reward him instead of stealing credit—the real power behind the Ministry for the Suppression of Error: Lady Sula. She would surely put him in charge of a more thorough interrogation of all Ronnie's Citadel lovers, maybe including Rosamund herself; their self-serving and conflicting statements would quickly be revised; an important Freethinker or Christian or Eggist spy would be revealed and questioned to discover his crimes and co-conspirators; and the inspector would vault over lesser mortals to his rightful place—maybe chief of division! Or higher!

Goodbye to drudgery, he thrilled, like that suffered by the bitter woman at the next desk, who'd been ordered to task some clerks to compare on old guest list with birth records and then follow up to identify somebody of a certain age and appearance who'd been in the VIP enclosure for the sailing of the *Wind of ZAH*–two years ago, no less! Some kind of high-priority target, he'd heard, but they always said that.

36 - Misdirection

Eleven days out

Lady Clare lingered, perhaps not wanting to miss the main event, even if she was only occasionally conscious, as rumor said. Cornelius had sent a message to Nel regarding settlement of the bill and arrived the next mid-morning in a small carriage. The whole family collected in their good clothes to welcome him and express concern for their patron's well-being without actually naming her malady, then he and Nel adjourned to conduct business. When he left some time later, he beckoned the loitering Ronnie to accompany him to the carriage.

"She's in a bad way, Ronnie," he said to Ronnie's unspoken question. "Very weak, in and out of consciousness, but still taking some food and still with us. Doctors think she might make it."

Ronnie took his hand with both of his. "Thanks for telling me, Corney," he said. "And little Zander?"

"Being kept busy," said Cornelius, reaching behind the seat for something. "He asked about you."

Ronnie nodded but didn't comment, since he was under orders never to return to the house and would perhaps never see the boy again.

Cornelius set on his lap a large, flat slipcase, finely finished and varnished, not made by any woodworker of Ronnie's acquaintance.

"Lady Clare was planning to give you a gift, but never had the chance, so I put it together as she intended." He slid a thin, cloth-bound book as big as a lamp-table out of the case and for a moment Ronnie feared the trauma at the Clare house had so unhinged everyone that they were sending out death sentences as gifts. Involuntarily, he glanced out the window for police.

Don't worry," assured Cornelius. "It's just pictures. You can say where you got them if you're ever asked."

"Pictures?"

"Your drawings," he said, opening past blank pages to the Great White Heron. "She knew you intended to leave them, but she wanted *you* to have them and keep them safe.... See?... The drawings are separated by this special paper for protection, and you can take them out as you please.... It's all right, isn't it?" he said with a note of personal pride at what a handsome gift it made.

Ronnie ran his fingers lightly over the artifact. "Yes, he murmured. "I had no idea such fine binding was done now."

"It's done by the Vital Records office.... Part of the Treasury."

"Vital records?"

"Births and deaths and such." He gestured to the priestblood tatoos on Ronnie's earlobe. You'll be in them, somewhere."

"I suppose. I don't think about it."

"Well," said Cornelius, sliding the volume back into its case and handing it over, "a memento of better times."

Ronnie stood on the front steps with his gift under his arm as Cornelius's carriage pulled away. When it was gone, he started to turn back inside but felt his attention drawn elsewhere. He scanned the pedestrian traffic on the opposite sidewalk and found himself looking briefly into the eyes of Chatter, Trader Baladur's son-in-law, whom he hadn't seen in many markets. As soon as he was sure Ronnie had seen him, he looked away and walked toward the Square. Ronnie lingered and saw him turn left at the corner without looking back.

He had made contact and was now headed through Woodmaker Gate and back to the Meadow, Ronnie knew.

After showing Lady Clare's gift to the family and marveling over the weight of coin paid to the shop for his "work of art," Ronnie excused himself to check the committee's "message board" in the Square and to "chat up the traders." He carried his owl-branded leather tool satchel for cover and, once at the Meadow, dropped in a couple of small purchases from other traders before he got to Baladur's rig, which was looking more prosperous than last he'd seen it, with a free cleaning from Bil's Rigwash and an official transport pennant in its holder.

"Looking Good, Master Baladur," said Ronnie to the elderly man in the newish broad-brimmed hat and the century-old new teeth, coming back to the field's perimeter after setting the hobbled mules to graze. "Your rig *and* you!"

"Feeling good, my boy," said Baladur, trying for the sake of any witnesses *not* to pick up his pace and throw his arms around Ronnie as he might have done. When he drew near, he simply stopped and offered his fist in the common greeting, but said, "I embrace you, Ronnie."

"*I* embrace *you,* Baladur," said Ronnie, meeting the old man's fist with his own for a moment longer than convention demanded.

"And *I* embrace you, Ronnie," said Rae, stepping out of the van's front door with a baby in her arms. "As well as hug and kiss you."

"And I, you, Rae, if Chatter doesn't mind."

"He's not here, so I accept." She nearly grinned.

"And what's this?" he gestured up at her burden.

"This is a baby girl," she said, angling her down to be seen, "name of Melody, but we call her Meli around others. The child looked at the stranger with big-eyed wonder.

"Well, Melody, I embrace you, too. May you grow up to be like your mother."

Rae looked toward the nearby buildings to where Chatter could be seen carrying two wicker baskets. "Here comes lunch.... What say you, Dad? Inside? Or outside on the blanket like last time?"

Δ Δ Δ

"So you see, Ronnie, we owe you a lot," said Rae, taking a tiny sip of the brandy Ronnie had brought as Melody slept beside her in a wicker bassinet. "Once we could make ourselves presentable again, feed our animals properly and buy better inventory, things turned around. Then came the commission to carry official mail and we were respectable again, too. That helped a lot with getting your warning spread."

"And how was it received?" asked Ronnie.

Rae turned her head to her father. "Dad?"

The old man took a swallow and set his cup over in the grass. "First of all, Ronnie, thanks for giving me something important to do–I needed it. Now, as to the message and its effect, that's why we're here today and not a month ago or a week from now. We spread your message in all directions to the most trustworthy people and then we backtracked, up until yesterday, to collect information from these people about the government's preparations for pogrom. And hopefully we bring it to you in time to act on it. The equinox, you said. That's eleven days from now."

"Yes," said Ronnie with rising excitement, prepared to hear about intense recruitment and training, pre-positioning of materiel, furtive troop movements, couriers galloping on the road and more. "And what preparations did you discover?"

"None."

He'd heard Baladur just fine but couldn't help himself. "What?"

"Beyond about twenty miles from the city, *there is no major new military activity.*" He waited for this intelligence to be digested.

"But," began Ronnie, "but ... how can that be?... We constantly hear rumors now, about huge heretic armies on the frontier that must be confronted by the forces of ZAH. We assume the rumors are manufactured to justify mobilizing a large force and sending it far into the field, but that only makes sense if the rumors and activity are widespread in the *field,* so the communities will initially welcome the soldiers as *defenders.*

"Unless?" asked Baladur.

Ronnie stared. Then he changed position to sit back on his feet and made a gesture and an attempt to speak but stopped. Then he stood up and walked into the meadow among the grazing animals, who looked at him curiously. On the blanket Baladur refreshed his and Chatter's and Ronnie's cups as Rae turned her baby's hooded bassinet so the sun didn't reach her sleeping eyes.

When he returned, he lowered himself and took a swallow from his cup.

"When you first gave the warning," he began carefully, "was it believed?"

"Not by all, no," answered Baladur, "but it was *heeded* by all."

"Not believed by all," Ronnie clarified, "so can you say that some people might have been ... *disinclined* ... to see signs of impending pogrom, even if they were there?"

"I *might* have said that, if not for what we found when we checked back later. By then most had become convinced that something was impending in the Citadel itself—it just wasn't manifesting elsewhere."

"Then maybe it just represents, a new level of discipline in the army. They're just doing a better job of keeping the pogrom secret, so the heretics will be caught off guard."

"Unlikely," said Baladur. "Think about the movement of thousands and ultimately tens of thousands of soldiers. They need food and materiel caches, bivouac sites, a whole infrastructure; they need licensed transporters like us to precede the army, before the roads become clogged by refugees, so we'll be in position to load plunder. And we're not being pre-positioned like that."

"So you're suggesting ... what? That there is no pogrom? Or ..."

Baladur waited for him to work it out.

"Or, ..." Ronnie continued, "it's a pogrom confined to the city ..."

"Or?" Baladur prompted.

"Intelligence from a senior bureaucrat says it's a pogrom," Ronnie insisted. "but now I'm wondering if the leaders are not disinforming their own people, so that whatever leaks out is about a pogrom, and not about the real intent."

"Which is?" Baladur coaxed.

Ronnie looked around to see expectant eyes. "A military takeover," he said.

"Bravo," said Baladur quietly, then to the others, "I told you he'd figure it out faster than we did."

"We've had weeks to put it together," said Rae, "but it seems to fit what we've seen.... None of it can be good, but at least it's not a pogrom."

Ronnie didn't reply but instead descended into deep, frowning thought. When he didn't quickly come out of it, Baladur broke the silence.

"What is it, boy? What're you thinking?"

"We needed a pogrom," he said. "A far one, like they've done in the past, not a near one."

"You needed ... what are you talkin' about?"

Ronnie raised a hand for a moment to collect his thoughts and gauge the propriety of what he was about to say, then: "It appeared from all our intelligence that the army and a large part of the Guard would leave the city eleven days from now, making it as vulnerable as anyone can remember. So we all came together, and we made a plan ..."

"A plan?" demanded Baladur. "What plan?"

Ronnie looked at the old man, friendship still warring with operational security.

"To fight!" said an unexpected voice.

"Yes, Chatter," said Ronnie, turning to the normally taciturn man's now-burning eyes, "to fight."

"To fight?" said Baladur, a bit tremulously, his age suddenly upon him. "Fight the army? The Priesthood?"

"Overthrow them, actually, before they could inflict much damage on the towns."

"Over– How do you ..."

"Ronnie," said Rae, "you said you *all* came together.... All *who?"*

"Everybody. All the circles in the city, at least all we could find. Everyone's not going into combat, but–"

"My god, my god ... "murmured Baladur.

"How many?" asked Chatter with what passed for excitement.

"Several hundred, armed and trained, hopefully with more to join in later, after we've launched."

Rae clamped a passionate grip on Ronnie's forearm. "Are you *serious,* Ronnie? Is this *real?...* There hasn't been such a large uprising in the entire history of Zahdom. How ...?"

"I know. We *all* know. And yes, it's real. Brave people have already died to protect the operation. As for how, it's a complicated plan, and only good if the army sorties as expected, but it involves the capture of the Council of Messengers and capture or blockadement of several sites, like the Treasury and the Black Tower; followed by some bargaining with the army and bureaucracy."

"A classic coup," said Baladur, reviving. "Your idea?"

"Kinda. I mentioned it to some people–stuff from books. That's why I've got to get your information to our leaders right away. We need to develop plans for these other contingencies."

"How do you see those?" asked Rae.

"Well, I'm thinking if it's a *far* pogrom, like before, we're all set; if it's an army *coup,* we ride it out with the rest of the populace and look for a later opportunity; if it's a *near* pogrom, we try to get non-combatants to safety ... and the rest of us die gloriously in battle, so our people will have heroes. We'd be tortured to death anyway."

The others regarded Ronnie for a few seconds to see if he was making a joke–trying to lighten the mood. Finally, Baladur took up the brandy and poured a small dollop in each cup and set the bottle down.

"To heroes," he said, raising his cup.

∆ ∆ ∆

Ronnie was going to have a lot of explaining to do. In giving warning of the pogrom to Baladur's family and through them to the town and village circles, he'd violated the security protocols of his own family and circle. But the intelligence his act had generated was golden, and it had to be laid before the committee, whatever the consequences for himself.

He started the process with yet another breach of protocol, walking out of the Citadel onto the river road to catch a ride a mile north to Bil's Rigwash and there to give Bil a notice of meeting at the dairy that night as if it had come from one of the committee members. Then he took the bus south to the Square, knowing the four members inside the wall could be reached by Tofer by mid-afternoon, if Owlly didn't blow up and cancel, over the news of his by-then multiple transgressions.

In the event, after Ronnie had asked Brod and Jak to look after customers so Owlly and Nel could join him at the kitchen table, Owlly had a surprise of his own.

"This trader—Baladur—you say he's the one that brought you to the city three years ago—that he remembered you and your parents from the village?"

"Yeah," answered Ronnie.

"Describe him."

"In his sixties, maybe, leathery face, between your height and mine, wiry, wears a lot of clothes even when it's warm, plus a wide-brim hat over a bald head."

Husband and wife glanced at each other in what looked like amusement.

"What?" asked Ronnie suspiciously.

"Well, I give the man credit for discretion. He's the one that brought the message from your dad that you might show up—a few days before you did."

"What?... It can't be the same man. He was moving *south* on the river road when I got a ride. Besides, why wouldn't he have told me by now?"

"Why? Because the person who gave him the job—your dad—didn't authorize him to, and you didn't need to know. That discretion is why I'm prepared to trust him now. As for him being southbound when you saw him: licensed transports shuttle back and forth during a pogrom—to transport plunder. If he left the city after talking to us, that would put him on the road southbound with another load a few days later."

Ronnie simply shook his head in amazement. If Baladur was *that* discrete, he wondered if Hemma and Rae and Chatter also knew who he was at the time, that day they came upon him by the side of the road, offering his axe for a ride.

"Okay," said Owlly decisively, "here's what we're gonna do.... At tonight's meeting I'll present this intel as coming from a source I trust. The committee will have to decide how to address the possible scenarios. Now ... go task Tofer."

It was long after midnight by the time the colonel could get to the window in the bathroom. In the bedroom, Nuyen finally slept after returning from a disturbing committee meeting and he moved with caution to turn up the small lamp and compose his note with pencil and paper. When he was done, he stood with the lamp and moved it back and forth across the window, hoping the watcher who was now always on site after committee meetings hadn't fallen asleep. A minute later, the roughly dressed and hooded man dimly appeared below the window and the colonel dropped the folded note to him.

Less than an hour after that, a disheveled Sula came from her bedroom to receive the note from the night shift commander of her household guard. She read it and frowned.

"Summon Grotius," she ordered. "Now."

37 - Double Agent

Six days out

Ronnie was in the market when the first detailed reports hit. A frisson of morbid fear swept through the crowd as shoppers and vendors began to congregate around anyone who claimed to know anything or to have talked to anyone who claimed to know anything. The scene reminded Ronnie of the one in the street in front of Checkers's place, where Error agents had seeded the crowd with the appropriate misinformation and let human nature do the rest.

The rumors spoke of skirmishes at the frontier in many places at once as the heretic army tested ZAHdom's defenses. Many garrison troops and civilians brutalized and murdered, homes and crops burned. Most terrifying: entire fields of brave young recruits sent out just days before, lying dead and dismembered–with not a single dead heretic among them. It was inhuman, otherworldly. It had to be stopped.

Panic buying began and Ronnie extricated himself from the maelstrom to head back to the shop. He told the others what he'd seen and heard and received in turn the message that Lady Rosamund was expecting him at twelve bells. Like everyone, he had a million things to do to help prepare for the multiple contingencies identified by the committee, but he couldn't afford any drama from Rosamund just now, and anyway, she might be worked for some important morsel of information.

Something was wrong. Rosamund went through a lot of the same motions as usual—commanding him, using him, at times overcoming his faux-resistance, but something was different—beside her uncommon dryness. In place of her usual selfish lust was ... what? Fear? ... Embarrassment? ...

Finally he grew impatient with the charade they were both engaged in and looked up from her frightened nub, not with the expression of an ignorant teenage sex toy but with the knowing gaze of a man her own equal. He'd taken her hands while his mouth was against her and now, as he looked at her steadily and her eyes grew large in comprehension and as she started to tremble, he held them tight against the mattress.

"Don't cry out, Rosie," he said calmly. "I'll break your neck before they can save you."

She couldn't have been more shocked if she'd been a gourmand about to consume a lobster that suddenly stood up on the plate and addressed her with perfect diction.

"Do you believe me?"

"Let me go!" she ordered with false bravado, then, shivering, "What are you going to do?" and finally, "Please don't hurt me!"

"You're in a world of shit, milady."

"Who are you? Are you Freethinker?"

"A world of shit," he repeated, "and I'm the only one who can get you out of it."

That was worth listening to. "How?" she breathed after a moment, ceasing her struggle.

"I'm going to ask you some questions, some of which I already know the answers too," said Ronnie without blinking. "If you lie to me once, I'm just going to kill you, and myself."

"You wouldn't kill your—"

He was working the poison packet from the recesses of his mouth and now displayed it on the end of his tongue.

"What's that?"

"Death," said Ronnie. "Not pleasant, but sure. If I bite it and spread it on you with my tongue, we'll both be dead within minutes. Faster if I chew into you."

Her legs strained to close but she was pinioned.

"Now," be began, "first question." He pushed the packet with his tongue to hold it between his front teeth and muttered around it, "Is anyone in the apartment with us?"

"No."

"Outside?"

"No."

"Next," he said, tonguing aside the packet again, "where did you get the gold you gave me?"

"I ...," she began, and hesitated, until Ronnie slid down slightly and chillingly kissed her goose-bumped belly. "I borrowed it—from a special operations fund."

'You stole it."

"Yes."

"Next, what's happened since I last saw you?"

"What do you mean?"

"You know what I mean. What scared you?"

"A Ministry cop, a detective, calls himself 'inspector'. Said you were seen in familiar conversation with Lady Clare before she was attacked, then chased the attackers. Surveillance on you had revealed our connection here, so he asked what l had talked to you about—if we'd ever discussed my work. I told him no."

"Good, that's what we're gonna go with."

"How do you mean?"

He cocked his head. "Ever attended a torture session, Rosie?"

"No."

"But you've heard about them."

"Yes."

"Do you have any doubt that you'll reveal having stolen state monies to give to me or having revealed state secrets to me, if the inquisitors get ahold of you?"

"No."

"Do you have any doubt that they'll execute you for those infractions–once they're done with you?"

"No."

"Then we'd best put on a good show to prevent that, wouldn't you say?"

"Yes."

"He released her hands and drew the covers over her as he got up and sat on the side of the bed, still naked. He fluffed her pillows and helped her to a comfortable position.

"Now," he said in a pleasant way, "in exchange for saving your life, you're going to tell me everything I want to know about this cop and his investigation, about these special operations funds, and about these rumors of attacks at the frontier. Then we'll go from there."

"All right," said Lady Rosamund, settling into her role as traitor with surprising readiness, almost as if she viewed it as an adventure.

By the one o'clock bell, Ronnie was ready to wind down and adjourn to another time, but Rosamund wouldn't stop talking. She'd found her new passion: secret agent, or at least willing pawn of a naked and gorgeous and potentially brutal enemy agent. As Ronnie started to stand to get dressed, she reached out and touched his arm, letting the covers fall away from her breasts to reveal erect nipples.

"What gave me away, Ronnie?" she asked.

He thought about that a second, then answered with a little smile: "You were dry."

"Well," she replied, moving her hand to his bare leg, "I'm wet now."

∆ ∆ ∆

Striding back toward Woodmaker Street, the surprising turn with Lady Rosamund and the nearness of battle on his mind, Ronnie took stock of the last two and a half years of his life, during which he'd learned to be not just a military theoretician and a spy and killer but an expert lover of women, initially servicing unmarried priestesses according to their legal claim under the Protocols, but mostly whoring his way to those secrets of the Citadel held by senior clergywomen, usually married ones. During that time he'd never had a real girlfriend, never fallen in love even if pretended love was the seducer's best tool and could sometimes feel enough like the real thing to temporarily make one forget one's purpose.

In a few days—one way or the other—that would all be over, he told himself, as he automatically checked for a tail in the propped-open glass door of a shop he was passing.

What would he *do* in the new world—if it could be brought into existence? What would he *be?* A simple woodworker? Or maybe a teacher, a politician, or a diplomat? In the Zahist world, almost no one was qualified for these roles, but he was. He'd grown up studying and conversing about the history and nature not just of the lands now occupied by the followers of Zah but of those across the seas, sometimes, with Jenna, in the languages of those places. He wasn't the natural linguist she was, but he'd learned from her that once you've accepted the *idea* of languages and cultures very different from your own, you're on your way.

Jenna. There she was again, his childhood friend and mentor and first love, insinuating herself into his mind in these latter days despite his best efforts and despite the likelihood of never seeing her again. According to his State Ministry lover, Magnus's mission to faraway China was supposed to return after the coming winter, but Ronnie knew that might never happen if the rebellion was successful. Perhaps the diplomatic party would settle permanently in China, that wondrous place where, according to reports his informant had seen, electric lights illuminated the throne room of the warlord of Xian and what sounded like a pre-Cleansing automobile carried VIPs about the great courtyard with a whirring sound; he could imagine Magnus the emissary and Jenna the interpreter being taken for a ride in it with the warlord.

The tender feelings that still arose when he thought about Jenna made him feel uneasy about all the young priestesses whose bodies and emotions he'd clambered over to get what he needed from older, less-vulnerable ones. Most were not Zahist zealots but simple survivors in the world in which circumstances had put them, theoretically equal to men in Zah's creation but in modern practice mostly not. Many now earned a government stipend for raising children he'd fathered–children destined for government service whom he didn't have the luxury of caring about because he couldn't directly do anything for them. The best he could do was to help create a better world for them to grow up in. As he passed through the gate and neared the shop and prepared to return to the business of war, he hoped what he and his people sought to achieve somehow justified all the uncertainty and suffering that was coming to them and their mothers.

"She said the word filtering out of Grotius's office in the last few days was that the attacks began two days before Baladur showed up, but initially only a few people were privy to the intelligence," Ronnie told Owlly in the afternoon. "Maybe that's true and maybe not. More recently–the way it looks to me–they've sent contingents of expendable recruits, escorted by special operations troops. At the frontier, away from witnesses, the special ops guys kill the recruits, change gear and terrorize the countryside a little, and change back to straggle in with stories of heretic armies. Locals clamor for Citadel regulars to protect them, and now they're starting to be sent."

"That would mesh with their need to pull the whole army and part of the Guard into the field, wouldn't it?" said Owlly. "If their objective is a far pogrom."

"*If* that's their objective," said Ronnie.

"Anyway, good job, son," said Owlly. "I'll get this before the committee tonight.... You say you arranged to see her again in two days? Must have ended on good terms. Think she'll show?"

"Yeah, I think so," said Ronnie, remembering the moment when both he and Rosamund realized you couldn't just switch off an intense sexual relationship like they'd had, even if it no longer made sense, or at least not as it had.

In the late afternoon, as Ronnie and Slammer Jon went over battle plans in the library and Tofer rearranged books again, a man in the Black Tower was having one of those career-making moments.

"Dark hair and blue eyes, you say?" asked the acting deputy inspector of his next-desk colleague, trying to sound casual. "Late teens? Tall?"

"Late teens/early twenties *now*," she clarified. "We're talkin' more than two years ago."

The inspector had been doing his best to block out the woman's grumbling about the task she'd been given, until he overheard the exasperated complaint: "How many tall, dark-haired, blue-eyed teenagers could there have been? What if he was a trespasser?"

She'd exhausted the possibilities among guests with VIP passes and was grasping at straws among the two thousand or so Citadel boys of a certain age who could have been on the bridge that day. The idea that he might not have been a registered Citadelian at all, but instead a gate-crashing townie, didn't bear contemplating.

The inspector thrilled with the possibility that his colleague's high-priority target and his own Ronnie-the-carpenter might be the same person. If he could just make the connection between Ronnie and the bridge, he'd be set for life. He quickly made an excuse about going to see a snitch on a case to which he was actually assigned and went downstairs to Lady Rosamund's office.

He'd already seen the Property Department chief and received her oral report about her midday rendezvous, which she'd seemed to draw out and make more graphic when she realized how easily titillated he was. She'd said Ronnie had given no cause for suspicion and when asked about the rumors of his saving Clare, he'd explained it was a fluke. They were talking about cabinetry, he acted without thinking when he saw the archer, and was then ordered by the bodyguards to put his poor rent-a-pony to the fruitless chase. He was scared, he'd said, and worried about explaining things to Daisy's owner. As she'd concluded her report, Rosamund had unexpectedly asked if the inspector had adequate funding for his investigation and assured him she could dip into her own discretionary funds if he ran short. He'd filed the bribe offer away for a future conversation.

"The bridge?" she said now. "No, I don't think so, and I was there, in the VIP enclosure. Shall I ask my friends?" she asked, by which she meant the two senior bureaucrats he'd already talked to.

"Yes, very kind of you," he responded, enjoying his own fake politesse, knowing it was always best to keep the subjects hopeful and confident until the trap door to the interrogation chambers was opened beneath their feet. Then, armed with the new question, he was off to start descending the ladder of acquaintance, cataloging the women and pretending to be satisfied by their self-serving palaver until he could present his conclusions to Sula and get them all consigned to the inquisitors, and seeking, ever seeking, that woman who would say, "Yes, he was there."

38 - Spy Hunt

Five days

The powerful forces of history and hope and momentum were sweeping doubt aside.

History taught that the Priesthood did not conduct pogroms in the capital because they were too disruptive to tranquility and commerce; some even said that moderates on the Council of Messengers tolerated heretics among the populace—as long as they provided valuable services and didn't raise their heads—as a necessary evil or even moderating counterbalance to the militarists.

Hope surged because it had been so long suppressed and suddenly sensed soil and sunlight in which to grow.

Momentum gained as many signs began to point in the direction of a "far" pogrom to be initiated on the equinox: Under cover of the suddenly-made-plausible heretic threat, units were being readied to march out, secrecy was dropped in favor of preparing the populace for the opportunities and sacrifices of war, and—crucially for Ronnie—traders and others with suitable vehicles were being dispatched toward the frontier in all directions, as evidenced by the spoken message Rae had sent him as her family and others prepared to depart. So irresistible was the momentum toward rebellion among the Freethinker leaders that the coincidence of the new reports, coming soon after the committee had discussed their troubling absence, was only briefly considered before being disregarded. It's implication—compromise of the military committee—was too awful to contemplate, so it wasn't. Ronnie tried to raise a voice of caution through Owlly and Slammer Jon and Verjil, but the elders had now decided, and he could only attend to his duty.

In the afternoon of the fifth day, the rebellion—and Ronnie—fell into mortal danger.

Throughout the day Ronnie made himself available as a message center for Slammer Jon, puttering about the workshop and showroom, checking the already-counted inventory of fasteners as cover for noting quantities of other items, polishing already-polished furniture while watching for the well-dressed and mostly female couriers. Some time after two bells, a stylishly dressed young woman entered and he moved toward her. He thought he'd seen her before, though not like this—maybe at a fancy club. Early twenties, nose-tall to himself, fashionably short and shining red hair framing long-lashed brown eyes, wonderfully shaped and poised but today somehow tentative.

"Good afternoon, madam," he said as he approached. "May I ..."

"Hello, Ronnie."

"Hello ..."

He stopped. He'd automatically thought to banter or otherwise give himself time to ascertain if she was an unknown courier or friend-of-a-friend, or perhaps a priestess in mufti or ...

"Cinya?" he blurted. "Cinya, is that you?"

"It's me," she said, smiling nervously. "I didn't know if you'd remember. It's been awhile. You're all grown up."

"Not remember you?" he said, shaking his head. "That wouldn't be possible. It's just that ... "He gestured at her hair and dress and shoes and light civilian overrobe. "Did you get fired?" he teased.

"I'm in disguise," she replied, trying for an amusing tone.

"Well, it certainly worked with ..." He paused as he remembered how much she valued her waist-length hair. "You're serious?"

"Yes."

"Are you in trouble, C?" he asked, glancing over her shoulder to the street. "What can I do?"

"You're in trouble, too. Can we talk?"

Ronnie turned to Nel, who was standing at her desk near the back of the showroom as only one customer browsed. "Mom, can I have a few minutes?"

"Of course," said Nel. "Take your time."

He led Cinya to an arrangement of upholstered chairs at the side and pulled two close together and they sat.

"What's wrong?" he asked.

"The Error Police are asking about you." When he glanced again over her shoulder she continued. "Don't worry, they haven't gotten to me yet."

"What do you mean, 'gotten to you yet?'"

"It seems like they're going down a list of your girlfriends, farther and farther back. They ask general questions, but two specially."

"Yes?"

She watched for his reaction. "They want to know if you ever asked girlfriends about their work, and if they'd ever heard of you being on the bridge for the sailing of the *Wind of ZAH*, two years ago."

Ronnie felt the blood drain from his face and hands. The first question meant they were looking for a spy, the second meant the military committee definitely had a leak.

Ronnie's special value to the Freethinkers was that he was the only one of them, other than the Colonel, who could identify all eleven Messengers at a glance, thus making their capture more certain and their use more effective, with or without the Colonel. At a committee meeting the Colonel had—out loud to six other people—made the connection between Red Mask and the celebration on the bridge. Now the Error Police were trying to connect Ronnie to the bridge. Therefore, it seemed, they were trying to connect Red Mask to Ronnie. Ronnie *was* Red Mask, they meant to prove.

As Cinya saw Ronnie's mind working furiously, she grew worried.

"I'm scared, Ronnie," she said, now glancing over her own shoulder., "Should I be?"

"Yes ... I'm sorry."

"What have you done?" she demanded, a note of hysteria in her voice. "What *are* you?"

He took her hands as Nel looked up briefly from her work. "Calm down, C. Let's see what we have here exactly. You said 'they' were asking questions but hadn't reached you yet. First of all, how many cops are we talking about?"

"Well, I didn't mean 'they' literally. I think it's just one—a detective, by his badge, but calls himself 'inspector'."

"One detective?" By himself? No scary entourage? That's odd, don't you think?"

"Is it?"

"I think so. Makes me think he's trying to keep what he learns to himself."

"Which is what?"

"In a minute. You also said they were making their way down a list. Where are they on the list?"

"You tell me. I won't use names, but one's a department head in the Planning ministry—her secretary's a friend of mine—and the other is the mistress of a Guard Corps general. Ring a bell?"

"Yes. They've got a way to go."

"That's comforting," said Cinya with a note of pique.

"How did these women know about me being on the bridge?"

"Well ... I might have talked about you a little after you left.... I guess I missed you."

"How can you be so sure they didn't tell the cop about you and me and the bridge, if they knew?"

"Because we don't tell strangers more then we have to—even cops. But probably everyone will tell who introduced you or knew you first. Cops won't leave without that."

"They'll be back." said Ronnie, cryptically.

"What do you mean?"

Instead of answering, Ronnie, squeezed her hands and asked, "Cinya, why have you done this?"

"What, exactly?"

He held her hands apart to display her. "*This*," he said. "Cut your beautiful hair, put aside your grey robe for a—"

"Black."

"What?"

"I wear a black robe now, which sort of goes with being assistant catering manager at the Palace."

"Congratulations, milady."

"Thank you."

"And what about Iris? Where is she in this?"

"She's not. I never mentioned her by name to anyone, and anyway, she lives at Mount of ZAH now, with a husband and a child. *Your* child, as a matter of fact. A beautiful little—"

"Stop," said Ronnie, hand raised.

"I'm sorry," said Cinya, understanding. "Which brings me to why I'm here."

"I'm listening," said Ronnie, but then his attention was taken by a matronly woman in workaday clothes who entered and caught his eye.

"Excuse me just a minute," he said, and went to the woman to memorize some piece of information and then return, to find not the self-possessed priestess and assistant catering manager he'd left but a woman quietly weeping in remembered loss. He quickly found a clean polishing cloth and came back to scoot his chair closer so he could dab her tears, in the midst of which she laughed ruefully and rested her forehead on his shoulder.

"It's almost a relief," she sniffed.

"What is?"

"To know you dumped me for a string of other women because you were on some kind of mission, not because you didn't like me."

"Cinya ... I–"

"Don't," she said, and he fell to silently and almost imperceptibly rocking with her. After a minute she took the cloth and dried her eyes but remained close to him. "That day, on the bridge, I'd just been told I suffered from Sula's curse and–"

"What's that?" he asked softly.

"It's ... infertility. Do you understand?"

"Yes."

"Yes, of course you do.... Some women call it that after Lady Sula, the Messenger, in fear that it will turn them hard-hearted the way it did her when she realized she'd never be the matriarch of her own branch. She was my age....

"I'd been with a man who'd already fathered children," she went on, "but Iris convinced me I just had to try elsewhere, as many elsewheres as it took. It was she who pushed me to speak to you that day. I just wanted a baby, but–something about you–I fell in love. A few days later, when you moved on, I tried to feel it with others, but found only disappointment. Finally I just gave up and tried to concentrate on my work. Until now. I was afraid of how it would feel to see you again, but I couldn't bear to see you hurt if I could prevent it."

"Thank you," he said. "And there's no curse on you, Sula's or otherwise."

"So, are you going to explain it all to me?" she asked.

"Yes, but first ... there's something I want to show you."

"Show me?"

"Yes, it's this way," he said, taking her by the hand and leading her through the displays with a glance to Nel. At the stairway to the basement he descended a couple of steps and looked back.

"Is this where you bury the bodies?" she asked, half seriously.

"Not yours," he said, and put her hand on his shoulder to follow him down.

They meandered through the shelves of woodshop supplies until they got to Ronnie's personal space, clean and comfortable and well-lighted by the sheer-curtained ground-level windows and elevated from the concrete floor on a low, wood-planked platform. Cinya looked at it with amusement, then stepped up and commenced to wander about to study Ronnie's personal effects. Her eyes lingered on the utilitarian but very welcoming single bed.

"Did you expect a big round one, like in the love hotels?" he asked.

Instead of answering, she came to the edge of the platform and confronted him almost at eye level. "What did you want to show me."

"You have to close your eyes first," he said, and when she'd complied, put his hands at her waist and began gently to kiss her face and eyelids.

As Cinya slumbered on his chest, Ronnie slipped the poison packet back in his mouth and tried to puzzle it all out. The committee had a leak, he figured, but not necessarily direct to the police. The Colonel had made the connection between him and the bridge in front of six other people. Those six led to hundreds more, and the leak could have happened through any of them. Circles and individual members were expected to operate on a "need to know" basis, but there was no practical way of enforcing the generations-old protocol.

If the leak about Red Mask occurred below the level of platoon commander, it may not have been accompanied by details of the coming operation, since those further down did not yet "need to know"—again, theoretically. And that must be what has happened, he surmised, because the Freethinker community is not currently being ripped apart before it can launch a planned attack. Right?

One thing was for sure—he couldn't hide things from Mom and Dad anymore. There were too many possible explanations here—some relatively untroubling, some horrific, catastrophic. He needed help.

Cinya stirred, and he stroked her hair. She murmured something warmly against his skin.

"What?"

"Tenderness," she replied. "That's what you brought me down here to show me."

He continued to stroke her head and she moved to kiss his nipple.

"Maybe I thought you could use a little tranquility before hearing the bad news," he said.

She stopped moving and looked up at him, then propped herself on an elbow with her breasts squashed against his ribcage and waited.

"Putting myself in the mind of this cop," he began, "I think he's freelancing–maybe for a bribe but probably for career advancement. He's come across some information through the Clare thing and maybe stitched it together with something else and now he's almost got a package he thinks he can sell.

"He won't move until the deal's done and he gets authorization to proceed," he continued, "but if he gets it, things will get ugly."

"How so?"

"You and the other women will be arrested and consigned to the inquisitors, to see if you ever told me anything you shouldn't have."

Cinya shook her head in refusal. "No! He's questioning each one as he goes, writing it all down! Then he leaves!"

"That's just preliminary, to get you all to tell lies that can be thrown back at you during the sessions."

"The sessions?" she repeated in a strangled voice.

"Torture-interrogation sessions."

Cinya stared for a moment, then shuddered and began to look about in panic. She lurched from the bed to gather her clothes and try to put them on all at once.

"You can't save yourself," Ronnie said calmly, "even if you turn me in. It's their protocol, and no one *you* know is going to interfere with the Error police. However ..."

"However?" Cinya echoed, controlling herself, smoothing her dress and sitting on the side of the bed to put on her shoes.

"However, *I* can help."

"*You* can help," she said skeptically.

"Yes."

She looked at him for a long time before saying, "You know, you should have killed me instead of fucking me."

"Probably."

"Why didn't you?"

"Couldn't."

"Why not?"

"Dunno. Jus' couldn't."

She managed a tiny smile. "So," she said finally, "how can you fix this so no one has to die or be tortured?"

"Can't."

"But you said—"

"Can't fix it so no one has to die."

"You mean ..."

"Someone definitely has to die."

Owlly and Nel sat straight-backed across the dining table from Ronnie as they heard the evidence that the military committee might be compromised. It couldn't have been worse news.

"So your theory is that, since no Freethinkers are being arrested yet," said Owlly, "the story about the guy from the bridge who knows the Messengers must have leaked somewhere far beyond the committee itself, out of the context of rebellion."

"Possibly," said Ronnie, "unless it's part of a pattern of leaks." It was really a question, but Owlly didn't respond to it.

"What about the description. Do you think everyone you took messages to a few weeks ago realized you were the one in red?"

"I thought not, but how else would the description be so accurate?"

In answer, Nel reached across and took Ronnie's rough-palmed hands. Turning them up, she said, "Look, these are a craftsman's hands, but *these*," turning them over, "are the smooth, unblemished hands of a young man. What little hair there is on your arms is dark, like your eyelashes and eyebrows, and even in dim light one would probably say your eyes are blue. That's enough right there, I'd say." The men agreed.

"Can I make a suggestion about tonight's committee meeting?" Ronnie asked. Owlly nodded and he went on. "The fact that our two mustering places are still secure suggests that our group and Flame's are the most disciplined, the one's we can be most sure of. I know it's against protocol, but maybe you should communicate this new information–our suspicions–privately to Flame, so it doesn't get out and compromise more. Then, if we can neutralize this bridge thing on the side, we can return to relying on whether or not the army sorties in five days to tell us whether or not to muster and launch the attack." Owlly looked skeptical; Nel nodded approvingly.

"'Neutralize this bridge thing on the side?'" said Owlly doubtfully. "What are you talking about, son?"

"Well," Ronnie began, a little shamefaced, "I need your permission to do something, but first I need to tell you something *else*–something I left out before–about that day at Checkers's–something I did."

"What did you do?" they said in unison, staring.

"I killed two men."

Ronnie had barely gotten past being scolded and then reluctantly praised for his actions at Checkers's, then shocking his parents anew with his plan to "neutralize this bridge thing," to winning their acquiescence, when shouting erupted above their heads. Three hands immediately went to mouth while three tongues found and positioned poison packets. At the ready, they listened.

"Well I'm going!" said a surprisingly penetrating feminine voice. "And you can't stop me!"

A more muffled masculine voice answered with something like, "Now, you listen to me! I'm not–"

"Forget it! I'm going!"

Ah, a domestic argument, shocking in its novelty and intensity, but better than twenty or fifty Error paramilitaries storming through the doors.

All three went out to the showroom to see who else might be overhearing and to stop the feuding couple before they could say anything dangerous, but there were no customers, furniture shopping having fallen down the list of priorities as tension increased in the city.

"Hey, you two!" called Nel toward the loft. When the couple appeared she said, " *What,* in Zah's name, are you *doing?* There could be a bunch of customers down here—or a bunch of Error agents!"

"I'm sorry, Mom," Brod said anxiously, then pointed at his three-months-pregnant wife, "but she—she—she— *Tell them!"*

Suki stepped to the rail and assumed the pose as of a queen addressing her subjects. "I shall fight in the upcoming battle, in my brother-in-law's squad."

"See?" wailed her husband. "Mom, help me talk some sense into her, for god's sake! For the baby's sake!"

"I already tried," sighed Nel.

"What? You *knew*? ... and you let her—"

"My boy, you ought to know by now, there's no *letting* or *not* letting Suki do *anything*. I just promised to help look after Madi."

"But, but ..."

"Son," said Owlly, "you're both grown-ups, and this is husband and wife stuff, so work it out between yourselves. And do it quickly and quietly and don't wake Madi. Suki will be an asset, in the fighting or out of it, but if she's going to be *in* it, she needs some coaching, and there's not much time. Now go!"

Ronnie soon left the shop to deliver his collected messages to Slammer Jon at his plywood-manufacturing operation two blocks away and there received an assignment to reconnoiter the vicinity of the church—looking for signs of surveillance—before sundown. He took some of

Mom's fresh apple pie to Tofer and left by the "back door" with his leather satchel. His route took him past the armory, where he noted the still-open delivery gate and a couple of wagons at the dock. In the pleasant autumn weather the door to the office complex was propped open.

Walking the streets around the church where he knew Jak and a few others quietly worked, exchanging greetings and occasional pleasantries with the locals, he detected nothing unusual. Then, his circuit completed, he considered how much time remained before his return to the alley would coincide with nightfall and turned the opposite way in the direction of the Palace. He made a loop around Clare's leafy neighborhood, walking purposefully, and came back downhill across the street from her long brick wall. A male bodyguard he didn't know watched him from the elevated terrace where he and Clare had stood, and a female guard paced the section adjoining the lady's private quarters.

Coming even with the gatehouse and the closed gate and seeing Bear in conversation with the gate guards, he slowed to a stop under a tree. Bear saw him, stopped talking, and the guards followed their boss's gaze to Ronnie. After a few seconds, Bear gave him a "move along" gesture with his head, but Ronnie remained placidly watching. Relenting, the big man glanced around and back to Ronnie and gave a thumbs-up sign against his chest. Ronnie returned a tiny nod and resumed his descent toward the darkening alley and home.

Lady Clare yet lived.

39 - Boy on the Bridge

Four days

The future of the Citadel and thus of the known world was coming down to the timing and order of a few crucial events. In the homes and secret meeting places of Freethinkers and others who would be rid of Zahist tyranny and in the Palace of Messengers and the Ministry for the Suppression of Error—and wherever else such tyranny was challenged or defended—collective and individual interests pushed and pulled on the machinery of the future's creation.

Throughout the morning and early afternoon of the fourth day before equinox, the acting deputy inspector of detectives, in pursuit of private interests with consequences far beyond himself, eschewing an official carriage and instead taxiing about for secrecy, braced women in their homes and offices and beauty parlors, on occasion encountering husbands or boyfriends who were asked to leave with the intimidating assurance that, at this stage, it would be in everyone's interest if the lady and the policemen kept the matter between themselves. The inspector made a show of writing their names and their big and little lies in the notebook he kept inside his leather jacket and moved one, not wasting too much time with women who had independently come to know Ronnie after the celebration on the bridge but knowing that he was getting ever closer. Their time would come later anyway.

∆ ∆ ∆

Dawn of the fourth day found the late-sleeping Minister Grotius rousted out of his lover's arms by Lady Sula's bodyguards and hustled without girdle or makeup to his office down the corridor, there to explain to the incipiently homicidal black-robbed woman why his people were getting distracted from the real plan by the phony one and why one potentially troublesome young heretic couldn't be identified so all his kith and kin and coconspirators could be rounded up, if they appeared to threaten her private objective. Functionaries scurried about for the answers.

At midday in the Shopping Street hideaway, Ronnie claimed more than he knew to terrify the still-fully-dressed Lady Rosamund into believing she and others would be arrested and tortured if the inspector's freelancing efforts were not stopped.

"I'll pay him!" she wailed, standing in the middle of the floor as he sat on the end of the bed. "I can pay him!"

"He's not doing this for the money, Rosie. He wants promotion. There's probably not enough money to—"

"But ... there must be a—"

"If you're gonna pay somebody, pay somebody to *stop* him, and get the book he carries."

She stared at him open-mouthed, incredulous. "You mean ...?"

"What choice do you have?" he asked reasonably,

"But ... *how?"*

"Don't you know somebody?"

"Not like that," she said, then, grasping, "Do you?"

"Sure, but killing an Error detective is a big deal. I don't know if they would take the job. How much can you pay?"

"You should pay, too!"

"Can't, Rosie. What you gave me was for others. It's gone."

She glared angrily for a moment.

"You *could* just try to escape to the mountains," he suggested. "If you're not robbed, you might be able to make a life." Now she just looked miserable at the prospect of trading her wealth and position for a sheltering tree or cave and a brutish "protector."

She looked away in thought, then back. "I can get twenty ounces of gold," she announced.

"Then I think you'd best go to the market and spend them on some warm country clothes and boots. Winter's coming."

"How much, then!"

"Another hundred, I'd say."

"All right, all right!" she cried in defeat. "What do we do?"

"First of all, you go get the money and get it to me at the shop between two and four bells," he instructed. "Is the cop expecting a report from you?"

"Yes," she said. "At two bells. My office."

"Good. If he asks why we were so quick today, tell him we did it in the hallway with our clothes on–give him some juicy details; he'll like that. Then–now listen carefully–you tell him this ..."

A messenger sat patiently on a bench at the side of the Black Tower's lobby, observing the traffic and occasionally glancing toward the uniformed man and woman at the reception counter. Near two bells a formidable-looking black-leather-coated man entered and headed for the stairs; the woman at the counter signaled and the messenger rose to intercept.

"Inspector?"

"Yes?" said the policeman, slowing.

"Message from a lady, sir. 'The Guardsman's friend', she said."

"Go ahead," said the officer with satisfaction. The seeds of fear he'd planted were starting to sprout, first with the Guard commander's mistress, the courtesan Mona, who'd had an "exchange of professional courtesies" with fellow player Ronnie.

The messenger went blank-faced and droned: "Quote: 'I

remembered a story about Ronnie meeting someone on the bridge. I think her name is Cinya and she works in the catering service at the Palace.' Unquote."

"Cinya, she said?"

"Yes, sir."

The detective smirked and turned away without tipping the messenger. He climbed to the fourth floor and headed for Lady Rosamund's corner office overlooking the river, passing the assistants' desks where poor Janelle–from whom Rosamund had taken Ronnie–still worked.

In an age-old ritual he was made to wait a few minutes to establish his inferior rank, which the thought of Lady Rosamund being brutalized in the basement made tolerable. Then she came out to rescue him.

"Inspector!" she cried, glancing accusingly at her secretary. "I'm so sorry you were made to wait. Please come in. How goes the investigation?"

"It moves along, milady," he said, taking a proffered chair. "How goes the affair?"

"The *affair?"* she repeated with a certain amusement, settling behind her large desk. "That might be overstating. Why, today I'd barely gotten through the door before ..."

She stopped and put on an uncertain look. "Excuse me, Inspector, I'm sure you don't want to hear the sordid details."

"Perhaps I *should.* It might give me insight."

"Well," said Rosamund confidentially, leaning forward slightly as the officer did the same, "I was still dressed, but I wasn't wearing underwear, so ..."

When the inspector had left and reflected on the interview, he realized that the only new information of interest he'd collected was regarding subject Ronnie's social life away from the priestess. It seemed he'd taken to spending most nights at a club called Scarface, where he was treated like a VIP because so many male customers had disappeared into the army: special table overlooking the dance floor, discount drinks, the works. He was planning to go that very night.

For the inspector, the planets started to come into alignment.

First, he spent an excruciating hour in his poorly ventilated sixth-floor walk-up office, pretending to work on an assigned case, until his boss left and he could get on with his real work. Then he caught a cab for the Palace, showed his badge and got directions, and found the catering office but not anyone called Cinya. She was due back, they said.

He wandered back toward the high-ceilinged lobby to look up at the patched skylight and the elaborate marble staircases and columns that still impressed despite a century of smoke and water damage. His eyes fell and he found himself looking past a guard station down the broad corridor that housed the private residences of the Sword and his fellow Messengers. Down the stairs at the end, he knew, was a formal audience hall.

As he gawked, he heard sharp steps approaching from behind and turned.

"Inspector?" asked a young woman in black. "You're looking for me?"

"Ah, *Lady* Cinya, I presume," he said, in recognition of the status conveyed by her costume. "Thank you for seeing me." He showed his badge and gave his name and lifted her hand toward his forehead and waited for her to invite him back to her office, but she did not.

"Could we ...?" he started to ask, gesturing back down the corridor.

"Actually, Inspector, I'm a little pressed for time just now. Was there something ..."

He was disconcerted by her lack of deference and by her attractiveness. Time to put her in her place.

"Very well, milady," he intoned in his official voice. "It has come to the Ministry's attention that you are acquainted with one Rondak, a woodmaker of the town. Can you confirm this?"

She tilted her head slightly. "What's this about, Inspector?"

"Do you refuse to answer?"

The priestess took half a step back at the policeman's confrontational tone. "Perhaps we should ask my boss to join us," she said.

"Perhaps you should answer the question before you get yourself and your boss in trouble."

Now she was getting scared, like he was used to. He felt himself on firmer ground, and becoming aroused.

"Then no, I don't know anyone by that name," she answered.

The inspector gazed at her with a certain sadness before taking out his fat black notebook and writing a few lines in it. He poised his pencil to write a few more.

"What about two and a half years ago," he asked mildly, "on the bridge, at the sailing of the *Wind of ZAH?"*

"What about it?"

"You were there."

"Yes, along with hundreds of others."

"And you claim you didn't meet anyone there."

"*Of course* I met someone there; I met a *lot* of someones; I ran out of cards."

"But not Rondak—that's your claim?"

She shook her head in exasperation. "Inspector, how do you expect a ... 19-year-old woman to remember every man who wants to meet her? I just don't know any named Rondak."

"Boy," said the officer.

"What?"

"Not a 'man', as you said. More of a boy ... about seventeen at the time."

"Ah ... yes ...," said Cinya, suddenly falling into a reverie. "A teenager—a virgin teenager."

"So you *do* remember him!"

"I remember his cock," she said with unexpected frankness. "It was lovely."

"And his name?" asked the inspector, rigid with anticipation.

"Definitely not Rondak ... Ronnie, maybe."

"And his appearance?"

She put her head to the side again, thinking. "Good looking, I'm sure, but ..."

"Height? Coloration?" quizzed the policeman impatiently.

"I think ... honey-blond hair and ... no, that was another guy."

"Would you recognize him if you saw him now?"

"Maybe. For sure if I saw his cock."

"Good. You're coming with me."

"What? *No*, I'm not going with you! I have a date after work and– "

"Look, Cinya," he said harshly, tactically dropping her honorific, "you're in a lot of trouble for even knowing this guy. I'm giving you a chance here–a chance to avoid the inquisitors. So far, I'm working this alone. If *they* have to get involved, I won't be able to help you.... So, what's it going to be?

"Right now?" she asked in a small voice.

"No. I'll pick you up around eight bells. We'll go to a club called *Scarface*. He hangs out there. Do you know it?"

"In the town, yeah," she said. "I'll have to change."

"You've been there," he asked.

"No. It's a little raunchy for us–has a love hotel attached–but they say the music's good."

"Really," he said sarcastically, knowing exactly what she meant. He hated the new, pounding rhythms.

She looked him up and down. "Are you going like that?" she asked. "I mean, you're a good-looking man and all, but you look like a cop."

"No, of course not," he said defensively. "I've worked undercover before. Just give me your address and I'll see you at eight bells."

After Cinya walked away the inspector took a deep breath and stood still for several seconds as he let it out, his eyes closed and his arms slightly away from his sides, fingers splayed, basking in the glory and triumph of the moment. He'd found the boy on the bridge! –or as good as found him–and his life would never be the same again. First, with his new title and salary he'd move out of the bachelors' quarters in the Tower and into a proper house. He'd ditch the hookers and big-cop groupies for a respectable girlfriend and maybe even start a family. His new peers would treat him with respect and he could finally be the one to mete out disdain and humiliation to underlings.

Opening his eyes, he again regarded the Messengers' residence wing and with a surge of self-confidence thought, *Why wait? Why not do it now? What could go wrong?* Suddenly his feet began to move and he found himself crossing the cavernous lobby, across the flow of traffic, toward the guard station at the corridor's entrance.

As he approached, the two men at the counter and the dozen or so others loitering beyond looked at his poorly fitting cop clothes and his unfashionable haircut and facial hair and the stupid, faux-superior expression on his face, and decided from experience that he was no one they needed to be deferential toward. But he might be some kind of madman, so they watched him.

"May we help you," said the immaculately uniformed man down his nose, reluctantly raising a pre-Cleansing fountain pen from a paper he was writing on.

"Yes," said the policeman, fumbling for his badge, the surge of animal vitality already starting to ebb. "I have a message for Lady Sula."

"I'll take it," said the guard, holding out his hand.

"No, it has to be delivered in person."

"In person," echoed the guard.

"Yes."

"To Lady Sula, *the* Lady Sula." Someone behind snickered.

"Yes, it's ..."

"You're not one of the regular Ministry couriers, are you? Who do you represent, exactly? Which Department? Shall I send for Lady Sula's personal assistant?"

"No. I mean ..." The surge was gone. "Look," he said, patting his pockets and bringing out a dog-eared card on which he'd changed "Detective" to "Inspector", "I'll just write it." He began to use his pencil but stopped and asked to borrow the man's fountain pen, which was handed over with all the enthusiasm of a mother handing over her baby to a curious vagrant. He wrote*: Lady Sula, Messenger of ZAH, I have taken the initiative to discover the identity of the boy on the bridge your looking for and for security will give it only to you personally.*

When he handed it and the pen over, the guard took them as if they'd been dipped in urine and started to read the card.

"No, don't–" began the inspector, but surrendered with a gesture.

"That's it?" asked the guard dismissively.

"Yes."

"Lady Sula is out. Do you intend to wait?"

"No. I'll be at the Ministry after about ten bells tonight."

"Very well," said the guard, putting the card in an envelope, writing something on it, and handing it over his shoulder to a woman who immediately started down the corridor with it.

Watching it go, the inspector had the sensation that he might shit his pants.

Lady Sula laughed low at a cruel joke some sycophant had made at someone else's expense and those around her joined in.

Before her arrival at the dinner party given for a couple dozen of the city's clerical and commercial elites in honor of one of their own, everyone had been enjoying themselves, conversing in small groups and laughing naturally. Now they were all concentrated on pleasing her, and the effort was already becoming exhausting. Then an old-fashioned miracle happened, and the party was saved.

Just as a liveried servant entered with a small bell to announce dinner, a minor commotion erupted somewhere else in the house. Heads turned toward the hallway, where, within seconds, the house's majordomo and a couple of household bodyguards appeared one step ahead of Sula's own security chief and the personal assistant she'd left at work at the Palace. The assistant held up a wrinkled business card and Sula went to take it from the young woman's trembling hand. She read both sides quickly and fixed her dark eyes on the assistant.

"When? How?" she demanded.

"The Palace guards' station. About three hours ago. It was irregular, so–"

"Arrest her," said Sula as she moved, and the cluster of servants and guards parted for her. "Take me back to the Ministry."

Cinya was fearful as she opened the door of the house she shared with two absent priestesses but immediately found amusement and relief in the policeman's appearance: his "undercover" dance-club clothes looked almost identical to his regular cop clothes, if a little tighter-fitting to display his weightlifter's body and incidentally the fat notebook in the left inside pocket of his leather jacket.

Behind him in the street stood not an official vehicle but an ordinary cab, supporting Ronnie's belief that he was freelancing.

"Let's go," he said with an authority that belied his surprise at seeing her. As she reached back for a short jacket, he saw that the fluid-moving top she wore nearly exposed her breasts, and that the thin, red-leather pants disappearing into matching lace boots threatened to cleave her in two. He was sure there must be something in the laws or Protocols against ZAH's servants dressing so provocatively; he'd have to add it to the list of charges after her arrest.

Cinya, for her part, smirked at the attention she felt him give as she walked to the cab–recalling her days of promiscuity–and concluded her decision to borrow her party-girl housemate's club clothes had been inspired.

∆ ∆ ∆

"Not here?" said Sula with a chilling timbre. She was sitting in Grotius's mammoth chair, all the lamps burning bright.

"No, milady," said a night-shift functionary. "We've checked the gym and the stairs he sometimes runs at night, and we can't find him. Lobby guards report him leaving on foot around eight bells. We sent people to his favorite spots, and Minister Grotius should be here soon."

The detective's section chief entered the office between two beefy guards, his feet skittering along the floor. When he was parked at the edge of the desk, Sula pushed the detective's card across its surface with two manicured fingers. "Read that," she ordered.

Wordlessly the man read the front of the card, shook his head slightly, then turned it over. Blood drained from his face. He looked at Sula in confusion.

"You were put in charge of identifying someone who may be a Palace insider," she seethed, "a traitor.... Now one of your people–who isn't even assigned to the case–is advertising that he knows who the Palace traitor is. And where does he announce this? *At the Palace!...* How is this possible?"

"Ma'am– My Lady ... I'll find out! His records, files ... maybe a co-worker ... I–"

"You have until morning, then you'll be executed." She looked to her security chief. "See to it," she said, to his brief nod.

"HE'S NOT HERE YET," shouted Cinya over the pounding beat as she returned to the table.

"Are you sure?"

"There aren't that many guys here, and I don't recognize any of them.... Did you see that scarface one?"

"Yeah, I saw him," said the cop. "Stay on the job ... and stop drinking! You've had too much already."

"I wanna have fun! You made me miss my hot date." She suddenly took his hand. "C'mon! Let's dance!"

"No, I'm not dancing! And neither are you! Sit down!" He pulled her down by the arm and for a while she sat still, her priestess's hauteur aroused, offended to be roughly handled.

For the hundredth time, the inspector glanced toward an elevated area from which patrons at tables could look out past a rail and over the dancers to the bandstand, where degenerate-looking youths too skinny for the army invented new percussive and vocal sounds as they went. He took this raised area to be reserved for favored customers, and the ones already there, being served by a separate bar at the back, did indeed look more prosperous. One table was vacant and had its chairs tilted against the table, and he thrilled in his bones with the conviction that his quarry would soon be seated there, obscenely spending the money and the military deferment he'd extracted from foolish women, which was doubly ironic because such establishments had only been allowed in the first place as a recruiting tool and a venue in which to spy on the young.

His eyes were drawn back to the dance floor, and to two young women dancing together. There were other pairs and groups of females, but something about these two was mesmerizing. They moved in unison, their hips rhythmically dropping and thrusting in a way that others noticed and tried to emulate. Occasionally, in mid-thrust, they glanced at *him*.

Despite the coolness of the night, the club grew warmer with body heat. Cinya took off her jacket and draped it on the back of her chair. At a moment when the inspector was looking toward the VIP area, she suddenly stood up.

"FUCK YOU, I'M DANCING!" she shouted, and was out of reach before he could stop her.

She went to the edge of the crowd and started to move, head down, red hair brushing her cheeks, just her and the syncopated beat. The cop glanced once at the empty VIP table and settled down to watch her. Soon the two girls nearby took her hands and drew her to dance with them. When she tried to copy their moves, they put her between and showed her how. Within minutes, the three were moving with erotic, pulsing synchronicity and the cop couldn't take his eyes away. When the music stopped, he had no idea how long he'd been watching and jerked his head nervously to see the VIP table still empty. When he looked back, the priestess and the others were gone and he stood up to look for her. There she was at the bar, he saw, her hair tossing as she laughed at something said in her ear. Unexpectedly, she and the girl who'd made her laugh looked his way.

As he watched, Cinya and the others took shots of liquor from small cups and then got bigger ones. The three exchanged cheek-kisses and Cinya began to move through the crowd. The inspector unwound a fraction: she seemed to be making a complete circuit of the club, looking at all the young men but not long enough to invite approach. When she returned to the table, she was flushed, alive.

"This is from my new friends Keera and Jane." she said, setting the drink before him. "They want to fuck you."

"What?"

"You heard me. Fuck. You. They think you're sexy, and I told them we were friends, not lovers."

"Lady Cinya," he said in his official voice, "you forget yourself, and why we're—"

"Look," interrupted the priestess. "He's not here. It's too early for a player." She pushed the cup at him. "Just chug this, take those poor, love-starved girls next door, and give them a half hour of your attention. I'll hold the table and come get you if he shows."

He stared at her open-mouthed for a moment, then shook his head and took a sip of what turned out to be hard cider.

"It's very nice of the young ladies," he said, "but I'm not going. I'm here to work. So are you." And with that he resumed his surveillance, taking occasional sips of his drink. Cinya sat back dejectedly. After a while she put her jacket back on.

As the band re-formed and got ready to play again, the cop glanced at his informant and found her staring at him. The cider had relaxed him a little and he lingered on her and almost smiled before turning away. She scooted her chair closer beside him and leaned in.

"Can I ask you something?" she said seriously, if a little drunkenly.

"What?"

"Do you have a wife? Girlfriend?"

He regarded her a moment before answering. "No, and no," he said. "Not steady, anyway."

"Why not?"

He took another sip of the soothing cider. "Women I'm attracted to don't usually like cops. Women who're attracted to cops–big cops like me–don't stay long."

"Why not," she repeated.

"Cause 'cop-style' gets old," he said candidly.

"What's 'cop-style'," she breathed, passing her hand under his arm and moving so that it was cradled against her. He looked down at the new arrangement and decided not to challenge it. He could see where this was going. He lowered his head toward hers and spoke confidentially.

"It's subduing and cuffing a struggling or frightened female and fucking her, usually from behind–however she likes it."

Cinya remained perfectly still, as if stricken by the image. The inspector took a gulp of cider.

"Did you ever do that to a priestess," she asked finally.

"No."

"Do you think about it sometimes?"

"Yes."

She hesitated, then said, "When you grabbed my arm before, I was mad at first; no one's ever touched me like that.... But ... it turned me on."

He pulled back and looked at her squarely.

"Let's go next door," she said hoarsely.

Δ Δ Δ

"*But it's not my fault, Lord,*" cried the obstinate woman to a profusely sweating Grotius, who loomed over her menacingly to impress the watching Sula. "His desk is right next to mine. Research clerks came and went. We were given no secure area for our work and no special security protocols. We looked at thousands of people. He overheard something about a boy on the bridge and reacted to it. That's all I know."

"And all this?" demanded Grotius, gesturing to a long conference table stacked with the detective's files, being poured over by Grotius's personal staff. "There's nothing here to connect your investigation to anything he's working on. How do you explain that?"

"I can't, sir," she said, "unless it was burned."

"Burned? What are you talking about?"

"A week ago. He was ordered to purge some files of the officer who was killed. Maybe he found something and kept it."

"Kept it where?" He looked to an assistant, who said, "Nothing here, Lord, nothing in his quarters."

"Maybe he has it with him," said the woman.

"No! You mustn't!" cried the handcuffed Cinya. "You're not allowed!"

"Shuddup!" growled the big cop, slapping her hard enough across the back of the head to send her sprawling face-first on the bed in the lamplight and turn her pretend indignation to real fear. She choked down the impulse to end the game–just a few more seconds. Now she begged and cried real tears as he found the drawstring of her tight leather pants and pulled them down to her knees. He kneaded her flesh with his big hands and gloated at his conquest as he positioned himself to enter her. Then, just as she looked back to watch him thrust home, playtime ended.

He saw it in the tiny shift of her focus to a point beyond him and in her beseeching expression and instantly his experience overcame the effects of the mildly drugged cider and the priestess's performance to make him duck his head and throw up a forearm in an explosive spasm of self-preservation. The weighted sheepgut garrote snapped tight not on his bare throat as intended but across his wrist, pinning his right arm but leaving the rest of him to fight for his life—and he had a lot of fight in him. He powered up with Ronnie on his back and attempted to throw him off while elbowing, headbutting, and searching for eyes and testicles with the free hand that couldn't yet get to the knife at his ankle. Ronnie knew he was overmatched and in desperation suddenly gave up the useless garrote for a bear hug, pinning the muscular man's arms to his sides from behind and bringing him down on top of himself, making a tremendous racket that he hoped Tom's wife Polly had prepared for when she selected the room.

"Now what, you pussy?" gritted the cop, trying to turn and bite Ronnie's nose and face and neck. "You gonna hug me to death? I'm gonna kill you and—"

"C!" called Ronnie, "get a towel! From the dresser!"

"feed you to your little pet!"

Cinya, who'd gathered herself onto the bed with her pants still around her knees, regarded the entangled men with fear for a second, then moved to retrieve a folded towel and offer it to him as if he had a free hand to take it.

"Stuff it in his mouth!" he ordered.

Now the man saw real danger and thrashed about. Ronnie tried to trap his legs and hold him—as he'd once held Jenna's frail father Clarence when he lay dying from the poison he'd taken to unburden his fleeing family of himself—but the cop was too strong, and too determined to live.

"Hold his nose!" said Ronnie. "Make him open his mouth! You can do it, C!"

The cop clawed with his trapped hands at Ronnie's forearms, bloodying them. As Cinya diffidently touched the cloth to his clinched mouth he finally took fright and started to yell, and Cinya's hesitation evaporated. She grabbed his nose and squeezed it closed. When he started to gasp and to bite at her still-cuffed hand, she pushed more and more of the cloth in. The cop grew wild-eyed and tried to push it out with his tongue but now she clamped her hand forcefully over his mouth and leaned her weight on his head to keep him from thrashing. She looked away and cried as he struggled.

The door opened and a horrible creature appeared, the deep cleft down its face accentuated by the lantern it carried. In a second the monster comprehended all and was at Cinya's side, its hands over hers. When the cop gave a final shudder and lay still, it spoke.

"I've got this, milady," said Tom kindly. Then, over his shoulder, "Girls, take care of her."

Keera and Jane came and stood her up away from the scene of death. Jane pulled up her pants and tied the drawstring at her belly while Keera patted her face with a second towel and combed her hair with her fingers.

"Better?" asked Keera.

"Yeah," said Cinya. She attempted to turn to where the men continued to hold the cop to make sure he was good and dead, but Keera stopped her with a soft "No." Now she noticed the woman from downstairs who'd taken her coins and directed her and the cop to this room, standing guard at the half-open door.

Ronnie came to her, blotting the blood from his clawed arms with the towel that had been the murder weapon, the inspector's black notebook in his waistband. He used a small key to uncuff her hands and held them both as he drew her to the door.

"Polly and the girls are going to put you in a special cab—the driver's a friend of ours," he said. "I want you to go home and forget all about this—put it out of your mind and live your life. If trouble comes, just stay calm and keep your head down. You'll be all right." He looked around at the others and back to her. "Ready?"

"Will I see you again?" she asked.

"Yes," he said, kissing her on both cheeks. "Now go."

Δ Δ Δ

As Ronnie read the folded-up surveillance report that tied him to Lady Rosamund, and by extension to Cinya and the bridge and Red Mask, he breathed a sigh of relief. He had all the freelancing detective's evidence in his hand. He and his family and circle were therefore now in no more danger than usual, which felt like reprieve from a death sentence.

A mile away, behind the wall, Sula waited in vain. She knew the detective would not have left such a note as the one in her hand, and then made himself unavailable, on purpose. The foolishness that made him write it had surely gotten him killed. Well, she mused, he had to die anyway, since he was privy to evidence of her connection to the attempt on Clare's life, as was his section chief. She would just have to proceed without him, and without solving the mystery of the boy on the bridge–even if he was a member of her own elite circle.

"Take me back to the party," she ordered, coming to her feet. Whether the dinner would have been held, for the three hours of her absence, was not in question.

"And these two, milady?" inquired her security chief, indicating the woman investigator and her section chief.

"Execute them," she said, raising her black hood as a phalanx formed around her.

The section chief immediately started mewling, but the woman stood up and gritted, "You. Stupid. Bitch."

Sula stopped and regarded her, eye to eye.

"No," she amended as she resumed her exit, "execute him, promote her."

"Yes, ma'am."

40 – The Proposal

Four days

It was the last market day before equinox and the city crackled with electricity as before a storm.

With the military committee meeting every day, Ronnie and Jak no longer needed to check for the members' summons, but his duties still took him to the Square. Owlly and Slammer Jon had detailed him, when he wasn't otherwise occupied, to take the tenor of the city, and the marketplaces were the perfect venues for that.

Arguments and even fistfights broke out among some marketgoers over whether the army was getting ready to sally to defend ZAHdom from a horde of mutant, cannibalistic, and even horned and fork-tailed heretics, or whether it was all a scam designed to justify raising taxes on the common people to support the lavish lifestyle of the Priesthood and its favorites. But most people reserved judgment or didn't care and just went about their business and their lives. Then there were others who unexpectedly gave Ronnie hope.

Squeezing through the crowded market, where some vendors were doing everything they could to encourage panic buying, he was reminded of the day in the market at his home village of Firstportage when, as a boy not yet sixteen, he'd challenged the soldiers who came to take Jenna away. When the confrontation was over and he found himself still alive, thanks to Jenna's restraining hand as he moved to draw his dagger, he'd looked around and met the sympathetic and supportive eyes of brother and sister Freethinkers who were sprinkled through the marketplace. But there'd been a few strangers, too, and even then he'd wondered how many ordinary-seeming people were like him and his friends and family, and just had different generations-spanning security protocols that kept them unknown even to others of their own kind, be they followers of banned religions old or new or of gods-free reason, also banned and punishable by death. Now, in the great market that occupied most of Citadel Square, he repeatedly caught the same look in the eyes of others and began to suspect himself of wishful thinking. Maybe what he was seeing was simply the shared excitement that accompanied great events—the prospect of *change* from an unsatisfactory status quo. Still, if it could be harnessed at the right moment ...

He passed through the main gate with his leather tool satchel across his chest and his small Citadel work badge on his collar, as usual noting the number and practices of the Guardsmen on duty there. Once again he concluded that trying to pass with a fake badge was too risky to be a central element of their plan, even though they had a few made of metal and others of wood and paint; therefore anyone too fearful to make the passage through the drains would just have to be left behind to other duties.

He wasn't dressed for the smaller and more genteel companion market through the gate in Chaplin Square— serviced by vendors with Citadel passes and attended by Citadelians who shunned the masses— so, to avoid drawing attention, he made only a single purposeful pass down each aisle, then turned west to again reconnoiter the armory and church and back northeast to the Citadel Guard compound, appropriately situated on ground overlooking the army's facilities. He knew of the plan to retard the Guard's response to the Freethinker attack in two days' time, but he wasn't in on the details, so he simply collected visual and aural impressions as he moved past.

Looking south through trees, he could see that the army compound teemed with men and horses and that ranks of loaded and tarp-shrouded wagons stood at the ready on the training field. More men could be seen in the three partly skeletonized mid-rise buildings which constituted their barracks, doing domestic chores or exercising, talking or scuffling in groups, cooking over open fires like cavemen or pissing into space in disregard of laundry strung on long lines between the buildings.

He moved on around the hill, eventually to Shopping Street, where the pace had picked up quite a bit. At eleven bells, the available curbside space was mostly taken by private carriages and the parking valets were doing a thriving business, hopping up beside drivers with number paddles to direct them to nearby off-street parking even as customers alighted onto the sidewalk. Studying the shoppers and the shopkeepers who awaited them at their doors, he sensed not a dread of advancing heretic armies but a certain party atmosphere, as if the mutant cannibals had already been vanquished and the profits made in the vanquishing were already being counted up and celebrated.

At the end of the high-end shops, where the street name and the ambience changed, he stopped and considered his next destination, knowing that if he went two blocks *this* way and one block *that* way, he'd end up at Cinya's house, according to her description. He made the turn.

Ever since Cinya mentioned that she was assistant catering manager at the Palace, he'd been duty-bound to question her about arrangements for the breakfast three days hence, but silencing the Error policeman had taken precedence. Now that the fatally ambitious and chain-bound man rested in the mud at the bottom of the Husson, his interment rewarded with twenty ounces of his ministry's own gold, distributed among Tom and Polly and the club girls, it was time to remember that Cinya was first and foremost an intelligence asset, and always had been.

When he arrived at the location, he found a two-story pre-Cleansing house which had, like many other structures, been retrofitted with extra fireplaces and chimneys. Very nicely, in this case. Ronnie found it surprisingly homey looking.

He'd thought to leave a message with a servant or housemate, but it was Cinya herself who peeked out past a curtain. He was prepared to follow her lead, perhaps to pretend to be a repairman, but she opened the door wide for him to enter and embraced him on bare tiptoe.

"I take it we're alone," he said after a while.

"My housemates are at work," she murmured. "I have the day off."

She took him up the stairs to the master bedroom and they made love, though that hadn't been his intention. Afterward, as they lay together, both wondering what they were doing and where it would lead, Ronnie trying to formulate his questions, Cinya spoke.

"This is my parents' bed," she said against his chest.

When he raised his head to see if they might be coming through the door, she squeezed him still and went on.

"My dad died about five years ago, when I was sixteen, my mom last year. They both worked at the Interior Ministry."

"Endorian?" he asked, naming the clan of the reigning Sword, Lord Endo. She looked up at him.

"You know the clans?"

"Yes."

"Why am I not surprised," she went on rhetorically, snuggling again. "We're supposed to be neutral, so we end up with neutral jobs, like assistant catering service manager ..."

"What exactly do you–"

"... or Sword of ZAH," she went on, "when the other clans need someone uncontroversial between them. Sometimes we're even used in arranged marriages, to smooth out divisions, remind everyone that we're one big happy family."

She didn't sound that happy.

They were silent for a little while, Ronnie stroking Cinya's back. Finally, "C, why are you telling me these things? You never did before."

"Before, you were a seventeen-year-old country kid with a good sense of humor and a nice body, and yeah, I kinda fell for you, but there was no way I could see you as part of my life–the life of the Citadel. Now you've revealed yourself, whether you meant to or not, and I like what I see. I think I know what you and your people are, but I don't care. I'll even help you find others like yourself, if that's what you want. But first you have to cross over."

"Cross over?" he said with foreboding.

"Into the Citadel–as my husband."

He stopped stroking. A minute went by. Two.

"Are you going to say anything?" she asked peevishly.

"I'm processing."

She got up on her knees to face him. "You're *processing?* See, you don't even *talk* like a townie! –much less an ignorant country boy– when you let your guard down."

"I'm trying to imagine how *you* imagine I could make that transition, and why you would want *me*, over all the Citadel men you could have."

"I like *you.* I'm comfortable with *you.* I trust *you.* Especially now, after what we've just been through."

"You're talking about the bonding effect of murdering an officer of the law together?" he said. "It might wear off."

"Don't be an ass,':' she retorted. "You know what I mean."

They stared at each other for a long moment, then, "C, you're a priestess of the god ZAH, creator and owner of all; I'm a woodworker with ... unconventional beliefs. How could this be made to work?"

"Simple," she said, reaching for his left earlobe, already marked with two strokes. "We'll make you a priest."

He looked like he might get up and storm about the room, waving his arms in consternation, so she straddled and sat on him while she made her case.

"Just listen," she said. "Are you listening? Good.... It's all about *perception.* Your parents were both priestblood and you'll be in the books at the Treasury. So you already have a good start. The rest is just politics and process and patience."

"Explain," he said.

"Look, it's not unheard of for clergy and non-clergy to marry. But most of those non-clergy spouses don't make the transition because they don't know how to act, how to play the game. *You*'re very smart; you'll figure it out. Plus, I'll bet you can read. We'll get you tutoring in the texts and rituals and in priestly behavior and then we'll socialize a lot. People will come to disregard your background if *you* do. They'll only care what you are *now*—what you *aspire* to be. If that's something attractive to them, they'll invite you in."

"Just like that."

"Yeah, just like that."

"Just ... leave the past behind. Friends, family, neighbors ..."

"Yes.... Well, there wouldn't be anything to stop you from visiting, but you'd find it awkward. So would they."

"What do you mean?"

She cocked her head to one side as if surprised that he didn't understand. "Because you'd be master and they'd still be slave," she said.

After a moment of silent horror, he was grateful that she'd put things in such stark terms. He gently moved her off and swung his legs down to begin putting his clothes on.

"Why do you hesitate, Ronnie?" she asked sincerely. "You're just going to come back to me."

He started tying his boots.

"What holds you back?" she asked. "Is it that girl?"

"What girl?"

"Jenna."

He stopped tying, then finished and turned, the question implicit.

"I *heard* you, *saw* you ... that day on the bridge." she said. "You told Iris and me you were looking for a lady. Then later you went crazy, yelling at someone on the *Wind*. Who was she? Some childhood sweetheart?"

He stood up. "It doesn't matter anymore."

"So you say, yet the memory of her makes you turn down the best offer a country boy ever got."

That almost made him smile. "It *is* a good offer for a country boy," he said, "but right now I have to go. Things to do."

"Well, I'll be here, during the day, if you want to talk."

"Here?" he said. "Don't you have to work?"

"Not for the next three days," she answered.

"Why not?" he asked, coming back on-mission.

"They're getting ready for ... "

She stopped and studied him–studied him long enough to make it clear she knew what he was doing–then gave him what he wanted.

"They're getting ready for a breakfast conference with the Messengers and the Sword in attendance," she said plainly. "When they do that, they use a special, vetted catering crew. This time they'll even have extra food-service people from the army."

"Why the army?"

She shrugged her shoulders. "I do weddings and such, so I'm not sure, but I suppose it's because the top brass will be there, along with a bunch of back-office people–analysts and secretaries and such." She gave a slight sardonic smile. "War with the heretics and all that."

"How big is this army contingent?"

She shrugged again. "Big enough to take over our upstairs offices. Not nicely, either. They acted like soldiers"

Taking a taxi to Woodmaker Gate with the morsel of intelligence, Ronnie looked out at the Citadel with new eyes. In their last conversation, before he turned back from pogrom to find Jenna, his father had admonished him to find some camouflage in which to enter the enemy camp and to get "ever closer to power" once there, saying that the Priesthood, in scanning the horizon for enemies, might overlook one at its own feet. So far, he'd cloaked himself as a needed craftsman and a gigolo to gain admittance to the physical Citadel, but he could never become part of the *idea* of the Citadel like that. Cinya was a minor aristocrat and marriage to her—in priestly robes—could change everything. In that guise he could, over time, sabotage from within, possibly with the help of the "others" Cinya had alluded to. Most importantly, he could live longer than the next three days to try it, and wasn't there something to be said for that? Can't do anything for anybody—or the cause—if you're dead, right?

Nel looked up as the doorbell rang, then went back to the customers she was attending. In the workshop, Owlly pretended for a moment to carve on a chair leg, until he saw who it was, then retrieved a piece of paper he'd hidden and picked up a drawing pen to resume writing. He caught Ronnie's eye and directed it across the room to Brod before putting pen to paper. Ronnie took the cue.

"That for Suki?" he inquired as he arrived at Brod's worktable, where his brother was using a stone to sharpen a machete held in a vise; the weapon had somehow already been cut down in all its dimensions. Lying on the table next to it was a stiletto—not long like the one he often wore at his back, but long enough to pierce heart or liver or lung or eye in the hand of a quick, small person.

"Yeah," said Brod hoarsely, then cleared his throat and started again. "Yeah, jus' givin' her some options, ya know? She says her squad's got a small spear for her but, ya know—" He'd forgotten to inhale and ran out of breath. Uncertain of his own voice, he went back to sharpening.

"I'll be back in a minute," said Ronnie.

He went to Owlly and reported his new intelligence about the breakfast at the Palace. Neither was prepared to be certain of its significance.

"It would be odd for the Palace Guard, being protectors of the Messengers, to countenance the army being close to them in force,"

Owlly mused. “Which suggests they’re just part of Sula’s “heretic invasion” charade, with maps and such.”

“Remember,” said Ronnie, “she said they acted like soldiers.”

“I won’t forget,” said Owlly. “Whatever they are, they still represent a potential obstacle to be dealt with. I’m writing to Flame and Verjil now; I’ll add this to it.”

“Am I taking it to them?”

“No. Tofer’s back on the job full time. We need him in these final hours—plus, he’s loving it! He’s out now to Slammer.”

Ronnie left Owlly to his miniature coded writing and went back to Brod.

“She still determined, Brother?” he asked.

“Yeah.”

“Where is she now?”

“Upstairs with her sisters,” said Brod in a resigned monotone, “talking about how to raise Madi, if ...”

“May I make a suggestion?”

“What?”

Soon Brod, Ronnie, and Suki were in the library while one sister looked after Madi and the other helped Nel in the showroom. Following Ronnie’s lead, they’d donned gloves and taken armloads of scrap lumber and trim strips down the stairs and Ronnie had backtracked to get the mattress from his bed and stuff it in the tunnel opening to the alley, to deaden their noises. Now he set the big lantern from the table on a tall stack of books and confronted his sister-in-law, a three-months-pregnant woman not much bigger than a healthy twelve-year-old.

“Suki,” he said, “I don’t mean to interfere with your squad leader’s training, but I’ll feel a lot better if I know you’re ready for the chaos and violence you’re about to encounter—and that you have a way to fight men that won’t just get you killed right away. Your husband’s afraid for you, but maybe he’ll be able to concentrate on his own job better if you show him you're ready."

She nodded. "What do you want to see?"

In response, Ronnie took a deep breath and let out a country boy's full-throated bellow that sent Suki stumbling back and falling and her husband stooping to her aid as he held up a warning hand to Ronnie. Instead of relenting, Ronnie went storming about the large space in an apparent paroxysm of rage. He heaved the heavy oak meeting table on its side with a crash and pushed and kicked and slammed his body against it and then picked up a piece of lumber from the pile and noisily attacked it and then took his grunting fight to the former parking garage's concrete wall.

"GET UP, COWARDS!" he yelled over his shoulder. *"FIGHT!"*

As the others got to their feet, Brod retrieved a suitably sized piece of lumber and offered it to his wife.

"PUT IT DOWN, DUMMY! YOU'RE NOT GOING TO BE THERE TO HELP HER!"

Brod left his wife and joined the imaginary fight, in full voice for the first time in his wife's presence. Soon she was with them, yelling her heart out and stabbing and smashing wood against concrete.

"STOP!" yelled Ronnie, and the others complied with flushed faces and panting breath.

"Enemy soldiers might be young and beautiful and look like nice people at home," he said. "You have to be ready to destroy even something you would otherwise cherish. And with that he yelled and ran across the room to attack the end of the first bookcase. *"C'MON! GET 'EM!"*

Now the next two bookcases were getting mercilessly pummeled and gouged by the others.

"HELP ME HERE!" he yelled, and they rushed to his aid. *"WE HAVE TO PUSH THIS WAGON OVER IN THE ROAD!"* And with the slightest hesitation it was done, with three bookcases toppled and hundreds of precious books scattered, hopefully undamaged.

"STOP! ... SUKI, ATTACK ME!"

She lowered her weapon. “Can’t I rest first?” she asked, only half in jest.

“YELL IT! AND NO, YOU CAN’T!”

Her smirk became a snarl. *“FUCK YOU, THEN!”* she growled, trying to bring the lumber down on Ronnie’s head. *“I’LL KILL YOU!”*

Ronnie stepped left and closed on her and violently batted the wood from her hands as she swung. Then he pushed her down, pressing her down by the shoulders so as not to jolt the baby. Brod put a restraining hand on his shoulder.

“*BACK OFF! YOU’RE NOT HERE!”* he barked, pushing the hand away. *“SUKI, GET UP AND FIGHT ME!”*

In a flash she was on him, swinging, kicking, trying to gouge his eyes. Ronnie effortlessly grabbed and flung her into her husband’s arms; Brod moved to attack him.

“STOP!” he held up a hand, and all held position.

“Suki,” he said now as Brod glared a warning, “do you accept that you can’t defeat a trained soldier head on? –that you need a different way to fight?”

“Yeah, show me,” she said, her eyes burning.

“You have to be a *harrier*–a fighter that hits and runs, or drives or lures an enemy into a kill box–do I need to explain that to you?”

“No.”

“I hear they have a short spear for you. That’s good. Plus you’ve got the dagger and machete.”

“What?”

“I didn’t show them to her yet,” said Brod.

“Okay, listen,” said Ronnie, taking her hands and drawing her to stand before him. “When a man gets *stabbed* in a fight, he often thinks he’s only been *struck*, especially if he doesn’t *see* the knife, because a hard blow masks the penetration. Understand? That means, if you repeatedly attack a soldier from behind, one who’s already engaged with one of us, you may be able to injure him fatally, or at least distract him enough that the other fighter can kill him. Got that so far?

Remember: hard blows, bury the knife to the hilt and jerk it out quick, and hold on tight, or it could be wrenched from your hand by his reaction."

Suki nodded seriously, like she was engraving his words on her mind.

"Okay," he continued, "do you know where my heart is?" She pointed to the left side of his chest.

"More to the center—and strike me with your fist! —we're not being polite here!" She did as told.

"My liver?" She wasn't sure and he showed her, then went through lungs, kidneys, throat, and face, all accessible from the back and sides. "The face is important because you may deliver a fatal blow that doesn't disable for several minutes; in the meantime you have to terrorize and discourage. If you find yourself in the position, yell like crazy and stab viciously and repeatedly in the eyes and mouth. Got it? Okay, let's practice."

For the next hour the three alternated positions and scenarios, yelling and striking and defending, using pieces of wood in place of weapons. Suki learned how to strike hard with the knife in either hand and withdraw it in one motion to escape before a sword came around to decapitate her, how to stab into the anus or testicles and get underneath the scapula or under the arm to the heart—especially if the enemy was in armor—how to chop at heads and necks and arms and legs with her machete, and how to cut throat once an enemy was injured or worn down, holding his head against the shoulder and drawing the knife in one quick, strong motion from one side to the other— and moving immediately to the next fight and the next, until there were no more.

Finally the imaginary enemy was vanquished and the three paused to enjoy their victory, fatigued but alive to their fingertips.

Ronnie looked to Suki. "Ready, Sister?"

"Yes."

Then to Brod. "Ready, Brother?"

"Ready."

"Good," said Ronnie, tossing his wooden weapon on the floor with the rest of the mess to be cleaned up later. "Let's eat!"

Ascending the stairs behind the others with a candle, he was happy to see them holding hands.

Most of the rebels were not so fortunate as to have underground bunkers where they could yell and smash things. On this, the last night of scheduled training for most units, after dinner or in lieu of dinner, hundreds hid themselves together in stables or warehouses or barns or walked out into meadows far from any house to talk and practice. Some youths pretended their exercises in darkening streets and squares were mere horseplay or perhaps some game that, being illegal anyway, required them to flee from police or pay customary bribes to avoid the indignity of a summons to the next priestly lecture at the precinct house.

Most units now practiced with imaginary weapons, since their real ones were already at the church and the bakery. Jak's team of skinny youngsters had made so many trips through the drains with long wrapped bundles that they now moved in the dark with the speed, stealth, and confidence of sewer rats.

Elsewhere, other teams planned and practiced too, but not with imaginary weapons, and not with the aim of letting aborning freedom breathe but of smothering it in its crib.

41 – Setting the Stage

One

At dawn on the last day, small units of the Army of ZAH, watched over by Guardsmen at the battlements, quietly exited the Citadel by the main gate just as street cleaners were getting started on the debris from the previous day's market, which had stayed busy until police forced the last vendors to leave with the approach of night. Three-man teams of men wielding big push-brooms and scoop-shovels and leading ponies harnessed to trash carts stopped to gawk.

The column was heavy with well-mounted archers and moved at a leisurely pace. Interspersed along its length were four mobile pigeon coops. At the end of the square it divided in three, with one coop going south, one west, and two east, presumably to divide again at the bridge with one crossing over and the other turning north up the river road.

An hour later more than a hundred mufti-clad professional rumormongers employed by the Error police hit the streets and shops to plant the seeds of what by midmorning would grow into conviction that the force had been deployed to invest the countryside around the city, first to catch and execute draft evaders and deserters from the army, and then, once the main force had passed, to follow it and prevent desertion from the front. It was a perfectly reasonable and plausible explanation and few questioned it, even among the

Freethinkers, even if there was no actual "front" and even if it made monitoring the main force's departure problematic.

Despite having only imperfect information, almost all the players in the drama were now prepared to believe the denouement would see their enemies vanquished from the stage of history and themselves taking the bows. Only the most secret and subtle of them, Lady Clare, was uncertain and anguished.

If the picture her spies painted was accurate, then everything she held dear, everything her family and clan represented and had worked generations for, was in danger of annihilation. To have risked all by too direct a role in the current affair would have been irresponsible, she repeatedly told herself; she could only nudge, plant ideas. Yet she ached to do more. Today she staggered about her bedroom, steadying herself on the walls and furniture—the closest thing to pacing she could manage. She needed more time to recover from the effects of the poison, but there wasn't any. Nor was there anyone to take over for her. With her husband and children murdered, her uncle Mortimer a mere placeholder on the Council of Messengers, and her brilliant and charismatic brother Magnus kept out of play on the other side of the world, there was no one else—not yet, anyway.

Stumbling past her dressing table, she stopped and looked at herself in the ancient beveled-edge mirror. She was a wreck: stooped, pockmocked of face, and with the roots of her hair all white. What she saw made her angry and she straightened up and combed her hair back with her fingers.

She moved to sit at her desk, found paper and a screw-cap fountain pen, thought for several minutes, wrote a brief note in trembling hand, started to write another, and paused in thought.

"Not yet," she murmured, screwing the cap back on.

In the afternoon, after conferring with Slammer Jon and others, Ronnie returned to the shop to find what he knew to be one of Lady Clare's household carriages standing at the curb. The driver saw him and knocked on the cab and Cornelius stuck his head and arm out to beckon him.

The older man made space on the single seat and exchanged pleasantries, giving the brief assurance of his lady's improving condition that he knew the boy would want but wouldn't presume to ask for. Then he reached under the seat.

"You left in such a rush last time," said the majordomo with a sardonic tone as he slid Ronnie's owl-branded toolbox to him, "that you left this behind–sorry it wasn't returned earlier.

"Ah, yes, thank you."

"Also," said Cornelius, glancing at the pedestrian traffic as he reached into his jacket, "there's a note for you."

He took the folded paper out but extended it only halfway. "Shall I read it to you?"

In answer, Ronnie held out his hand and Cornelius gave him the paper. He glanced out the window, then unfolded the note and read it. It had no salutation or signature and was shakily written.

He read it a second time.

"Do you understand?" asked Cornelius.

"The words, yes," said Ronnie, "but the meaning ..."

"Something from an old proverb, I think," said Cornelius. "Maybe she thinks you'll understand it some day when you need to.... Can you repeat it? word for word?"

Ronnie recited the note without looking at it and returned it to Cornelius's waiting hand.

"Well, young man," said the older one, putting the paper away and offering his hand, "I think we must say goodbye, or as they say across the water, *au revoir.*"

"À bientôt, j'espère." See you soon, I hope, said Ronnie with a conspiratorial half-smile, reaching for the door handle.

∆ ∆ ∆

That night Freethinker families and their family-less friends gathered to break bread, to quietly cherish each other, and to remember those who were gone, everyone understanding that if they were killed in the coming battle there would be no one left to remember the ancestors. By unspoken consensus, talk of the rebellion was put aside in favor of variously amusing or shocking anecdotes about those living and dead, with frequent laughter and holding of hands and speaking of names in the Freethinker way. By the time the dishes were washed and put away and the candles snuffed and the lanterns turned low, even the doubtful and the frightened were ready.

42 - Ghost Soldiers

Equinox Day

The city awoke under a clearing sky to unusual quietude, with most people heeding the generally anticipated but suddenly announced ban on non-essential street traffic. Soon a hum of activity began to develop as the several thousand men of the Army of ZAH main force prepared to go to war against the heretic enemy. Soldiers still in their sleeping apparel thronged the window openings or sheer drop offs of their many floors to peer first at the ominous horizon and then to call to each other between floors and buildings with the affectionate abuse common to young soldiers through the ages. Many made small fires for tea or breakfast, as always depending on the breeze to carry the smoke along the blackened ceilings and out the sides of the buildings, or on the former elevator shafts that served as chimneys. Others hurriedly donned their ill-fitting green uniforms and hunter's hats to take their breakfast at the lower-level dining halls and get to the parade and assembly areas, there to mingle with their comrades among jostling wagons with their resigned horse- and mule-teams and the sharp-eared and eyed steeds of the cavalry. By midmorning the laundry had been taken in and the fires had been extinguished and the soldiers had mostly disappeared from the windows and ledges. On the assembly grounds units began to collect to receive their orders.

At the armory a few blocks away, where staff and workers had been kept on site in the last days to make sure all was in readiness, racks of swords, spears, axes, bows, incendiaries, and other implements of war were wheeled into position behind counters over which signs depicted the different weapons distributed there according to the corresponding patch sewn to each man's sleeve below his rank. Citadel Guardsmen at the portals prepared to admit unarmed army soldiers through one revolving gate to receive their weapons and to see them out another one to be monitored until they left the Citadel, maintaining the supremacy of the Guard within the wall.

In Chaplin Square crews finished festooning the reviewing stand, with the Messengers destined for chairs throne-like and draped against the elements on the top level–though the day was fair–Ministers and the like given cushions on the one below, and lesser invited guests consigned to wooden benches below that, though they would have the consolation of being separated from lesser mortals by a low barrier patrolled by Guardsmen.

By eleven bells the seating was prepared and a steady stream of fancy horses and carriages commenced to pull up in front of the reviewing stand to disgorge the merely rich and important, who descended with practiced nonchalance and found their places with the assistance of uniformed ushers. Many wore the black robes of their station while contriving to give glimpses of the elegant gowns and suits and footwear and jewelry beneath.

Across from the reviewing stand and behind another cordon of Guardsmen, gawking Citadelians who preferred the company of the elites to that of the townspeople beyond the massive doors and lowered portcullis, tried to find the best locations in the quickly thickening crowd.

As both sides of the square were nearing capacity, a line of carriages that had pulled up behind the stand received a signal from the event director and started delivering its cargo of government ministers and other dignitaries. Error Minister Grotius was first and had to be carried up the back stairs in a special chair, followed by a small army of sycophants. Others came with family and attendants and as they arrived and began to settle in and to visit with nearby acquaintances, the event director gave another signal, which was relayed by flagmen on rooftops to the waiting army.

Following custom, the commanding general of the expeditionary force and his senior staff led the column out of the army compound on horseback and were followed by an elite special-operations unit on foot. At the armory the officers relinquished their mounts to grooms, led the troops through the revolving entry, and emerged into a holding area fully armed, less the light armor and shields that would follow in wagons and be distributed near the field of battle. Released back to the street and remounted, they formed up behind flag bearers and drummers and sent a message that they were ready. So far they comprised less than five hundred armed men—against more than two thousand professional Guardsmen on duty for the occasion.

The event director gave another signal and a line of ceremonially dressed Palace Guardsmen emerged from the former bank building across the narrow street from the back of the reviewing stand, some starting up the stairs while others followed and formed a corridor and then turned outward as if to repel attackers. One by one the Messengers, who'd been made secure and comfortable after earlier arriving on the other side of the building, walked through it with their attendants and started up the stairs.

At another signal the drum ensemble in an enclosure next to the reviewing stand struck up the quiet cadence of a slow heartbeat. At the top level the fancy-dress Guardsmen stepped out one by one past their commander to advance with deliberate, exaggerated movements across the upper level behind the chairs and turned to face the square, an arm's reach from each other. The drummers stopped with a flourish, let the silence linger dramatically, then resumed with the Messengers' processional. All came to their feet and faced the upper tier.

One by one the Messengers were ushered to stand before their seats, starting with those at the outside. Some of them stood stoically, others smiled and acknowledged their acquaintances on lower levels, a couple even raised a hand to the crowd across the square, which elicited cheers to go with the drone of applause. The tenth one out was Sula, who elicited not pleasure or excitement but awe, accompanied by polite applause as the crowd studied her in fascination. She'd come into view with the hood of her embroidered-edge silk robe up and was too far away for most to see well anyway, but as she reached to lower it there was a collective holding of breath. Pale skin suggested someone who spent most of her time in chapel communing with the god; dramatic dark eyes and almost-black hair suggested agelessness; red lips mesmerized—the men anyway. The women were waiting for a glimpse of the fabulous gown she must be wearing under her clerical robe, but she didn't deign to reveal it.

Lord Endo, the Sword of ZAH, was an anticlimax, starting with the fact that he didn't wear the Chaplin's beribboned white uniform, which was far too big for him. He came out to half-hearted cheers, even though he was theoretically the most powerful person on Earth, and was followed by a very tall man bearing on a cushion the sword itself, the very one ZAH supposedly gave the Chaplin one-hundred nine years before to wield in his name. Arriving at the elaborate center chair, Endo turned and faced the crowd, while the sword on its cushion was placed on a low stand in front of him. The bearer retreated behind the line of chairs; the director—now unobtrusively standing at the end of the tier—nodded to the conductor below, the drummers gave another flourish and ended, and the Messengers took their seats.

The crowd had barely turned its attention back on itself and begun murmuring when the sound of the marching drums drifted from around the corner and all heads rotated to the end of the square. A cheer broke out as a line of young men bearing the sword-bequeathing-hand-of-ZAH ensign came into view, followed by a row of even younger drummers. The flag bearers and drummers and then the mounted officers and the expertly marching men made the turn and, as they approached, the conductor, on the director's signal, had his ensemble match the marching drums to more dramatic effect. In front of the reviewing stand the formation smoothly reordered itself to face the Messengers and on a glance between the drumline's lead drummer and the conductor suddenly stopped and stood at attention.

The Sword stood and all rose. He raised his hand toward the men below and spoke of "brave soldiers of ZAH" and "generations of order and peace" and "heretic hordes" and, "threat of annihilation," but not in his own voice. Endo's voice was weak, so the tall man who'd born the sword spoke over him in a voice that could be heard across the square, where it may have been thought to emanate from the nondescript portly man himself, though those below in the stands knew better.

When the director heard the end of the scripted remarks he nodded down to the conductor and a drumroll ensued, which signaled the column to reorder itself toward the closed gate. Then, with another flourish and stop, the Sword stepped forward, picked up the circa-2000 regulation full dress sword of an officer of the United States Navy, slowly drew it from its scabbard so it glinted in the midday sun, turned and raised it in the direction of the gate, and pronounced–in the tall man's voice– "Let ZAH's will be done!"

All at once the drum corps erupted, the marching drumline took the cue, the column started moving, As Citadelians clapped and cheered and the inner doors began to move on their tracks into the tunnel–revealing the already-open outer doors and the heavy iron portcullis just as its man-piercing spikes were cranked from the pavement–it seemed as if a great beast were being let out of its cage. Then, as the flag-bearers and drummers passed through the fifty-foot-long passage under the gatehouse and emerged into Citadel Square, and as a second column entered Chaplin Square behind, the puny emanations of the well-mannered Citadel crowd were obliterated by the raucous yelling and whistling and banging of pots and pans of the enormous crowd waiting beyond the wall, which set the horses to high-stepping and bobbing their heads and gnashing at bits on tight rein.

To the outside-the-wall townspeople—whatever their thoughts about the heretic threat—the sallying of the army was an excuse to party. Even the families of young men recently drafted were prepared to revel, secure in the knowledge that in living memory no force had long stood up to the Army of ZAH and most men had returned undamaged. In fact, its members had been enriched by wars against heresy, with booty bags by the thousands being returned to the Citadel and outlying towns and ownership of fixed properties accruing to the state or to the elites or to local facilitators.

The celebratory mood was encouraged as usual by uniformed and plainclothed-but-obvious Error Ministry policemen moving through the crowd and by the sight of numerous prisoner-transport vans stationed around the perimeter of the huge space, with a few prisoners already peering forlornly through the barred windows for effect.

Many Freethinker men and women had arrived early enough to secure standing room at or near the curb that separated the commercial and pedestrian areas of the square from the broad avenue that ran up its middle, and now they used these vantage points to study their adversary. Ronnie's spot was near the gate with Slammer Jon and his family. Both had children on their shoulders and both children had small cardboard horns purchased from one of the many vendors moving through the crowd with food, drink, drugs, noisemakers, and souvenirs. Over the children's constant tooting they shared observations. To Ronnie's eye, most of the mounted officers leading the column under it today looked more like the beneficiaries of connection than possessors of martial skill, but the unit following behind its own wolf standard was different: comprised of men more mature and competent looking than the usual soldiers. Ronnie felt himself recording their faces.

Once past the gate the column slowed its march to allow following units to catch up. By the time it reached the south end of the square it was joined up. There some units turned west, some east, and some continued south between government buildings and the stone columns that marked the beginning of the restricted-use highway.

As the units passed, the quality of soldiers seemed to go down but the noise level at the curb to go up, as families recognized their recently inducted young men and called out to them, causing them on occasion to lose step or get tangled with their unfamiliar weapons. Then Ronnie saw something unexpected: a face he'd already seen—not in the crowd or on some other occasion, but today, in this very column of soldiers.

He'd been trying to memorize the faces of officers and a few others but hadn't hoped consciously to remember those of the thousands of common soldiers. Nonetheless, there one was, among the draftees: the face of one of the elite soldiers of the Wolf brigade, marching now with head lowered into hunched shoulders in the unprofessional way of those around him. Ronnie opened his mouth to bring Slammer's attention to the man but hesitated. What if he was mistaken? A bad or implausible identification would undermine others' confidence in his previously trusted memory. But then he saw more faces. "Slammer," he shouted, and the tall man leaned to him. "I know it sounds crazy, but I'm seeing some faces for a second time."

"Whaddaya mean?"

"It's like some of these guys are passing for a second time," said Ronnie. "Like him!" he pointed with his eyes. "Second row, second guy. He's got his hat different this time ... And that one! Marching out of step."

Slammer Jon drew back to regard Ronnie, looking for something. "Are you sure, Ronnie?" he asked. "We've seen thousands of faces. They're all blurred together to me."

"Pretty sure, Slam," he said with a nod, depending on his commander to read his lips in the din.

"How many?"

"Several dozen seem familiar so far," he shouted. "From the first two units."

Slammer Jon leaned as close as the wriggling burden on his shoulders would permit. "Keep watching, report after," he ordered, and Ronnie nodded.

Ronnie watched. Through the tunnel he could occasionally glimpse the lower part of the VIP seating area and it looked to be emptying out already. He surmised that the Messengers and ministers had probably departed once the first few units were past. He kept watching, estimating numbers, noting weapons and the units' different comfort level with them, and whatever else he could absorb. By the time the column had turned from troops to supply wagons and chuck wagons and mobile smithies and myriad other less-interesting articles of war, the crowd in the square was dissolving into its constituents, some melting away to their homes, others to food stands and taverns and other nearby establishments, stretching the exciting day out toward sundown.

Unburdened of the children on their shoulders, Ronnie and Slammer John stood at a kiosk munching fruit-filled pastries and puzzling over what it all meant. Ronnie claimed to have seen many faces a second time and others a third–as many as several hundred men, from the special operations units, at first, but then from others. Where had they ended up? What had been the purpose in recycling them?

"If you're right," said Slammer Jon, "then my guess is it's a scam.... Ghost soldiers.... The generals or the Ministry get paid by the Treasury according to how many soldiers they have. On an occasion like today, when they have to be put on display, they can only make their numbers by recycling. Simple." He smiled at the logic of his own conclusion.

"Maybe," said Ronnie, "but how would they do it?"

"Look," said Slammer, "everybody's been *here*, in the Square. The surrounding streets were probably empty. Getting back in through another gate wouldn't have been that hard.

"Yeah, but–"

"Let's wait to hear from the other watchers."

Citadel Guard troops, not having far to go and not seeking the public's attention, waited an hour before riding on horseback and in troop wagons past the empty reviewing stand and out the gate to garrison nearby towns, so that army units there could proceed to the front. This was the move predicted by the Freethinkers' intelligence—crucial to the success of the attack—and numerous eyes watched it as carefully as they had that of the army. These men—and even a few women riding separately in wagons—looked altogether more professional, not least because they traveled in their distinctive silver-themed costumes, albeit with the straps of their light, boiled -leather-and-metal armor loosened for ventilation and polished helmets held in laps or placed at feet. To Ronnie's eye, they seemed to comprise about three fourths of the Guard force—also as predicted—with no funny business regarding the numbers this time.

According to calculations, the Citadel was now as lightly manned as it had been in living memory.

As Ronnie feared, his observations about the army numbers got lost in the flood of other intelligence from the day, particularly once reports from the high lookout points arrived near sundown.

Freethinker spies had been prevented by troops investing the nearby countryside from following the column as it split up and headed for the horizon, so hawkeyed watchers had been stationed on midrise rooftops within the Citadel from which they could see as much as twenty miles of road, even as it dipped out of sight and reappeared. These reported that even after it had become impossible to distinguish the column itself, they had still seen its receding dust cloud, as much as fifteen miles away. This news negated all previous reports suggesting the departure of the army was a mere feint in a plan to launch a "near pogrom," and the momentum toward rebellion increased.

A backyard telescope set up on the roof of the 44-story Error Building knew better. At its eyepiece, Lady Sula smiled as she observed what was clearly an ersatz army of fabric and straw, being manipulated down the road with ropes and poles by a few soldiers, the rest having turned off miles before into a field sufficiently distant and obscured from the Citadel hill. Since that point, wagons spaced through the fake army had been dragging fat knotted ropes to raise dust, and in the lowering sun the effect was entirely convincing.

“It’s good,” mumbled Sula–uncharacteristically– as Minister Grotius and the military planners standing a few feet away awaited her judgment. They breathed a collective sigh of relief: none of them would be executed today.

Tomorrow was another question.

43 – Point of No Return

Equinox night

There came a moment in every Freethinker household when there was nothing more to say or do. Wordless embraces were exchanged, hands clasped, faces memorized, and then it was off to war.

That evening hundreds of men and women and teenagers set out singly or in small groups to go fishing or for a stroll or to visit family, as they would tell anyone who questioned them, depending on where and how they were encountered. Many would embark for the storm drain, in rowboats already positioned upriver on the far side, fewer from the more heavily populated near side. Others would walk in the dusk or faint moonlight to the reed-covered bank near the bridge or to the bakery or to smaller venues close to their objectives.

Not unexpectedly, the unusual movement of so many people resulted in the first fatalities of the rebellion, not counting the three men Ronnie had already killed in preparation for it. On the east bank a country policeman had seen a group of people carefully walking single file through a field to get to a waiting boat and, accustomed to being feared and obeyed, ordered them to accompany him to his local outpost. They'd rushed and throttled him, tied his pantlegs closed and filled them with rocks, and consigned him to the river. Near the bridge it had been an innocent but troublesome drunk, who, alone among his several fellows, had refused to take gifts of money and liquor to move away from the vicinity of the drainpipe, commencing instead to yell and fight and eventually to wave around a rusty knife, until there was no choice but to smash his head with an oar and send him floating away, his death to be lamented when there was time, even if it would have to be excluded from the inspiring story of the founding of the new order.

For the fighters who would sally from the bakery and smaller venues there was nothing traumatic about filtering into the location during the day or being escorted in from many directions in the near-dark, but the gaping maw of the storm drain was something else altogether. Very few knew what they were getting into before they saw it, and many may have shared with most people of the era a fear of the underground, where disease and death lurked. But there was nothing for it but to get them in one end and out the other ready to fight, one way or another.

"Welcome, Uncle," (or "Auntie", "Sister", or Brother") said Jak and the other young sewer rats to each new arrival at the pipe, shaming the frightened ones to act bravely in the presence of the youth of their tribe and to get in line and step up on a makeshift stair and look into the almost-black hole, seeing the first few pairs of boots and then nothing else before a faint light at the end.

This is a rainwater drain," said the young guides by rote. "Just touch the ceiling and follow the others to the lamp and sit down against the side. Do you need one of us to go with you?"

The answers, in front of not only the kids but the black-masked Slammer Jon and the red-masked Ronnie and a half dozen who watched, ranged from a tremulously whispered "Yes, please," to a flat "No," to an enthusiastic "No thank you, little brother!" Some arrivals had to wait a few turns to stop trembling and get up their nerve, but even they were eventually swept along into the traffic of their friends.

A girl in workpants and boots at the end stood faintly illuminated by a lamp mounted on a staff that she moved farther and farther back with her. *This side please, this side please*, she would say, alternating. *You can hold hands, but don't talk.*

Finally they were all in, more than two hundred by number and thousands more in spirit. The remaining boats had been pushed into the current, the step and other evidence removed, and the area otherwise returned to its normal state. *Behind* no longer existed for them; there was only *ahead.*

Slammer Jon and Ronnie made their way to the light with some of the platoon leaders while others remained at the opening. The subordinates moved on behind as Jon thanked the girl and took the staff from her, but when he held it near his own, black-masked visage, which had his eyes and mouth floating in space, a disconcerted murmuring ensued and he drew the girl close again.

"Everybody settle down, please," she said in the tone of an experienced babysitter. "Quiet, now. Our leader is going to speak to us.... Listen, now." She stepped aside again.

"Brother Fox?" said Jon low into the silence, and waited.

A small directional lantern held by one of his commanders at the other end continued to burn.

"How about now?" he asked at a conversational level.

The light continued to burn.

"Now?" louder. The light was obscured.

"Brothers and sisters," he began at the middle level, "this is as loud as I can talk, so I hope you can all hear what I have to say. We're only going to take a few minutes, and then we can move to our destination, which is a spacious and comfortable place above ground, so keep your mind on that.

When we get there, there'll be low light but we have to remain quiet until morning, so be patient. Find your squad leaders and do as they say.

"Now," he went on, "some of us are wearing hoods or masks, others not. That was a choice you were all given, and you may change your mind if you choose. Most of the commanders are covered, but you should know that we're all wearing different colors or designs. I'm supposed to be the only one in black, so you can address me as 'Black' or 'Black Mask'. My adjutant here—my assistant—" he drew Ronnie into the light, "is supposed to be the only one in red, so he's 'Red' or 'Red Mask'. Our brother at the back is 'Foxface'— You get the idea.

"Now Red Mask is going to acquaint you with our route, but before he does, I want you all to know that he and his young crew have been working for weeks to make this passage possible, so show your appreciation by listening carefully and doing what he tells you. There will be no questions.... Red?"

Ronnie accepted the staff-lantern, nodded to the few rapt faces he could discern before him, and began in a version of his fake voice to lay it all out: the time and distance, the increasingly confined space, the need for silence, the absence of rats or the mythical Dead, the low danger of flooding, the assurance that their chosen weapons and more awaited them, the fact that bigger men like Black Mask had made the passage, the efficacy of holding onto your predecessor's belt in the early stages, the promise that awkwardness would yield to rhythmic movement, the best way to get over the wall quietly, and the necessity of relieving oneself on the move, if necessary. He ended with the instruction that, when the movement began, anyone who felt they might hold up the column should remain seated until others had passed, before joining the flow. Then, tutorial complete, he passed the staff back to Black Mask.

"Red Mask leaves it to me to mention some harsh realities," said Slammer Jon. "First, there may be some among us who know they can't do this. Those people should stay right here, under guard, until signs of battle begin in the morning, then come out and do what they can. The reason we allow this is so we won't have to kill a brother or sister behind us or ahead of us to keep them from losing control and compromising the mission. Second, as many of you will already have guessed, this passage will be made in complete darkness."

A faint murmur of dismay arose. He waited for it to die away.

"Let's practice together," he said. "Foxface?" The light at the other end was extinguished.

"Now, I'll put this one out, but there might still be a little moonlight." He waited for an outcry, and when there was none, he turned the wick down to nothing.

"Good," he soothed. "Now take your neighbors' hands, if you don't already have them, and close your eyes." He waited a minute, then, "Now take your hands back and sit silently. Take deep breaths, if it relaxes you."

After another minute he went on: "There will always be the sound of movement around you, so this is as isolated as you're going to feel. If you can sit like this, you're going to be fine." A couple of nervous chuckles confirmed it.

Another pause, then, in the cadence that must have moved the followers of Priestbane before a caravan was attacked: "It's time, Brothers and Sisters.... Now join hands again and speak a last word out loud, but low, and make the word 'ready', if that's what you feel. Tell me now, what is your condition?"

"Ready," murmured the many voices in unison, like many wills become one.

The bakery and its carriage house and stable had, like the basement of the church, been light-proofed so fighters could move around without banging into things. Many fighters here were unmasked, especially those already compromised by their association with the bakery, who would have nowhere to return if the attack failed. The baker, his daughter Katren—known in meetings of the military committee as Flame—and the workers therefore freely showed themselves as they welcomed and guided more than two hundred fifty new arrivals to their places and got them settled according to their unit and mission, treating as family not only those they knew by face or voice but complete strangers.

Seriousness of purpose vied with nervous high spirits as groups sat on the floor among the ovens and tables and racks and talked low among themselves. Some fighters who'd donned numbered hoods specific to their unit as they came in from the dark now decided to doff them, feeling themselves among their kin and kind.

Just before the night's final bell at ten, all ears and eyes strained to make out the half-dozen figures who entered from the alley and began circulating among the groups, silently acknowledging the fighters and being acknowledged in turn. All were unmasked, except for an imposing figure in a snug grey hood, who carried himself with authority even while showing deference to the group's obvious leader, himself a handsome, self-possessed man in his mid-thirties, who made his way to a worktable near the front and climbed atop it.

Stand-mounted candles were placed nearby to illuminate the man and he looked out over the clusters of fighters until he was sure he'd attracted their attention. Then with one hand he put a finger to his lips for silence and with the other beckoned the fighters closer. Some of the forty members of his own circle, all unmasked, made way and urged the others forward, until they were all close enough to hear. "Brother and Sister Freethinkers," he began, not too loud, "welcome to the revolution. My name is Verjil, and it is my great honor to have been selected by your military committee to lead you into battle in the morning." He nodded around the large space and others returned the gesture.

"I speak to you quietly now so we can't be heard out on the street, but be assured, come nine bells and a half in the morning, after more than a century of being quiet, we're going to make some noise." Several people chuckled at the prospect. "A *lot* of noise." Soft laughter. "In fact, noise is crucial to our plan, so get your most terrifying, merciless, and blood-curdling battle cries ready. As for the details of the attack, you'll be given those by your squad leaders, but here's the overview ..."

He laid out the committee's strategic vision, so they'd know what they were trying to achieve and why. When he got to the part about securing the Messengers, he gestured for the grey-hooded man to join him on the table.

"This is Brother Grey, or 'Grey Mask'," he said. "He will help us identify the Messengers, who may leave their places and try to escape in the crowd. During the attack he's going to be wearing a striped jacket like those you see on convicts doing road work. Those of you assigned to secure the Messengers, or who may be in their vicinity, should follow his directions until they are all accounted for, or until countermanded by me. Understood?" Heads nodded in the candlelight. A couple of young people started to speak but were silenced by their squad leaders. Grey Mask stepped down. Verjil waited a moment before going on.

"We are small in number, but if we can win the first few minutes others will join us and we will win the war. To do that we have to be vicious, to terrorize and confuse, so fight fast and hard until the enemy surrenders." He looked around to more nods. "Now, let's all try to get a few hours rest. Your squad leaders will take most of you across the alley to the workers' quarters above the carriage house or to the stable and show you where to bed down and where to relieve yourselves. The bakery will begin operating as usual before dawn, but then close for an unscheduled cleanup some time before eight bells. The alley gates will be closed at both ends. You will be brought back to receive your weapons and be put in order by your squad leaders. You will be given something to eat. As you've been told, some of you will proceed to the target by bread van, some will follow on foot. Those of you in the vans must not talk or make noises with your weapons or move about until the doors open at the target, then you must follow your leaders to create a path for those who follow, which means killing anyone who resists you or gets in your way, not stopping to tend our own wounded. Once the Messengers are taken and the room is barricaded, the politicians among us will take over for the next stage and we can see to the wounded, but you must all remain vigilant. We believe the Guard will stand down to prevent the Messengers being killed, but we can't relax too soon. Stay alert." He paused, nodded to a group standing near the table, and announced, "My brothers and sisters will come among you now to guide you to your rest. May it be peaceful."

Δ Δ Δ

Along with Slammer Jon and some of the other leaders, Ronnie weaved among the clusters of fighters sitting or lying on the floor of the meeting room and utility rooms in the church basement, occasionally stopping to grasp hands in greeting and brotherhood, commiserating about knees skinned by the last stretch of pipe, seeing but giving no special attention to Brod, Jak, and Suki. His demeanor and gruff voice made him seem older than his years and he was treated with comradely respect.

"Red Mask, sir," said a boy almost his own age, "will someone wake us up if we sleep?"

"Yes, Brother," he replied. "The bats will do that for us."

"The bats, sir?"

Ronnie stooped down to the teenager. "Upstairs is a sanctuary for thousands of bats. Right now they're out hunting mosquitoes and such, but they'll come back right before dawn. They make a noise like wind in trees, but we still mustn't move around and disturb their routine until light is let in and street sounds cover us. Okay?"

"Okay."

"The bats won't bite us?" asked a furrowed-brow woman who might have been the boy's mother, though family members were mostly separated so they wouldn't get distracted trying to protect each other at the expense of the mission.

"No, Sister,' said Ronnie. "They try to avoid us. You can go right among them and wave your arms around and never touch one. Trust me."

She studied his eyes a moment and said, "I do."

He straightened up and continued his circuit, here and there hearing snippets of conversation that he knew must be about children left behind and understanding. To maintain security, most fighters had been told of the impending action only this day and sharing the information with the young or making elaborate arrangements for their safety had been discouraged, lest domestic drama and the break in routine catch the attention of neighbors and police and put all in jeopardy. There was barely time to recruit grandparents and other non-combatants to look after the children so the fighters—whether parents or older siblings—could simply walk out as if on some errand. Morning, and the progress of the attack, would tell the caretakers whether to flee with their charges or kill them or bring them into the streets to celebrate.

At the many-chimneyed house on the side of Citadel Hill, the gate was smoothly opened and then closed behind the horse-mounted Cornelius and two accompanying guards. On the moonlit terrace Lady Clare observed them, standing back out of arrowshot and peering past the rail. As grooms took the horses, she withdrew into her rooms and waited, supporting herself on the back of a sofa. When Cornelius entered, she stood erect.

"Well?" she asked.

"It's done, milady," he said, handing her note back to her. "Mortimer will pass your concerns on to Endo and the Guard tonight without revealing their source. He's confident that enough of the others will agree to the change. Sula will be outmaneuvered, if she's indeed up to something."

Clare wobbled a little and resumed leaning on the sofa. "Outmaneuvered but not defeated, Corney," she said weakly. "She'll be back at our throats by morning."

Pacing her bedchamber with Endo's note in her hand, Sula was showing her age—still indeterminate but with the frown and the crow's feet marking her closer to fifty than the thirty she pretended to be. Household sycophants and bodyguards stood about nervously, illuminated by candles that flickered with the high priestess's agitated passing.

How could this happen? she seethed, the breakfast meeting's venue suddenly changed on the Sword's order from the large, many-windowed hall, which was accessible by the back stairway to her elite troops hidden on the floor above, to a smaller one on the other side of the service area that was without such ready access, on the basis of a rumor that a group of anti-draft demonstrators would collect to throw rocks through the large hall's windows. She didn't buy it, of course, although she knew the timid Endo would have. Someone had discovered or guessed her plan and wanted to obscure that fact.

Could anyone have discerned its main objective–to kill the other Messengers under cover of a terrorist attack, and the terrorists too–or were they just spooked by the presence of the large military staff on-site for the meeting–larger than they knew, in fact. She stopped and bit her lip. It was too late to stop the attack, as she knew not its staging point, but perhaps something could still be salvaged from it. She snapped her head to her recently elevated new assistant.

"Summon the Wolf."

44 - Clockwork Pandemonium

Plus One

In the Guards Tower, the timekeeper watched the second hand of the ancient gold timepiece that he kept on a silk cord around a beltloop. When it completed its circuit, he pressed his hands to his ears and nodded at the two burly and deaf men who stood on either side of a great bell that had been rescued from a burned church and hauled up the side of the 34-story building in one of the Priesthood's first public displays of ascendancy. The men now raised huge sledgehammers and struck it alternately, glancing at the timekeeper after each blow to know if they were to strike another. When he removed his hands and raised them before him, they stopped; a few seconds later smaller bells outside the walls to the north, west, south, and across the river began to relay its message: nine bells of the morning.

Gates opened and real and counterfeit yellow bread vans began to issue at a leisurely pace from the alley of the bakery and from three other venues across the city. They rode stiffly on reinforced suspensions and their specially selected animals labored a bit on inclines, but no one took special notice of the ubiquitous sight.

Taking different routes, three vans set out for the Treasury, four for the Guards Tower, five for the Error Building and its adjacent steam plant, and six for the Palace. Only two headed for the abandoned church to pick up passengers.

At the church all was in readiness. Fighters variously stood quietly in the side galleries of the sanctuary cradling their weapons or sat in the outer rows of pews, avoiding the grey-white, head-high deposit of guano that ran up the middle of the space and overflowed the inner pews. At the front, just down the steps from the alter on a cleared patch of concrete floor, stood a stoppered bathtub dismounted and brought from the basement and an assortment of trash bins and pots, all partially filled with crude oil bought from numerous vendors over several weeks to avoid suspicion.

From the guano-free space near the now-unbolted but still-bricked-up double doors—in front of which lay an obelisk-shaped and rope-wrapped tombstone from the cemetery—Ronnie looked around at his people in the low light of the dirty clerestory windows. Many curiously studied the bats, some of the animals in turn awake to the changed environment, though at this hour they should have been sleeping off a night of feasting on flying insects. When his eyes fell again they met those of Suki, who wore a plaid hood with the number eight painted on the forehead. He studied the war-fighting garb that hid her growing belly and concluded she could easily be mistaken for a young boy, well-armed with sheathed machete and dagger and with a steel-tipped wooden spear that stood a little taller than herself.

She raised her spear a few inches from the floor in salute and Ronnie acknowledged with his own weapon, the whistling bush axe that he and his father had made together and that he'd brought with him from Firstportage Village, its freshly sharpened, hooked blade gleaming and the oiled cover removed and belted across his belly under his clothes for whatever protection it might afford.

He sought Jak but knew his little brother was probably still downstairs unwrapping the last of the weapons with the other youngsters or helping Brod's squad prepare for its special task. His eyes moved on and noted how fighters studiously ignored the piss on the floor in a couple of places. He thought of Owlly and Nel and the other non-combatants who must be struggling to conduct themselves normally this morning even as their friends and children faced death.

A frisson of excitement passed through the fighters as Black Mask and his sub-commanders entered the sanctuary from behind the alter and made their way around the side. Since last night many fighters had become newly aware that Black Mask, whatever his real name, was in fact the notorious highwayman once known as Priestbane, and they parted for him with respect, which engendered a certain swagger in the man himself. At least he had led men in battle and killed many priests and their guards, they told themselves, even if he hadn't done either in twenty years.

In the church sanctuary made even dimmer than usual by the canvas that had been draped over the hole in the stained-glass window just an hour before, Black Mask motioned for first one seated group and then another to quietly stand and move slowly down the side galleries. When all were assembled to his satisfaction he consulted the jeweled watch on his wrist, once stripped from a dead priest and now wound up for the occasion of the Priesthood's demise.

Twenty minutes after the hour. The breakfast was scheduled for nine bells. Even the VIP guests knew better than to be late and the Messengers themselves would certainly have arrived and taken their places by now. The seconds began to feel like minutes, the minutes like hours. He looked up at a figure in the front loft, who in turn glanced at a sharp-eyed youth perched at the narrow clerestory window nearest the street on the north side, and then back to Black Mask to slowly shake his head in an exaggerated way.

Struggling not to check his watch again, Black Mask observed the preparations at the dais at the front of the sanctuary. There a man set aside the glass cover of a burning lantern, turned up the wick, received from the hands of a young helper a long-handled straw broom, and fixed his eyes on Black Mask in readiness.

A moment later the man in the loft raised his hand. When Black Mask looked to him he touched the corner of his eye, raised two fingers, and concluded with a thumbs-up. Half a minute later the iron-shod wheels of the two bread vans could be heard rolling from left to right and stopping just past the corner to obscure as best they could the remarkable sight waiting to unfold in the dead-end street at the side of the church.

Brod peered over the cemetery wall, saw the vans in place, and rolled over the top to land smoothly on his feet, weaponless. Nineteen more fighters followed, to the utter amazement and consternation of a man sweeping his front steps half a block downhill and of a couple of women approaching on the sidewalk beyond him. The fighters calmly walked to the opening doors of the vans and boarded, ten in one and ten in the other, following the instructions of Verjil's man within each to sit around the sides and not yet to touch the pile of weapons in the middle. As the door closed, a watcher at a south side window of the church sent his signal back through the relay in the loft. Black Mask acknowledged and checked his watch, then silently pointed a command at the broom-bearer, as Priestbane might once have done in the forest with one of his archers, with authority. That man dipped the broom in the bathtub, rubbed away the dripping excess on its rim, and, as everyone watched in fascination, lit it over the open flame of the lamp; it burned steadily and, in the way of heavy petroleum, emitted thick black smoke. Now the man moved the burning straw toward the collection of containers on the floor and, unknowingly, into the vapor cloud that had been forming since the thick liquid began to be poured from cow stomachs at first light.

The cloud erupted with a flash and a low whump that startled warfighters and bats alike and threw the firestarter back on his rear, but within seconds it was obvious that the oil was well-lit and creating the dense column it was intended to. Many bats had dropped into confused flight with the concussion and more followed by the second as the high clerestory started to fill with smoke from the roosting place in the exposed rafters down toward the floor, beginning to seep out the covered window and signaling the bread vans to begin their three-minute journey.

As the bats swirled in fear and frustration, unable to get out, their noisy swarm sank lower and lower and many fighters began instinctively to duck and swat and to raise their weapons defensively. Some appeared on the verge of hysteria, clutching at neighbors.

Ronnie sensed Slammer Jon's concern and followed an instinct to step forward twenty feet down the center aisle to where the ridge of hardened guano started and to climb atop it, into the dark and now-roaring and squeaking maelstrom. He stood with perfect calm, his axe at his side, untouched by wing or claw or tooth even as the swarm sank below his red hood and shoulders. Seeing this, others took courage and stood too, and the moment was past. He returned to his place.

Now Black Mask turned and pointed to the makeshift granite battering ram on the floor by the door and its knotted rope-ends were immediately taken up by six big men. He pointed to the dais where several youngsters including Jak departed to open the church's now-functional back doors and windows. He looked at his watch and the accumulating smoke, waited a few seconds until bats started to drop to the floor, and pointed at a woman holding a rope, who pulled on it to tear away the canvas covering the hole in the stained-glass window above, almost invisible now in the boiling, living cloud.

Liberated smoke and bats poured out the hole on the cross-ventilated westerly breeze like water from a suddenly collapsed dam, but nearby pedestrians and carriage drivers and passengers and neighbors, made curious by the bread van incident, barely had time to be shocked by the sight when, with a great crash, the dry oaken doors of the church, closed since the Cleansing, were shattered by the pointed end of the heavy obelisk, sending the bricks enclosing them flying out into the street.

As the stone was let go and thudded down the steps to the sidewalk and the growing crowd breathlessly awaited the next wonder, the million-voiced howl of Christian ghosts or of some great monster emanated from the gaping doorway and a river of howling and clattering and banging bodies surged forth. Pedestrians fell back trying to get out of the way and horses bolted, careening their burdens down the street in fear.

Black Mask and his subcommanders led downhill at a jog as Ronnie held back behind the leader's right shoulder. By the first intersection the fighters had stopped yelling to conserve breath and surprise and fallen into a rhythm, moving smoothly through now-stopped traffic and ignoring the beat cop who simply stared. Two blocks to go.

Ahead and one street over, the two bread vans moved at a normal speed closer to the open loading-dock gate of the four-story, slit-windowed one-time secure storage facility, its smokestacks confirming normal activity within. Two of the four Guardsmen on duty at a hut outside the gate–representing the Citadel Guard's legal control of the armory–came into the street to look past the vans for the source of the strange noises and saw the black smoke billowing into the sky beyond nearby buildings. They fell into animated debate with each other and with the contingent of soldiers stationed on the other side of the open portal–representing the army's actual management of the facility–about who should mount up to report the fire. They were silenced and stilled by the sound of a distant bell; the same bell as before but rung rapidly with lighter hammers and without cease. The Citadel fire alarm.

Elsewhere, at the bakery and in the vans slowly approaching the Treasury and the Guards Tower and the Black Tower and the Palace, others heard the signal they'd been waiting for.

At the side of the bakery, young men blocked traffic, to the displeasure of shouting drivers, as the alley gate swung open again and ten more yellow vans issued in an unbroken line. These men boarded the last van as others ahead ignored irate but unarmed traffic cops to block the next four intersections. By the time the caravan reached the last corner and turned to bring the palace into full view, the other eighteen vans were delivering their payloads.

At the Treasury, shouting fighters simply alighted at the curb and at the rear service entrance and stormed through unprepared guards and into the public-access lobby. As information-desk attendants and visitors and workers variously scrambled to hide or slammed office doors or stood paralyzed in disbelief until knocked down, fighters carrying chains and locks set about securing the doors. Within two minutes the building was locked down. True, the Priesthood's treasure could not yet be taken from the secure inner sanctum of the building, but neither could the treasure or the rest of the guards on duty get out of it. The Priesthood's money was now unavailable to it, and no one had died.

Not so at the Black Tower, where attackers and defenders fell as guards and loading dock workers and steam-plant workers fought back, screams and shouts and clash of metal echoing through the tower lobby and elevator bay and blood smearing the path to the two sets of stairs. There, friction-fused incendiary satchels were thrown to explode both upstairs toward the police and military offices and down toward the guards' quarters while arrows were unleashed to discourage anyone from trying to get through the smokey fires as they consumed themselves on the fireproof stairs. As office workers and residents began to break second and third floor windows to flee, workers at the coal-fired steam plant next door were being forced at spearpoint to vent the boilers and snuff the fires, disabling the tower's elevators.

Remarkably, most denizens of the Guards Tower a few blocks to the northwest remained unaware of the alarm bell madly ringing at the top of their own building, until one of the bell-ringers' children raced down past sparsely occupied middle floors to tell them. By then the yellow vans were pulling up to the east and west entrances of the tower and the north and south entrances of the stable/carriagehouse not far away, in the park between the Tower and the Palace. As shouting guards demanded to know what in ZAH's name the drivers thought they were doing, the drivers' helpers pulled pins to disconnect their animals and lashed them away to safety while fighters inside activated fuses and bailed out the back door already on the run, some of them nocking arrows as they went. Despite the novelty of the situation some guards understood and gave warning, just as the first van exploded in plywood shrapnel to scatter burning tar all around the entries and arrows came back from the nearby archers, discouraging men and horses from coming out for at least a few minutes.

The nearly simultaneous nearby explosions brought occupants of the Palace to the windows, and service-area workers and Guardsmen out onto the docks, just as the first two innocent-looking yellow bread vans were pulling up to the dock and as four more were making the turn into the service lane and as the final ten were within seconds of catching up. Mesmerized by the smoke beginning to rise over the intervening trees, the thirty or so gawkers took a moment to realize that a man had casually stepped out of the first van onto the long dock with a homemade sword drooping from his left hand and a dagger from his right. In the time it took for all to transfer their attention to this apparition, and for the guards to put hand to sword, the man was quietly joined by twenty others and the doors of the arriving vans were flying open. Then the man took a deep breath and the spell was broken.

"KILL THEM ALL!" Verjil yelled, and charged the nearest guard, who stumbled back and fell before he could draw his sword and died with a cleaving blow to his unhelmeted head. Two others summarily broke and ran for the door amidst the jumble of fleeing civilians but the other eight or ten on scene stood their ground even as they rapidly became outnumbered and perished at the hands of multiple attackers and even as they killed a few of them in turn. Service workers clambered over each other and cowered against the walls as shrieking fighters barged through the short corridor and into the kitchen to hack and stab and bludgeon anyone who didn't instantly submit, quickly turning the smooth floor slick with blood so that crowding fighters repeatedly fell atop those mortally wounded but not yet dead and struggled to their feet to be swept forward by the pressure from behind. Pots and pans and dishes flew and terrified shouts rang out, and then the real fight appeared to start.

Drawn by the crashing din, a dozen or more Guardsmen came through the double swinging doors ahead on the left with swords drawn and engaged. Not pausing to wonder why there were so few, or why others peering through the glass of the right-side doors stayed back, Vergil's personal bodyguards surged around him and mostly fell before the professional soldiers, until the soldiers were themselves overcome by sheer numbers. The fighters trampled the fallen of both sides to reach the metal-faced doors and burst through and down a short passage, on guard against an onslaught of defenders, but there was none. Instead they were momentarily dumbfounded by the sight of as many as three hundred mostly black-clad men and women and numerous waiters and event staff either standing stoically at their places or crying out in fear or shouting in outrage or desperately trying without success to get out of the room. Then Grey Mask pushed up to Verjil's shoulder in his distinctive striped jacket and pointed at the scrum of people at the door.

"STOP THEM!" he shouted, even as he noted something amiss, and Verjil motioned his fighters into action.

"ON THE FLOOR!" they yelled as they moved across the room, stabbing and hacking at anyone who didn't comply. People screamed, chairs and table toppled, dishes shattered, and even the stoics broke and got down. More and more fighters flooded into the room to find not the battle they expected but a mass of supine and frequently whimpering priests and priestesses.

The door was secure, apparently locked from the outside by palace guards to contain whatever was going on and now chained on the inside as well, as attention turned to a head table and to the nearby door in the corner that led into a complex of event-management offices into which a few figures had fled. Grey Mask strode through the field of bodies to the four tables set end-to-end at the side of the room, followed by Verjil and his guards. When he got there he roughly handled a few of those on the floor to see their faces and then stepped back to Verjil as guards took position over them.

"The woman at the end is the Civil Service chief," he said privately.

Verjil looked at the colonel's exposed eyes and mouth with incredulity. "And the others?"

"Don't recognize them. No Messengers, No VIPs. These people are bureaucrats."

"Then ..."

"The Messengers must have been switched to another room."

"*We have to find them,*" Verjil said urgently, starting to turn for the chained door. Grey Mask grabbed his arm. "It'll be suicide now," he said. "There may be a hundred Palace Guardsmen on the other side of that door."

"We have to try!" said Verjil, pulling away. "It's our only chance!"

Suddenly a commotion erupted in the kitchen that made the fighters still filing into the meeting room look over their shoulders and then turn in fright as those behind them frantically tried to push past the swinging door, knocking others down.

"ARMY!" yelled one to Verjil as he tumbled into the room just before a steel arrowhead appeared in the middle of his chest.

"BARRICADE THE DOOR!" shouted Verjil to those near it.

"But sir!" protested a squad leader.

"DO IT NOW!" Verjil ordered as he sheathed his sword and moved to overturn a heavy wooden table against the still-crowded swinging doors. Others fell to helping even as arrows flew through the narrowing doorway and then the glass and as twenty or more fighters were cut off with no choice but to turn and fight the fully armed and armored soldiers who'd swept from a commercial building across the street to attack their rear and drive them into the kill box. As fighters hopelessly watched the bodies of their own people pile up through the broken windows, Verjil beckoned Grey Mask toward the chained doors to the main corridor and demanded in his ear, "If not here, where?"

"Well," said the colonel, playing for time, "two doors down on the right, I'd say, but ..."

"But *what?* Quickly!"

The colonel's eyes darted to the side and his head jerked fractionally as a new locus of yelling and banging started up past the event manager's door, through which a few of the fighters had gone to round up stragglers. Underlying the sounds of men and women dying was the unmistakable low rumble of dozens of pairs of boots clattering down stairs.

The colonel looked back and Verjil saw the crinkle of his eyes and the smirk on his mouth, "but it's too late," he finished, stepping out of Verjil's reach as the door slammed open to admit the already-blood-splattered men of the Wolf Brigade.

At the armory the two Guardsmen in the street had seen the nearby smoke and heard the fire alarm bell and now they decided as a precaution to lock up as soon as the two bread vans were past. But as the first one reached the gate it suddenly turned in and accelerated toward the building in defiance of the yelling guards in the street as well as the army ones who bolted out of the inside gatehouse to try to grab the second horse's bridle as it too was turned in. One of the soldiers glanced back up the street and registered the amazing sight of a river of rough-dressed figures rounding a corner a mere half-block away, carrying steel saws and sharpened pokers and myriad other re-purposed or homemade weapons, and he darted in after the second van to begin madly ringing the small alarm bell hanging from the eave of the gatehouse. An arrow through the neck from an archer who'd popped out of a trapdoor in the second van's roof stopped him even as another archer appeared from the first van to target ahead and even as an unmasked Brod and his fighters spilled out the side and rear doors to slay the other soldiers, send the Guardsmen fleeing–as Ronnie had suggested in private– and secure the gate just as the main body arrived in full cry.

The loading dock doors were closed but the office complex door was unlocked, if the two men who'd been standing outside it in conversation were any indication. Realizing what was happening, they got tangled with each other trying to get through the door and close it behind them; one caught an arrow in the shoulder and the other drug him through and locked it and shouted a warning behind as he looked fearfully through the door's mesh-reinforced window.

As the last fighters arrived and took defensive positions in the street, others checked the employee's entrance—locked and likely to have guards behind it anyway—as still others went to work on the office door with the large crowbars they'd brought. The corridor beyond filled with incredulous office workers who were soon supplanted by guards in army gear, at first outraged and shouting at the vandals' affrontery and then scared as the tools distorted the door frame. When it popped open and a murderous howl erupted from the nearly two-hundred fifty attackers, office workers and guards both fled to the last office and disappeared.

"C'MON!" yelled Black Mask, leading the charge with sword high followed by Red Mask and his bush axe and Brod and his shock troops wielding their own wicked-looking instruments of death. At the last open doorway, both Jon and Ronnie darted across to draw bowshot but there was none.

"Which one?" demanded Jon after a quick look located three identical doors in the back wall beyond a counter, and Ronnie replied, "We're told the middle."

"Brod! Open the middle door on our silence, wait for our shout plus three beats, then charge!"

"Got it!" said Brod, moving into the room with his men to take up positions on either side of the door, whose inside lock was in the open position.

Black Mask now raised his sword to the fighters crowding the corridor, put a finger to his lips and followed with a motion across his throat, and they fell silent. Brod opened the door to an eerie silence, Black Mask telegraphed his intention by gesture to those in the corridor, and then he and red Mask bellowed a death cry that was instantly picked up by all.

A fusillade of arrows from nervous defenders within the armory flew through the doorway to strike the counter and the walls behind and through the office door to bury themselves in the corridor wall; then, as those archers nocked new arrows, Brod bolted diagonally out the door.

"CHARGE!" he yelled, and immediately caught a more disciplined bowman's arrow in the side. The point glanced off a rib and re-emerged at his flank to his sharp "Ah!" and he instinctively reached to hold it out of the way of his sword arm as he sought a target and as the fighter behind him dropped his own short spear and fell clawing at the arrow protruding from his face. A barrage of smithing tools and half-formed metal objects took down more of the fighters poring through the doorway and then steel met steel.

The two dozen army swordsmen and the handful of office workers before them were terrified by the screaming horde, fighting desperately for their lives. Arrows from archers sheltering behind fixtures quickly grew erratic and stopped. Within half a minute the remaining soldiers and workers broke and ran, clambering up stairs and down as the room filled with attackers. One soldier tripped and was swarmed.

"DON'T KILL HIM!" bellowed Black Mask, striding over and pushing the wounded man on his back with his boot and placing his sword tip at his throat.

"Where are the others?" he asked quietly enough to cover the man's anticipated betrayal of his fellows.

"What?" the man croaked, already speared once in the kidney and leaking badly.

"You heard me. Where would they shelter? The other guards, the workers ... Speak if you want to live."

"But ... they're gone! They ... Please don't kill me!"

"Gone? Gone where? Speak or die!"

"Most workers were give tha day off, sudden like ... smiths told to leave fires burn.... Just guards–two squads ... Don't know where ... I–"

Black Mask drove his sword point through the horrified soldier's carotid artery and moved to the next task as the man tried to stifle the spraying blood with his hands.

"You there!" He pointed to a squad leader in an evil-clown mask,

"Get the doors open." then turning, "Medics! Tend our wounded." Turning again, "You and you, to the basement! Yell 'Contact' if you need reinforcement.

"You Brod!" he jabbed his long finger again, then hesitated upon seeing a broken shaft being pulled out of the young man's side by one of his squad members.

"Good to go, sir!" said Brod.

"Upstairs, then! Floor by floor! The rest of you follow by squads to rearm yourselves from the stores and come back to relieve those on defense until everybody's got a decent weapon. Got it?"

"SIR!" shouted the fighters packing the room and still pushing in, excited by the prospect of getting their hands on real soldiers' weapons even as they stumbled over their own dead and wounded.

"Archery Two and Three! Gather all the shafts you can and bows if you want and get to the roof."

"SIR!"

"Engineers to the steam plant! We need the elevator if we're going to arm the people by nightfall."

"SIR!"

"I'll send further orders by Red Mask. NOW GO!"

A raucous roar accompanied pounding workboots and suddenly, as Ronnie glimpsed the childlike form of Suki ascending the open staircase with her squad, he and Slammer Jon had their first moment of privacy since the attack began. Ronnie leaned close and spoke in Jon's ear.

"Slam, did you catch the part about the smithies being told to leave their fires burning?" But the thoughtful Jon was absent, and the eyes that scanned the action from behind the black hood were those of a man possessed by the moment of triumph.

"It's *working,* Ronnie!" he exulted. "We're going to win! A hundred and nine years of oppression and now ..." His voice trailed off in wonder.

"Yes, but–"

"Let's take a look from the roof!" Jon said excitedly, already sheathing his sword and in motion, ordering a lieutenant to take over below as he started up the stairs three at a time.

The fighters already inside the four-story building had bounded up to get their new weapons in a party mood, not even bothering to look for the half-dozen hiding fugitives, but as the two passed the second level it seemed the revelers were now about the quieter business of selection, shunning swords in racks and littering the floor along with the weapons they'd brought and instead trying to pry open oil-filled barrels marked as containing fifty swords each; others examined the steel tips of lances with apparent awe. On the next level crates of shields and body armor were beginning to yield to crowbars even as fighters excitedly strapped on the few loose pieces lying about.

The top floor was the bow shop and fletchery, and here the party atmosphere survived as some archers traded in old bows for strong new ones and everyone gathered canvas-wrapped 100-arrow bundles and ascended one at a time to the roof up the less rickety of the two wall-mounted staircases.

Emerging on the roof with Ronnie and the archers, Black Mask glanced over the street-side parapet to see a proper defensive line set in the street and then basked in the morning sun and in the moment of glory, slowly turning with his hands away from his body. Three blocks to the northwest, the oil fire at the church still billowed. On the hill to the north, smoke from the lower regions of the Black Tower and the Guards Tower showed those operations had been carried out as planned. In the vicinity of the Palace itself, the tiny figures of spectators collecting on rooftops and in the streets gave evidence of that most-crucial one as well. By now, Black Mask knew, the Messengers and the Sword of ZAH himself would be in Verjil's custody and the threat of counterattack eliminated. Soon Owlly and the Baker and the other politicians would–

"SLAM!" gasped Black Mask's second lieutenant against protocol as he struggled through the trap door with a bundle in his arms, followed by several others with other burdens.

"What?" said the commander in irritation.

The group managed the treacherous stairway onto the roof and hurried over to spill their cargo into a common pile at Black Mask's feet as the archers who'd taken shooting positions and started to unwrap their bundled arrows looked back.

Ronnie saw Black Mask shrink as he gazed at the collection of weapons. When he reached down for an oily sword, his hand trembled. In bright sunlight, the deception was obvious.

"All fake, boss," said the lieutenant, normally Jon's shop foreman. "Wood, clay, papermash, boiled sugar, tin. We've been tricked! Better get out of here, if we can."

Black Mask couldn't move–until one of the archers called out.

"LOOK!" said the eagle-eyed woman with her hair braided behind her left shoulder, away from her bowstring and quiver. She had instinctively glanced back at the nearby wall seeking an escape route and seen the dust; now all followed her gesture and found the brown smear in the middle distance to the south.

"AND THERE!" called a bowman, pointing to the road east of the river.

"And there southwest," said Ronnie, spying a column emerging from a tributary valley so close to the city that vehicles could be distinguished in the cloud they created, not more than a few hours' march away.

"Is it the heretics?" asked someone, and all were silent with what they had believed was the absurdity of that notion. Finally, Ronnie spoke the obvious.

"It's the army," he said. "The entire army. They must have been hiding."

"So it's the 'near pogrom' after all," observed the lieutenant evenly.

"Maybe more," said Ronnie, and the older fighters looked at the precocious teenager. "A military-coup, I think."

"A coup? But ..."

"Our attack inside the wall gives the army reason to enter with its arms," said Ronnie. "They could wipe out the Guard and take over."

"That bitch Sula," mused the lieutenant after a moment, as all contemplated the tyranny that would surely follow the ascendancy of her clan.

"Maybe," began Slammer Jon weakly, "we could force our way out and disperse into the woods, like in the old days. Verjil's people must be seeing what we're seeing. Maybe–"

"SOLDIERS!" yelled one of the archers at the parapet overlooking the street. "Getting ready to attack!"

The officers rushed over to see twenty or more green-clad archers in two rows taking up position on the roof of the two-story uniform shop across the street, with the obvious intention of raining arrows down on the fighters noisily milling between the street and the loading dock and with apparent disregard of opposing archers looming two stories above them, though several did appear to keep watch on the armory's roofline. They stood back out of sight of the rebels with arrows nocked, waiting for something.

"Slam," Ronnie said calmly, as if he were telling someone they had a terminal illness and had only a few minutes to live, "those men are Wolf Brigade; I recognize some of them. If they're *here,* they must also be at the *Palace.*"

"Fuck!" blurted a nearby archer as he prepared to nock the first arrow from the unwrapped bundle at his feet.

"Zah's balls!" said another.

"I can't believe it!"

"Fucked now, for sure," predicted another.

"What now?!" demanded an exasperated Black Mask.

In answer, the woman with the archer braid left her position to hand an arrow to her commander, who inspected it impatiently. Fine steel point, straight shaft, feathers angled just right. Then he saw it. The arrow had no notch for the bowstring. It was useless. They were all useless.

Black Mask snapped the arrow with a guttural cry and threw it down. He turned to look at the ever-nearing dust clouds and back with anguish toward the Palace and down at the "ghost" soldiers he'd failed to inform the committee about, now edging forward, and he broke.

"My god, my god ... what have I done?" was all Ronnie could hear, as two hundred heavily armed and armored killers of the Wolf Brigade jogged out of the alley behind the uniform shop and pandemonium descended.

45 - Terrible Beauty

At the palace, in the rage and terror and melancholy of annihilation, Freethinkers died, bravely defending their place in history and memory or in hatred of their killers and solidarity with those beside them or foaming at the mouth in desperate suicide or scrambling under tables to steal the robes of priests for escape or in last-second peaceful communion with loved ones, but they died nevertheless. Every last one. Numerous clergy too, as Wolf Brigade soldiers surreptitiously daggered them during the melee and archers standing behind a defensive line shot them with civilian arrows as they cowered, all to besmirch the Freethinkers and to make the threat of them more fearsome in imagination then they could now be in fact. Through it all the renegade colonel stood immune in his striped jacket, observing the encircling carnage with satisfaction, until the rebels were all dead or dying. Then he was respectfully escorted into the presence of the Wolf and efficiently stabbed to death, thus obscuring Lady Sula's role in enabling the Freethinker attack. He died with a look on his face that said he should have known.

As the slaughter was winding down and some Wolf Brigade dead were being stripped to hide their numbers, the effort to breach the door into the other venue, where surviving kitchen workers said the Messengers had been moved, was winding up, with claims of concern for the safety of army and Error personnel at the breakfast shouted through the glass pane of the locked service door.

"That why you're in Error black now, Colonel Gregor?" shouted the commander of the Palace Guard over the clamor of the milling bureaucrats.

"Indeed, Colonel Vorhees," said the Wolf. "Made para commander yesterday. Told you were shorthanded and might have trouble this morning–demonstrators or some such–so we came by to help. Saw the terrorists and did what we could. Now you've got a roomful of dead terrorists and a lot of live and grateful clergy, and we need to get where we're needed."

"Told by whom? And when?"

"Lady Sula, this morning. You can thank her yourself."

And with that he turned toward the rear dock even as Vorhees did the same, coming out nearly simultaneously among milling and injured clergy and tense Guardsmen and paramilitaries.

"We're not done here, Gregor," said Vorhees.

"Got to be for now, colonel. City's under attack, if you haven't noticed. I'll retrieve my dead later. Six or seven, in black like me."

The battle at the armory still raged. The simultaneous appearance of archers on the opposing roof and troops jogging around the corner threw fear into the Freethinker ranks extending out into the street. Black Mask came out of his stupor as the first arrows struck the jumble of fighters already confused and disorganized by the rumor that they'd been duped. He started to yell down as screams rang out but lurched back when arrows whizzed by his head and peppered the protective parapet. He turned to see all eyes expectantly upon him.

"Right!" he said, getting control of himself. "Archers! Consolidate the good arrows you brought with two or three shooters. The rest of you go downstairs ... try to find tools ... pliers, cutters ... maybe something to make a split to hold the string–"

"Suggestion, sir!" offered Ronnie.

"Speak!"

"Vices on some of the workbenches below. Mash the ends or break them off ... might leave a surface that–"

"You heard 'im!" ordered Black Mask. "Go! We'll send you help!"

To the lieutenant and Red Mask he barked. "This way!"

He strode to the east side of the roof and flung open the trapdoor over the other stairway and moved to step through.

"Better let me test it, sir!" said Ronnie hurriedly, and Black Mask motioned him into the lead. The apparently disused stairway, its handrail wobbly and the entire structure barely hanging onto the wall by a few loose bolts, sagged under his weight but held. Black Mask started down before he'd reached the bottom and the lieutenant followed. By the time they'd crossed the room to the main staircase one of the archers at a workbench reported, "It's gonna work, sir!"

"Good job! Now give me a thousand just like it! There's a lot of enemy to kill!"

"Yes, sir!"

Passing the third floor, Ronnie spotted Jak and his squad of girls and boys still looking for viable weapons. "Sir," he said, his hand on Black Mask's arm. "Those are the tunnel kids. They can help!"

"You, there!" shouted Black Mask, and a half-dozen young faces looked up at him as he placed a hand on Ronnie's shoulder. "Quickly now! Red Mask has new orders for you!" Then to Ronnie as he drew his sword, "Join me at the front when you finish!" and he was gone.

Ronnie imparted the problem and the mission to Jak and the other youngsters and dispatched them upstairs in seconds. When they were gone he rushed to the sound of men and women battling shoulder to shoulder for their lives. The front was still exposed because those trying to push into the fight prevented those ahead from retreating through the now-open loading doors; every few seconds another Freethinker just behind the line of contact went down, bowshot with near impunity by the archers a mere thirty paces away, whose opposite numbers were almost out of arrows to restrain them. Searching for Black Mask, Ronnie saw his two lieutenants desperately trying to get fighters to back into the building or behind the wall, but they continued bravely if suicidally to press forward. Then he saw him, ahead of the line, perhaps atoning for his failure, slashing and butting and kicking in the company of a few plaid-hooded fighters who fell one by one. Every few seconds he turned and tried to order a retreat into the building but his intentions were heard by no one in the cacophony and understood by few. Ronnie guessed he was still alive only because the archers were loath to hit the comrades engaging him hand to hand. But their hesitation wouldn't last.

Red Mask raised his double-sided and hooked bush axe over his head, gave a yell that created a path through his own people, and headed for his commander. Within seconds, four soldiers were mortally wounded by the unusual weapon, which with its wrist strap could be thrown a few inches and retrieved or swung in a wide arc. But no sooner had he created a little space than he glimpsed archers rise to punish his rash act. Still, it was not yet his time.

Several enemy archers suddenly crumpled and others held fire to shelter behind the lower building's inadequate parapet as a salvo of army-issue arrows struck. The bowmen's leader reached out from cover for a shaft buried in the tarred roof and found that the end of it had been mashed to splinters so that it would hold a bowstring. He remembered from his briefing that the rebels would have access to thousands of such supposedly useless arrows; at such short range they would be lethal enough. Time to retreat, but not before one task was done.

Black Mask and Red Mask saw each other and started jabbing and hacking in the other's direction. They'd almost joined up when surviving archers on the shop roof suddenly stood and let fly at the tall man in the black hood, hitting a couple of their own and being themselves mostly cut down. Black Mask arched and his eyes flared as a half-dozen arrows found his back. He fell heavily to his knees, then on his side. Red Mask knelt to him as the battle closed over them.

"UNCLE JON!" Ronnie called to him, affectionately for the first time. "Slammer Jon" Woodmaker, once notorious as the highwayman Priestbane, couldn't draw breath to speak, but he had a final message. Just before his leaking heart stopped and his eyes fixed, he reached to pull off his hood and shoved it into Ronnie's hand.

Freethinkers were risking their lives above Ronnie and there was no time to grieve. He lashed out at one attacker's shins with the front edge of his axe and stood to lead the others out of the pocket as friendly arrows broke the enemy's attack and Freethinkers struggled to close the armory gate. Soon, army archers were repositioning and shooting from the interior of the uniform shop and, at greater distance, from other buildings, while the gate, increasingly littered with the dead and dying, still could not be closed. But the two forces were separated for the moment and a moaning, crying, and pleading respite descended.

That was a problem for the Wolf, just arrived on horseback from the Palace with Sula's admonition still ringing in his ears: whatever the course of events, keep the thousands of spectators collected in the area and indeed the whole city in a fever over the existential threat posed by the enemies of ZAH, which could only be defeated by the returning army. Breaks in the action—at least ones like this that the people could see out their windows and down the street—were not useful. Reinforcements from the Palace were arriving behind him and he'd already given his order for the next act in the drama when a voice from the armory stayed him.

"ARMY COMMANDER!" yelled Red Mask from behind a column, elevated by circumstances and selected for a voice that could pierce walls when turned to full volume.

"WHADDAYA WANT, HERETIC?" came the reply after a long moment.

"SHALL WE RECOVER OUR WOUNDED?"

"LEMME THINK ABOUT IT."

A minute went by, then another. Suddenly a fusillade of civilian arrows streamed from the shop's windows to strike not the armory or the Freethinker wounded, who were left to suffer in the street, but the Wolf Brigade's own mortally wounded. With this signal, troops already blood-smeared moved along the sidewalk behind the sheltering wall from both directions and charged through the opening to reengage Freethinkers sheltering on the other side. Strangely, army troops now fought with a certain restraint, as if they were trying to delay the denouement, and Ronnie realized they might be attempting to keep up the appearance of a mortal threat to Zahdom until the main body of the army came within the wall in force, whereupon the rebellion would be ostentatiously crushed and the Council of Messengers overthrown or demoted. For the Freethinkers, and freethought itself, the comparative lull in fighting could mean survival.

"We can't let them get in the building or they'll fire it," said Red Mask to the surviving lieutenant and several squad leaders watching the action from cover through the one open loading door. "But if we can *delay* them, and *then* let them fire it, or fire it *ourselves*, I think we can escape."

The others looked at him with skepticism or derision or pity, until Brod spoke up: "How, Brother Red?"

Within a couple of minutes, heads were nodding and the operation was agreed. Some departed to make arrangements on the second floor, others to join the fencing match outside. Brod gave orders to his fighters and they recovered the tools they'd used to breach the first door and bounded up the stairs.

On the roof, archers at the eastern parapet remained vigilant over the two unoccupied walled courtyards below—through which soldiers had just yesterday come and gone to receive their arms—and over Brod's squad as it worked at the trap door and on the rickety stairway. As two men kicked the broken handrail away below, others on the roof secured the top of the stairway with ropes. Then, with Jak's crew helping, the stairway was pulled away from the wall at the bottom while the men with crowbars worked directly on the loose bolts and soon the whole structure was hanging by the ropes. Pulling from above and pushing from below and using the dismounted handrail for guidance, the stairway was taken through the portal and laid on the roof, all twenty-five feet of it.

Within minutes the fight below intensified, watchers apparently having seen part of the stairway as it was raised above the parapet and guessed what it portended. Now there was no time to lose.

As the roof archers pored arrows into the enemy ranks, Ronnie and the lieutenant ran downstairs to call a fighting retreat. Fatigued enemy soldiers would have let them go but were forced to remain engaged all the way to the loading dock's edge, beyond which was certain death from the archers positioned within the building.

The metal door came down and was locked as the last fighters cleared the opening and enemy arrows peppered it and skittered across the floor. In seconds it was being hammered with sword and lance butts and the office corridor, now choked with furniture and other obstacles, was being probed. "EVERYBODY TO THE ROOF!" yelled the lieutenant. "WE'RE GETTIN' OUTTA HERE!"

No further encouragement was necessary, and the fighters trooped up the stairs as fast as their tired and damaged bodies would take them, not stopping to ask how escape was going to be possible. Ronnie saw Suki moving head-down among a mere three or four surviving members of the plaid-hood squad. She'd lost or discarded her short spear but walked with the machete her husband had made in one hand and the dagger in the other. She was covered in blood.

At the first landing, barrels of oil meant to have contained swords had been maneuvered into position and awaited deployment. The second and third floors, strewn with fake weaponry, were almost depopulated of fighters. On the top floor they congregated at the remaining wooden stairway and ascended it two at a time, with comrades underneath supporting it as high as they could reach.

On the roof Brod and Jak and the others had brought all into readiness. The stairway was lined up with its rope tethers tied to the skylight frame and a team of the strongest men was being put in order to launch it. Fighters were preparing themselves and each other and sharing water from bladders that had survived the fighting.

When Red Mask and the lieutenant made the roof, the leaders spontaneously came together in a huddle.

"Bridge first, then fire?" suggested Brod, and all concurred. The lieutenant turned to Ronnie.

"Red, this is your idea," he said. "Direct us."

"Right!" said Red Mask, turning to the others. "You men! You're gonna have *one chance* to make a bridge for us, so put your heart into it! Brod, you're the strongest–you push from the end at the last moment!... Now listen ... we need to elevate the front, like this"–he demonstrated with his hand– "and launch it like we're aiming for the far southern sky. Got it?"

All nodded; some shouted "Sir!"

"Okay! We'll move back and forth twice for practice and then launch on the third pass. Got it?"

"Sir!"

"Okay ... lift!"

The seventeen men raised the stairway to their shoulders and at Ronnie's command backed up twenty paces. He stepped to the wall and looked at the target: the top of a wall of a destroyed building about twenty feet away, against which the debris that comprised the wall was piled up on the far side. Below was a sheer drop to an inaccessible field of trash that had been collecting since the wall was built. If they were unsuccessful, it might soon contain their bridge as well. He turned back to determined-looking men and boys.

"On my 'Go', start slow and don't trip, pick up speed, and think about pushing and getting out of the way of those behind as you reach the wall. Ready?"

"Sir!"

"Go!"

The men moved out clumsily, making their burden look unwieldy.

"Stop!" he barked as they reached him, disheartened. "Again!"

They backed up and tried again. Better. They needed more practice and some rest but there was no time. They backed up again.

"Okay, are you men ready to get us out of here?"

"Sir!"

Red Mask stepped aside. "Ready?"

"Sir!"

"Go!"

The men moved out as one. By the time the first ones reached the wall and peeled off, they were growling and then with a mighty shout and heave they launched the stairway into space. Brod's final push took it to the end of its two tethers. and one snapped, skewing the missile to the side. As it crashed down on the top of the parapet and onto the opposing wall it seemed sure to bounce and plummet into the abyss, but it wedged itself in debris and held—barely.

A moment of stunned silence yielded to cheers, and then Ronnie, seeing the lieutenant gesturing at the trapdoor, called for attention.

"Red, lead us out!" said the lieutenant. "I'll get the fire started." And with that he was gone.

"Rope!" demanded Ronnie, and a knotted coil from the third-floor stores was placed over his head and draped from one shoulder. He climbed onto the parapet and then onto the bridge and then let go of helping hands. He moved to the middle, bounced a couple of times for all to see, and turned back with a grin.

"Let's go, Brothers and Sisters. Follow me!"

Downstairs at the second floor landing the first barrels of oil had barely been spilled down the main staircase or rolled to burst open on their own when a howling mob breached the loading dock door and flooded into the first floor. Even as the lieutenant threw the torch to light the spill some soldiers got by and fell upon those at the top of the stairs, most of whom had sheathed their weapons or put them aside while they worked. All were mortally wounded within seconds, including the lieutenant.

"SMOKE!" yelled one of the streetside archers over her shoulder, and Brod nodded in satisfaction as he herded the dwindling fighters toward the bridge. Enemy bowmen to the east had started sniping at those crossing over but at the distance had hit only three, one of whom made it across on hands and knees with an arrow in the flesh of his buttock. Red Mask stood atop the wall as a beacon, out of the snipers' line of sight, and watched those who'd already crossed over descend the rubble-cliff with the help of the knotted rope tied to a bit of mangled iron sticking out of the wall near where Suki sat, her eyes fixed on her husband, willing him to hurry across.

Spread out below was a sight as amazing and horrifying as it was welcoming: the Heretic Graveyard, which he'd known would be there from his study of maps in the secret library. What had once been a traditional cemetery of the city of All-Boney had come to be the depository of the ashes of almost its entire pre-Cleansing population, as well as those of hundreds of thousands of strangers who'd been killed in fear of disease and then hundreds of thousands more killed and burned as heretics, along with the books claimed to have condemned them. Altogether, more than two million during the reign of the Priesthood of ZAH, now lying mixed together in long, meandering ridges covered with weeds and shrubs and surrounding the periodically smoke-belching crematorium in the middle, where the provisionally condemned were given the opportunity to shovel and glean the ashes of the dead in hope of reprieve.

Ronnie knew the cemetery well, because that's where he's chosen to bury his personal treasure, in three separate locations. He also knew that no soldier of ordinary superstitions and phobias would venture there but wasn't so sure about those of the more-disciplined Wolf Brigade. If his people could just get across to the wall and drop the bridge behind them ...

"Brother!" he yelled to Brod. "Cut the tether at the far end and bring that end across with you. We'll drag it off the building from here."

"Got it!" came the reply.

Fewer than twenty remained on the roof, plus the lieutenant and the eight or ten who'd started the fire. Brod cut the bridge's tether loose and awaited them anxiously at the trapdoor, peering into the increasingly smoky interior. Suddenly he spasmed in pain as an arrow appeared under his right ribcage and Suki screamed his name. He lurched back and drew his sword but could do nothing about the arrow or the dark liver-blood that seeped over it. As Suki struggled to break free of Ronnie's arms and would have stabbed him if he hadn't been holding her hands, Brod roughly pushed stragglers onto the bridge. Behind him archers who'd rushed to the opening and begun shooting to cover them–at a disadvantage against a bright sky–fell back one by one as well-aimed arrows flew through the portal. At the end, there was only the woman with the archer-braided hair, mechanically reaching down to her packet of squash-ended arrows, nocking as she stood, leaning forward to shoot down the stairs, and repeating. Ronnie and the few others on the wall watched her with admiration and morbid fascination until finally an arrow caught her under the chin. Without drama, she let the bow slip from her hand, lowered herself to her side, and was still. Brod pushed the last man across the bridge and staggered to replace her but turned back as if having forgotten his keys or money and with an agonized grunt pushed the bridge along the parapet a few feet and off into the abyss.

"NOOOO!" cried Suki as the stairway plummeted.

Brod was already turned to his duty, merely raising his sword in farewell. When he reached the opening, he stepped purposely through and was down about two steps when three arrows struck him in the chest. He jerked, drew his big chin in to survey the damage, threw his sword down the stairs, and toppled in after it.

The others on the wall started their descent, but Ronnie lingered with a keening Suki in his arms. In a moment a head rose through the opening to regard them. Seeing no remaining threat, the man it was attached to emerged and walked to the parapet, sheathing his sword. A dark-complected, brown-haired, grey-eyed man in his late thirties, intelligent of expression and with a curious shape to his face that made him look a little feral, he broke eye contact with Ronnie only long enough to glance into the gap at the shattered bridge. When he looked back, he nodded and smiled toothily, and Ronnie realized the man was not named for his unit, but his unit for the man: The Wolf.

As two bowmen who'd used their leader for cover suddenly split to either side and let fly their arrows, Ronnie rolled with Suki below the ridge of the wall, toward the knotted rope. The arrows sailed harmlessly into the vast cemetery and no more were wasted. Now he put Suki's hands on the rope and bade her descend, as one of her waiting squadmates accompanied her. Then he lay back for a moment, listening to the Wolf shouting orders.

With the rope in one hand he looked into the near distance one final time and saw that all three army columns were close enough to discern vehicles and cavalry and marching infantry.

They were all headed for the great square from whence they'd departed and would start to arrive within two or three hours, as he'd previously predicted, but there was a new element.

As he stared, he could faintly discern, moving just ahead of the army columns, the silver-themed costumes and armor of the Citadel Guard, who'd apparently left the nearby hamlets and villages they'd been assigned to invest in order to get back before the army. Contemplating the scene, Ronnie remembered the note from Lady Clare that Cornelius showed him but wouldn't let him keep.

He nodded to himself, murmured "Thank you, milady," and took the rope to descend.

46 - Madman to the Fore

Hmmm ..." mused Lady Sula as she watched the scene through her telescope, her retinue standing in attendance nearby.

Freshly arrived on the first elevator to make the ascent since the steam plant was put back in operation, she'd been apprised of the events of the last hour at the armory as she watched their conclusion. Now she stepped away from the glass and began to pace. The regular observer resumed his place at the eyepiece.

"The bridge is gone," stated the man blandly. "Did you see what happened, milady?"

"The criminals pushed it down," she answered as she came close and turned. "How many crossed over?"

"More than a hundred, we think." He continued watching as the Wolf's men on the ground fixed ropes for those on the roof of the armory to descend as the interior fire mounted higher.

A general spoke up: "We were thinking of having the Wolf go around to cordon the cemetery ..."

Sula looked at him witheringly as she passed; guarding a perimeter nearly a mile long with army forces vitally needed *inside* the wall would be counterproductive.

No one else ventured a suggestion as the high priestess paced. Her mind working furiously, she began almost to smile, despite the partial failures of the morning. *So what* if the rebels got away and fled to the woods or dispersed to their homes? Their survival and continued threat would merely support the maintenance of martial law. But there was an even more valuable service they could provide–right now.

"Show me the first column," she ordered; the observer moved the instrument and stepped aside.

At the eyepiece she studied the silver-clad Guard hurrying ahead of the green-clad army and demanded, "How much time between the Guard and army?"

"Maybe thirty minutes?"

"And the three columns will arrive together?"

"Looks like it, milady. In about two hours.

She observed for a few seconds more then turned to her audience. "If the rebels head for the Square, let them pass. Their interference may delay the guard and allow the army to catch up."

Heads nodded, understanding. In the confusion that might follow, the army could easily force its way through the main gate.

"Set some more fires in the meantime," she added thoughtfully, "assassinate a few disfavored people from the lists, and, ..."

They held their breaths for something typically outrageous and difficult.

"when it's over, bring me the head of the boy in the red hood."

"Yes, milady," they said in chorus to her receding back."

Lady Clare didn't have such a good view from her more-distant terrace and her eyes weren't so good anyway, but the hawk-eyed teenage girl standing arm-in-arm with her made up for these shortcomings. She'd come to report the smoke and the remarkable flight of bats from the old church and stayed to describe occasional glimpses of the dense body of attackers rounding corners near the armory and of unusual activity throughout the city. When fires broke out at the Error Building directly behind them and then at the armory near the wall, she moved about with her mistress to supply detail to the picture of panic in the streets both uphill and down, of the dust clouds foretelling the return of the army, of the tiny figures on the roof of the armory, and finally of the ant-like exodus over the wall and the downing of the makeshift bridge.

With Cornelius and Bear and a couple of maids and assistants now collected behind her, she let go of the girl and drew herself erect.

"My carriage and four, Corney. Let's go have a look."

"Yes, ma'am," said the majordomo without emotion, though he was enormously troubled that she would go out at a moment of such uncertainty and in her still-delicate condition. He looked an order to an underling who left to carry it out.

"Now, my dear," she said, turning to the girl, will you help me dress?"

"Where are we?" asked a young woman who'd already lost her two best friends, now crouched with the others between two shrub- and small-tree-crowned berms of ash and bone fragments and dirt. She sounded shaky and leaned on her neighbors.

"Somewhere no one's going to attack us, I think," said Red Mask. "Zahists are afraid of places like this."

"Me too!" said someone in the back, and a nervous but healthy titter passed through the fighters, who, *in extremis,* were now family to each other.

"I know the cemetery well," said Red Mask. "I can get us out. The question is, where are we going?"

The question hung in the air a moment, then, "Do you know what's going on, son?" asked a long-limbed and gaunt middle-aged man, belying Ronnie's attempt to inspire confidence by seeming more mature. In respect, he gave up the pretense and answered in his natural voice.

"I do, sir—at least I *think* I do. Shall I tell you all?" Many nodded.

He scooted onto the slope of the berm, elevated a little. "Our brothers and sisters attacked several places across the city," he began, "intending mainly to take advantage of the absence of the army and most of the Guard to capture the Messengers and use them to take control. Instead, *we've* been used–to create excuse for the army to return and take over inside the wall ... take over *everything*." He let the awful consequences of that sink in for a moment.

"They'll be back in the Square soon, and I'd say the forces that attacked us will help them get through the gate before the Guard can reestablish control."

"Can't we join up with the others? ... fight them?" asked a boy whose molded mask left the spiky strip of hair up the center of his skull exposed.

Red Mask looked down, without words.

"There *are* no others," said the gaunt man. "Right, boy?"

"I fear not, sir. We were the only ones with an escape route."

"Which you created, I think," said Gaunt Man.

Now Ronnie recognized him as one of the squad leaders, without the hood he'd worn and apparently bereft of his entire squad. He remembered the form and the shouting voice of him as he struggled with others to protect the fallen Black Mask.

"Whaddaya mean?" asked someone.

"The bridge, and the fire to delay the soldiers–his ideas," he said. "I was there."

"The arrows, too," said one of the members of Jak's squad. "The ones we found were no good, but he figured out how to make 'em work."

Everyone remembered how the battle had turned when the arrows finally started flying in quantity, and several murmured their approval.

"So, Red Mask," said Gaunt Man after a moment, what do you think we should do now?"

Ronnie looked over the hundred-plus fighters, torn and tired and wounded, so far suffering stoically the loss since morning of many who were dear to them, and a great weight of responsibility descended upon him. He knew what he wanted to do, but how could he ask or sway any of these men and women and boys and girls to join him in what surely amounted to a suicide mission?

He glanced back at the top of the wall to orient himself.

"I guess most of us live *that* way," he said, pointing east and south.... We *could* just leave our weapons here and return to our homes—hope the army's pogrom won't take us and our families anyway ... *or*, we could go to the Square and *fight*—try to keep the army from getting through the gate and making our world even worse."

"But we'd be wiped out in minutes!" said a man with incredulity, merely stating the obvious.

"Possibly."

"So why do we fight?"

"For history ... for legend," answered Red Mask, to general mystification.

"Speak on, son," said Gaunt Man after a few seconds.

"We may have lost more than four hundred brothers and sisters this morning," said Red Mask, warming, "cut down in private, with none but their killers to say how they died. In future, the Black Tower's rumormongers and the priests will portray them as degenerate cowards, enemies of Zah *and* the people, and even their families left behind will lose confidence in themselves and their hope for a better world. But if we leave here right now, *with* our weapons, and go straight down Stonecutter and Woodmaker Streets to the Square, and we station ourselves before the gate, and we fight bravely, in front of thousands of witnesses, then we write a story to inspire those who follow us, and if that's the best we can do today, I say it's enough."

Ronnie let his eyes fall, declining to challenge anyone's mere pride.

"I'll go," said somebody's grandmother, finally.

"I'll go," said a greengrocer-cum-history teacher.

"I'll go," said a nanny-cum-biology teacher.

"I'll go," said a horse breeder.

"Me too," said a tailor's apprentice.

"Me too," said a carpenter.

"We'll go," said Suki and Jak, their hands held aloft together.

They committed themselves to each other in ones and twos and threes until all had spoken, then fell silent again.

"Who will lead us, then?" asked Red Mask, and directed himself to Gaunt Man. "You, sir?"

The man studied him before speaking. "Tell me, son," he said, "when Black Mask was with you on the roof, and he came down and led the charge that killed him, why weren't you with him?"

"He'd sent me to direct the tunnel rats to make arrows," answered Red Mask. "Why?"

"I think he made that charge because he saw we were doomed and he wanted to show us how to make a statement with our deaths, just like you're suggesting we do now. I also think he saved you on purpose. That's why, when you came down and saw him and started killing your way to him, he tried so desperately to reach you–not to escape, but to protect you."

"Maybe," said Red Mask. "I–"

"When he fell, and was dying, he took off his hood and gave it to you. Do you still have it?"

"I do," said Red Mask, reaching into his shirt behind his axe's leather cover and withdrawing the blood-spattered cloth.

"Why do you think he gave it to you and not me or one of the others?"

"He couldn't speak then."

"I think he meant for *you* to lead us if he fell. That's why he kept you close. And you *did* lead us. You led us *here*. You might as well *keep* leading."

Ronnie stared at the squadless squad leader, then at the crumpled scrap. The fighters murmured among themselves.

"Put it on," said Gaunt Man.

Some of the fighters immediately nodded. Seeing this, Red Mask held the black cloth aloft in his fist and sought the approval of all. They nodded quadrant by quadrant, all the way to the back.

"If you trust me to lead you, then I'll trust myself to do it," he said. "I accept your commission. But I won't become Black Mask. I'm not yet worthy of that, and besides, if no corpse at the armory is found wearing a black hood, then Black Mask is not dead, but fights on in secret, and if some of us survive to spread his legend, he'll be a ghost for tyrants to fear every time they step out their door or take to the road. For now, before we die as gloriously as we can, we have some allies to go meet and a giant army to outwit."

He stood up and looked around, cradling his axe and grinning at his suddenly gape-mouthed comrades.

"Are you ready?" he asked, back in his mature command voice, as if he were inviting them to join in the harvest dance back in Firstportage Village. They glanced around at each other and struggled to their feet.

Allies to meet?

Giant army to outwit?

Omgod! –what kind of young madman had they chosen?

47 - Citadel Square

Peeking over the head-high wall in various places toward the Square, Red Mask could not find a spot where there were not spectators collected on the far side of Cemetery Road. It was a tough neighborhood of slaughterhouses and tanneries and some carried the tools of their trade, though most seemed merely to point and speculate about the fires and the unusual movement of vehicles and people. There were no police in sight.

"Okay," said Red Mask to his new lieutenant, Gaunt Man, "we're out of time. Get everyone along the wall in pairs, one to hold the weapons while the other climbs over. When you and I go, everyone follows. Move with authority but without threat. No awkwardness or hesitation. The scariest-looking group is right here, opposite us. We'll confront them first. Got it?"

"Yessir," said Gaunt Man.

Some of the spectators had seen movement behind the cemetery wall, but none were prepared for the coordinated appearance of more than a hundred armed and bloodstained fighters, led by a tall, lithe figure wearing a snug red hood and carrying a well-used axe with a long, hooked, double-edged blade. They fell silent, waiting.

Red Mask and Gaunt Man handed off their weapons and walked purposefully across the street toward the bearded behemoth whose body language and that of his companions identified him as the leader. He stopped a few feet away and regarded the man, who seemed more curious than afraid, with his hand casually draped over a meat cleaver in a bloodstained holster strapped to his thigh. Many of those around him were armed as well.

"You in charge here?" asked Ronnie.

"Sorta," answered the man. "Name a Big Hog. You the ones come over the wall? –the rebels?"

"You saw?"

"Yeah ... hell of a thing.... You Priestbane?"

"Priestbane wears a black mask and goes by a different route. For today, I'm called Red Mask."

The big man nodded, then, "The elders said you might need help."

"In the worst way, and right now."

"Whaddaya need?"

"The army returns to the city as we speak, to invade the Citadel under arms and take over. They'll kill a lot of people outright. We're going to the square to stop them passing, but we could use help slowing them down until the Guard gets back in place."

Big Hog looked past Red Mask to the tattered remnant across the street and smiled. '"Stop them passin'?" he repeated. "The whole Army a ZAH?"

"Yes."

The big man's smile faded. "Where they at now?"

"Three columns, all with Guard troops returning before them. The nearest comes by the west road." He pointed south. "They should be right over that way within the hour. If you could harass them, get others to join in ..."

"I get the picture." He looked around at his neighbors with concern. "It'll be bad for my people if the army wins and comes for revenge."

"Yes."

Big Hog looked into the eyes of Red Mask and the lanky man with him and at the calm determination in the demeanor of those across the street, who had to know they were going to their death, and decided his people could not but honor such courage.

"Let's do it, then. What's first?"

△ △ △

By the time Red Mask led the "rebel army" into Stonecutter Street, it was obvious the politicians had laid the groundwork well. Big Hog's runners had raced ahead to spread the word and thousands of people had come into the street from neighborhoods to the south, even as beat cops made themselves small and disappeared and flagmen at the infrequent stations atop the wall a block to the north sent ineffectual semaphore messages to the weakened Citadel Guard. Traffic turned off or moved aside as excited kids raced down the street ahead and fast-paced fighters briefly grasped the hands of loved ones or bumped fists with strangers.

By the time they'd reached Patty's Pub and Stonecutter Street had become Woodmaker Street, a hundred or more new fighters had fallen in behind with their weapons, many wearing headcovers or hastily fabricated masks. One of them, to Ronnie's eye, was unmistakably Tom, whose cleft face could not easily be hidden behind a snug, honey-colored hood. Striding past him in front of Patty's, he'd raised his axe in salute and Tom and a dozen others with him had replied with a variety of helmet-splitting and armor-gouging instruments.

Half a block later, Owlly stepped from the crowd on the sidewalk and angled to meet the pace. Red Mask beckoned him past those fighters who'd made themselves his bodyguard and they grasped each other on the move.

"Report!" ordered Owlly.

"Time's short, Dad! The Guard and army will start returning to the Square within minutes. All our fighters are dead, I think, except about a hundred of us, plus these others now. Jak and Suki live; Brod sacrificed himself to cover our escape. It was a trap, Dad, allowed to happen to give the army excuse to invade the Citadel and take over, I'm sure. We go to stop them–give the Guard a chance.

"I've asked for help from the east side, too, but I fear you won't last five minutes, Son."

"The Guard arrives first; we'll see what happens."

"They're no friend to us; they'll kill you too!"

They were coming up to the shop, where on the porch stood Nel and one of Suki's sisters, holding Suki's priestchild Madi in arms. Owlly moved to peel off toward them, looking back toward his adopted son.

"We go to our duty, Dad!" shouted Ronnie. "Tell our story!"

A moment later, at the corner, he looked left to see the narrow portal at Woodmaker Gate closed tight, with two scared-looking guardsmen peering through peepholes and two watchmen in the small booth atop the wall readying their flags to report the rebels' passage.

In the last block he studied the behavior of the young people spilling into the Square ahead of the column to gauge the danger that awaited. He turned and walked backward for a few seconds without slowing down, making eye contact with those he could and checking everyone's position, then turned again as the huge square opened before him.

It was empty.... Empty of enemy, at least, though hundreds cavorted or strolled or excitedly exchanged gossip, hundreds more filtered in from side streets to form a perimeter like at a sporting event, and hundreds more already watched from windows and rooftops, some bearing the pots and pans and whistles they'd employed just yesterday.

Suddenly, as the column passed into the square, one of its members stooped as others shrouded him and then stood and moved past Red Mask into the lead.

"Look!" exclaimed a spectator to his friends. "There he is—the one in the black hood! They say he's Priestbane! My dad told me ..." And thus was the famous highwayman of legend resurrected and put back in command.

Black Mask and his red-hooded adjutant led the rebel column into a wide arc across the square, creating a semi-circle with the imposing gatehouse at its center, staying out of accurate range of the twenty or more archers of the depleted Guard corps who stood at its lower battlements twenty feet above ground, along with a few officers, infantrymen, civilians, and one wobbly high priestess with her attendants. The space behind the line was quickly filled with other fighters and unarmed sympathizers and altogether the mass of serious-looking people gave a formidable appearance, even if no more than four hundred of the thousand or more were armed.

“Perfect,” breathed Sula at her telescope, trying to bring Red Mask into better focus as he and the other man faced the gate’s lowered portcullis and closed oaken doors. She gave up, moved the scope to survey the pitiful collection of Guard troops assembled inside the gate–she couldn’t see the front battlements from her vantage–and returned to focus on the other man.

“You told me their leader was dead,” she said mildly, without looking to Minister Grotius and the generals flanking him. “‘Black hood ... may have been Priestbane,’ you said.”

“Yes, milady,” Grotius replied carefully, “hit in the back more than ten times as he tried to flee, we’re told. That right, General?”

The bemedaled and beribboned man cleared his throat, chilled by the lady’s tone. “Yes, minister, milady,” he assured. “That’s the report.”

“Then how do you account for *that?*” she challenged, stepping away from the instrument.

Grotius moved to look for a moment then stepped aside and glared at the general, who took his place. After watching the two masked men apparently conferring with each other for a few seconds, the general got control of his voice and said, “A common ploy, milady. A leader falls, his people prop him up or put someone in his place.... Not the same man, I’m sure.”

“We’ll see,” said Sula cryptically as she resumed the glass, thinking she might prefer that the *threat* of Priestbane not die with the actual *man.* She hadn’t decided. For now she was just reveling in the scene, with the heretic forces stupidly arrayed toward the gate when the real threat was at their rear.

"How long now?" she asked of the regular observer, to the chagrin of the officers.

"The Guard troops should arrive–more or less together–in about a quarter hour, milady. The army was closing on them but now seem to have fallen back."

"Fallen back?" said Sula, surprised. Why had no one told her before?

"Yes, ma'am. It appears they're being engaged–from the side streets."

"Engaged? Show me!"

In a moment she was peering at the force approaching on the west road, making small adjustments on her own. What she saw shocked and enraged her, for there, on public display, was the feared Army of ZAH apparently being harassed by youths launching rocks and hunter's arrows and other missiles while others ran from cover to strike or stab a soldier or horse and run away. As she watched, a cavalry officer trying to drive attackers away from the column found himself on the ground being pummeled after his horse was tripped, only to be saved by foot soldiers in a time-wasting rescue.

"When this is over, I want that neighborhood destroyed," she seethed.

"Yes, milady," said Grotius and the generals in unison.

In the Square, Black Mask and Red Mask conferred one last time and then Red Mask started toward the gate by himself. Excited spectators increased their noise level in anticipation of some dramatic development.

At fifty paces he stopped, let the axe fall from his hand on its swiveling wrist-strap, and, with a twisting movement of the torso, started swinging it about his head. In a moment a deep thrum began, so unusual and compelling that it soon imposed a watchful silence on the several thousand spectators. Then he caught the axe in his left hand, took a breath, and spoke so the whole echoing square could hear.

"CAPTAIN OF THE GUARD!" he shouted in his Red Mask voice.

A bemused or perplexed stirring and looking of one to another ensued at the battlement, then a beribboned senior officer standing with the priestess gestured and a younger officer spoke.

"WHAT?" came the fainter voice.

"I HAVE A MESSAGE.... PERMISSION TO APPROACH."

More conferring, then, "COME AHEAD."

Archers' arrows remained nocked but bows undrawn as Red Mask neared the gatehouse. By the time he arrived he'd realized that the senior officer was in fact General Krono, commander of the Citadel Guard, and the priestess, whose clan, he remembered, was allied to the one that dominated the supposedly neutral Guard, was Lady Clare. He wasted no time worrying about the implications of their apparent acquaintance, or whether Krono knew that his own mistress, the courtesan Mona, was one of his intelligence assets.

"General," he began from about thirty feet away, speaking past the junior officer, "time is too short for protocol, so my leader's message must go directly to you–right now."

"Speak," said the general.

"As you may already know, this–" Red Mask twirled his finger around to encompass not just the Square but all the events of the day– "is all a ruse, cover for the army to invade the Citadel under arms in about thirty minutes and kill *you,* and this *lady,* and anybody else who stands in the way of its rule."

"They won't get in," said the general defensively, puffing himself up.

"Oh yes they will. With Wolf Brigade troops already inside and a raging battle going on out here, the gate will be compromised. You know it. That's why you look ready to shit your pants."

"I–"

"You think your returning troops will cut right through us, but they won't. We'll fight, they'll slow down, the army will catch up with overwhelming numbers, the Wolf will kill you all and open the gate, and it will all be over—*unless* ..."

"Unless *what?"* asked the general.

"Unless we *don't* fight."

"If you don't want to fight, why are you here?"

"We're here to fight the *army*, and you too, if necessary, but I— but my *leader* proposes a brief alliance, lasting, say, twenty minutes."

The general slowly shook his head in wonder. "Unbelievable," he said. "And what makes you think the Citadel Guard would make an alliance with the likes of you, however long?"

"Because, as a wise person once said, when you run out of friends, you must seek out the enemy of your enemy." He glanced at Clare, standing behind with Bear and Cornelius and a maid, but she didn't react. "Right now we're both short of friends."

The general looked around, thought for a few seconds, recalled the report of the rebels sparing his men at the armory gate, stared at Red Mask for a few more seconds, and said, "What do you propose—exactly?"

To Lady Sula's frustration, Red Mask and whomever he spoke to had been out of sight for several minutes, obscured by the gatehouse structure and the wall. At first she'd smiled sardonically to herself to imagine what the leader of a band of rebels could have to say to the defenders of the Priesthood of ZAH—a surrender demand, perhaps—but she'd grown uneasy. Now, with the creature in red on his way to rejoin his wrong-way-facing confederates and the army once again closing on the Guard units, she relaxed. It was almost done.

Red Mask had barely reached and conferred with others and seen his simple order passed down the line and filtered into the mass of volunteers, when a group of horse-mounted scouts passed between ZAH's Columns to enter the Square at its southern end. Attired in the polished metal and silver-grey cloth of the Citadel Guard, they stopped four abreast and marveled at the scene: thousands of spectators at windows and rooftops and spilling off sidewalks, and in the square itself a great mass of civilians, many armed. Eventually one of the scouts noticed that a flagman at the far gatehouse was signaling, but none of the four was a flag-reader. After a quick exchange, two of the riders turned their mounts to canter away toward the main body.

Within minutes, the two thousand or so men and a few women of the Guard force that had been sent to garrison nearby towns and villages began to stream into the square, spreading out with lance- and sword-armed cavalry in front, as if preparing to ride the rebels down. In the middle were the grim commanders, also on horseback, and next to them in a cart, one sitting and peering through a pre-Cleasing pocket telescope and the other standing with his flags at the ready, were two signalmen. When the flag-reader recited to the colonel next to him the order of his general at the gatehouse, the colonel looked to see if there was any uncertainty, then said, "Acknowledge."

Sula was exultant. As she rapidly changed her view between the Guard force, now on the verge of attacking the rebels, and the first army unit a mere few hundred yards away, she mentally urged the soldiers forward to fall on the backs of the already engaged combatants and create the chaos that would signal the hidden Wolf Brigade to move against those paltry forces guarding the gate. The gate would be flung open, the army would push through triumphant, and the new age—the Sulan Age—would begin.

She moved the glass again to enjoy the fear and despair and the well-deserved suffering of those who would challenge the legitimacy and the natural supremacy of ......

Something was wrong. The rebels were not falling into disorder as she expected, but were instead calm, now arranged mostly sideways to the gatehouse and the Guard formation, with half of them facing the other half up the middle. The hairs began to stand up on the back of her neck and her armpits became moist.

As she intently stared, Black Mask and Red Mask entered the mass of rebel fighters at the center and made their way shoulder to shoulder straight through to the side facing the Guard, followed in pairs by all the Freethinkers, until their single line formerly facing the gate was now a double one dividing the fighters up the middle. Black Mask took a position before them while Red Mask continued into the open space between the two forces. He turned toward his people, performed the curious ritual with his weapon, yelled something, and finally, as if cleaving Sula's hopes and dreams asunder, used the weapon slowly and symbolically to divide the rebel ranks in two.

"NOOOOO!" screamed Sula.

In the square, as the parallel lines of Freethinkers took the cue and turned to motion their allies back, the two halves neatly unzipped from south to north with a rumbling of short steps until a path more than fifty paces wide was created. Red Mask moved to the side and gestured.

The Guard colonel urged his mount forward and the formation consolidated itself behind him to pass through the opening. The crowd had, at the cleaving, reacted with a collective gasp; now it broke into clamoring argument about its significance. A few threw insults and brickbats at those they thought had been cowed and broken, while others—supporters of the Guard or those who understood why it had to be let through—urged patience.

Red Mask struck a non-threatening but watchful pose, with the blade of his axe resting on the paving stones and his hand on the butt, ready to be betrayed but hopeful. In the rebel ranks beyond him, some people surreptitiously grasped hands for courage as the Guard commanders and cavalry clopped past, nearly close enough to touch, their lances raised and bows slung, both sides studying the other. Unlike the often feral- and undisciplined-looking soldiers of the army, these select troops' dress and equipment and manner spoke of competence, and all were glad not to have to fight them.

Next came the vigilant infantrymen, who kept their attention on the rebels' homemade but serviceable weapons even as they studied their faces with curiosity. Then came the few supply wagons that could be thrown together after lookouts had informed of the army's unexpected return, and the column was through.

At the gatehouse, the iron portcullis began to be cranked from the pavement and the heavy doors to be drawn open on their tracks. Now followed the most dangerous moments, when the Guard column could turn on the rebels, secure in the certainty of being reinforced from inside, and crush them between themselves and the army. But the general had not sworn falsely, and the flagman had not conveyed a secret message of betrayal; the last carts passed through the portal and, as the sound of hundreds of clopping horses and thousands of tramping feet began to be heard from a new direction, the portcullis fell into place with a resounding thud.

48 - Legends

In the vast Square, a murmuring, funereal quiet descended, as even the revelers and the sceptics came to understand what was happening, and that there would be no further preliminaries; this was the final act in a drama the like of which they'd never seen.

That it could have come to this state confused and unsettled many townspeople, for neither in living memory nor in the telling of parents and grandparents had any such thing ever happened. Never since the Chaplin's first missions of enlightenment to settlements outside his home village, where ZAH first commissioned him to His service, had anyone resisted the god's servants in an organized way. Only deranged and pitiable and often book-reading troublemakers had ever said otherwise, and they and their lines had been exterminated just like potentially diseased strangers were in the early days, and for the same reason: to prevent transmission.

As the footfalls of horses and men and the clatter of equipment and the rattle of wagons and the muffled cries of skirmishing grew louder, the spectators in the square watched the rebel formation with a certain impatience, waiting for those in it to break and run for their homes as even reckless teenagers did when caught vandalizing audience halls or painting anti-Priesthood graffiti or mocking the clergy in the streets. The situation was becoming serious, and it was high time everyone came to their senses. But the rebel force remained, even as its composition changed by the minute.

Only the Freethinkers themselves knew exactly what had transpired behind the wall this morning–that hundreds had already fought and died for the simple freedom to hold and follow their own beliefs–but as their stories had been sought by those near them and had filtered through the assembly, and as the allies and others had studied their torn and bloodstained clothing and their wounds and their nicked or bent or broken weapons and above all their faces and eyes, the reality and the immediacy of mortal danger compelled them either to slip away or to cleave together with whatever weapons came to hand.

Red Mask and Black Mask did not exhort, nor do anything to appeal to pride or passion, save grasp the hands of those they walked among. Nor did they announce any complicated tactics–there was no time to learn them. There was only time for companionship and for reflecting on the lives they gave and the family and friends for whom they gave them, and, for the practitioners of banned religions old and new–some of whom now displayed the symbols of their faith–for reflecting on the teachings of their gods.

Taking a position beside Black Mask a few feet in front of the others, Ronnie contemplated the two stone columns in front of him and remembered the day he'd passed between them with the trader Baladur and his family. He'd left his own family and Freethinker circle to make their way to the mountains just ahead of pogrom and come to the Citadel in search of Jenna, only to find her in the arms of a powerful man and on her way with him across the sea. He knew now that the sting he'd felt when she'd turned away from his desperate call, as the *Wind of ZAH* raised sail and passed down the river, had been what led him to emulate her, training and using himself as a weapon to get what he wanted from the elite women of the Citadel. That had worked to win information and money and connections for his co-conspirators, but it hadn't worked to make him forget her.

Still, at the end, he couldn't hate her. He'd come to hope that, when she returned in the spring or summer, they might be friends who laughed together about their childhood in Firstportage Village, and even now he hoped she'd remember him fondly, even if the official history of today's events painted him as a fool who caused the deaths of thousands, even if–

Ronnie the sentimentalist instantly reverted to Red Mask the de facto battle commander upon spying the column moving directly toward him on the south road, the broad ceremonial avenue that continued across the Square and by which he'd arrived three and a half years earlier. The increasing sound of skirmishing to both east and west suggested those columns were being harassed and perhaps prevented from reaching the Square by side streets, but the middle one, the one led by the expedition's commander, General Jovan, was coming on relatively unimpeded–and fast.

"Don't you see?" demanded lady Sula. "It can still be made to work!"

She found herself pleading with a mere colonel, Minister Grotius and the two generals having slipped away to a lower floor for safety when her earlier expectations regarding the Citadel Guard weren't met, knowing she could lash out at anyone nearby at such moments.

"We just have to make sure the army conducts the pogrom as we said it would," she continued, "as soon as these criminals are disbursed. Just send a message that–"

"That's–"

"How dare you interrupt me!... What is it?"

"That's what I was trying to tell you, milady. The Guard is refusing to flag our messages out, and it's too far to signal from here. We have only what the birds have brought in and so far their intention is unclear, in the absence of orders. With the loss of surprise, it probably depends on what happens in the next minutes."

Sula glared at him for a moment as if she might have her bodyguards throw him off the roof, then turned back to the telescope and focused her hatred on her red-hooded nemesis.

Δ Δ Δ

Lady Clare focused on him too, but not with hatred.

Despite her attendants' attempts to get her to take a comfortable chair they'd brought from below, she still stood at the gatehouse battlement, despairing to overhear General Krono making arrangements with his officers for disarming of the troops and rapid collection and cremation of the rebels' remains as soon as the disturbance was over—the usual practice. Could a dream long-dreamed end so ignominiously, in the same ovens to which she was responsible for consigning books?

The Army of ZAH, which had never lost a serious battle but also never fought one, entered the square with a casualness calculated to belittle, with officers and cavalry on horseback and archers and infantrymen on foot contriving to ignore the nearly one thousand mostly armed civilians as close as sixty paces in front of them, or to lean to each other to make jokes at their expense. So they were surprised when—before a thousand of their own six thousand had even passed the stone columns—the rebel's apparent leader started writhing and swinging his weapon about his head to create an arresting low hum, suddenly stopped, yelled "KILL THEM ALL!" in a murderous bellow, and charged them with a band of screaming maniacs on his heels. More than surprised, they were momentarily stunned into immobility as the distance closed between them and some in the crowd yelled warning. Then, with archers still struggling to unsling their well-crafted bows and infantrymen to unsheathe their shiny swords and cavalry to ready their needle-sharp lances, they were set upon in a most unseemly fashion. The first rank stumbled back upon the second and the second upon the third, gouged in the face or viciously hacked across the limbs and back by unfamiliar weapons until unarmed rebels started picking up *their* dropped weapons and using them on the next rank.

In the lead with Black Mask at his flank, Red Mask had sprinted toward a point off-center only to veer at the last moment directly at the expedition's commander, Jovan, who'd chosen to surround himself with sycophants instead of real bodyguards. His horse screamed in terror and jerked its head back as the bush axe came down across one eye and then went strangely off-key as a second blow with the hooked side tore through its windpipe. Red Mask clambered over the blood-pumping and dying animal even as it tripped and crashed into another rider and repeatedly brought the axe's point to bear on the stylish but light armor around the trapped general's neck and chest until he too was pumping blood, and then he was gone to the next target and the next and the next.

The army gained a respite only when the field of dead and dying fighters and animals grew so broad and tall that it formed a sort of barricade behind which soldiers could regroup. The south-approaching unit's officers had been decimated and many of its infantrymen and archers killed, but those of the east and west units were mostly functional and soon merged to push not only between the stone columns but more ruthlessly through side streets, emerging a few at a time all around the rebels.

Starting the fight with a thousand private armies-of-one had been effective at first but had devolved into spontaneous and ever-changing alliances as partners fell and new threats distracted. At one point Red Mask found himself working with Plaid Mask Number Eight–Suki–and doing very well. She'd learned to harry with a certain rhythm and grace, waiting for a swordsman to commit to a swing and then darting in to stab his thighs or kidneys or hack at his calves before the sword could be brought back her way. She worked her routine a couple of times and then he lost sight of her, until a moment of calm occurred in the storm.

"Ronnie!" she called as she holstered her bloody weapons and joined him for a drink from a bladder he'd cut from a soldier bleeding out at his feet.

"We *did* it!" she cried, and drank deeply.

"Did what, Sis?"

"We showed 'em!"

"Showed 'em?" He looked around to see if he'd missed something.

"Suki, they're about to wipe us out!"

"Not *them,* silly," she said, gesturing to the field of bodies in which they stood, *"Them!"*

He followed the sweep of her hand to take in the thousands of spectators at windows and rooftops and side streets and even standing weaponless among the combatants, mostly yelling like crazy and seemingly *not* for the army. To illustrate her point, Suki took Ronnie's axe-hand by the wrist and raised it and the weapon between them. Immediately the spectators at nearby buildings cheered as if the two had scored a goal at play.

"Yeah, I see what you mean," he said, suddenly more comfortable with the bloodlust and thrill of power he'd been feeling. "Maybe we *did* show 'em."

"Brod would be so proud of you, Ronnie. You led us to make a good history for our children."

Ronnie touched Suki's little baby-bump with the back of his hand. "Let's make sure his child gets home safely; he or she is going to be needed."

The levity in Suki's voice was replaced by solemnity as she pressed Ronnie's hand to her belly. "My baby and I are needed *here,* Ronnie," she announced. "We fight with *you.* We all fight with *you!"*

Sula's lip curled in disgust to see Red Mask's weapon raised as if in triumph, probably to the howling of the inconstant and soon-to-be-sorry populace of the town.

"They say it sings," commented the observer next to her as he looked through a pair of folding opera glasses.

"What are you talking about?" she demanded rudely.

"The weapon, milady," he replied mildly. "One of the gate guards told one of our spies that it makes a noise when he swings it around."

Really? she mused, and turned to the loitering colonel. "Did my reward get advertised?"

"Not yet, ma'am," he answered. "The Guard is still preventing all communication."

"Get it out *somehow*, Colonel," she threatened, "and make it five hundred ounces if the red one's weapon is also taken; it's a talisman of failed revolt. I want that weapon!"

"Yes, milady."

"And get the others up here. This is almost over."

"Yes, milady."

Ronnie and Suki quickly shared news as they hurried to another fight: Jak lived and had developed an amazing technique for killing archers on foot, rushing at them with jinks and feints until the arrow was wasted and the archer found himself with a sword blade in his belly; Big Hog had been bashed in the head and appeared dead; Scarface and a couple of his crew still fought; Black Mask hadn't been seen lately. Then they were engaged and again lost sight of each other.

As the sun moved to the west and the sky began to cloud up, Ronnie grew weary, staggering a little between encounters, his arms and shoulders rubbery from swinging the now-dull axe against armor and blade and lance. At one point a man who'd come with him over the wall rushed up to shove a crumpled black hood in his hand with the news that "He's fallen," at another he paused to look across the square to see that so few of his people remained that soldiers could surround and kill them with increasing ease. Citadel Guard officers, covered by bodyguards and numerous archers at the gatehouse battlements and on top of the wall, had even walked out of the pedestrian passage next to the main gate to confer with army officers, and some soldiers went about the square killing the wounded and robbing corpses of both sides, under a barrage of insults from spectators.

One group of a half dozen soldiers seemed to be on a mission, skirting fights to make their way toward the southeast quadrant of the square where he found himself virtually alone among scavengers who were too busy to engage him. The longer he looked at them the surer he was that their mission was *him.*

It was inevitable, of course; the fight had to end with him dead or fled.

He emptied the water bladder he'd earlier taken from a dead soldier and tossed it away. Then he regarded the nicked, scarred, and generally sad state of his axe and briefly considered trading it for one of the many swords or lances scattered about, but he could not–at this final moment–part with this link to his past and his family.

He cradled it in his arms and waited.

Lady Clare knew about where Red Mask was but couldn't see him clearly in the waning light. Her hawk-eyed young maid, however, could see him sharply enough to describe an air of resignation that brought Clare's fist to her heart in anguish. The intent of the soldiers hurriedly weaving around last-gasp resistance to get to him was clear enough, and so was Red Mask's. She couldn't bear it.

"General!" she commanded in her high-priestess voice, expending a large part of her remaining energy. "A word, please!"

"Where is he?!" Sula shouted at the telescope.

"Somewhere in that line of government buildings, ma'am." said the ever-calm observer. "At this angle we can't see their fronts."

She glared, willing Red Mask to come into the open to meet the soldiers who searched for him and to die in her sight. As she scanned back and forth along the roof edges, she saw part of a large black carriage-and-four moving rapidly south on the west side of the square, surrounded by a mounted bodyguard. It had turned out of the shadow of the wall and so could have come from inside, and now, as it approached a building abandoned when the fighting started, it turned into a courtyard and disappeared.

△ △ △

"THAT'S 'IM!" shouted an overaged sergeant to his handful of scruffy men. "That's the red-mask one! See the bush axe?... We're rich, boys! Jes take yer time, only not so's to let anybody jump our claim!"

Ronnie was too tired to attack so he just waited, looking beyond his executioners and noticing the gate's doors beginning to open behind the still-lowered portcullis and thinking how the Citadel would be back to normal not long after his death was confirmed. When the six surrounded him, he let his weapon drop on its leash and swung it around a couple of times to show them the folly of that approach. They switched to a multi-pronged frontal attack and set about trying methodically to stab and bleed him with sword and short spear. Hurt and provoked, he rallied and chopped one man's sword arm to the bone but then fell back, dragging the dull axe on the pavement. Another poke and then another and another, some ineffective, thanks to the thick leather axe-cover belted to his belly under his shirt, others adequately so at creating more holes for his life to spill out of.

The burning eyes and greedy grins on the faces of his attackers told him he was almost finished. When his heel struck a wall, he realized he'd been maneuvered into a grassy triangle bounded by the driveway and the front of the empty government building and the wall of its courtyard. He wasn't going to make it out of here even if the remaining men decided to take a lunch break.

Suddenly the attackers looked over their shoulders and sneered in disgust at the veritable cavalcade of claim-jumping mounted archers who clattered into the courtyard followed by a careening and skidding armored carriage. Then the sergeant realized that the fine livery and accoutrements of this troop identified private security and he puffed himself up to order them to move along. But they had other ideas.

At a sharp command, half the troop stood in stirrups and drew bow. Ronnie let his eyes close, thinking that at least it would be harder to make up stories of cowardice over his corpse; all the arrows that killed him would be in the *front!*

A chorus of shocked and terrified cries snapped his eyes open to reveal an inexplicable sight; five soldiers with arrows protruding from torso and neck and himself still unshot and alive. Nor did it make sense to his fatigue-addled mind when several of the horsemen dropped to the ground with short sword to dispatch and mutilate the five writhing soldiers in front of him and a sixth nearby nursing a ruined arm and then to go about pulling arrow shafts from bodies or breaking them off. Only the familiarity of the men's livery spoke to him, but he couldn't make sense of its message.

The horsemen quickly remounted and moved to create a cordon between the street and the events in the courtyard. The carriage lurched ahead with the door already opening and Bear stepping onto the running board. Now he alighted on the pavement and held the door open.

"Ronnie!" cried Lady Clare through the haze. "Come this way! Quickly!"

He was immobile, looking at the faces of Clare and Cornelius as they beckoned. He was confused; it wasn't supposed to end this way.

"My boy, you have to *live!* There's work to be done! We need you!... *Come!"*

Ronnie looked behind the carriage and past the horsemen to the Square, where the battle seemed suddenly to be over, with even civilians out looking for loved ones or robbing corpses under cover of looking. There was no one left to fight beside, but there was still a history to be written. He'd thought his role in that history was to die fighting in front of witnesses, but now the battle was over, soon-to-be-cremated corpses of heroes and cowards were beginning indiscriminately to be stripped and piled up, and he was being invited to *live.* Would he dishonor his dead brothers and sisters and himself if he didn't join them? Did history have a different role for him?

He couldn't figure it out, but some instinct compelled him to put one foot in front of the other toward the open door of the carriage. When he got there, Bear stepped in front of him.

"Your weapon, Master Woodmaker?" he said, not unkindly.

Ronnie merely stopped moving, his axe by his side as it had been all day.

"I think, today, the man and his weapon are one, Bear," said Lady Clare. "Let him pass."

Sula was dismayed at the battle's sudden cessation. She was sure that could have happened only if the rebel's real surviving leader, Red Mask, was dead or fled or at least perceived to be. Still, she scanned the areas where she thought he could be, hoping to see someone showing off his severed head and weapon. In looking elsewhere she and the professional observers missed the black carriage and its retinue turning back onto the southbound street at a walk among wagons detailed to collect the bodies before they could become diseased. With the battle over, her obsession with Red Mask moved to the back of her mind and practical matters of political and physical survival replaced it. She beckoned Minister Grotius and the two generals to a more private spot and shooed others away.

"I'll have to make a report to the council before nightfall," she said. "Before then, we need to identify the dozen or so bureaucrats and officers responsible for this fiasco. They'll probably want to take responsibility and kill themselves right away to save their families. See to it."

"Yes, milady," said the three, relieved to be the executioners and not the targets of such an order. Then one of the generals inquired delicately, "And the fellow in the red hood ... any follow-up there?"

"No, not now," she mused, already starting to consider how his legend might be used to her advantage. "I have a feeling he'll turn up, sooner or later."

∆ ∆ ∆

Fearing that they'd been seen rescuing Red Mask, Lady Clare had her driver approach the city's outer edges in several locations and sent her horsemen to scout others, looking for a place where Ronnie might be delivered to the relative safety of the forest, but the army had established a cordon and Ronnie was in no condition to make it on foot, even with money, food, clothing, and Bear for a helper. He'd lost too much blood and his wounds needed tending, and even now he had to be propped on the floor between Bear's knees, still wearing his hood and clutching the axe in his lap.

Finally the party was back at the south side of the square, whose restricted-access central avenue was now cleared of bodies and devoid of regular traffic because of the closed gate. Waiting near the columns for other traffic to be stopped in too-slow deference to the symbols of her station on her retinue's tunics and flying at the corners of the carriage's cabin, looking out the window at the forbidding iron portcullis and the frustrated soldiers still milling about dangerously, she made a decision. What were twenty immaculately liveried and mounted guards and a fancy carriage and intimidating ensigns good for if you couldn't just go where you wanted when you wanted to, high stepping all the way and silently commanding gates to fly open before you by sheer force of will, especially if you've already bribed the gatekeeper once. The moment required her to curb her secret egalitarian impulses and to be Clare, direct descendant of the Chaplin through highest clergy on both sides, niece to the Messenger Mortimer, sister to the likely next Sword of ZAH Lord Magnus, and not someone to be made to wait.

She summoned Kemal to her window and gave him instructions that made him snap a salute and straighten his cap before taking half his troop forward to preemptively stop all traffic in the intersection ahead, to the cowed consternation of the warden on his platform. Then she leaned forward and touched Ronnie intimately for the first time since he was a baby being hidden away for his own safety, placing her hands on his cheeks through the red fabric, raising his face to her.

"Ronnie," she said, "you have to trust me now! ... *Do you trust me?"*

He looked at her for a moment, let go his axe to reach up and pull off the mask.

"Yes, Mother," he said with a tired smile. "I trust you."

She smiled back at him, raised her head and shouted an order, and the carriage pulled ahead and turned down the central avenue, gaining speed.

Into the Citadel.

Please enjoy the continuing story of Ronnie and Jenna and all the others in

RED MASK

Book II of Into the Citadel

Beginning with ...

1 - Clare's Gamble

FASTER!" yelled Lady Clare, poison-blanched hair steaming as she leaned out the window of her armored carriage.

"PORTCULLIS'S DOWN, MA'AM!" returned the driver, who'd started to slow the four horses from a run.

"*FASTER,* I SAY! PRESS THEM!"

"YESSUM!" yelled the man, lashing the horses into a gallop and forcing them to maintain it despite the fearsome sight before them.

The Citadel Guard general at the gatehouse battlements suddenly leaned on his hands and stared in disbelief. The crazy woman meant to drive her fine horses and large carriage and her twenty mounted guards and herself right into the impenetrable iron portcullis that blocked the Citadel's main entrance. Social acquaintance, inter-clan amity, and the expectation of a golden thank-you had moved him to order the great oaken doors and portcullis opened minutes before—even with heretic rebels and coup-making regular army troops and rambunctious town youths still thronging the great square—but the deal hadn't said anything about a galloping return through the hundreds of armed men near the gate who craved nothing more than an invitation to rush and secure it for their own treasonous purposes.

The troops had already given up on their dark plan once and settled down to the still-achievable goal of slaughtering the rebels who'd unwittingly given them the pretext to return under arms from a fictitious operation and who now insisted on dying gloriously for their cause. The first surprise-opening of the gate had given them hope and they'd almost braved the Guard archers at the battlements before backing down, but now, seeing Clare's carriage and guards racing up the central avenue, they abandoned the rebel-mutilating and corpse-robbing and shop-looting and whatever else they were doing to head for the still-closed gate on horse and foot from every direction.

The general glanced at others at the battlements and over his shoulder in the direction of the obscured 44-story Error Building—the Black Tower—and took about two seconds to consider several things: the rank and wealth and influence of Lady Clare, the extra gold that might come his way if he raised the portcullis again for her, the effect on his life and career if she crashed to her death in front of the thousands of witnesses still populating the sidewalks and rooftops in the square, and finally, whether the remarkable event he thinks he's just witnessed could have been observed at this angle from the roof of the Black Tower, where they were reported to have a pre-Cleansing telescope. Then, out of time, he broke for a nearby portal into the winding room and bellowed within repeatedly until he saw the gears start to move, then dashed down the stairs into the fifty-foot tunnel under the wall to give the high priestess a piece of his mind—if she survived the next few seconds.

The great doors had been left partly open so guardsmen could look out but still shelter behind them if the frustrated soldiers started shooting through the portcullis. The general shouted his trailing junior officers and guards into action and lent his own shoulder to help push a door along its curved track as the spiked portcullis crept upward feet away. *Too slow!* He rushed forward to push on the iron with other men while the hurtling formation bore down and threw himself against the sidewall at the last moment. Heaving horses thundered past as the two men on the seat ducked low and the foot-long spikes of the still-moving portcullis raked the luggage rails off the roof of the carriage. Close behind, the mounted guards were mere feet ahead of a howling cavalryman who led an impromptu wedge of soldiers in rushing the opening under a fusillade from the Guard archers at the battlements above. The rump of the last horse had barely cleared the portcullis's line when an operator jerked a lever that sent it plummeting, impaling the cavalryman and his mount. The door rolled home with a boom to shut out the screams of man and animal and the Citadel was once again secure from its own army.

The carriage sped on, to the general's dismay, out of the tunnel and up the hill. Only after he'd come out and stood in the street with hands on hips looking after did it stop. When it started up again at a more relaxed pace, a rider came back at a canter. It was Kemal, captain of Clare's horse guard. He slowed his animal to a walk, then stopped and dismounted.

"General Krono," began the handsomely liveried man, "I am instructed to convey Lady Clare's profound–"

"What in Zah's name was *that,* Captain?" gritted the general. "You nearly got yourselves and half of us *killed!* Not to mention–"

"If we may, sir?" interrupted the captain, suggesting with a gesture that they speak away from others standing nearby. The general glared for a moment, then spoke over his shoulder.

"Major, return everyone to their duties," he ordered. "Offer to take in the army's wounded under guard through one pedestrian gate if the rest back off. And raise the portcullis enough for a small crew of them to drag away the mess there."

"Yes, sir," said the major, herding the others away,

"Now..." said the general, waiting.

"As I said, sir," began Kemal, "my lady sends her profound–"

"You said that. Get on with it."

The captain nodded and changed tack. "A hundred kilos of silver, sir. How shall it be delivered?"

"A hundred ..." marveled the general. "For what, exactly?"

"For helping in the rescue of my lady's servant Cornelius."

"Cornelius?" said the general, confused. "But–"

"Yes, sir. My lady came from her home to express concern about her man Cornelius being trapped in the square during the fighting. She saw him in danger, and you let us go out to get him. She's very grateful."

The general could only stare, open-mouthed. He knew Clare's majordomo Cornelius perfectly well, and he also knew the dignified older man had arrived on the battlements with her and stood to her rear the entire time. If someone in the square was rescued, it wasn't Cornelius.

He and Cornelius had in fact been watching as, in the distance, one of the rebel leaders–the man wearing a red hood who'd negotiated safe passage of the returning Guardsmen–had finally been driven into a courtyard, out of sight. Just then Lady Clare, still wobbly and going white-haired from what the whole city knew to be a recent assassination attempt, had claimed to have seen one of her servants and insisted on being allowed to get him away from the fighting, even though it was almost over. He'd relented only to see her and her guard proceed directly to the courtyard's entrance and block it from view with her big carriage. The implication of that, combined with the galloping, no-inspection return, and the fabrication about Cornelius, was too stunning to contemplate. Best to put it out of mind–as long as the price was right.

"A valuable retainer like Cornelius ..." mused the general, glancing around, "all the others who helped ... Shall we say three hundred?"

"Two, sir?" returned Kemal.

"Done. Sundown, my house, one market from today."

"General," nodded the captain in agreement, remounting and cantering away up the hill where, raising his eyes to the leafy environs of Clare's mansion near the Palace, the general glimpsed the black carriage that might or might not contain the only survivor of the first organized rebellion against the Priesthood of ZAH in its 109-year history, a man whom his soldiers and officers were already calling by the name they'd heard shouted by fighters and spectators alike during the day-long battle in the great square.

Red Mask.

Acknowledgements

Dr. Bernard Bos
Michael Collier and Patti Valdez
Eli Collier
Timothy Day, Esq.
Martha Emery and Stephen Harper
Julie Johnson
Debbie Jones
Byron and Sally Lee
Jeff and Soledad Lee
Edward and Yanis Nicholas
Nancy and David Pierce
Harrison and Kayla Pierce
Michael Scherzer
Jerry Zachow and Laura Lambder

and, *in memorium,*

James Harrison Campbell, Jr.
Dana Albertina Davis Campbell

Without whom . . .

About the Author

James Harrison Campbell is a former international trade specialist for government and industry, a former maximum-security prisoner and seven-year escapee, and a perpetual student of human nature. Previously at home in Tokyo, Paris, Lima, Atlanta, and Phoenix, he now lives alone on the banks of the Tennessee River where he is thrilled to be alive and unexpectedly free thanks to a federal judge who credited him with having "changed the lives of many inmates and their families" through mentoring and education.

Into the Citadel, his debut dystopian trilogy, defeated prison walls every time he picked up his contraband mechanical pencil to write it.

(Learn more soon at www.intothecitadel.com)

Made in the USA
Columbia, SC
14 December 2023